GUARDIAN OF THE GOLDEN CITY

BOOK 2 OF THE SĪHALT SERIES

AUSTIN REHL

Edited by JOEY QUINCE

Edited by ALICIA COFFMAN PHELPS

Edited by ANNA L. REHL

LOCK10 PRESS LTD

Dear Reader,

Thank you for reading the next installment of the Sīhalt Series! If you have not yet read the first book, **Guardian of the Sunshine Bride**, check it out. It's a great story.

It always makes me feel happy when I can deliver the next book for my fans. I don't mean to leave you hanging in this series, but this book must end somewhere, and the story arc isn't finished yet. Remember, I'm a reader too. I know how it feels!

Consider yourself loved (and warned) for deciding to read this book in the first year of its publication — while I'm working on the next installment. Happy reading!

—Austin Rehl

Dear Reader

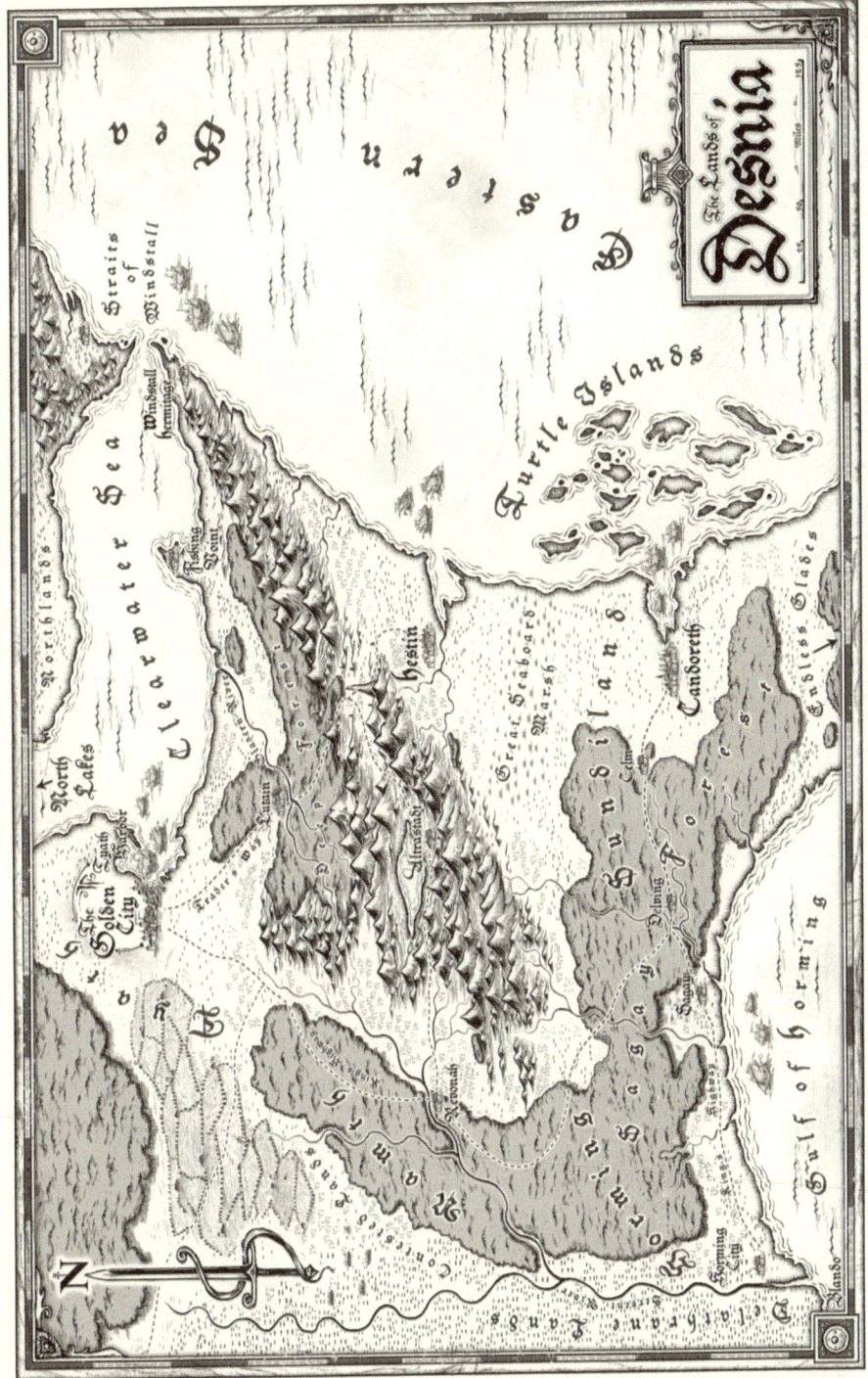

THE GOLDEN CITY OF

TYATH

Harbor
of
Tyath

Smuggler's Quarter

Eastern Gate

Merchant Quarter

South Gate

Middtown Quarter

Hightower Quarter

West Gate

Palace Complex
Library
Great Cathedral
Academy
Infirmiry
Arena
Market
Harbor Walk
Lighthouses

BLANDO

REFOUNDING SONNET

Like a seed of the spring flower,
  She was carried on the wind.
  From sun-lit shores, to frozen lakes,
  An Empire she would mend.

She would break the shining walls,
  And many of those within,
  Shower her light, and Talented might
  On the darkness that descends.

-Attributed to
  Emperor Heathron Dol Lassimer,
  Third Age

1

SWORN PROTECTOR

Kathleen climbed the steep steps to the top of the city wall. Her vision blurred from the tears in her eyes, but she wanted to see him off. She wiped her eyes again and felt the warm wind blow heavy against her face when she finally looked out, over the ramparts.

He was leaving. Her Sīhalt Guardian, her protector, rode his black horse across the Amaranth Plain, down the road, heading west toward the Delathrane Lands. Kathleen waved the white cloth above her head. She knew that he would be able to see her, even from a great distance. The man was a Sensor. If he chose to look back, he would clearly see her mouth the words, "I love you."

Would he truly return from the Delathrane Lands? Kathleen wondered.

She knew that Jared was a skilled warrior. She had seen him in action and knew that he was formidable in combat, but could he stand against so many enemies — alone?

After seeing the Serpent King so bent on revenge, she was not sure the Sīhalt Guardian would be safe. Jared would do his duty and seek out Seth no matter what. Yet his brother may not even be alive. Who could live as a captive among those barbarians and not expect to be so fully broken they were unrecognizable even to their loved ones? Kathleen's heart ached. So much had been overcome, and yet to see her Sīhalt Guardian departing left an emptiness inside her heart that she feared might never be filled.

"Father Abbath, bring him back safely to me," she prayed.

The wind howling over the embattlements disguised the soft steps of a man approaching.

"I am sorry, Your Highness. I have not had an opportunity to ask for your forgiveness for my failures."

Kathleen jumped slightly, and turned to see Captain Channing Dur Ruston bowing low. He swept his elegant hat back into place dramatically as he stood upright again. His eyes flicked towards Jared's receding form on the horizon.

"I am also sorry that you have lost a man to whom you have grown so...attached," he said, without a hint of ridicule. Kathleen could sense that he spoke with sincerity and she appreciated it.

"Your Highness," the captain continued, "I swore an oath to protect and obey you. Until your wedding day, I will keep my oath. Even if I must remain with you another year, far from my home. As a man of Marth, I am your faithful servant, and I will stay with you here in the Golden City of Tyath until you are happy and secure in the bonds of matrimony."

Kathleen noted the flourish with which the captain spoke. Any 'man of Marth' worth his sword knew the ways of eloquence. Captain Dur Ruston was like a Sīhalt Guardian in that way. The people of Marth Island, the largest of the barrier islands of Sundiland, were full of a love for courtly ways, but they were also known to be stubborn and proud.

"I am willing to release you from your oath, Captain. No one could have predicted the events that disrupted my Wedding Procession. I cannot in good conscience keep you here as part of my entourage. You have done your duty," Kathleen said.

"I was the one who lost you in the wilderness. Though we fought bravely, the barbarians were fiercer than we could have imagined. When we finally realized that you had been separated from us, I rent my cloak and commanded the men back into the fray!"

"You did the right thing, Captain. Without your leadership, many more of our people would have died. You saved my best friend, Lady Albodris, for which I will be forever grateful."

She really did not want him to feel obliged to shadow her steps. She remembered her discomfort in Candoreth when the Sīhalt had done such a thing — always lurking about. It had nearly driven her mad. Even the presence of a strikingly handsome man like Captain Channing Dur Ruston would grow tiresome.

"I no longer require your services, Captain Channing."

As soon as she had spoken, Kathleen regretted it. The man looked utterly crestfallen, as if his whole world had been destroyed. He took a step back, eyes wide in shock.

Kathleen quickly spoke to repair the harm she had caused him. "...At least not within the walls of Tyath," she said.

Relief flooded into his face. He took a hopeful step forward.

"Where would you have me go? What quest must I fulfill? Just say the word, Your Highness, and it will be done."

Kathleen looked over the ramparts again. She could just barely see Jared.

"You must follow the Sīhalt Guardian. He travels west to the Delathrane Lands. The journey will be fraught with danger." Kathleen noticed with a hint of humor that even she began to speak more floridly as she spoke with Channing.

Captain Channing nodded without hesitation. She continued, "He has promised to return within the year. I do not want him to travel alone, with no one to trust or turn to for help. I saw how equally matched you were in the arena in Candoreth."

At the mention of how he rivalled the Sīhalt in martial skill, the man of Marth puffed out his chest a little more. Kathleen felt it was appropriate, even if something of an embellishment, to demonstrate confidence in a man she might be sending to his death. After all, he had lasted longer in the arena against the Sīhalt Guardian than any other man she had seen.

"Swear to me that you will use your sword to protect and defend the Sīhalt Guardian!"

Her voice rose in royal command, the captain pressed a closed fist to his chest, his eyes intense with loyalty for his Princess.

"On my honor, Princess Kathleen Dal Sundi! I will do as you command."

"Then make haste good man. He rides west!"

Kathleen pointed out over the wall toward the distant green forest. Captain Channing swept the edge of his short cloak with a flourish as he turned to run down the stairs. His tight breeches made Kathleen want to laugh in spite of the seriousness of the moment. The man probably needed the assistance of at least two servants to get his breeches on!

He would have been too much for the Ladies of Tyath anyway, she thought with a grin.

The captain made no delay. As soon as he descended the steps, Kathleen saw him ride west on the same road Jared had taken, his horse galloping, Channing urging it on, with shouts of exultation.

2

MEETING MAXWELL

Jared rode out of Tyath determined not to look back at the Golden City or at Kathleen until he reached the tree line.

He shook his head as he considered the twists and turns that love and life might take. As he approached the shade of the first large tree, he heard a familiar voice.

"Could you use a hand in your search for Seth?" the dry, cracking voice asked.

Jared brought his stallion to a halt in the cool of the shade and looked for the speaker but could not find him.

"I figured you would be back in Tyath enjoying the ale," Jared said with a smile, still unable to locate the person.

"I'm headed to Windstall Hermitage if you are. Do you have room for my skinny bottom on that enormous horse of yours?"

"Anytime, Maxwell," Jared said, "but I'm headed west."

"Master Tove said you would want to go directly to the Delathrane Lands. I'm in!"

There was a rustling in the trees, and then an old man, rail-thin and covered in dirt, dropped from the overhead branch and landed on the saddle right behind Jared.

"Well, what are we waiting for?" he asked, flashing his gap-toothed smile. He raised a thin hand and smacked Steed play-fully on the rump. The stallion looked back at the riders.

"He has killed men for less than that," Jared warned.

The old man chortled. "Giddy up, Steed!" he said.

The great horse moved forward as Jared gazed back at the gleaming walls of Tyath. On the highest parapet he saw a red-haired girl waving goodbye with a white handkerchief. He thought, even from this great distance, he saw her lips form the words,

"I love you."

I love you, too, he thought, sending the message her way.

"So, what are you going to do about the girl?" Maxwell asked. He had an uncanny way of sensing people's utmost concerns and cutting to the heart of them.

"You mean the Princess?" Jared replied.

Maxwell smiled.

"That is the girl you just spent the last number of weeks with, right?"

Luckily Max was sitting on the horse behind him, otherwise he would have seen the tears welling in Jared's eyes, which he would never have let go unchallenged.

"They didn't really want you in that city if I caught their meaning," Maxwell said.

"The time was far too short," Jared replied, speaking of his time with Kathleen.

"Well, I couldn't wait for you to arrive," Maxwell said, patting the Sīhalt on the shoulder.

"How long did you wait for me?"

"Not to worry," he said. "I arrived just in time — as always. I always assume you DeTorre boys will need me to get you out of trouble."

"How on earth did you know I would end up in the dungeon? Even I didn't predict that," Jared said.

"Just a hunch, I guess. When I saw the report from Richard

and Cara, I read between the lines. I figured if you were falling in love with the girl, that might get you in trouble. It always does that to me."

Jared frowned. As they rode, Steed tossed his head, wanting more slack in the reins.

"You've never been in love Maxwell."

"Well, I suspect that when it happens, it will be troublesome," the old man on the back of the horse replied philosophically.

"I got in trouble because of a misunderstanding. I was knocked unconscious, and so was Kathleen. Otherwise, we could've explained."

Maxwell sucked on his cheek. He squinted, as if he was considering the truthfulness of that statement.

"All I know is that if I paid a man to bring my sweetheart safely to the wedding altar, and he married her instead...there would be trouble," Maxwell explained.

"The very idea of you having a sweetheart is troubling enough," Jared replied.

"Hey, my time will come!" Maxwell protested.

"Not looking like that," Jared replied dryly. "You need a bath...and some teeth."

"You're not looking so young yourself anymore! I see some gray in your black hair," Maxwell cackled.

"The only girl you are likely to attract, looking as you do, is the old hag, Jinx, who served breakfasts at that tavern in Fishing Point," Jared retorted.

Maxwell shook his head and pulled it back as he screwed up his expression as if he had sunk his teeth into a bitter fruit.

"That's nasty! This is just a disguise. I did it to help you!" Maxwell laughed.

"Right, well, you managed to get yourself to smell the way you look. I can barely stand it."

Just then, Steed shook his head and snorted from both nostrils.

"See? Steed agrees with me," Jared said.

"After all I've been through to rescue your sorry little..."

"Well, my fake wedding was a disguise, too. So, stop teasing me about that. I didn't really marry her," Jared said.

"Which is why Prince Heathron let you live," Maxwell noted.

"I could have handled the situation. But it was rather hairy for a moment," Jared agreed.

"That seems to be the only way you know how to operate," Maxwell's wrinkled, gapped-toothed grin turned even further upward. "That is why I like to be around you," he said.

"How did you actually get into the dungeon?" Jared asked.

"I found a little opening in the exterior wall, near a grate, and snaked my way through it. Luckily the dungeon is constructed against the exterior of the city wall."

"I'm sorry to hear that. I know it is distasteful for you to imitate a reptile. And the old man?" Jared asked.

"He was already dead, but I got the general idea," Maxwell said gazing down at his skinny arms and legs. "Besides, you're like a brother to me. I'm happy to do it for a price," Maxwell laughed as Jared shook his head.

"Speaking of brothers, have you received any word regarding Seth?" Jared asked.

"Master Tove sent me over. He thought you might need a little assistance in finding him."

"I believe he's alive," Jared said.

"Do you have any clue as to where he might be?" Maxwell inquired.

"There is a barbarian chieftain, calling himself the Serpent King. I believe he knows where Seth can be found. He is the one who led the Delathranes to attack the Wedding Procession."

"The Serpent King. That sounds dramatic," Maxwell said.

"You know how the Delathranes are."

"True. But I kind of like it," Maxwell replied.

"You would."

"Maybe I should start calling myself 'The Eagle King' soon," Maxwell said in a grandiose manner, gazing out into the blue sky.

"I'll call you whatever you like, as long as you go report to Master Tove. Tell him I completed my assignment for House Dol Lassimer. The Princess is safe in Tyath, and I am going to find Seth. You can meet me again on the road westward."

3

A WILLING SWORD

J ared watched as Maxwell dismounted and prepared himself to Shift. The disguise Maxwell often chose in human form was that of a miserable, malnourished old man.

"Why do you prefer the look of an old man?" Jared asked.

"People underestimate me like this," Maxwell replied, gesturing to his emaciated body.

Jared could understand that. Maxwell had grown up with Seth and Jared at Windstall Hermitage. He was no more than a few years younger than them. His Talent as a Shifter made him more useful as a spy or assassin to the Order, and so although he was trained as a Sīhalt, he did not wear the black cloak of a Guardian.

"I dress in rags too, because I never get my clothes back. Will you hang on to these?" he asked. Maxwell began to untie the fraying rope about his waist that served as a belt.

"You want me to hold that thing?" Jared grimaced.

"I'll just put it in your saddlebag. I mean, I am traveling hundreds of miles for you, after all," he replied.

"Can't you bring back something to wear from the Hermitage?" Jared asked.

"I suppose," Maxwell said. "But people just might wonder why an eagle is flying by with a brand-new change of clothing in its talons."

Jared smiled at his friend. "Thank you for coming to help me."

"It's my pleasure. I can always count on an adventure whenever I'm with you or your brother."

After he removed what little clothes he was wearing, Maxwell crouched on the ground and began to Shift. It was always a bit unsettling to watch his friend change from man to beast.

"Couldn't you do that off in the woods a little ways?" Jared asked, "You don't want people to see you."

"I need room to spread my wings," Maxwell said with a smile. "You'll be fine."

Spasms that appeared involuntary shook Maxwell's frame. He cried out, but the shrillness of his voice increased as his shoulders shifted back. His voice became a piercing screech. Feathers sprouted along his arms and torso.

Jared could hear the approach of galloping hooves.

"Hurry, if you are able," Jared said. "Someone is approaching."

Maxwell cried louder. His legs shrank as his toes became elongated into long, sharp talons. His eyes widened and drifted toward the sides of his head, his profile becoming sleeker, more aquiline. Jared tried not to grimace at the sight. He looked down the road to see none other than Channing Dur Ruston, the Captain of Candoreth riding hard toward them.

For a moment he wondered if the man was in danger. But then he saw his bright, gleaming smile. Whatever the reason for the rush, Channing was happy about it.

Channing rode into the clearing just in time to witness Maxwell's final patches of human skin be replaced by the smooth feathers of an eagle.

"Can I believe my eyes?" he asked.

"What are you doing Captain? You seem to be in a hurry," Jared replied.

His horse was panting. The mare was a fine animal. Steed nickered in recognition of her.

"The Princess sent me to join you on your journey," Captain Channing said breathlessly, still looking at the green rock eagle nearby.

"Why would she do that?" Jared asked, his brows furrowed.

"I intended to guard her, but she said you traveled alone. She said she wanted someone to be with you, someone that you could rely on to protect you."

"And she believes that person could be you?" Jared asked doubtfully.

Captain Dur Ruston straightened in his saddle. His pride was in need of protection as well.

"She commanded me to come. On my honor I swore to her that I would bring you back within a year," he said.

Jared rolled his eyes. He looked at the eagle and shook his head slightly.

"Could we use another pair of hands on the mission?" Jared asked.

The eagle blinked twice.

"Maxwell doesn't want you to come."

"So, it is a man!" Channing said. "I thought my eyes deceived me! I heard the stories when I was a child, but I didn't know Shape-Shifters still existed."

"Go back to the Golden City and take charge of the men you still have left there. Our journey will be very dangerous, and King Lukald will have need of you in Candoreth."

"I am not afraid of danger," Channing replied.

"Even when you should be?" Jared raised an eyebrow.

"My oath is to Princess Dal Sundi. She commanded me to follow you, to be your protector and friend."

"You think you have the ability to protect me? You think I want you as a friend?" Jared's words were sharp.

"Even a weak ally may tip the scales in your favor during a hard-fought battle," Channing quoted a well-known Sīhalt truism.

Jared considered this. The eagle nodded his head.

"I thought that during the royal Wedding Procession, perhaps we had formed a kind of friendship, if only bound by duty," the captain said.

"I suppose I should not spurn the willing sword of a man who seeks my friendship. The eagle screeched, extended his wings, and scratched at the ground.

"You must be willing to sacrifice yourself for the good of the mission. We go with that understanding," Jared said sternly.

"I am willing to place my duty above my safety," the Captain replied.

"If you ride with us, you will do what I say. I am your commanding officer," Jared insisted.

"As long as nothing you command me to do is contrary to that of the Princess's wishes, I will obey," he replied.

"She commanded you to keep me alive. As soon as we find my brother, I will return to Tyath. I plan to stay alive."

"It's settled then," the captain said.

"Where is your gear?" Jared asked, for he could see no saddle bags on the mare.

Captain Channing patted his sword. "I only brought this. I came as quickly as I could. I was afraid that if I delayed, I would never find you."

"A wise choice on your part," Jared said. "Maxwell can you bring a bed roll and a few necessities for the Captain when you return?"

The eagle screeched — it didn't look happy. It blinked in understanding, but only once this time.

"Okay, give my regards to Master Tove. I'm sure you'll give him a full debrief, love story and all," Jared said, shaking his head.

This time the eagle winked. If it could have smiled, Jared was sure it would have been that of a gapped-toothed old man.

Then the bird extended its expansive wings and flew eastward toward the Straits of Windstall.

Channing and Jared watched him go.

"That's Maxwell, a good friend of mine. He will be joining us again soon. We head west," Jared said.

4

INVITATION ACCEPTED

D ays passed. Gazing at her reflection in the mirror, Kathleen reached up to touch her black and blue cheek. The bruises had gotten worse, if that was possible, and there was a yellow tinge around the darkness.

"Is this very noticeable?" she asked Larissa. "I had hoped to just blend in," she asked, attempting humor.

"Your Highness is yet very beautiful," she said primly.

"I hope they don't treat me like that," she said.

Kathleen would have gladly turned to Melva for a touch of Healing. The cost of a few days of age would be worth it if she could present herself in public without reminding everyone of the drama that had unfolded upon her arrival.

"You don't suppose they will say 'Here is the pitiful Sundiland Princess. She barely showed up to be married but was thrown from her horse and lay unconscious while the Marriage Day passed!' instead?" Kathleen asked.

"They will say whatever they like. You will need to give them other things to talk about. Inundate them with new stories, and they will cease to speak of the old ones."

"I don't need their pity. My bruised face will have to do."

"I heard that Prince Heathron is keeping his word and is sending food to Candoreth. We should go to watch the wagons being loaded near the city gate," Larissa suggested.

"Are you willing to go with us?" Kathleen asked Melva.

"My bones prefer to sit right here, but I'll go if you insist," the old woman said.

Kathleen pulled the Healer to her feet.

"Come on, Melva, I am already feeling bad for bringing you to this hostile place. If I had realized how you would be treated here, I would not have required you to accompany me on the Wedding Procession."

"It has been my honor, child. You would not have been able to keep me away. I'm happy to be your lady's maid and remain primarily within your personal chambers if needed."

"Well, come get some fresh air with us today," Kathleen insisted.

As they neared the city gates, some people gave Melva a sideward glance, even as they bowed to Kathleen.

"They do not have to do that," Kathleen whispered to her companions.

"Accept all the deference they are willing to give," Larissa replied. "If they want to treat you as their future Empress, by all means, allow them to do so. It can only give you more influence."

Line upon line of heavy wagon wheels turned under the weight of the grain, meat, and cheese that was being sent to Candoreth. Prince Heathron supervised as his clerks checked off the list of items. Kathleen watched him give directions to the stewards and ensure that the heavy canvas covering the goods was fastened tightly. The loaded wagons would save her people.

"Many nobleman would not have deigned to involve himself in what could be considered menial labor. Yet, there is the Prince, taking his time to make sure your people are cared for," Melva said, raising her eyes to gaze at Heathron with a different perspective. She seemed to approve.

"That is so sweet, isn't it?" Larissa said. "You aren't even his wife yet!"

Kathleen closed her eyes and offered a silent prayer of thanks. The Prince was under no obligation to send aide to her homeland. He could have justifiably given her people nothing.

Heathron walked toward Kathleen, smiling after he caught her watching him.

He smiles often, Kathleen thought to herself, *so different from Jared.*

This morning, Heathron wore a forest green doublet with tall, brown leather boots to match. A golden band ran around his forehead and disappeared behind his sandy blonde hair.

"Heathron, will you make sure that the drivers make a stop along the Delving River?" Kathleen asked. "The destitution in those villages remains severe."

"Anything you wish, Kathleen," he said, revealing a perfect set of bright teeth.

"I'm truly grateful for your generosity," she replied.

"My generosity is inspired by my admiration for you." His wide smile shone bright, boyish, and sincere. "You will make a lovely Empress, and it is my pleasure to be of service to you."

Kathleen smiled in return. "Thank you."

"I have one year to win you over, and I intend to use every moment of every day to do so." He turned and went back to checking the wares in the closest wagon.

Kathleen looked down at her arm and hand. The bruises were fading there, but she knew the skin on her cheek remained a deep blue, with the border tinged in yellow where her face had smashed the flagstones. Kathleen felt self-conscious about it and was thankful that the Prince had acted as if she were as unblemished as a dew-kissed dawn rose.

Jared's departure had taken its toll on her. She had felt powerless ever since she had arrived in Tyath — trapped like a fish in a weir. It was good to get out and feel the sunshine on her face.

*The Prince of Tyath is everything any young lady could desire —
handsome, fabulously wealthy, and most importantly kind,* she
thought.

She missed the Sīhalt Guardian dearly — the image of Jared's
changed appearance flashed across her mind's eye again. She
thought of the peppering of gray in his hair, his powerful stance,
and the depth of his voice. He had sacrificed many years to the
healing Melva had given him, but the changes he had endured on
her behalf only made her feel more obligation toward him.

Kathleen planned to wait for Jared's return, as she had
promised. Despite the innate goodness of Prince Heathron, she
hoped that in time, the Prince would better understand the bond
that had formed between herself and the Sīhalt Guardian. For
now, she knew that she must navigate the political intricacies of
the Golden City and the advances of an imperial Prince. Kathleen
saw no reason to crush Heathron's hopes. Time would tell what
the true outcome would be.

"Anything could happen in a year," Melva said, standing by
her side, almost as if she had read her thoughts.

Kathleen blushed and looked at the ancient Red Grower who
smiled at her. Melva was more like family to Kathleen than a
servant.

"I'm just saying, a girl needs to consider all her options," the
old woman said.

Kathleen knew this was true.

"I did not intend to fall in love with the Guardian. The
emotion caught me unaware," Kathleen said softly so that only
Melva and Larissa could hear.

"The consequences of persisting in that relationship would
have caused our people great pain. Your father could have been
deposed by now," Melva reminded her, gently touching her on
the arm. "Love will do what it will, but the realities of living
should not be ignored."

"I know, Melva," Kathleen said as she watched Heathron interact with the teamsters checking the harnesses.

"A wise woman once told me when I was younger, and being pursued by a man, that 'anything can happen if you let it'."

"Let me guess, my mother said that?"

"No, mine," Melva replied. Her gaze seemed to drift off in remembrance of younger years.

"I have felt little desire to socialize. There is less risk if I keep to myself" Kathleen said.

"This is the first day you have ventured out despite the invitations from Heathron and other members of the nobility. He asked you to attend the Arrival Festival. She declined! Can you believe that?" Larissa asked, her inquiry laced with disapproval.

"She needs a bit more time. Kathleen will not stay isolated forever. A flower needs sunlight," Melva said.

"Remaining cloistered in your room, writing love-sick letters to your absent warrior is no way to live," Larissa observed.

"I haven't written him any letters."

Kathleen knew that Larissa was right. She had spent her first week mostly alone. Melva remained close but seemed to be allowing Kathleen time to grieve.

"I had hoped the nobility of the Golden City would forget that I am Talented," she said to Melva after another group of women walked past. She received a few sidelong glances again.

"They will never forget," the old woman said. "Don't give them a reason to hate you by ever displaying your powers, child. Among the nobility there is already reason enough to find fault with a foreign ruler, let alone one who is Talented. Prince Heathron is walking a dangerous path among his supporting houses. I can feel the tension of all the political maneuvering in this city."

"I did not seek this. Can't they see that?" Kathleen sighed.

"We are all born with the capacity to be angels or demons.

They think the Talent is demonic. I don't agree with them, but I see why they are afraid and behave as they do."

"I regret not telling him from the beginning I am a Green Grower," Kathleen said, watching Heathron. "He is a good man."

"Would it have made a difference?" Melva asked. "His parents knew of your mother's abilities. He considered it too."

Kathleen felt the wave of obligation mixed with gratitude wash over her.

"I should go to the upcoming dance with him," she remarked.

"Are you ready to venture out into society?" Larissa asked. "That would give the young ladies something else to gossip about."

"Larissa has been like the tiny honey-sucker, buzzing her wings and visiting every open blossom in the city," Melva said as she flapped her hands close to the sides of her body and dipped her tongue down quickly, mimicking the honey-sucker.

Kathleen laughed at Melva's antics as Larissa faked an affronted pout.

"I do have a taste for sweetness," Larissa finally said smiling. "Have you seen the young Lord Naystrom? His lips and eyes put me in the mind of smooth nectar."

"You girls be careful. Sometimes the most beautiful blossoms bear a bitter fruit in the end," Melva said.

"You are wise, Melva. Will you go with us to House Turlin's ball? I could use a friend by my side if I am to be navigating the social seas of Tyath."

"I'll be with you the entire time," Larissa said. "I'll help you get acquainted with everyone."

"Honey-suckers are energetic, but the little birds are not known for their intellect." Kathleen winked as she said it, and Larissa flipped her hair.

"Well, we do have fun!" she said.

"I should not go with you, Kathleen. I will remain in our chambers. My presence would only cause you greater distress in the end. Child, you look the part of a Princess that should rule. I will help you in our dealings with the Tyathian nobility, behind closed doors, if I can. I don't want to risk your acceptance by standing beside you. I would serve as a constant reminder to them that you are very different from them. Go with the Prince. Enjoy an evening of dancing and feasting. That is what you should do," Melva counseled.

"Larissa said I was a fool to miss the Arrival Festival thrown in my honor. Is this all that the nobility does in the Golden City? Party after party?" Kathleen asked.

"Is there a better use of our time?" Larissa shrugged.

"Every people and every nation have a class of people at the top. They live on the fruits of the people they rule. Their duty is to rule with justice, go to the dances, and attend the festivals, child. It may be the best way you can do your duty to your people and to yourself," Melva said.

Kathleen nodded.

"You are wise, Melva," Larissa remarked.

"I am old," Melva laughed. "But I've seen a thing or three in my years."

Kathleen saw the Prince speaking with a group of merchants and a few men in military attire. Kathleen overheard him talking.

"I'm sure the Delathrane barbarians would love nothing more than to steal this shipment," Prince Heathron said. He looked up and was surprised to see her standing there.

"Hello, Princess Kathleen," he said. "We are at your service."

The soldier bowed reverently to Kathleen, while Heathron inclined his head.

"I would like to accept your invitation to the dance at House Turlin," Kathleen said.

"I would be delighted!" the Prince replied.

Kathleen glanced towards Melva.

The old woman nodded approvingly. The younger golden-haired girl clapped her hands quickly with excitement.

"Shall I have the pleasure of your company on the way there? The Turlin Estate is a few miles outside the city. I would be pleased if you and your friends would accompany me," he said.

"Lady Larissa Albodris will be attending," Kathleen said.

"Shall I arrive at sundown on the appointed day then?"

"Splendid," she replied. "I will look forward to seeing you then."

The Prince bowed and Kathleen walked back to the comfort of her friends, trying to remain composed. She was sure the blush that ran from her cheeks to her neck gave her away. Kathleen felt excited. This was good.

"You're going to have so much fun!" Larissa squealed.

"Calm down, Larissa," Kathleen said. "Don't make a scene."

"Oh, we're going to make a scene," Larissa promised. She smiled devilishly. "These Tyathian Lords of the Northern Realms are going to be reminded of what they've been missing when we arrive."

5

KICK THE DOG

"Azrah, heal the wounded," Cedric said, as he dismounted from his shaggy horse. The animal was the stoutest of the Delathrane mounts, and it had taken a few scrapes from their attack at the Golden City. Cedric berated himself. He had taken risks that were not wise. His anger had overcome his good sense. He had been beaten by the Sīhalt again.

Even shot through with arrows, the Sīhalt Guardian outmaneuvered him. Cedric took a few steps toward his abode. *Certainly, no man could survive so many arrows*, he thought.

The black felt tent stood beneath the shade of a cottonwood grove. In front, tied to a post, sat the blue-eyed prisoner, the brother of *Der'Antha*. Cedric planted one foot firmly in the earth and swung his other boot in an upward arc toward the prisoner. The broken man cowered on the ground, pathetic. He was not even good bait.

"I killed your brother, *Handri!*" the Serpent King shouted, trying to find some amount of satisfaction, or some small victory, in his obvious defeat.

"Then where is his skull?" the prisoner asked softly as he lay in the dirt coughing, holding his left side where Cedric's foot had landed.

Defiance? Resistance now? thought Cedric. *Why?*

Cedric had felt certain he had beaten any remaining defiance out of the man. The one called Seth was a shrinking wreck of a person, a mangy ghoul with blue crystals for eyes.

Cedric frowned, his nostrils flaring as he breathed. The sight of the man kindled his anger. He needed to calm himself — he needed a plan. The visions had shown him the end. He would walk the streets of the Golden City with a great army of Delathranes. He needed to discover the path that would lead him there.

"Did you miss me, *Handri*?" Cedric inquired, as he stooped over and scratched the man behind the neck like a dog. "I am sorry for kicking you, but your brother is very sneaky. I do not have his skull yet. But he may be dead."

Cedric turned to the Meat Witch administering to the wounded.

"Azrah, have you ever Healed a man with an arrow in his back?"

"Many times, my Serpent King." She managed to mumble through her asymmetrical jaw, her chin shifting to the left.

"How about eight arrows? Have you ever Healed a man that looked like a porcupine with arrows for quills?"

She looked upward toward the sky for a moment, trying to recall, then shook her head.

"No, my King. You were the greatest Healing I ever managed." She murmured through her misaligned mandible.

"And don't forget it!" he laughed and slapped Seth's back.

"You see, I do not believe he lives, but you never know," Cedric admitted.

"He's alive...I can feel it," Seth said.

"Can you do such a thing, *Handri*?" Cedric asked, looking closer with squinting eyes.

"Loving families can often do that, and Jared is my twin, born just moments before I arrived," the prisoner said.

Cedric huffed. He was not sure if he believed the Sīhalt.

"And, he's not sneaky," the prisoner said. "He is predictable. I beat him in every game of *Chendris* we ever played."

"You and your brother play...*Chendris*?" Cedric asked. "I thought only the People of the Serpent played the Game of War."

"We played the game of Circle and Destroy often in the long cold winters in Adisfall, but we did not call the game *Chendris*, and we were very young."

Cedric's interest was piqued. He loved the game of strategy. Before his Healing, he had beaten every young Delathrane within three years of his age, and those who were older refused to play for fear of losing to 'Little Cedric'. The little boy that still remained within the Serpent King wanted to match his wits against anyone who might offer a decent challenge.

"I did not realize you played the Game of War. What did you call it?" Cedric asked.

"We called it Circle and Destroy," the prisoner said.

"We must play, *Handri!*"

"I cannot. I am starving and would not be able to focus."

"Then you shall be fed!" Cedric exclaimed.

The Serpent King barked orders to his men. They pointed to Seth, and their women folk brought over bowls of steaming stew to Seth. He used his shaking fingers to sweep the savory meat and vegetables into his mouth.

"I don't want any excuses about being hungry when we play tonight," the Serpent King said. He was now glad he had not killed him. He had never beaten a *Handri* at *Chendris* before.

The Sīhalt Guardian nodded quickly to Cedric as he ate.

"I will play," he said through mouthfuls of stew.

～

Sᴇᴛʜ ʙᴇᴀᴛ Cedric in their first game of *Chendris*. It was a close match, and Seth knew he risked death whether he won or lost, but without his usefulness as bait, Seth surmised that he would be killed either for sport or retribution. He believed his brother was still alive — he needed Jared to still be alive!

Seth's calculation proved correct, however. The Serpent King did not immediately kill him for the victory. Instead, he raged at the loss, then began to laugh hard slapping his thigh.

"I will not kill you, Sīhalt. Not yet. You are the best competition I have had in a long time!"

The giant of a barbarian looked at the board with the pieces placed in the final movement as he scratched his neck. Cedric studied the layout.

"I see what you did here. This is new to me!" he laughed again, then turned to Seth.

"You will play again."

Seth knew that he did not have a choice.

Cedric set up the *Chendris* pieces once more.

"We will play again," he said, nodding to himself.

Seth was tired, and he didn't feel like playing anymore. The best meal he had eaten in months lay comfortably in his stomach. He wanted to curl up and sleep, but since his life depended on the pleasure of the Serpent King, he roused his faculties to prepare to play again.

In spite of himself, Seth smiled at how Cedric's defeat reminded him of all the times his brother Jared would insist they play again, especially if his little brother won.

"Why do you smile, *Handri*? Do you have another trick up your sleeve?" the barbarian asked.

"This reminds me of my brother. He would never let me be the winner. He made me play again and again until he could stop at the win for the night. Sometimes I would lose to him just to be able to go to sleep."

"I am nothing like your brother," Cedric said. "He has no honor. *Der'Antha* did not even come for you."

"My brother will come for me. And when he does, you will know that he has honor."

"Your brother left you here to rot while spending his time with another man's betrothed. And you call us barbarians?"

Cedric placed the pieces of bone on the board again, taking more time do so than he did in the previous game.

Seth always liked this part. It gave him time to plan. Every unguarded statement from the Delathrane gave Seth a clue as to the happenings of the world beyond his captivity. So far, he had learned that Jared had escorted the Princess of Candoreth to Tyath. They had been wounded greatly. If Jared truly was alive, Seth knew that he would come for him. Just as if their situations were reversed. He intended to use the *Chendris* game to buy himself more time. Seth realized he could, at least for the short term, use the game as leverage for food and news.

His chances of survival were now a little better than it had been before. If the Delathranes no longer believed Jared would come to his rescue, he needed another reason to be kept alive.

He would move carefully.

Seth sat across the board from the Barbarian King as they played each evening. They often played in silence, but at length Seth spoke to his opponent.

"Like this game, Cedric, you have much to learn. You still call me *Handri*. I am not," Seth ventured.

"I will call you *Handri* even if you don't like it. I will do as I wish," Cedric said, studying the board.

"I am not offended by the term. It is accurate for many of the people I live around, the people of the Golden City and Horming, but not for me. I am not a *Handri*."

The Serpent King seemed to consider this. His hulking frame sat heavily on the floor opposite the *Chendris* board.

"What do you call yourself?" he finally asked.

"My people are of the same line that founded the Windstall Hermitage. We come from the far north. In the oldest books, we are called Sons of Jurlen, though most have forgotten that name."

"We have old stories, too," Cedric said.

Seth nodded. "Some time I would love to hear the song of your storyteller."

That was the first night Seth was allowed to sleep inside the tent. As he lay looking up at the fabric over his head, he could feel the tethers holding him tightly to the central pole inside the tent. Seth smiled to himself. His chances of survival were improving.

6

PURSUING THE SERPENT KING

They rode in relative silence and camped in the evenings far enough into the forest that they would not be seen. Only a few people passed them on the road. They were settlers from the contested lands moving back east. The Delathranes had not let up. It was not safe for the citizens of the Empire to live so close to the barbarians now.

Jared kept watching the skyline for Maxwell's return. He needed to know that Master Tove had given his blessing. There was a small part of him that worried. Perhaps Maxwell would bring word that Seth was no more. It was possible, but Jared pushed the thought from his mind.

Seth is alive, he told himself again.

Flying over the treetops, a great eagle flew on silent wings. It suddenly passed low over their heads. The enormous bird of prey reached out with its razor-sharp talons to knock the luxurious, feathered cap of Captain Dur Ruston to the ground. Channing ducked at the last moment and reached for his sword, but the eagle was already gone. The bird screeched and spooked the mare. She bucked, kicking her hind legs high in the air, nearly making Channing fall out of his saddle.

The bird landed in front of them, some way off, and didn't rise again. When they finally calmed the captain's horse, Jared and Channing could hear laughter.

"I heard you coming, Maxwell," Jared said.

"Not a chance! I saw with my little eagle-eyes you both nearly fell off your horses! I surprised you, and there's no denying it," Maxwell said through fits of laughter. "I dropped your bed roll and supplies over there, Captain," he said, pointing to the high grass. "Now you and Jared don't have to share a blanket."

"The Lord Sīhalt and I did not share his blanket!" Captain Channing began, incensed.

Maxwell rolled on the ground laughing, not wearing a stitch of clothing.

"Ignore him, Channing. Max, put some pants on," Jared said throwing the ragged pants to Maxwell.

"Why don't you be a little quieter?" Channing said. "There are barbarians in these lands."

"I'm not worried. We can out-fight any group of savages," Maxwell said.

"Says the one who can just fly off whenever he likes!" Channing observed.

"What did Master Tove say when you reported?" Jared asked.

"He commended you for fulfilling your duty," Maxwell said, more serious now. "He said he's proud of you."

The words touched Jared's heart and he gulped, surprised at the emotion that sprang so readily at the message of praise and approbation from his master.

"Most of the latest news had to do with the Emerald Coast," Maxwell continued. "The pirates are more numerous. They've set up shop on the Turtle Islands near Candoreth. The navy of Sundiland is having a time of it. No one knows yet where they came from or what they want. They are not from the Gulf of Horming, like we initially thought. It's probably best that Kathleen isn't home."

"That's not good," Jared replied, thinking of the close call Kathleen and Girdy had suffered at the hands of the pirates.

"They must be coming from across the Eastern Sea, or at least that's what Master Tove thinks. Their ships don't look like any we are familiar with, but if Master Tove is trying to get to the bottom of it, we will know the truth soon."

"What about the Delathranes? Any word of Seth?" Jared asked.

"There are many reports coming in about the Serpent King. He's got the clans all stirred up. They say he is gathering the largest host of warriors since Dumal Wells."

"Yes, I met the barbarian," Jared said with a sigh. "He was the enormous warrior that led the horde. He almost killed me at the gates of Tyath."

"I missed that? Too bad I was in the dungeon waiting for you," Maxwell said.

"The one calling himself the Serpent King has a vendetta against me," Jared replied.

"What did you do to him, go steal his girl too?" Maxwell teased.

Jared shook his head and narrowed his eyes. "No, Maxwell," he said. "I killed his father."

Maxwell frowned and nodded.

"That would work to start a vendetta," he stated plainly.

"Are you ready to ride with us?" Jared asked.

"I've been waiting for this," Maxwell said. "It's good to be back on a journey with you."

"It's not my first journey with a Sīhalt Guardian either," said Channing.

Maxwell turned to the captain.

"Did you almost die?" he asked.

"Yes, come to think of it, I did almost die," said Channing.

"Exciting, isn't it?" Maxwell beamed.

"Why don't you fly ahead and take a look for us to see what's going on? We are nearing the river and I am feeling a bit...un-nerved by all the silence of late," Jared said.

"I'm tired of flapping my arms, and I need to stretch my legs," Maxwell said, standing up, still nude. Both Jared and Channing looked away, rolling their eyes.

Maxwell threw the pants to Channing now and said, "Hang on to those for me, Cap!"

Maxwell sat back on his haunches. He gritted his teeth and growled toward Channing. The captain put a hand on the hilt of his sword but did not draw the blade.

"Easy, Captain," said Jared. "He's just teasing you. Don't give him the reaction he wants."

Maxwell Shifted into a timber wolf with yellow eyes and black fur. His lip curled revealing sharp fangs, and he ran off into the grass.

"I don't think I'll ever get used to that," Jared remarked.

"Why didn't he make himself bigger?" Channing asked, intrigued.

"He makes an impressive wolf, but why not be even bigger?"

Jared explained as they rode.

"That's a common misconception about Shape-Shifters. There is conservation of mass. Notice how the wolf was about the same size as the man?"

"It makes sense, but can he turn into anything? Like a dragon?"

"The more familiar he is with the animal, the easier it is for him to make sure it is accurate when he Shifts. I suppose he could turn into any beast as long as he was familiar with it."

They crossed the river into Delathrane Lands without inci-dent. They passed territory that had been used as a barbarian encampment in recent weeks, but they did not encounter a single war band.

"They are all moving westward, it seems," Jared noted.

"All quiet to the north and south," Maxwell said, when he

finally came strolling into the camp Jared and Channing had made. "I ran as far as I could in both directions. We don't need to worry about being flanked. Now I really am tired," he said. Channing threw the pants back toward Maxwell who caught them and nodded to the captain.

"We can camp in the valley tonight, and in the morning, we will climb out of the floodplains," Jared replied.

"And into the lands of the Serpent King? Who is this man, anyway?" Maxwell inquired.

"He is the son of King Raldric."

"Clan Razewell?"

"Yes," Jared said. "He was caught in the fighting as Seth and I tried to leave the Delathrane encampment. It was my blade that gave him the scar he wears."

Channing nodded in understanding.

"He is an ugly one from what I've heard," Maxwell said shivering at the thought. "He has a vertical scar down his face and a split tongue. Talks like a snake."

"We met again in the forest of the mountains. We were lucky to escape with our lives," Jared said.

"If Seth is still alive, I hate to think what he has been through if that man is his captor," Maxwell continued. "The barbarian king came out of nowhere. The reports about the clans living in the Serpent River Valley said nothing about him until just this past year."

"A year ago, he was just a small boy," Jared said. "I am the one who gave him the scar. Well, really the wound," Jared said, trying not to show how much the moment affected him.

"In war, terrible things happen," Maxwell said, picking up on the solemnity.

"You struck a child?" Channing asked in surprise. "Even if it was a Delathrane child, I think I would find that difficult to do."

Jared scowled at Channing.

"It happened in an instant," he said.

"What was a child doing in the midst of a battle?" Channing asked.

"You were not there. The entire encampment was against us. I do not harm children, but Seth and I were hard pressed. The boy stabbed me in the back of my knee. I swung at him. It was reflexive," Jared said.

"Well, he's no little child now. Have you seen him?" Maxwell asked.

Channing nodded. "He is a monster of a man."

"I would say he is a monster now," Jared said. "Look at the tracks, those were made by Delathranes. Let's follow them toward the river."

7

CHENDRIS

"H*andri*, are you ready for the next game?" Cedric asked. He seemed frustrated as he came into the tent and settled down, waiting for food to be brought to him.

"Set up the pieces," he commanded.

Seth grabbed the pieces, which were carved from bone and placed them on the circular board.

He would be defending again. The Serpent King loved to go on the offensive.

Every day the barbarian chieftain came back to the encampment, insisting on games of *Chendris*. Seth suspected the recruitment was not going as well as Cedric would have liked. The encampment had not been moved in weeks, and Seth had not seen many other Delathrane tribes joining lately. Once they had moved beyond the flood boundaries of the river to the lands westward, the tribes had less respect for the legend of the Delathrane King with the split tongue.

When the strong liquor flowed after the cooking fires burned low, Seth noticed that the Barbarian King initially played even better than usual. Sometimes so well that Seth barely managed to win.

"I cannot even beat the *Handri*!" Cedric cursed and threw his drink to the side. Seth thought he might be struck, like in days past, but the Serpent King restrained his fist.

"Why do you always beat the Serpent King?" a sneering barbarian warrior asked, leaning over Seth with breath that reeked of strong liquor.

"Stay away from my slave," Cedric barked at the sneering warrior. "I want to compete against the very best player, and the *Handri* slave is better than all of you put together."

"He needs to learn his place," the warrior insisted.

"He is trying to stay alive," Cedric explained.

Then, turning to Seth, the Serpent King spoke deeply. "If you allow me to win, simply because you're my captive, I will kill you. You know that, don't you?"

Seth nodded — glad he had not tried that strategy.

"I have too much respect for you and the game. I would not do that," Seth said to the ugly-faced barbarian.

"So, when I beat you, it will be a true victory for me," he growled as he began to set up the game once more.

This time Seth placed his queen in the middle and surrounded her with pawns. The second ring held archers. He built a wall around the archers and placed cavalry on the outside. Cedric frowned at the new set up.

"What are you planning for me?" he asked. "You placed your pawns next to your general.".

Seth looked at Cedric, who raised an eyebrow.

"I might yet make adjustments. Go ahead and put your formation on the board."

Cedric placed his army around the perimeter of the board unlike his typical set up. He left a few spaces between the pieces that were light and dark. Cedric had by now ceased to allow an audience to form around the games. Only the highest-ranking warriors were allowed to watch. Cedric didn't want to endure the shame of his constant failure in front of his people. Seth made sure never to present himself with hubris. He maintained an even temper and used the game to strive to build rapport with the Barbarian King.

"How long do you think you'll keep me here?" he asked after one particularly good match.

"You will never leave," Cedric said flatly.

Seth was unsure if that meant he would be captive forever or die a slave at the hand of the King when he was no longer interested in him for their *Chendris* matches.

Seth was no longer staked to a pole like a dog in the rain. Now he had been given a place to sleep within the royal tent. The transition from despised captive to treasured pet was not enough though. Seth wasn't sure which situation might be worse in the end.

In the silence of the match, Seth took a risk and spoke to Cedric directly.

"I can be of great service to you...alive," said Seth. "You are not having the success you want. I can be of service to you."

Cedric glared at him, searching for any sign of insubordination.

"How dare you speak to me of service, *Handri*?" he growled.

It was a dangerous strategy, and Seth knew his life hung in the balance. His next words, if accepted, would determine his future. Seth knew he could not be kept as a pet forever. He saw what happened to pets in the Delathrane encampment, both the human and animal kind. He swallowed and continued.

"I am trained to be a counselor, my King. I can offer my words of wisdom to you, if they would be of any benefit."

The offer hung in the smoky air for the length of five of Seth's heartbeats. The warriors closest to the Serpent King watched the interaction carefully.

"Sīhalt, you are the only one here who has bested me in the

Game of War. Maybe you do have ideas I may not have considered," he finally said.

Seth noted that he was not called *Handri* this time — a good sign.

The Sīhalt Guardian waited for the Delathrane leader to say more, but he did not. He looked at Seth through eyes half-lidded and dark. The fire suddenly spat in the central cooking pit, sending sparks dancing up toward the night sky.

"Gathering followers is not the same as defeating enemies," Seth began.

"I will make the greatest force this land has ever seen in order to drive the prideful *Handri* of the Golden City out to the sea. Why would you help me? Would you turn on your own people?"

"As I said before, I am not *Handri*. I am a Sīhalt Guardian. We have fought on both sides of many conflicts and advised on many more. Those of my order serve faithfully when sworn to do so."

The Serpent King remained silent for a moment, and then stood up and pulled his knife from its sheath.

Seth flinched but held his ground where he knelt. Perhaps he had said too much.

This is the end? he thought.

The hulking warrior approached him, and slowly drew his knife across his own forearm as he stared at Seth. A line of blood welled up and ran down his skin, toward his elbow, where it dripped to the floor.

"To be in my service, you will be blood-sworn to me, Sīhalt," said the Serpent King.

"I did not know your people still use the oldest of oaths," Seth replied, trying to fathom the seriousness with which the barbarian acted. Was this a trick? Was he being taunted?

"Open your mouth and take my strength into yourself. With this act, you swear never to leave me, nor to do anything to my detriment. Even your Gods will hold you to this, no?" Cedric said.

It was not the typical way to engage the services of a Sīhalt

Guardian, but Seth would accept it as an advancement of his station. He didn't suppose Abbath would object, given the circumstances. Seth did not hesitate but turned his head upward and opened his mouth to become blood sworn.

Seth watched the enormous fingers of the barbarians place the game pieces back on the board.

"Do you prefer the attack?" Seth asked.

"I prefer the fight — attacking or defending, both are sweet to me," the Delathrane King said.

Seth watched him closely, trying to be discreet as he did so.

The Serpent King had become better at the game. Much better, in fact. It now took Seth effort to beat him.

"What about you?" Do you prefer to defend or attack?" Cedric asked.

"I prefer to defend...the weak and innocent," Seth said, waiting to see if the barbarian caught the irony.

"There are no innocents in this war, Guardian," the Serpent King replied.

"What about the children or the aged?" Seth asked.

"Do the old ones not harvest the grain to feed your troops? Do the children not pray for the success of the Tyathian soldiers? Wolf pups grow to be hunters, no matter how soft they are when young," he said in his forked-tongued, guttural way.

"Who treated you the worst as I slept? Was it not the old women and the children? They tormented you daily, covering you with glowing embers, just to watch you squirm. Are they innocent?"

Seth looked down at the countless scars made by the scorching ashes the youngest of the Clans had pressed against his skin for sport. The barbarian had a point.

"Perhaps they simply fight the battle in the form it is presented to them?" Seth said without malice. "Children follow the traditions of their fathers and mothers. If they are hateful, it is because they are taught to behave this way."

The giant shook his head slowly, both ends of the white scar lining up as he pursed his lips.

"No *Handri*, children are naturally cruel, as are the aged. Even a grandmother, bouncing her grandchild on her knee, would gut you like a spring rabbit if I gave the order."

"It's your move," Seth said quietly.

Cedric began this time with the pieces set in the spiral pattern. Seth had learned that technique from Master Bradshaw when he was convalescing one summer after a fall when he was twelve years old. The barbarian seemed to understand it perfectly. Seth set up a defense, but the barbarian executed his attack perfectly.

"Who taught you that style?" Seth asked.

"I created it a few years ago when I was eight years old," Cedric replied. "You like it?"

He smiled wickedly.

Seth nodded, impressed. "Has anyone beaten you when you have used it?"

"No *Handri*, if the chance to strike is offered, I always take it."

"Why do you call me *Handri*?" Seth asked as he moved his game pieces to shore up his defense.

"All the people that came across the sea are *Handri*," Cedric replied.

"You're wrong again," Seth said.

He moved the *Chendris* pieces to stop the slowly tightening spiral at the center of the board, breaking through the offensive with a concentrated strike in the opposite direction.

Cedric looked up with surprise.

"I am not *Handri*. My people come from Addisfall. We are not of the Golden City," Seth explained.

"How did you do that?" Cedric asked, confused.

"You wish to go back? Perhaps I can show you another game," Seth offered.

Cedric nodded, "You will show me another game."

And so, I live to see another day, Seth thought.

"Tyath was founded by one people. Addisfall was founded by others, as were Candoreth and Horming. We did not come from the same country across the ocean," Seth explained.

"Were you enemies, then?" Cedric asked.

"At times, in the distant past, we were," Seth said.

"We have been at war among our people long before your people came. I have heard the songs of our singers," Cedric said.

"You are strong. Yet, you do not know your enemy as well as you think you do," Seth said carefully.

Seth moved his pieces outward and expanded them, shifting from defensive to offensive.

Cedric made counter moves to try to stop his advance.

"I am learning," he stated.

Seth paused his hands on one of the game pieces.

"As your blood-sworn, I will serve you until you release me, or until I die," Seth stated seriously.

Cedric nodded, "That is right," he replied.

"May I give you advice? You have grown rapidly but unfortunately, still lack experience. Your childhood was cut short and you were thrust into this role suddenly."

"I do not need your pity. After all, it was your brother who gave me purpose and made me stronger," the Serpent King said. Cedric held up an arm, wreathed in muscles.

"I saw the look on my brother's face after he struck you when you were a child. He was mortified."

"But then he ran, like a little girl, and left you to be captured," Cedric replied.

"We planned to meet back and gather the remains of our sister. He did not know I was captured."

"Yet still, he did not come for you. I waited for him."

"As did I."

"Instead he decided to guard a woman on her wedding

journey for money," the giant warrior said with a scowl, as if he intended to spit the bitter words out of his mouth.

"He did his duty," Seth said.

"How can you see it this way? Brothers-in-arms, if they're still alive, will defend one another!" Cedric replied.

"Our master gave Jared his mission," Seth said.

"Did your master tell him to kill my father?"

Seth hesitated. "No, that was an act of vengeance and anger. I am as much to blame as he is."

"Your brother, *Der'Antha*, is a very fierce warrior."

Seth nodded.

"He is a good man, even if he is your enemy."

"I would like to drink from his skull, but he is sneaky," Cedric said as he moved one of his pieces against Seth's. "Like you."

"He made it to the Golden City, didn't he?" Seth replied.

Cedric nodded, and frowned. "Only barely — we almost had him. We pierced him with many arrows. I believe he no longer lives."

Seth exhaled.

But you didn't see him dead, he thought.

"If he's alive, he will come for me," Seth said.

"I see the concern you have for him. How can you serve me and my enemy?"

"You will understand your enemy better, by hearing my words," Seth suggested. "And, the other chieftains will see that you have a Guardian sworn to serve you. This will bring you more honor in their eyes."

Cedric considered this.

"I know that you are good with the blade, how do I know you will not kill me in my sleep?" Cedric said.

Seth held his wrist together and knelt on the ground.

"Bind my hands daily if you choose, but I will not attempt to escape or to harm you or your people until I die or am willingly released from your service."

Cedric leveled his eyes at Seth and reached forward with a giant hand that had grown calloused since the Healing. He moved the final pieces on the *Chendris* board, killing Seth's remaining forces, one by one in a masterstroke.

"I win, Guardian," the Serpent King said.

8

A LETTER FROM HOME

Larissa smoothed the green silk she wore and adjusted the long, white gloves that reached past her elbows. She walked over to Kathleen. Her hips swayed in the suggestive way she always moved. Any men within eyesight would turn to gaze upon her golden locks bouncing upon her bare shoulders.

"That dress is fabulous Katie, you should wear it more often," Larissa said. "And this is going to be the most fantastic dance you've ever attended."

Immediately, images of the dance Kathleen had shared with Jared in Altrastadt came to her mind. She remembered his passionate embrace, the graceful movements they had shared together on the dance floor in front of a crowd that believed them to be newlyweds.

"I doubt it, Larissa," Kathleen said.

"No, you don't understand. The dances here are splendid! The music, the decorations, and all the lords and ladies in attendance, it's unlike anything you have in Sundiland. I can see it in your eyes. You are dreaming of it now, I can tell," Larissa said.

Kathleen kept the memories of the dance with Jared to herself.

"I am sure it will be beautiful," she agreed.

The clip-clop of cantering hooves could be heard approaching. It was a quick pace of a half-dozen horses. Around the bend came the royal carriage emblazoned with the Acorn and Fox of House Dol Lassimer, circumscribed by scrolling, gilt acanthus leaves. The horses were white and black in alternating matched pairs.

"I am so glad we are traveling with Heathron. We are going to arrive in style," Larissa said.

The door of the carriage opened, and the Prince stepped down.

"Good news, Kathleen," he said. "I have a letter for you."

He extended his hand and Kathleen rushed to greet him.

"From my father?" she asked.

"The courier arrived just as I was leaving. I hope the news is good. I don't want to dampen our evening, but I couldn't bear to delay. I knew you would want to read it."

Kathleen held the letter in her hand, and carefully turned the folded paper over.

It was her father's stationery. She held it to her lips and inhaled, wondering if she might be able to pick up his scent on the paper.

With trembling fingers, she lifted the blood-red wax that sealed the letter closed.

"Do you mind if I read it before we go?" she asked.

"By all means, Kathleen, I wouldn't expect you to wait," Heathron said.

Kathleen unfolded the pages and began to read. After all she had been through since leaving, this was the first letter from home.

Dearest Daughter,

Word has finally reached me that you have arrived in the Golden City. I thank Abbath that you have made it there safely.

Rumors came back to our city that you had been killed. Other rumors said that you were stolen by the barbarians. Against Queen Renata's wishes, I led what men we could spare to search for you. When the people of Horming City said your Wedding Procession never arrived, I truly feared I would never see you again. We traveled north to Revonah only to find devastation. We turned back, harried by Delathrane barbarians all the way through the Sagav forest.

I privately grieved for your loss but tried to present a respectable face of hope for our people. The pirates and brigands have been bad enough, but to have Delathranes within our borders was a severe blow.

You cannot imagine the joy and consolation I felt to see the relief come from the Golden City. To find out you were alive! I know now, that although you were not married, the man to whom you are betrothed is worthy of your love.

The food was most graciously received by our people. Many a small child in Sundiland was protected from starvation by the generosity of House Dol Lassimer. In truth, I owe my kingdom to Heathron. I am forever his loyal vassal. If we are able to establish a better harvest this coming year, I will travel to Tyath to witness your wedding at Midsummer next year.

Your little sister, Elayna, has asked that I give you a message. She says not to forget that you are invited to come home anytime. And she may visit you after all. She was told about ice skating and thinks the cold winters may not be so bad after all.

Please send us word of all you are learning and enjoying.

Your loving father,

Lukald

Kathleen felt tears welling up in her eyes.

"I am sorry, Kathleen, I tried to send help in time," he said.

Kathleen felt the elation of relief. Her tears flowed from joy, not sadness. Reading her father's words made her feel as if she could burst. She suddenly threw her arms around Heathron.

"Thank you, thank you," she wept. "Everything is okay!"

Heathron placed his arms around her waist. Kathleen realized that his arms were strong as she pressed her body against his, but she had a sudden thought that she must pull away. She felt almost as if she were doing something improper. A flash of the Sīhalt crossed her mind.

It is not wrong to thank him, she told herself.

She patted his shoulder and pulled back, breaking the embrace.

Larissa handed Kathleen a handkerchief.

"It's a good thing you don't wear very much makeup, Kathleen, I never know when you're going to burst into tears or need a hug from the Prince."

Kathleen took the handkerchief and was grateful for the small amount of privacy it provided as she wiped her eyes.

"It's good news then?" he asked.

"I think it's safe to say that King Lukald is happy to join our realm with the Empire. Your assistance has saved my family. I am so grateful."

Heathron looked at Kathleen. "We all have reasons to be thankful."

"I'm so happy that letter is adding to the joy of the evening instead of ruining it. I have been looking forward to this party," Larissa said.

"Now I feel like I could dance all night," Kathleen said.

"I must warn you," Heathron said, "I am an energetic dancer, I might take you up on it."

He wore the brightest smile Kathleen had seen yet.

Kathleen wished that things were not so complicated. As she entered his carriage, she hoped that during the year she would spend in the capital she and Heathron might become excellent friends. Kathleen gazed out the window towards the setting sun in the west, and wondered where the Sīhalt Guardian might be.

Larissa talked excitedly the entire way to the Turlin Estate.

"You're going to love it, Katie. There are so many young people in the capital, and the Turlins, although not my favorite house, know how to host a ball. The music and the food are always supremely delicious."

She stopped to place a hand on her stomach.

"Not that I need any more of that," she added.

Kathleen smiled at her talkative friend. Larissa made it easy for her. There was no need to hold up her end of the conversation if she couldn't get a word in edgewise.

"And there are a number of young nobles that I would love for you to meet," Larissa said.

"Larissa, in case you hadn't noticed, I'm not the most desirable friend to have around at the moment," Kathleen said.

"You have done more good for your people and provided more gossip for the Golden City than any girl I've ever met," Larissa said. "Besides, Prince Heathron remains steadfast."

"I see no reason not to!" Heathron exclaimed.

"I'm glad that I can provide some entertainment," Kathleen laughed.

"All the girls of the high noble houses are wondering if you really are a Plant Witch. That rumor is spreading like wildfire. I think the Church is a little overbearing about it if you ask me. I mean, even if you were cursed, you couldn't help that."

"I would appreciate it if you didn't refer to me as cursed or speak of my abilities to anyone," Kathleen said.

"You know what I mean, but your secret is safe with me," she said. Larissa flipped her hair in an air of frivolity. "I'm just glad you're going to the dance."

9

TURLIN'S BALL

Heathron's carriage drove up the long drive leading to Lord Turlin's palace. The matching pair of horses that pulled the royal carriage arched their necks regally. The Turlin Estate commanded a view of a gentle, green valley a few miles north of the city. The walls surrounding the estate were strong and well-guarded. The barbarians had not destroyed the estate, like they did some of the villages east of the city. Guards dressed in silver and white livery opened the tall iron gates. They passed stone lanterns burning at intervals to light the private road. Two more gates were opened and closed as they passed through. Finally, the carriage turned along the central avenue that cut across the bowling green, which was lined with cherry trees.

"You should see it in the spring," Larissa remarked. "The pink cherry blossoms are breathtaking."

"I don't think I have ever seen a home more beautiful," Kathleen gasped as they rounded a curve in the road, providing a view of the central stairs leading to the estate.

As the carriage rolled to the front of the house, the horses slowed to a stop. Prince Heathron and one of the Turlin footmen opened the carriage doors to help Kathleen and Larissa step down.

"Hello, Prince Heathron. It's so good to see you," a sultry female voice said from the stairs leading upward to the palace.

Kathleen looked out of the window and saw a tall, blonde-haired girl dressed in a soft, white gown rush forward and throw her arms around Prince Heathron. She looked as though she might be related to him with the light-colored hair and dark brown eyes.

"I didn't know if you were going to make it. You didn't respond as to whether or not you were coming," she said coyly.

"Who is that?" Kathleen mouthed to Larissa quietly.

"That is Jessica Turlin," Larissa replied.

"I was only made available recently, Miss Turlin," Heathron explained.

"Please tell me that you'll save me a dance," Jessica insisted in a voice so flirtatious Kathleen realized she was not likely to become the girl's friend.

"Did you bring someone with you? I wouldn't want you to be alone," Jessica said.

The girl knew full well that Heathron would come with his betrothed, if he came at all, Kathleen thought.

"I am accompanied by the Princess Kathleen DeLunt Dal Sundi this evening," he said, gesturing toward the carriage.

Jessica looked at the carriage and pretended, as if for the first time, to notice Kathleen sitting inside.

"I see," she said, inclining her head toward Kathleen and offering a slight curtsy with barely concealed disappointment at seeing Kathleen in tow.

"She's unfamiliar with our customs here in Tyath."

"I'm sure she will learn very quickly," Jessica said. "I took the liberty of preparing a welcoming line for the young nobility within the high noble houses. Princess Dal Sundi will be able to meet everyone that is important to know tonight," she said.

Kathleen stepped down from the carriage, and tried to smile sincerely.

Jessica returned the smile with a practiced expression of her own — a healthy mix of patronizing disdain and dismissiveness.

Heathron and Kathleen walked up the steps of the ancestral seat of the Turlin family. Young men and women throughout the Capital City had gathered there this day. They were dressed in their finest apparel. Many of the men wore decorative military uniforms with assorted ribbons and medals. Most of the men wore swords at the hip, although some were merely decorative. The women wore dresses that fit tightly on the waist and bust line, but expanded outward at the hips to three times the size of any Kathleen had ever seen.

Heathron moved up the stairs and turned away from Kathleen as they arrived at the spot where the stairs divided into two — one to the right, one to the left.

"I will go up the left side, you go up the right," Heathron said, letting go of her arm. "The ladies use the stairs on the right," he explained.

"Alright," Kathleen said. "Should I expect this every time I climb a flight of stairs?" she asked.

"If there are two options, young ladies stay to the right," he said.

"Why is that?" Kathleen asked.

Heathron paused, "You know, I am not sure. It is just the way we have always done it," he said.

"Then I will see you at the top," Kathleen replied as he bowed to her. Then he turned and joined the other young men who were making their way up the left side of the stairway.

Kathleen's gown was larger than the dresses she was used to wearing but not nearly as extravagantly sprawling as those worn by the other guests. She was careful to place her feet securely on each step as she climbed. It would not do to take a tumble at her first social outing in Tyath.

"I am not used to wearing a dress with a hoop built into the petticoat," Kathleen said to Larissa as she smoothed the folds of the expansive fabric.

"How are we supposed to dance in these?"

"Very carefully," Larissa joked as she tugged the strapless bodice upward to fit more comfortably beneath her arms.

"I miss the sleek styles of Candoreth," she said.

"We don't wear the hoops all the time, just for the summer season," Larissa explained. "It's tradition."

When they finally reached the top, Prince Heathron took her by the arm and whispered in her ear.

"They will probably start with a dance of some kind. This helps us all get to know each other. When the music begins, just stand across from me. As long as we are at the end, we can just do what every other couple does in the dance."

For a moment, Kathleen was taken, for a moment, back to a memory of Jared, her Sīhalt Guardian, whispering to her, "Just follow my lead..."

"Kathleen, did you hear me?" Heathron asked. He stood there, holding the door open so that she could enter.

"If you don't want to dance with the Prince, I will," Jessica Turlin said as she dragged her long nails along Heathron's shoulders. "We could show you the way this one goes and then see if you are capable of keeping up?"

"I'll manage just fine," Kathleen assured her. "I'm sure if I trip on this oversized skirt, Heathron will catch me."

"Of course, I will," Heathron said.

Kathleen cocked her head and smiled with a look that invited Jessica Turlin to try again.

"I'll introduce you to all the guests after this dance is over," Jessica said. Her lips parted to show her teeth again, but Kathleen couldn't quite describe it as a smile.

She is certainly less dismissive this time, Kathleen thought, with some amusement.

10

A TALENTED WITCH

Throughout the Tyathian Reel, Kathleen held her skirt hem above the floor to keep from tripping and she laughed as she twirled around the arm of Heathron and the next young noble man in the line then back to Heathron and so on down the line. Kathleen found herself giggling and smiling.

"I am glad I followed your advice," she said to Larissa who clapped and stood beside her in the line of the dance.

"I told you it would be fun!" she said, then sashayed forward to swing around the arm of a handsome, dark-haired young man across from them.

More carriages rolled in, one after the other, around the circular drive. The approach was lit by torches in the darkness, the flames casting shadows which seemed to dance in time with the music. Even the firelight appeared to be excited about this party.

Well-dressed footmen helped the girls exit the carriages as they were escorted up the long flight of stairs. At the top where it split into a balcony in either direction, Kathleen walked with Heathron and looked up at the stars in the clear summer night.

She could see the Hunter and the Hare in the constellations above her.

"Oh my goodness!" said Larissa, running past Kathleen and Heathron with arms outstretched.

She ran to greet a young lady with light brown hair and bouncing barrel curls. The diameter of their gowns did not allow the girls to hug normally, so they leaned forward for a quick embrace.

"I heard you were coming!" the girl said excitedly.

"Kathleen, this is my wonderful friend Hannah Aviella. And this is Kathleen Dal Sundi," Larissa said, pulling Kathleen forward by the hand. "She is from Candoreth," Larissa said, introducing the two of them.

The girl curtsied and smiled sincerely.

"Is it true that you're betrothed to the Prince?" she asked, her eyes wide with amazement.

Kathleen curtsied in return. "It is my pleasure to meet you," she said.

"Kathleen, you don't have to do that," said Larissa. "Hannah is from a lower house, you shouldn't curtsy to her." Larissa giggled and thankfully so did Hannah.

"This is all new to me," Kathleen said. "In Candoreth we don't make distinctions to that degree."

"In the north everything seems more rigid," Kathleen observed. "Everything you do here in Tyath seems to have a rule attached. In Sundiland we can eat what we want for breakfast, make friends with whomever we like — even servants, and we curtsy as a form of respect to another person whether they are higher than us on the social ladder or not."

Hannah's mouth fell open. She moved her hand to cover it and spoke in a softer voice.

"You mean to tell me, that a Princess would curtsy to a commoner or a slave?" she asked.

"We don't have slaves in Sundiland," she said. "My great-grandfather outlawed that a long time ago."

"Oh, but I was told you came to Tyath with your Delathrane slave woman?" Hannah said.

"It is very good that Melva did not hear you say that. She doesn't take kindly to being mistaken for a Delathrane," Kathleen said.

Larissa shook her head. "And she is not a slave," Larissa stated emphatically.

"But she is a witch?" Hannah asked.

"Melva is a Healer," Kathleen said.

"Aren't you worried that she will taint the air? Aren't you worried that her sorcery will bring the Plague upon your house?" Hannah asked.

Kathleen could see that the girl was being sincere, so she wasn't angry with her. Hannah could not help the fact that she had been fed lies, or at least had learned from people who were ignorant and prejudiced.

"I wouldn't be alive without her. She has Healed me a number of times," Kathleen said.

"Well, I suppose it's better to take the risk, if it's a choice between life and death," Hannah said.

As they spoke, another group of young people made their way up the steps. Some of the women cooled themselves with ivory fans as they peered at her condescendingly, and walked away to whisper to each other.

Jessica Turlin arranged the guests in a line, and Kathleen was able to meet them one by one. The faces became a blur of smiles and sidelong glances. Some were clearly genuine in their welcoming words. Others were more reserved and still others seemed hostile.

"Don't mind them, Princess Dal Sundi," Hannah said. "They treat everyone as if they are lesser than they. Just because some of us are not related to the houses within the Council of Nine, doesn't mean they should be so cruel."

"What council?" Kathleen asked.

"Nine of the high Houses get to help enforce laws with the Emperor and Empress. During the year, each of the Nine Houses must sponsor a social event — usually a dance like this one. House Turlin always takes this month," Hannah said.

"They put on a fantastic party, even if it's just to show everyone else how much better they are. I'm actually looking forward to it," Larissa admitted.

When the music began to slow again, the young men and women descended from the balcony above the dance floor. They were announced by a master-of-ceremonies who pounded his staff on the floor loudly and proclaimed the names and titles of the distinguished guests.

Kathleen took Heathron's arm. He walked gracefully down the stairs, as if he had been born for this. Kathleen prayed that she wouldn't stumble or humiliate herself in front of this crowd. After Hannah's comments about Melva, she wished that she hadn't worn green, even if it was one of her favorite colors.

She didn't need anything to remind the people of her Talent. She hoped that Heathron wasn't just tolerant about her true nature, but was genuinely willing to accept her as she was, even if his people were not willing to do so.

Because of the prestige the Prince enjoyed, there were a number of people who would not approach them. Most bowed respectfully as they passed. Only the highest-ranking guests saw fit to approach and strike up a conversation. As the night wore on and the drinks flowed more freely, Kathleen noticed the redness in the faces of some of the nobility. Girls who had once held themselves with more decorum, now laughed heartily and sometimes stumbled as they walked. Kathleen saw one girl wipe her face with her arm and spilled a little wine in her lap.

Heathron grimaced at the scene. "I'm sorry," he said. "Not all of Tyath is as practiced in moderation as I would like."

"My father rarely lost a bet when he was sober, but he likes to drink when he is gambling. He rarely wins the bets he makes late in the evening under the influence of wine," Kathleen replied.

"You don't drink, Kathleen?"

He swirled his wine in a crystal goblet, peering down at its contents.

"I decided when I was young that I would stay away from it," she replied.

"It's never been a true desire of mine either. I drink when there's a ceremony that might require it, but other than that, I could do without it. Would you prefer that I set it aside?"

"Oh, that's not needed Heathron," she said. "I'm just glad you're not getting foolish like some of the others here this evening."

As if on cue, a group of inebriated noblemen began to argue. Their shirts and jackets were blazoned with the various symbols of their houses. The heraldry denoted who was a member of the high houses and who belonged to the lesser ones.

A red-faced guest staggered forward, fumbling with a ceremonial sword on his hip. He lost his balance and the weapon clattered down on the table.

"Hey...Heathron!" he slurred, his voice accentuating the first letter of each word. "I'm glad you didn't marry the Sundiland Plant Witch. Do you think I will get a chance to meet her tonight?"

Heathron stood tall as they approached. He gestured to Kathleen, and she stood up as well.

"Lord Naystrom, allow me to introduce Princess Kathleen Dal Sundi, my betrothed," he added with emphasis.

Kathleen extended her hand with the long white glove. The young man, dressed in a crimson doublet with an embroidered wolf adorning in the upper left breast, smiled stupidly. The white sash he wore almost slipped from his shoulder. He kissed her hand and looked at her with bleary, brown eyes. He seemed to be searching for words.

"You may call me Aidan if you wish," he said to Kathleen and then turned to Heathron.

"Why, she's beautiful! I've never seen a lady with hair the color of fire this close. Can I touch it?" he requested, then burped, covering his mouth.

Kathleen drew back slightly and furrowed her brow.

"I'd rather you didn't," she said.

Prince Heathron stepped forward and interposed himself between the tipsy nobleman and Kathleen.

"You are mistaken, Aidan" the Prince said. "While it is true that Kathleen comes from Sundiland, she is no witch. Perhaps you're thinking of her servant, the old woman?"

"Oh yes, the Delathrane witch," the nobleman drawled.

"The very same!" Heathron said. "She has had the woman as a household servant since she was a child."

The nobleman frowned, disgusted by the idea.

"How can they live like that? I can't imagine spending my days with anyone who carries the curse of Abboth," he said.

"They could hardly cast her out!" Heathron said. "She had become part of the household by then."

"I suppose that's true, I have a couple of hunting hounds that aren't worth much, but I still love them," he said as he laughed, as did Heathron.

Kathleen fumed.

Hunting hounds? Melva is family to me! she thought to herself in outrage.

"Oh, that's good to hear!" the drunken young lord said. "Because rumors are flying around, and I could not imagine you marrying a Plant Witch or any other of the cursed ones. The Council of Nine would have something to say about that, I'm sure. I'm glad you have the sense to steer clear of that sort of entanglement. It really is a pleasure to meet you, Princess Kathleen," he said, bowing to her, oblivious that she was seething, and he continued across the dance floor with his raucous group of friends from lower houses. Kathleen caught a glimpse of the white dress of Jessica Turlin in the mix and felt even more anger rise in her breast.

Kathleen turned to Heathron.

"Why did you say that?" she demanded.

"I just don't think everyone needs to know your...personal matters," the Prince offered.

Kathleen frowned for a moment considering his explanation.

"Are you protecting me...or yourself?" she asked.

"I just don't want to make things hard for you, Kathleen," Heathron said. "There's a lot I'd like people to learn about you before they...," he trailed off.

"Before they find out I am a witch?" she cut in sharply.

"Much has changed in the city over the past few years. I believe the situation will get better, but the people need a bit more...time."

"You want to lie to people? You are willing to tell them that I'm something I am not?" she demanded harshly.

Prince Heathron paused and then started again.

"Kathleen, I just want to make things easier for you here," he said. "It's true, I think we should not emphasize the fact that you have a Talent. I thought we had an understanding about this."

He looked around, anxious that someone might overhear. "And since you were not planning on doing any dramatic demonstrations of your Talent, I thought it would be okay to deflect the unwanted attention," he said.

"I want you to accept what I am," she replied. Kathleen felt bitter anger rising in her stomach, born of the frustration of knowing that she was trapped. She couldn't leave the city, and now she realized that she was forbidden to exercise freely the Talent that was hers—inherited from her mother.

Didn't my mother do good with her Talent? Hadn't she built the navy for Candoreth?

"I refuse to believe that Melva, or my mother, or any of the Talented brought 'Abboth's Plague' upon our lands," she said, her voice overflowing with emotion.

"Kathleen, none of this matters to me. I just want to give us a chance."

"I want to go home now," Kathleen said. "I have had enough entertainment for one evening."

Heathron nodded and asked a servant to call for the carriage.

Larissa walked across the ballroom, when a servant told her Kathleen was leaving.

"What is the matter?" she asked, surprised by the sudden change in plans. "The dance is far from being over. Why are we leaving so soon?"

Heathron gestured to Kathleen.

"I am not feeling well," she said.

"Do you mind if I stay and ride home with Hannah? There are some noblemen with whom I'd like to become better acquainted."

The one wearing the crimson wolf and white sash waved to Larissa across the room.

Of course, thought Kathleen. *Larissa would go for that one.*

11

A GREEN GROWER'S GIFT

Kathleen sat on her side of the carriage with her hands folded in her lap. At times Heathron tried to break the silence by commenting on some of the evening's more light-hearted moments.

Kathleen made few remarks. She had no appetite for reliving the dance. Finally, Heathron fell quiet too. He gazed out the carriage window, up at the stars on his side. The silence between them grew more protracted, and Kathleen began to wish that she could run from the carriage into the forest, which she perceived in the distance beyond the fields. Couldn't she make her way back home to Candoreth, or live quietly by herself in the woods?

I could make my own food, Growing what I need, she thought.

She didn't have to be his prisoner or anyone else's. But deeper inside, she knew that she could not run away. Like so many women before her, she knew her heart would not let her abandon her duty to her people and her loved ones. She could not seek the solitude of the wild in a sudden dash for the solace of the wilderness of trees and leaves. Too many people, far from these city walls, were counting on her.

"Kathleen, thank you for coming with me this evening," Heathron said, breaking the silence.

"You probably wish I hadn't come," she replied.

"I didn't get to show you all my skills on the dance floor, but I will treasure this memory as the very first dance we shared."

"All we did was twirl and spin and run up and down the line," she said.

"But I saw you smiling as we danced."

Kathleen bit her lip.

She had enjoyed the energetic music and back and forth of the Tyathian Reel. When she had met back up with Heathron after spinning down the entire line of dancers, their hands had met and formed the bridge for all the others to pass beneath, and she had laughed out loud along with him.

"If only the whole night could have been like that," she said.

"It will get better, I promise you. And I am truly sorry for the part I played in ruining your evening."

Kathleen turned her eyes back toward the dark of the night. She did not want him to see how much his words had hurt her.

Heathron slid closer to her on the seat and placed a hand on hers. She decided not to pull it away. She felt more hurt and alone now, rather than angry.

The enormous city walls of Tyath loomed large on the horizon as they came closer to the northern gate. The lanterns at the guard towers punctuated the long walls, extending in both directions.

"I hurt you this evening with my inconsiderate words," he said, almost reading her mind. "I do accept you for who you are, for what you are," he said softly.

Kathleen kept her eyes averted. Heathron laced his fingers between her own, and she felt her heart begin to pound faster. She turned to him.

"What am I to you, Heathron?" she asked. "Am I a Plant Witch? One cursed by Abbath? Or do I have at least some redeeming qualities? Maybe it's just my exotic red hair," she said bitterly, pulling at one of her curls.

Heathron moved closer.

"When I look at you, I do not see a witch, but rather a woman. I see a lady with whom I would spend my life and have a family. I see a girl who is fun and beautiful and kind."

Now he held her hand between both of his, and she returned his gaze. The sincerity in his words touched her heart and seemed to wash away the pain he had inflicted on her.

"And I do like your hair. I find it irresistible," he said with a wrinkled nose and a smile.

Against her will, Kathleen laughed and blinked away the tears that had welled in her eyes.

"Men are so strange," she said.

Heathron nodded.

"We can be crazy, especially when we are falling in love," he said.

Kathleen had to admit to herself that love was not logical. Even in her limited experience with romance — and romantic feelings, she found them to be a torrent of emotion, rather than thoughtful considerations. Heathron gazed at her with an expression Kathleen remembered seeing on Jared's face. Kathleen felt an impulse to respond in kind, and tell Heathron that she loved him too, but she didn't feel ready to say it, and she could not bring herself to give precocious voice to something so precious. Instead, she took his face in her hands and gave him a brief kiss on the cheek.

"Thank you for apologizing. I rarely saw my father do that," she said.

When they got back to the palace Kathleen exited the carriage nearest to her private rooms. The Prince touched her on the arm.

"I didn't want to show you this yet," he said, "but after our conversation tonight, I think there is somthing you need to see," he said.

"I forgive you, Heathron. I was acting like a baby," Kathleen replied. "I'm sorry for making us leave the dance early."

"May I show you something in order to make amends?" he asked.

His face was lit with excitement, and Kathleen wondered what could make him seem so animated.

"Are you sure it isn't too late?" she asked.

"We would have been dancing most of the night if we had stayed at Lord Turlin's ball. No, tomorrow won't work," he said. "I must show you now. I know you do not consider this city your home yet, but I still have ten months to win you over. That was our deal, and I think this will make you happy."

He grabbed her by the hand and pulled her down the hall. Kathleen lifted the hem of her dress and took quick steps to keep up. Kathleen's resistance began to melt.

In an effort to be fair, she had to recognize that part of her frustrations stemmed from the circumstances she was in. It wasn't Heathron's fault. She wondered what an entire year in the Golden City would do to her. She didn't want to feel trapped, surrounded by beautiful people and beautiful objects, but not beautiful living things.

"I hope you have enjoyed your quarters," he said, "but I have put a lot of thought into this, and I wanted to surprise you."

They walked briskly through the halls of the royal palace. He led her up a flight of stairs and turned down the labyrinthine hallways.

"I don't think I could find my way back to my room without you," she said.

"We are going to the other side of the palace, to the side built nearest to the exterior walls. I wanted to find a beautiful place that was south-facing," he explained, "for the sunlight."

"What is it?" Kathleen asked.

Had the Prince commissioned some statue in her honor? What could it be? she wondered.

They came to a door and Heathron paused.

"Close your eyes," he said.

"Okay, I'm ready," she said.

Kathleen tried to walk forward as Heathron kept his hands covering each of her eyes. She laughed with delight.

"Hold steady," he said. "I don't want you peeking."

"Why would I peek? I don't even know what this is about." Kathleen took another step forward and felt a strand of her hair brush her cheek as if a breeze had disturbed it.

"I've been working on it since the first day you arrived," he said.

"I can feel the open air, are we in a courtyard?" she asked.

"You will just have to wait and see," Heathron said, his breath warming the back of her neck.

Kathleen inhaled deeply. A sweet scent hung on the air.

Gardenia!

"Heathron Dol Lassimer, what have you done?" she cried.

"I have my own ways of finding out what I need to know," he said. "Are you ready?"

Kathleen inhaled deeply.

"Yes, let me see it," she said.

Heathron removed his hands from her eyes. They stood in the center of a garden. A spacious room extended before her. The ceiling was supported by tall columns carved with every manner of plant and flower. Heathron smiled as he ran his finger along the intricate carvings. Kathleen noticed how alive even the sculptures seemed to be.

To the right was a bed and a wash basin. Along one side was a closet for clothes. Kathleen looked up and saw an expansive metal framework that held panes of clear glass. Two of the largest ones were open, allowing a breeze to filter through the room.

There was moisture, too. A trickle of water bubbled up from a small fountain that spilled over and into a reflecting pool. Then it meandered its way around to another corner of the room where it emptied into a discreet drain. Flowers and vines clung to the gleaming walls. Fragrant shrubs grew along the small brook, and Kathleen stroked her fingers on the underside of a small tree that was just beginning to establish its roots in the soil in the middle of the room.

"How have you managed to do this?" she asked breathlessly, bending to touch the soft leaves of the plants at their feet.

"I thought perhaps you would enjoy the privacy," he said.

"This is stunning. You have no idea how much this means to me."

"So, you like it?" Heathron smiled.

"It's beautiful."

"Some of the plants are local to our region here. But I had the royal botanist bring some tropical plants from the greenhouses. I thought that perhaps if you felt more at home, you would enjoy your stay here a little more."

"I don't know what to say, Heathron. It's as if you brought my dreams to life."

Heathron walked over to the crank on the wall and as he slowly turned the shaft, the window above closed. "You can adjust this for wind and temperature, and if there is rain outside you can easily close them. I made the roof steep enough that snow should slide off. I expect you will especially enjoy the garden in the winter."

Heathron squatted down beside the brook and dipped his fingers into the crystal waters.

"Even when the weather gets cold," he explained, "I have this water filtered through the steam chambers. It'll stay warm all winter long. The work is not yet complete, but you can at least appreciate the beauty of the room."

"This gift is so unique and so thoughtful," Kathleen said. She was impressed with the detail Heathron had built into the garden room, and by the grandness of the gesture.

"Did Larissa tell you of my love for gardenia?"

Kathleen sat down on the small patch of turf. She took off her shoes and savored the feeling of the blades of grass peeking up between her toes.

"This is breath-taking," she said.

Heathron walked over and put his arms around Kathleen. She allowed him to do so.

"I'm glad you like it," he whispered in her ear. "This area was built privately. Few people know that it exists. The only windows are those above in this room. Here you may do whatever you like...in your very own garden."

"I am sorry for accusing you of not respecting me," Kathleen said. "Now I understand how you see me."

"I spoke in haste this evening. I just wanted to make sure that you were protected from the prejudices of the nobility. I would never ask you to be something you are not, nor would I want you to be anything other than what you are," he said.

Kathleen drew in the smell of gardenia. It was not a scent she ever expected to experience again while in Tyath.

They sat close to one another and listened to the gentle sound of the brook flowing. It was peaceful and made Kathleen feel at ease.

"The royal botanist ensures me that the plants can survive over winter as we keep these chambers warm, and there will be plenty of sunlight during the day. I wanted you to have a place free from prying eyes. Guards have been stationed along the rooftops to keep people away until the construction work is complete. When I am done, you will have privacy as well as sunlight and security," he said.

"How did you even conceive of this?" she asked.

"I did some studying in the library, and there are some ancient texts that speak of houses made of glass where plants could be grown all winter long. I decided I would spare no expense in creating such a wonder for you. In some of the texts it was referred to as a 'greenhouse'. This one is for you. A greenhouse for a Green Grower."

"I don't suppose I can sleep here tonight?" she asked with a smile.

"The workmen will come early. It's almost the start of a new day."

"Then we should be going."

"Thank you for going to the dance with me," Heathron said.

"I let my worries get the better of me," Kathleen said with a look that begged an apology.

"Well, next time, I get the better part of you. Your worries will get nothing," he said.

"If you insist, Prince Heathron. I do believe this garden you have made for me will lift my spirits significantly," she said.

Kathleen looked at the surrounding vegetation and up at the expanse of clear glass and saw the blush of a sky just dawning.

"It's almost like being home," she said.

"You are home," Heathron said earnestly.

And for the first time, Kathleen believed it might be true.

12

WORSHIP TOGETHER

Once the structure was completed, Kathleen moved quietly into the Garden Apartments with Melva and Larissa.

They were the only two, besides Heathron, invited into Kathleen's private greenhouse.

"This is a man determined to win your love, my child," Melva said as she surveyed the vast room and its exotic contents. "It brings back memories of my home in the endless Glades," the old woman said, running her hand along the bark of the slender tree and dipping her foot into the warm pool of water.

"I like the privacy," Larissa said. "You could do just about anything you want in here and no one would be the wiser," she said.

"Hello," a voice called from the front room.

"That's Heathron," Kathleen said, turning quickly to go to the foyer of the apartment.

Melva and Larissa looked at each other. The old woman raised an eyebrow and winked at Larissa.

"She didn't hesitate now did she?" Larissa said knowingly.

"Would you worship with me?" Heathron asked. He stood

before her in a deep blue jacket. His high, stiff collar was tied with a matching cravat about his neck.

"It is a bright morning on this first day of the week," he said. "And if we catch the first service, it will not be too hot."

He seemed very cheerful. Kathleen looked to Larissa.

"It has been a long time since I have gone to worship publicly," Kathleen replied, looking down at her dress.

"You look fine as you are for a worship service, Kathleen. I've made other plans, but you should go see the Great Cathedral," Larissa said.

"I think it would be important for people to see us together in public again," Heathron said.

"My father stopped taking me after my mother died," Kathleen explained. "Is there very much difference here in Tyath when it comes to worship services?"

"The cathedral is spectacular. I love the architecture, and the stained-glass windows are like nothing you have ever seen."

"In which case, I would love to go with you," Kathleen said smiling and curtsying.

Larissa and Melva exchanged amused glances again.

THE BELFRIES of the Great Cathedral rang loudly with a traditional melody. Kathleen was certain that every person within the walls of Tyath would be able to hear the lovely sound.

The bells rang in a series, one sound overlapping across another, until a harmonious air played on the wind.

Heathron held out his hand to escort Kathleen to the carriage.

"Do I look alright?" Kathleen asked, running her hands across the front and side of her dress.

"The only one we're trying to impress is Abbath, and I'm sure he's simply pleased we'll be there. But yes, you look beautiful, as ever."

The carriage stopped in front of the Great Cathedral. All four bells rang. Kathleen had to raise her voice to be heard over the sound.

Crowds of people streamed up the front steps through the front doors of the cathedral. Clergymen and women who dedicated their lives to the Church wore dark brown robes to indicate their devotion. They gathered alms for the poor from the faithful that made their way up the stairs. Some offered candles to be lit during prayers.

The crowd on the front steps parted like oil and water and Imperial Guards flanked both sides on the front steps as Heathron and Kathleen stepped from the royal carriage. People bowed in their direction.

The bowing stopped once they began to ascend the steps of the cathedral.

"Do the people of Tyath not bow to their ruler on Sunday?" she asked.

"It is tradition that once we are in the cathedral or even walking up the steps, the people of every station bow only to God."

"It doesn't work that way where I am from, but I like this tradition. It keeps a Prince humble."

"Or a Princess," he said with a smile.

Heathron dropped a few coins into the hand of a monk and received four candles in return. They walked reverently toward the doors. Kathleen looked up before stepping inside. The gleaming walls were supported by flying buttresses made of stone. The sight was inspiring.

The edifice reminded Kathleen of a sandcastle she tried to build as a child, when she would wet the sand and stack it up by dribbling it into piles of elegant mounds. She could imagine a giant mixing stone and water in a colossal, ornately molded bucket, and slowly removing it to reveal this elegant cathedral.

Stonecutters with ropes and scaffolding had dressed the

surface of the stone with images from nature and history. Above
the doors she caught a glimpse of ships sailing across a stormy
sea and figures laying their faces on the earth as they reached the
shore. Other carved figures were in the act of planting grapes on
the shores overlooking the Clearwater Sea. In one scene a Sīhalt
Guardian stood beside a man wearing a crown. Kathleen thought
of Jared.

Images of the saints glistened silently above her as she walked
inside. Alternating male and female statues depicted the people
that had built the foundation of their society centuries before.
The oldest statues showed the most signs of wear. Countless
hands of the faithful had touched their marble feet during
prayer.

The Prince placed his hand gently on Kathleen's back and
guided her past the columns to the impossibly high ceiling of the
central area. Three chandeliers lit with white candles augmented
the splendor inside. Thousands of pieces of cut glass, arranged in
a spiral, hung from the ceiling above them by an intricate system
of ropes and chains.

The morning light streamed through a large window above
the altar. An image of Abbath descending from the clouds shone
brightly.

Smaller windows around the dome were open, allowing air to
circulate. Fresh air entered the doors at the ground level and
gently blew across the faces of the faithful. The air rose upward,
carrying the smoke and prayers of the people skyward.

"The faint rush of wind is supposed to remind us that Abbath
is always with us," Heathron said to Kathleen.

Kathleen closed her eyes and considered what prayers she
might offer. It had been a long time since she had attended
worship of any kind. On this holy day of the week, surrounded by
so many people vibrant with heartfelt devotion, Kathleen found
herself wanting to renew her efforts to have a relationship with

her Creator. She tried to remember the lessons she had learned as a little girl when it came to prayer.

First, she was supposed to trust God.

Dear Abbath, she prayed silently.

Then she was to express gratitude.

Thank you for my family. Even Renata. Thank you for protecting me on my journey to the Golden City. Thank you for softening the heart of the Prince and for the food he is sending to my people.

Next, she offered her own silent supplication.

Please protect Jared in the western lands. Help him to find his brother and bring him back safely. Please let my sister know that I love her. Strengthen my father to be a good king, and help me, dear Abbath, to know what I should do when mid-summer comes again.

She touched her finger to each hand the way her mother had taught her as a child. She then lit two candles and placed them on the wooden prayer shelf. Heathron did the same as he knelt silently in prayer beside her.

Kathleen felt like she belonged here. She felt peace during her silent contemplation. No suspicious glances were cast in her direction. No people showed displays of deference to her rank as a Princess or derision for her foreign looks or abilities. It did feel like home. She felt accepted.

"Can we do this more often?" she asked.

"Every week ,if you wish," he replied.

He reached for her hand, and she placed hers in his gladly.

They walked back down the central aisle as the harmonious chanting of the monks began to swell. They were halfway down the central corridor when the sound of breaking glass startled them.

One of the great chandeliers swayed precariously and then began to fall. The sound of rope running through pulleys disrupted the silence of God's house. People in the pews screamed and scrambled to get away from the danger. Kathleen and Heathron stood directly beneath the chandelier.

Imperial Guards instantly lunged toward Heathron in an effort to protect them, but Heathron was faster.

Placing an arm around her waist, he swept Kathleen off her feet and dove to the nearest pillar. His feet barely cleared the shattering crystal and polished metal that crashed to the floor of the cathedral. The heavy weight would have smashed them to pieces.

Heathron rolled over Kathleen, throwing his arms up to shield his face from the shards of glass that flew in all directions.

Worshipers who were injured cried out in pain as the chandelier landed.

Kathleen felt her back pressed against the stone column. Heathron pushed his hand against her chest. He stood in front of her, and she watched as he reached with his right hand into the back of his jacket and withdrew a short sword. He held the blade in front of him, looking in either direction for anyone who might attack them.

Clergyman in their long brown robes rushed to the rescue of the wounded, their sandals crunching the glass beneath their feet. Kathleen took a few deep breaths, appalled at the scene before her.

"Come with me," Heathron said desperately.

He led the way as they walked between the pews to the outer perimeter of the cathedral away from the crowd. He looked up along the wall where the rope system had been secured.

"You cannot have a weapon in this house," a voice said.

When he looked at the monk, the man opened his mouth in shock.

"I'm sorry, Your Highness. I did not realize it was you."

"Please, good brother, go help the wounded. I fear there has been an attempt on Princess Kathleen's life."

"Why would you suggest such a thing?" the monk exclaimed.

"Because the cords to secure the chandeliers to the ceiling did not simply break on their own, at the exact moment my betrothed happened to be directly beneath it."

He held up a rope as thick as Kathleen's arms that had been wrapped around the anchors in the wall. He brought his short sword down and cut through another section of the rope. The clean cut looked exactly like the rope that had failed.

"This rope was not worn, it was cut," Heathron said.

The monk touched his forehead with his fingers and held his hand outward in a sign to ward off evil.

"Political schemes in the house of God? What are we coming to?"

"I do not know, but we will not remain here to find out today," Heathron said.

Kathleen and the Prince walked discreetly and quickly along the outer wall, making their way towards the side door. When the Prince was certain it was clear, he led Kathleen back to the royal carriage.

"Are we waiting for the other guards?" the driver asked.

"They're likely in the presence of Abbath as we speak. Drive on," he commanded.

As the carriage rolled away from the tragedy unfolding within the cathedral, the tolling of the bells began again. This time their tone seemed mournful and afraid.

13

GUARDED FRIENDSHIP

The very next day, Heathron visited with Kathleen again. "You must be provided with proper protection," Heathron said. "Yesterday proved that."

They walked across the wet flagstones of the palace courtyard. Summer storms soaked the Golden City each afternoon, so Kathleen walked carefully among the shallow puddles that were scattered along the walkway. The wind that blew from the Clearwater Sea had abated this afternoon, and the humidity of a Tyathian summer drenched them. Kathleen wiped her brow and looked at Heathron.

"Do you mean guards like yours?" Kathleen asked, looking at the ever present but silent warriors that stood ready to defend the Prince.

"The guards for the imperial family come from a special rank of fighters. You will be able to choose two of them."

Kathleen was somewhat taken aback. She wasn't sure she wanted personal guards.

"Your guards are almost perfectly silent and stern. I once tried to speak with one of them, and he stood unflinching as if he were a statue," Kathleen remarked.

"They move only when I move and speak only when I direct them to speak. They respond only to me and anticipate my every need. In truth, it is easy to forget that I have guards," Heathron explained.

Kathleen agreed. There were many times over the past weeks when she had forgotten about the Imperial Guards, dressed in gray, who were ever present, ready to defend him. They became invisible to her. She didn't like the fact that she was growing accustomed to ignoring human beings in her service.

"It was never like that in Candoreth," Kathleen said. "I had guards there, too, but they were almost like friends. And they would wait in the hall when I needed to be modest, or if I asked them, I could have some alone time."

"Once they're assigned, the Imperial Guards will never leave your side," Heathron said. "Eventually you will get used to them and not even think twice about their presence, no matter what you are doing."

"If I'm changing? If I'm going to the bathroom? What then?" Kathleen asked. She didn't like the idea, as stoic and statute-like as the guards may be. "They will be an invasion of my privacy," she said.

"Kathleen, you must understand," Heathron explained, "Tyath is full of intrigue. I could never list the number of political murders, blackmail, or kidnappings that have happened in this city. It's not pretty sometimes, on the inside." He looked around at the shining wall, the flying pennants, and the people going about their daily lives.

"But it is my home, and I do love how it has become a beacon of hope for so many. Who else would stand again? The Delathranes? Candoreth? Horming? Certainly not Hestin. From our earliest days, the houses of the nobility have striven to rise above each other. Some say that it is designed to ensure no one ruler will gain too much power, but I don't know. Sometimes I think it just leads to continuous unrest beneath the veneer of calm. The Council of Nine was established to create stability. And for the most part, it works," he explained.

"Tradition often fills in when we are at a loss for what to do next," Kathleen said, trying to relieve the frustration she detected in Heathron's voice.

"The Imperial Guards were created centuries ago. They are an institution. It's beautiful here, when you look at our buildings — the architectural style and art. Think of your guards as part of that."

"I am not going to have any man or, for Abbath's sake, multiple men constantly in my presence. I honestly think I would rather die before giving up my alone time," Kathleen said.

"Oh, don't say that," replied Heathron.

"I'm serious," Kathleen said adamantly.

"They need not be men," Heathron said. "Men are the typical choice because they are larger and stronger — don't tell the ladies of the Imperial Guard I said that," he added with a boyish smile.

"Use female guards?" Kathleen asked.

"They are very skilled warriors. I have a few for you to choose from."

"So, you insist that we are going shopping for guards today?" Kathleen asked with resignation.

"In a manner of speaking," Heathron admitted.

"This is strange to me," she sighed.

"It is one of the greatest honors for a boy or girl in Tyath to be selected as part of the Imperial Guard. Be careful what you ask your guards to do, they will gladly die for you," Heathron said.

HEATHRON AND KATHLEEN were welcomed into the Imperial Guard training facility by a man in a gray tunic. "Line up!" he called to the students who were practicing.

The young guards quickly filed along one wall to be inspected.

"Princess Kathleen Dal Sundi is in need of protection. She will marry our Prince on Wedding Day next year. She requires a guard. Two of you will be chosen. Remove your masks, if you are wearing one, and your helmets also," the trainer said.

There was a general rustle and some clattering metal as young men and women removed their protective headgear. They stood perfectly erect and stared forward, like statues.

They stood, breathing heavily from the training session, perspiration soaking their shirts and running down the sides of their faces.

"You are given freedom to speak your mind to the Princess," Heathron said firmly to the assembled recruits. "She will want to know a little about you."

"How are they chosen for this duty?" Kathleen asked the trainer.

"Families that desire their children to become part of the Imperial Guard offer them as candidates when they are five years old. If the child demonstrates aptitude, they remain in the training program, if not there're then released back to their families to pursue a different vocation."

Kathleen nodded. Almost all of the potential guards looked like they could move fast. The first young man had a chiseled torso, golden hair that fell to his shoulders, a nose that almost looked like the beak of a hawk, and dark brown eyes — like Heathron.

"You may choose any two you like," Heathron said.

Kathleen looked at the young man. He was exactly the kind of guard she did not want in her room at every hour of the day or night. She moved down the line to the next one.

Kathleen had seen this woman during the practice routine. She had been defending herself against four attackers with nothing more than a long stick. She held the stick beside her, one end placed on the ground.

"What is your name?" Kathleen asked.

Without blinking the young lady replied, "My name is Lana, Your Highness."

"Where are you from, Lana?" Kathleen asked.

"I am from the Golden City," Lana replied. "I have spent my whole life here."

"Do you have siblings?" Kathleen asked.

"I believe so, Your Highness," she replied.

The trainer interrupted, embarrassed by the indirect answer she had offered.

"Lana is an exception to our normal recruit. She submitted herself for entrance into the Imperial Guard at the age of eight. That's the earliest a child can enter if they have no sponsor."

"Sponsor?" Kathleen asked, looking to Heathron then back to the girl.

"Your Highness, I was a street urchin. My family could not feed me, so they left me on the steps of the cathedral when I was a baby — or so I am told."

Kathleen grimaced.

"I haven't seen homeless people in the Golden City," she said.

"Then you haven't visited all the quarters of our beautiful city, Your Highness," Lana said softly.

"I choose this one," Kathleen said.

The touch on the girl's shoulder made her stand even taller. "Despite the traditions here in the capital, I expect us to become good friends," Kathleen said.

"That isn't possible," the trainer said. "Imperial Guards aren't allowed to be friends. They only serve."

"Anything is possible," Kathleen said.

"Yes, Your Highness," the trainer said as Kathleen continued down the line.

Kathleen stopped at another of the candidates, a girl with a slight build and straight black hair that seemed almost to possess a deep violet shade.

She reminded Kathleen of what Melva might have looked like when she was a young girl. She had the same heart-shaped face, but her skin was smooth and drawn tight, not wrinkled like Melva's was now.

"Tell me about yourself," Kathleen said.

"My name is Lilith, but my family calls me Lilly. I am twenty-one years old. I've been training since I was five. My father brought me to the Golden City to apply. I was born in the village of Fishing Point on the Clearwater Sea. I am not as strong as the others, but I am very quiet and fast," she said.

Her aura was one of confidence, not hubris. Kathleen stood taller than the girl by more than a head.

"You're very small — you don't look dangerous," Kathleen said.

"It would be a mistake to judge me to be as young and fragile as I appear," Lilly replied.

"You don't look twenty-one. You appear to be about sixteen years of age at best," Kathleen remarked.

"My mother has very good skin. I got my youthful looks from her," the girl said simply.

"You were born into a fishing family, you say. Do you sail?"

Lilly smiled despite her attempt at presenting a formal appearance.

"Oh, yes, Your Highness. Whenever I am allowed to visit my family I always go sailing with my father. He knows the best fishing spots on the Clearwater's southern coast."

"I choose Lilly," Kathleen said.

"Lana and Lilly, step forward," the trainer commanded. "Stand by your charge, the Princess Dal Sundi."

The two young women did so without hesitation. Kathleen looked at each of them.

"Have I chosen wisely?" she asked.

They nodded solemnly.

To Lilly, she said, "Why is it wise for me to have chosen Lana?"

"Lana never makes mistakes. She is strong and has known hardship. Whatever you ask her to do will be easier than that which she has already overcome," Lilly replied.

Then Kathleen turned to Lana.

"Why is it a wise choice to have Lilly as my guard?" Kathleen asked.

Lana hesitated, fighting against the training she had received. In order to look Kathleen in the eye, and speak as an equal, she had to put forth concerted effort.

"She is cunning and quick," Lana said curtly. "She sacrificed much to train. Lilly has been a mentor to all recruits. She is as compassionate as she is skilled."

"That is all I need to know. Thank you, Prince Heathron, for the gift of these Imperial Guards," she said.

14

OF HEARTS AND ROSES

"So that we may share the story of our lives together..." the letter stated.

"I wonder how much sharing she intends to do? I'll be interrogated, most likely," Kathleen said.

"Give the woman a chance. If she paid you no attention at all, there would be reason for greater concern," Melva assured her as she hustled Kathleen into the hallway. "Let me know how it goes," the old woman said with a half-smile.

"Come with me and hear for yourself," Kathleen suggested.

"You need to do this on your own. I'll wait here," Melva replied with her disarming smile.

"At least I have my own bodyguards," Kathleen said. "Do you think they will defend me from the Empress?" She smiled back at Melva and caught a slight hardening in Lana's eye.

She would defend me from anyone! Kathleen thought.

Kathleen knocked on the private residence of Rema Dol Lassimer. If the message had not been written so personally, she would not have come. A servant invited Kathleen in and gestured to a couch.

Now that she sat in the sitting room, waiting for the

Empress, her first inclination returned. Kathleen was sure she would be interrogated. She wished Melva had accompanied her.

Kathleen sat alone, sipping the herbal tea the servant provided. The thin, wafer-like confections they offered lacked any heft. They mostly melted on her tongue, infusing a slight hint of vanilla. *They weren't very filling. Perhaps only made to cleanse the palate?* she mused.

A door opened.

Empress Rema peeked her head into the sitting room.

"Set that down and come out to enjoy the sunshine," she said, waving Kathleen in her direction.

Kathleen was surprised by her friendly demeanor. She set the saucer down along with the elegant porcelain cup and placed what remained of the wafer beside it.

Beyond the door, the day shone brightly. Kathleen realized they were standing in a private, high-walled garden.

Kathleen turned in a full circle, staring up at the walls clad in green ivy. An ornate fountain bubbled happily in the middle of the garden. The greenery hid the stonework behind, and from the placement of the trees, Kathleen could have imagined that she was stepping into a deep, mature forest.

"I feel at home here. I love what your gardener has done," Kathleen said.

"No one is allowed in here except my closest friends and family. I don't even keep a personal gardener," she said. Rema spoke with the accent of the southern realms. Kathleen felt pleased to recognize the speech of Horming or Namth but didn't want to assume too much.

Empress Rema wore a large hat, its wide brim shading her face, and one of her hands rested on her hip, the other held a small set of pruning shears.

"If I don't keep these roses tidy, they get unruly, prickly and out of hand," she smiled. "Not unlike a man, wouldn't you say?"

Kathleen began to relax. Perhaps this might not be an interrogation after all.

"Ouch!" Rema exclaimed, pulling her arm back from the rebellious plant. A thorn was caught in her wrist just above the leather glove she wore.

Kathleen thought of the long night when she was a captive of the Delathrane barbarians. She remembered how her flesh had been scraped and torn by branches and thorns as she made a blossom trail for Jared to follow.

"You will be my daughter-in-law by this time next year," Empress Rema said. "If it hadn't been for the unfortunate events at the gate, you'd already be married to Heathron. Do I understand correctly?"

An interrogation after all.

Kathleen felt her face flushing. The Empress either did not know, or more likely chose to ignore the possibility that Kathleen might not marry Heathron next summer.

The words held more meaning than the Empress revealed.

"I feel fortunate to be alive," Kathleen said as she touched what remained of the bruise around her eye.

Empress Rema held a rose branch in her gloved hand and trimmed the errant portion with sharp shears. The separated cutting fell to the carefully laid flagstones at the Empress's feet.

Kathleen looked down.

She intends to prune me like the roses.

"My Wedding Procession was an adventure, to say the least. I looked forward to it from the time I was a little girl, but it didn't go the way I planned," Kathleen began.

"They rarely do," the Empress replied knowingly. "Even the best-laid plans often crumble as soon as the procession starts. I remember when I was a girl, leaving Horming was no small thing. I had very little time to get to know Kade. I saw him playing in a *Calvaris* tournament. He was very dashing — that was all I knew of him."

"I was surprised Heathron wanted to marry me," Kathleen said. "Although, I am grateful," she added.

"Oh, he's a very romantic spirit," Rema said. "I am surprised the weight of his increasing responsibilities has not crushed it out of him."

"How does a loving soul like Heathron survive in a city like Tyath?" Kathleen asked.

"There is a hardness about him I have seen grow. He is astute, even as he his kind. In his childhood, I watched Heathron befriend the boys that would tear him down and dance with the girls that would cut out his heart. He seemed to harbor no malice towards them. That is one of the things I love about my son."

She held the pruning shears level, and although Kathleen felt no threat, she wondered what a woman such as this might do to a girl who wounded Heathron's heart.

"Before I left Candoreth, I was given a painting of Heathron. I thought the artist had embellished the handsome looks, the smile...He hadn't," Kathleen said.

Rema shook her head. "My Heathron is quite the young man."

The woman turned and leveled her eyes at Kathleen, "And I want to believe that he is betrothed to a young woman worthy of him."

Kathleen reacted to the sudden intensity of the Empress. She curtsied, "Thank you, Your Majesty."

"Oh, leave off with the formality, Kathleen. I'm speaking to you now as the mother of a boy who loves you. I don't know why the dream of your existence helped him endure the challenges of growing up, but it did. I want you to know that."

Kathleen stood listening silently. The sweetness of the thought made her smile.

"So, I hope you do not let him down," Rema said.

"I feel like I have so little to offer. Why didn't he just choose another girl?" Kathleen asked.

"Heathron is a man of his word. Since he was a small child,

his oath of friendship would bind him, but he would pursue a vow of revenge with equal certitude."

Kathleen swallowed. "I see."

"Sometimes his obstinance does not end up working in his favor."

Kathleen braced herself for the opinion she knew was coming. She prepared her emotions to hear the criticism that would inevitably be aimed at her. Scathing criticism veiled in refinement — a product of almost every noble house in Desnia. She had received it before. In truth, she had dealt it before.

The Empress continued.

"This time," Rema looked Kathleen up and down, "I believe his willingness to endure his father's displeasure and keep to a commitment in the hope of true love, could be a blessing to him."

Kathleen flushed. She had prepared herself for a dressing down and instead the Empress disarmed her with a compliment.

"I'm not just speaking of your physical beauty, Princess Dal Sundi. I'm speaking of your heart."

The Empress moved closer. She spoke softly but her words were clear.

"We are both from the Southern Realms where the people and the weather are warmer. At times this Golden City will seem to be made of ice, not just in the long winters when every surface is covered with freezing crystals, but throughout the year. There are noble families that are political enemies of House Dol Lassimer. My son needs a woman with fire! He needs a wife that will protect him with the same ferocity with which she loves him."

Kathleen looked down again, not wanting Rema to see the hesitation she was sure must have been written across her face.

"I can see it in your eyes. They hold the fire, but do not yet have the love my son needs."

"If I had arrived in time, I would have married your son," Kathleen said honestly.

"And yet your heart was captured by the Sīhalt Guardian who all but took you for his own." Rema said the words as if she understood the difficulty Kathleen endured, falling in love with one man, while being promised to another.

It shocked her that the Empress was unstinting in her description of the situation.

"I did not intend for it to happen this way," Kathleen said.

"We seldom do. During this year in Tyath, I would like to meet with you often so that I can share what I've learned about how to succeed in Tyath. My husband grows physically weaker by the day. We are transferring power into Heathron's hands as quickly as possible. His half-brothers are of insufficient quality for imperial rule, as are his uncles. The people will not support them. By Marriage Day next year, you and Heathron must be prepared. That leaves us so little time. As Heathron's wife, you will wield imperial powers. Allow me to help you prepare."

Kathleen thought of Jared and then of Heathron as they had looked up at the starry night together in her own garden. Her arrival in the city, for all its attendant drama, had not stopped the political forces that moved her closer to Heathron. Imperial expediency weighed forcefully in the decision.

"I gladly accept your instruction. I do feel unprepared for the role of bride or ruler."

Rema smiled.

"Dear Kathleen, didn't you know those two roles are one and the same?"

Kathleen blinked and tilted her head, wondering if she had heard correctly.

"The men love to train with their swords and shields. They may boast at their prowess at war or in love. They call themselves the 'Head of the House', but a woman is the neck that turns the head."

"I saw that happen with my father," Kathleen said.

"It happens to most men. We underestimate the power we hold over them. Your mother was a lovely woman, though."

"I was speaking of my stepmother, Renata," Kathleen explained.

Rema waved her hand dismissively of the stepmother.

"Renata refuses to have any children. Any claim she might have had to the throne in Candoreth will not endure."

"She seeks only to fill her life with luxury," Kathleen opined.

"Yet she denies herself the greatest luxury of all — the chance of posterity! I do so look forward to grandchildren."

Kathleen had not given a lot of thought to the prospect of Queen Renata being a mother or of being one herself. There was so much she had not considered.

Empress Dol Lassimer clipped the stem of a dying rose and turned to Kathleen.

"When you were a child, I remember standing with your mother, Annalise, on the veranda, looking out over the blue waters of Candoreth. That day we spoke of her plans to build up the merchant fleet. She had singlehandedly strengthened the Candorethian Navy. She was a very talented queen. I hope you will be one as well."

If they were overheard, few people might have guessed at Rema's meaning, but Kathleen understood very well that Rema spoke of her gifts as a Green Grower.

"Has Heathron told you?" Kathleen asked, fearful that this knowledge might fall into the wrong hands.

"He has been discreet, but he was just a small boy and does not remember very much of Annalise Dal Sundi. I do."

Kathleen hung on every word the Empress spoke about her mother. Rema had a hardened edge to her soul, a polished blade that willingly divided the motives of those she met into friends or foes of their house.

"Are you ...like her?" the Empress pressed.

There was no use in denying her abilities. Kathleen nodded.

"I believe I might be a stronger Green Grower than my mother," she said.

Rema tilted her head back and exhaled a soft whistle.

"Kathleen, we must keep this quiet — for now. Staunch the rumors of your Talent that fly about the city," she said.

"I do not want my Gift to be a liability to Heathron's reputation and legitimacy. If it is better that I find a way to quietly leave, I am willing to do so. I have no wish to hurt him."

"Put such thoughts far from your mind, Kathleen. There is no way for you to leave quietly now. The only way for Heathron and House Dol Lassimer to maintain the throne is for you to marry him on the next Longest Day as you have promised you would do."

Kathleen felt the weight of responsibility rest heavier on her shoulders.

"I look forward to your introduction to the families of the Council of Nine. We have a dinner planned next month, and I wish for you to attend."

"It would be my pleasure," Kathleen replied, feeling much better about the kind of woman who wielded more power in Desnia than any other.

15

NEW FRIENDS

"How do you do it?" she asked, laughing. Kathleen donkey-kicked her feet in the air and tried to hold herself upright. Her arms shook with the effort.

"I can't do it," she said, her arms shaking, as she awkwardly tumbled over. She had completely forgotten that she now had an entourage. Two guards and a new maid were hers. They stood a short distance away, ready to protect or serve.

"Stop making me laugh," Heathron chuckled. "I can't do it if I'm laughing."

Heathron's shirt fell over his face, revealing a torso of muscled perfection. Kathleen had already fallen to the padded mat. She wiped her forehead and looked up at Heathron. He was still standing, or rather hand-standing.

"I should poke you in the ribs," she said, crawling a little closer to him.

"I'm blind right now. Don't you dare," he said, his shirt half covering his face.

Kathleen could see his muscles twitch, accommodating the movement of his feet in the air as he struggled to maintain his balance.

"How long did it take you to learn how to do this?" she asked.

"It was part of my training when I learned to sword fight and grapple. I love the tranquility that comes afterward." He struggled to say this as his feet teetered in one direction, then the next.

"This is the Hare Caught in the Snare pose," he explained.

Kathleen found her eyes drifting up and down the inverted form of Heathron, taking in the beauty of his young masculine form.

Who am I? Larissa? She scolded herself silently.

"Well, I don't know about you, but I'm getting hungry," Kathleen said, prising her eyes away from him.

Heathron finally perfected the pose and with one hand still down, the Prince spread his legs to counterbalance his weight as he raised the other hand off the mat.

"Now you're just showing off," Kathleen said. She placed both of her hands on the mat and moved to where she could see his face. He grinned broadly at her, straining to maintain the pose.

Kathleen squatted on the mat and brought her knees to the outside of her elbows as both hands were on the mat. She lifted her feet off the ground in the squat position.

"I only learned how to do The Frog pose," she said.

Kathleen puffed out her cheeks and made her eyes wide in imitation of the amphibious creature as she balanced on her hands in the squatting position.

Heathron burst out laughing, and collapsed onto the mat. He rolled onto his back and looked up at the ceiling still laughing.

He turned his head towards Kathleen.

"You are unlike any woman I have ever known — so at ease with yourself."

"Noble girls of Tyath can't have a little fun?"

"They take themselves too seriously. It's all about the political expediency of the moment. They do not seem to be able to share their true feelings or be vulnerable in any way."

"They can't all be that bad," she replied.

"I'm not saying it's their fault, but even the kind ones are motivated by reasons you wouldn't wish to fully understand," Heathron said.

"It's human nature to strive for power, prestige, and wealth. I understand that," Kathleen mused, thinking of her stepmother, Renata.

"The noble girls of the Golden City make an art form of it," Heathron said.

"Shall I bring in your breakfast?" inquired the servant as he walked into the exercise room.

"Pack the food in a basket. We are taking it with us," Heathron said. "Freshen up, afterwards, I have a surprise for you, Kathleen," he added.

Kathleen bathed quickly. The steamy rooms of the fieldhouse spa made her sweat. It left her feeling absolutely clean. Her muscles felt limber after the exercise.

The maid, Mara, had laid out three options of clothing for her.

Kathleen lifted the white, cotton dress. The expensive material was wrinkled but soft, and the length came down to her mid-calf. The neckline had laces that could be tied through embroidered slits at the front. She slipped the dress over her head. The pampering she could get used to, but the ever-present bodyguards were another thing. Had they been men, instead of the two girls she had chosen, getting dressed like this would have truly been unbearable.

Kathleen slipped her feet into the comfortable leather walking shoes and wiggled her toes. The shoe appeared dainty due to the wide opening in which to place her foot and the rounded toe. The snug fit along her heel held the shoe perfectly.

Even in Candoreth she never had much in the way of outfits and clothing. Melva and Sam had always been kind enough and made her life easier, but nothing at home compared with the wealth and opulence of the Golden City.

Mara began to work on her hair.

"I'll take care of this," Kathleen said and motioned the girl away. She quickly divided her hair into separate parts. Kathleen's hands worked quickly, and she wove tresses, plaiting her hair around to one side of her head so that the length of it fell over one shoulder.

"Would you like a ribbon to use for your braid?" the servant asked. Kathleen nodded and the maid reached into her apron pocket to produce a length of blue, corn-silk ribbon. Kathleen used it to tie the end of her hair.

"So, what do you think of what Prince Heathron said to me?" Kathleen asked Mara.

"Your Highness?" the woman replied, her eyebrows raised as if she knew nothing of what Kathleen had asked.

"Mara, just because most of the nobility treats you like part of the furniture doesn't mean I am oblivious to the fact you are person."

Mara stood blinking.

"I am absolutely certain you overheard the conversation I had with the Prince. Speak freely! All of you, speak freely in my presence," Kathleen said as she turned to look at the guards.

They all seemed resistant. She would have to try a different angle.

"I will not be disobeyed."

The maid and guards stiffened.

"You will speak to me as a peer and... a friend," she said, more softly.

Kathleen then turned to the servant again.

"I'm asking you, one girl to another, if you agree with the Prince's assessment."

The girl's eyes were cast down, almost in embarrassment. It was clear she wasn't used to speaking so candidly with someone of nobility.

"You mean, whether the other noble women can be trusted?" she asked.

"Is it as bad as he described?" Kathleen asked.

The servant closed her mouth and wrinkled it up to one side as she considered the question.

"I suppose it isn't their fault. But it isn't just the women, the men have their...motives too," she said.

The tone of her voice told Kathleen that perhaps Mara had already suffered at the hands of the nobility in one form or another.

"Do you feel safe here?" she asked. "I mean with me, as my servant, is there anyone who has put you in danger since you were placed in my service?"

"Not since...I have been in your service, Your Highness," Mara said. She blinked a few times almost as if she was holding back a tear.

"Promise to tell me if anyone threatens or abuses you," Kathleen said.

Mara nodded. "I will, Your Highness, thank you," she replied.

"That goes for all of you," Kathleen commanded, looking each of them in the eye.

"Just give me his name, Mara. I will take care of it," Lana said menacingly. Her fingers danced along the handle of her knife.

Mara shook her head. "That isn't necessary, Lilly. It will be okay."

"We will look out for each other," Kathleen promised. "Each of us will do whatever is needed to keep each other safe. We are friends. I am in your service as much as you are in mine...Do you promise?"

Mara, Lilly, and Lana each nodded in the affirmative. Lana began to smile.

"Candoreth must be a beautiful place if a Princess and her servants can be the best of friends," she said.

Kathleen thought back to her home and how free the people

were to speak their minds. She remembered the arena with the mixture of people from all social strata and the general happiness that was found amongst the various noble houses in Sundiland.

"We have our faults, too," she admitted. "But in Candoreth, you and I could easily shop, eat, and dance as friends."

Mara looked at her in amazement, almost as if she didn't believe it.

"Are you ready to go?" Prince Heathron called for Kathleen from down the hallway.

"You'd better get going," Mara said.

When Kathleen stepped out into the street, a strong gust of wind tugged at her dress. If her hair had not been braided, it would have blown around the back of her head and covered her face.

Prince Heathron held a hand to the white cap he wore to keep it from blowing away. He held the reins of a beautiful, chestnut gelding. The wind was warm, the sun was shining, and Heathron was smiling, as usual.

"So, where are we going?" Kathleen asked.

"Patience, patience!" he said.

From his pocket, Heathron pulled a dark blue handkerchief.

"I don't want you to see where we're going, this is a surprise.".

Kathleen shook her head and smiled. "Very well. As long as I can follow my nose to a good meal...I'm getting hungry."

He covered her eyes with the blindfold and tucked it tightly behind the back of her head. Then Heathron grabbed her broad-brimmed hat and placed it on her head at an angle which would allow the front brim to cover her face.

"Okay, that's enough," Kathleen laughed. "I am positive I cannot see anything."

"No peeking!" Heathron commanded. "Up you go!"

Kathleen tensed when he took her firmly by the waist and lifted her feet off the ground and onto the horse. The touch of his strong hands on her waist made her flush. She tried to regain her composure and reached up to steady the broad brimmed hat she wore.

"I'm going to be riding blind? Couldn't you have tied the blindfold on after I was already in the saddle?"

"Where is the fun in that?" Heathron asked. "Then I would have had no reason to need to lift you into the saddle."

Kathleen was glad the blindfold and hat covered her face. She could feel the heat in her cheeks and knew that the neckline of the dress she wore wouldn't hide her reaction to his sudden touch. The dress was loose-fitting and allowed her legs to move, but she was sure her whole neck was red at this moment.

"Let me help you," he offered, climbing into the saddle. Heathron put his arms around her and held onto the reins. "Are you all set?" he asked.

"I think so," Kathleen replied, her heart rate accelerating. She felt a surprising excitement being this close to Heathron, but the blindfold brought back memories of her capture at the hands of the Delathranes. Every day she was beset with memories of Jared and the time they spent together. She recalled sitting in the saddle, leaning against his chest. Kathleen remembered his scent, too.

Heathron took the reins, and the horse began to clatter down the street.

"We seem to be headed downhill," Kathleen observed.

"What else do you notice?" Heathron asked.

"The warmth of the sun is shining on my left cheek...so that means...we are headed to the east. Downhill means we are headed to the water," Kathleen said.

"Very good," Heathron said.

"I hear the sound of sea birds, too," Kathleen said.

The white birds cried louder as they approached. They circled in the air above.

"They always remind me of Candoreth," she sighed.

With the blindfold still on, Kathleen leaned back into

Heathron's strong arms and remained silent, thinking of what
had been and what might be.

THEY RODE along the edge of the harbor to a lookout park on the
windswept shore near the outer walls of the city.

Kathleen rested her head on Heathron's chest and enjoyed
the feeling of his muscled arms wrapped around her as he rode
and held her. She found herself feeling drowsy and with her
blindfold securely in place, she began to nod in and out of sleep.

She felt the horse's pace decrease and shade passed over her
face, gently waking her.

"Is she asleep?" the voice whispered.

Heathron must have nodded, because she didn't hear him
respond.

Kathleen tried to place the voice. It had a child-like quality
that made her think of her little sister Elayna, but it was likely a
young woman.

"I've spread the blanket over there. We have some pillows, too,
if you need to just lay her down and let her sleep. The poor girl
must be exhausted with all the new surroundings."

The girl from Turlin's ball, Kathleen thought, *what was her
name?*

"Hannah, are the others here yet?" Heathron whispered
softly.

That's it, Hannah Aviella, Kathleen remembered.

"My servants couldn't find Lady Albodris, but Lord Eldin is
here."

From the sound of her voice, Kathleen thought there might
be more meaning in that comment than the girl wanted to reveal.
Kathleen felt she might acquire an insight if she continued to
pretend to sleep, so she decided to maintain the charade.

Heathron swung his leg slowly over the saddle and

dismounted as he held her around her shoulders and waist to lift her gently from the horse. His clothing smelled of clean leather and a faint cedar scent.

His hands are so strong! she thought.

Kathleen heard the sounds of other people moving about when Heathron laid her gently on the ground and put a pillow under her head.

"What is it?" she finally mumbled, faking a new awareness at the disturbance.

"We've arrived," Heathron replied.

"Do we get to eat now?" Kathleen asked.

A few voices stifled laughter.

Heathron bent close to her and began to untie the blindfold.

"Are you ready?" he asked.

As the blindfold fell from her eyes, Kathleen caught sight of a three-tiered cake. A group of young lords and ladies stood with arms around each other. They began to sing. She did not know all of them, but there were friendly faces she remembered from the party. Hannah Aviella wore the sincerest of smiles as she sang with the group.

"Happy birthday to you,
On this day made for you!
Joyful memories we wish you,
On this birthday for you."

Kathleen clapped her hands in excitement. "I didn't know you knew!" she said to Heathron. "I have never had a surprise birthday party!"

The young men and women who had gathered to celebrate with her seemed just as happy to be providing the surprise as she was to receive it.

Kathleen looked at a curious box on the blanket in front of her. It was covered in thin sheets of silver. Intricate details showing flowers and birds swept across the surface. At intervals,

small openings were visible, but obscured somewhat by the fili-
gree metalwork. Kathleen wondered what was in the box.

"This is very fine craftsmanship," she said, her hands tracing
the patterns.

"It was made right here in Tyath," Heathron said, a note of
pride in his voice.

Kathleen unwrapped the letter that was attached to the silver
box and broke the wax seal of House Dol Lassimer.

She read the note inside.

Kathleen,
She reminds me of you,
With her coat all ablaze.
I hope she will remind you of me,
During these days
We are together.
I call her Kendra,
But you can choose
Whatever name seems best.
All my love,
Heathron

KATHLEEN TURNED TO HEATHRON. The sweetness of his words
touched her.

"Open it," he said, gesturing to the silver container.

Upon lifting the lid, a small, fox pup hopped out and darted
behind the box, hiding under the lid and looking back at Kathleen with dark, intelligent eyes.

"Hello, Kendra," she said softly. The tiny fox shifted its weight
onto short legs that appeared to have black stockings. The little
fox let out a small yelp of uncertainty.

"Oh, she's adorable!" Hannah exclaimed.

"That is quite a gift," Eldin Stellat agreed.

"Is this a fox? I've never seen a red one before! Our swamp foxes are all brown and grey," Kathleen said.

"These live in the fields and forests of the north. This one will turn white to match the snow during winter too," Heathron explained. "When they are raised in the company of a person, they will form a close attachment."

Kathleen coaxed the little fox to come closer, and Kendra suddenly jumped up into Kathleen's lap as she knelt on the blanket. The red fox hid behind her sleeve, peering outward. Kathleen stroked her fur gently.

"She is perfect. We even match!" Kathleen held her red hair against the fox's coat. The color blended perfectly.

"That is why I thought of you," Heathron replied.

"Throw in a few acorns and you have the living symbol of House Dol Lassimer," Eldin joked.

"I'm happy to see the joy she brings to your face. Abboth knows you have had quite a year. Happy birthday," Heathron said.

"Can I hold her?" Hannah asked with arms outstretched. Kathleen passed the small bundle of red fur to her friend and Kathleen turned to give Heathron a small kiss on the cheek.

The large picnic blanket was spread with the most delicious food. Ripened fruit was piled in woven baskets, with wedges of cheeses, meats, and small crusty loaves of bread. Bottles of chilled wine lay alongside.

Heathron cut the cake and stepped forward with two plates. He carefully brought a large piece to her.

"This is almost too much, but it looks delicious," Kathleen protested, eyeing what looked like raspberry filling between the layers of white cake. Her stomach growled.

"Happy birthday," he said with a broad smile.

Kathleen got to her feet and stood beside him. The warm breeze tossed about the white dress she wore, but otherwise it was a warm breeze on a beautiful Tyathian summer day.

"And now to honor a tradition from your homeland in Sundi-land," he said. "The first slice of the birthday cake is yours."

He held up one of the plates and offered it to her, keeping one for himself. Kathleen took the cake from him and looked for a fork. Heathron grinned and picked up his piece with his hand. Kathleen looked at him smiling, wondering why he was looking at her so expectantly.

"I can't wait to try this!" she said with a smile and decided to forgo a fork and use her hand.

When in a foreign land, just follow the customs as best you can, Kathleen recalled the mantra Melva had taught her as a child.

"And so you shall," Heathron replied, leaning forward to push the cake in his hand toward her face. The surprise at his sudden movement toward her made her open her mouth.

Maybe he intends to feed me the cake? she thought.

Instead, Heathron smashed the cake firmly into her face to the delight of the gathered guests.

Shock turned to dismay as Kathleen pulled back from the Prince's forceful delivery of the birthday dessert. The cake in her hand fell to the ground, and she raised her hand to wipe frosting and raspberry filling from her nose.

He stood there, grinning, while she tried to clean herself. Realization began to dawn on the young man's face.

"Aren't you supposed to return the favor? Don't you do that to me now, too?" he asked.

Kathleen looked down at her dress. It was soiled by the pieces of cake that fell from her face. The small audience laughed and clapped, evidently waiting for her to return the favor to the Prince.

Trying to speak through a mouthful of cake, Kathleen said, "We don't typically do that for a birthday - only for a wedding really."

"Oh, dear, I'm afraid I have made a dreadful mistake," Heathron began. He looked mortified.

Kathleen quickly realized the situation had only one remedy.

"However, on truly special occasions, my first surprise birthday party being one, it would be appropriate to grant a wish to the one who is celebrating her birthday."

"Anything you ask!" Heathron said immediately in an attempt to remedy the situation.

"And right now, my only wish is to..." Kathleen paused, stroking her cake covered chin, "...return the favor!"

Kathleen grabbed a handful of cake from the top tier and threw herself into Heathron's arms. He caught her with both hands, leaving himself completely vulnerable to her attack. Kathleen smashed the cake into his face and rubbed it through his sandy blonde hair.

Hannah Aviella and Eldin screamed with delight. Prince Heathron threw his head back and laughed as well, hugging her to himself.

A couple of carriages rolled up to the celebration. Kathleen thought she caught sight of Larissa sitting with Aidan Naystrom in the second carriage, but she could not be sure.

Jessica Turlin parted the curtains in the first one.

"What a ridiculous tradition," she said, eyeing Kathleen and Heathron. "You look like a couple of filthy Delathrane barbarians." The young noblewomen in her company shook their heads in disgust.

Kathleen went to brush a stray strand of hair from her face and ended up getting cake in her hair.

"Oh, shut it, Jessica," Hannah said. "You are just jealous because you were not invited."

"If we nobles cannot be the bearers of the flame of civilization, who can? We should be the picture of refinement, not follow the brutish customs of Sundiland. At least you are free from the eyes of most commoners," Jessica sneered and raised an eyebrow of condemnation toward the Prince.

Kathleen understood her meaning. She meant she didn't measure up. Anger flared in her chest at the snob in the carriage.

"Surely you are familiar with some of our traditions, Jessica?" Kathleen asked in her sweetest voice, as Heathron still held her in his arms. Kathleen ran her little finger down his cheek, scraping up some of the frosting, and placing it between her lips. When she removed it she was left with her little finger elevated in the direction of lady Turlin. "Some of them are quite delicious."

Jessica's face flushed with rage. She clenched her jaw in defiance at the gesture. Kathleen heard some of the guests gasp. There could be little misunderstanding of what Kathleen meant. Although the tradition had originated in Sundiland, it had spread, to all of Desnia. There was not a person over the age of eight in the Golden City who did not know the meaning of the raised little finger, or 'Candorethian salute'.

"I can't stay. We just came by to wish you a happy birthday," Jessica said through gritted teeth. "And remind you that House Turlin has decided to play for the opposing team in the Calvaris match this weekend.

"I suspected nothing less," Heathron smiled, "but thank you all the same."

His demeanor seems so sincere, Kathleen thought, *it must be maddening to the likes of Jessica Turlin.*

Jessica closed the curtains of the carriage and moved on.

Eldin Stellat began to laugh again when the Turlin party was gone.

"That was hilarious," he remarked.

Heathron passed a hand over his frosted face and shook his head.

16

CALVARIS MATCH

alvaris isn't something a lady gets herself involved
"C with in Candoreth," Kathleen explained to her guard,
Lana, as they made their way into the royal boxes
reserved for noble spectators in the arena of Tyath.
Lilly followed as well. Like the arena in Candoreth,
the enormous Tyathian structure was built close to the exterior
walls of the city for ease of transport of the livestock and crowds
that took part in the games. It dwarfed the arena back home.

"Are the ladies allowed to attend?" Lilly asked.

Both guards had become more open with her, and Kathleen
enjoyed it. They were more like friends than bodyguards and yet
they did not diminish the rigor with which they went about their
duty to protect her.

"They are permitted to attend the matches, and a few ladies
often do, but it is not considered a place becoming of feminine
refinement. My mother would only attend if father made a
specific request, or if the Candoreth team was playing Horming."

"What about the commoners? Was it frowned upon for the
peasants to attend?"

"Heavens, no!" Kathleen cried. "The commoners both male and female, old and young, love a Calvaris match."

"Another reason I am glad to be born a commoner," Lana said peering over the railing toward the larger more raucous seating of the peasants.

"I don't know," Lilly replied. "Lady Albodris doesn't seem to be bashful about her support for the players."

Kathleen looked further down the row of boxes and saw Larissa. She was wearing the face paint of an ardent fan and it was red —the color of House Naystrom.

She cheered loudly, almost excessively so, when the riders, dressed in crimson, rode onto the sand.

She is really striving to impress Aidan, she thought. I need to say something to her about that.

Trumpets blared to announce each grouping of riders. Every one of the high houses fielded a team and so did a few of the minor ones.

Riders were dressed in a variety of colors. Some wore yellow stripes, others sported a green tartan pattern as well as blue, purple, white, and silver. One rider for the opposition was dressed in all black. Their bucklers were painted with the emblems of their families, personal statements, or words of derision for their opponents.

On one side of the arena, Prince Heathron sat in his saddle, unmoving. His visor was up, and Kathleen imagined that he would be smiling, although she could not tell from her vantage point. The armor he wore shone brightly, polished to a brilliant gleam. Heathron held the long stick with the woven basket on the end across his saddle. Beside him a flag bearer held the Dol Lassimer crest aloft.

Opposite him, across the arena, sat the man dressed in black. He had his visor down and a swarm of players shouted and raised their sticks to cheer him.

"Who is that?" Kathleen asked.

"He is wearing black, so I doubt it is Lord Naystrom," Lilly said.

The figure dressed in black turned Kathleen's mind to Jared. If the horse he was riding had been larger, like Steed, she could have almost believed it was the Sīhalt Guardian, come back to Tyath as promised.

"What is the object of this game?" Lilly asked. "I've never attended a match before."

Kathleen pointed to the far gates of the arena.

"Do you see that circular opening mounted on the wall closest to the far gate?" she asked. "The players must pass the Calvaris ball through it to earn a point. When larger tournaments are held, they can open the gates of the arena and the players can even ride outside the walls. I don't know much about it except that my father lost a great deal in his bets on this game."

"Why are they wearing armor? Does the game ever get violent?" Lilly asked.

"There are no blades allowed in Calvaris. Notice the players are not wearing swords and all of the sticks have a basket on one end and a rounded knob on the other," Lana said.

The players began riding in patterns, weaving their horses in between the stone pillars set throughout the sand covered floor of the arena. They began to form allegiances, choosing sides that seemed to be led by Heathron or the black rider.

Some of the players seemed to be arguing about which side to ride for in the match. They rode to one side and spoke to the teams, then rode back to the other side, carrying notices or taunts from one side to the other. The yellow checkered shirts of the game judges moved out between the teams. The judges held batons that smoked at each end. They spun them in circles and used the batons to direct the players.

"Choose a side!" they cried. "The game is about to begin!"

Kathleen found herself thinking about the black rider.

The game has already begun for me, Kathleen thought, *and I have yet to finally choose. Will it be Heathron or the Sīhalt Guardian in the end?*

Kathleen looked across the arena sand.

She looked at Heathron and saw that his team was almost as large as those who had chosen to side with the opposition. Drums rolled and the trumpets blared again. With a shout, the riders on both sides surged forward as the judges on the raised platform in the middle of the arena dropped the white Calvaris ball.

A swift rider galloped into the middle of the arena for the opposing team. He leaned down and swept the ball up into the netting of his stick. He spun the stick in his hands, keeping the white ball in the basket at the end. He feigned as though he would throw the ball to a teammate, and the defenders swerved their horses to intercept. Instead the ball carrier hunched low over his saddle and passed the three defenders. His small brown horse was nimble, and he was able to make it past them. The crowd roared in approval at such an unexpected start to the match, and the race was on. He headed straight for the circular goal at the end of the arena. The only person left standing in his way was a final defender riding a large, gray draft horse.

The defender positioned his mount in front of the oncoming rider. He held his heavy stick, with a larger basket, aloft. Just when Kathleen was certain the two horses and riders would collide, the ball carrier swerved and stood up in his stirrups. He whipped the Calvaris stick though the air and the white ball sailed over the head of the defender in a high arc. The rider peeled off, turning the brown horse with his knees as he looked back to see the result.

The black rider had circled behind the defender.

Who is he? She thought.

He caught the ball expertly while his black horse was in full stride. In a fluid motion he moved the stick over his head and cast the ball toward the stone circle of the goal.

The ball passed through.

"One point for the defenders!" the goal judge called and the score was written above the stands in white chalk.

People roared in delight. Others shouted that the trickery at the beginning of the game had been unfair. Heathron saluted the rider in black.

"You are supposed to pass it to at least two other players before you make a ride to the goal!" Kathleen heard a man shout from the stands.

And so, the game went, back and forth, the sound of sticks clashing against shields while the horses whinnied. Men yelled and the carefully raked sand of the arena was churned like the waves of the sea.

Kathleen saw the score go back and forth. At first, Heathron's team was in a deficit. The defenders got off to an early lead and scored three points without a response from Heathron's men. Then, the Prince led his men in a brilliant charge. They cleverly hid the ball among them as they rode, then divided themselves as they continued to ride toward the goal.

The defenders did not know which of their opponents carried the ball. Kathleen found herself standing to see better, and she screamed with excitement both times Heathron advanced the ball and scored.

"It seems you are more taken with the sport than you first let on," Lilly said to her.

Kathleen blushed and passed her fingers through her hair to tie it back out of her face.

"It is an exciting match," she admitted with a smile.

"Who is the man wearing black?" Lana asked. "I've noticed that your eyes jump between him and the Prince."

She noticed? Kathleen thought.

"I don't know, but they are both formidable, aren't they?"

"Is that the word you use in Candoreth, for men like those, Your Highness? Formidable?" Lilly inquired.

"I suppose it is a fitting description, wouldn't you say?" Kathleen replied.

"I can think of other ways to describe them," the dark-haired guardswoman said with a smile.

"Be careful, you are in danger of sounding like Lady Albodris," Lana said.

"My very thought," Kathleen agreed.

Larissa's obnoxious cheers rang out loudly from further down the row.

"Go, Aidan!" she yelled, then screamed even louder when he waved in her direction.

"Is she inebriated?" Lana asked.

"I don't think so. She just sounds like it when she gets excited, and she loves the game of Calvaris," Kathleen explained.

Soon the score was even again when the judges called for the break at the midpoint. Heathron and his men took off their helmets and drank deeply from the water that was offered by the servants at the arena's edge.

Kathleen squinted across the playing field to watch as the rider in black removed his helmet.

Surely that cannot be Jared, she told herself, but she was straining nonetheless to see if she would recognize him. When he turned toward her and she thought that he might be looking in her direction, Kathleen felt a knot in her throat. Her breaths came more quickly, and she felt some anxiety at the possibility that he had returned early from his travels from the Delathrane Lands and was now within the city.

That cannot be him! She told herself.

But even in the telling, she remembered that Captain Channing Dur Ruston had suggested that the Sīhalt Guardian would be an excellent contestant on the Calvaris field.

"Would you like a drink, Your Highness?" a well-dressed servant offered. "I have the sweet lemon beverage so favored by your countrymen."

"Thank you," Kathleen replied. He seemed embarrassed by her gratitude to him.

"I humbly serve," he said before offering a drink to the next box of noblewomen.

The lemonade tasted just the way Kathleen liked it. Not too sweet, nor too sour. As she sipped it, a flood of memories returned to her. She imagined that if she could climb to the highest towers of the arena, she might be able to catch a glimpse of the Clearwater Sea. Those waters joined the Eastern Ocean and lapped upon the shores of her homeland. An intense feeling of homesickness swept over her, even as she steeled herself against the emotion.

Even if that were Jared competing with Heathron in the arena, was there any way he could sweep her away, back to the southern shores? Is that what she truly desired?

Kathleen thought of her father and little Elayna. They needed her here in Tyath. She could do more for them by marrying Heathron. Little had changed on that front.

Heathron waved to her before the drums and trumpets sounded again.

"Are you enjoying yourself?" he seemed to say.

Kathleen smiled and waved to him with the passionflower handkerchief.

"Excellent play, Heathron!" she called.

I should be elated to have such a man in love with me, she thought.

17

SAY MY NAME

The drums pounded in Heathron's ears. Then the trumpets sounded even louder. His blood was up, and he could feel that another victor was near at hand.

"You are taking risks today, Your Highness," one of his men said.

Heathron smiled.

"Could it be because you are trying to impress a certain someone?" he asked.

Heathron looked up to the box where Kathleen sat.

"She is a beauty, isn't she?" he remarked. "Enough to make a man fall on his own sword for her."

"Thankfully there are no blades or arrows here today, just a lively group of Tyath's finest having a bit of fun," the man said as he lowered his helmet back onto his head.

"Watch out for the black rider, he seems bent on unhorsing you."

Heathron rapped on his helmet and breastplate.

"That is why I wear these," he said. "Besides, I have a fresh horse. We can handle him."

"Give us a few more passes, and we will have this match

sewed up!" Eldin Stellat remarked with a smile. The skinny man squinted and held a Calvaris stick with a basket almost as large as the one used by the final defender of their team.

"Just hold that beast of a stick up in the air, and I'll get it to you, Lord Stellat. You won't need good eyesight if I hit your basket on the run."

"I'll do my best!" Eldin said and began to ride forward.

"Our goal is that direction for the second half of the match," Heathron said as Eldin galloped by.

"Right! Right!" Eldin said as he struggled to direct his spirited horse in the correct direction.

Heathron looked at the other men.

"Rally the men. We have a match to win. I do not expect to pay for their dinner tonight!"

He rode with Eldin and circled back toward the opposite team. With a shout, the Prince of the Tyathian Empire rode directly toward his opponent, the man dressed in black. Heathron watched as the other rider rotated his Calvaris stick in a circle. They circled each other, and Heathron caught sight of the pass sent to Eldin. Young Lord Stellat actually managed to catch the pass and began to ride toward the goal. No one was guarding him, as he was thought by the other team to be so unskilled that he presented no threat. Heathron needed to keep the black rider's attention. He slammed the visor of his helmet down and spun his own stick, twirling it above his head and yelling a challenge that could be heard by the crowd.

The black rider tucked the basket part of the sturdy stick beneath his arm and aimed the rounded knob of the other end like a lance at Heathron's chest. The Prince did not falter in his charge but rather stood forward in his stirrups to absorb the expected blow. The visor of his helmet obscured part of his vision, which was limited to a narrow slash of light, but even in that narrowed field of view, Heathron could still see his opponent clearly. He thought he recognized the man and growled.

"Come and get me!" he said with a fierceness he reserved for battle, rather than a game.

The black rider tilted toward him, the Calvaris stick unwavering. Heathron intended to knock the stick aside. He knew the armor on his forearms was strong enough to do the job. Heathron could hear the voices of the people in the stands roaring their support for the players challenging each other, man to man. He gritted his teeth and blinked the sweat from his eyes.

When the shaft was within reach, he threw his left arm upward and brought his own stick to bear, intent on striking the opponent's head. Heathron heard a crack as they met, and for a split second, he saw the broken wood of his opponent's stick. The strike from his forearm had broken the shaft at a sharp angle. The black rider held the shaft true to his target and the lance-like stick drove onward at the speed of two horses colliding. The polished breast plate turned aside the sharpened stake, but the narrow piece of wood found its way between the edge of the chest plate and the overlapping shoulder guards.

Heathron screamed as splintering pain shot through his left shoulder. He was torn from his horse as the black rider slammed into him. He turned briefly in the air, spinning like a maple seed on its way to the ground.

When his back finally collided with the sand-covered floor of the arena, his mind focused on one thought — *Kathleen!*

He fumbled for his visor with his right hand and lifted the metal plate. He blinked against the sand that was thrown into his eyes. He saw the man dressed in black dismount and run toward him.

He is going to kill me, he thought, and despite the pain of the wooden shaft piercing his shoulder, he rolled to a kneeling position and reached for the stick he had dropped in the collision. Blood soaked the sand where he knelt, and Heathron felt his heart pounding forcefully, pushing more of his lifeblood through the wound.

Heathron brought the Calvaris stick up in front, in a defensive position. Still the man in black closed the distance, sprinting toward him.

He will reach me before my guards, Heathron thought, I have been a fool.

The man in black reached up and tore the black helmet from his head. He slid to his knees in front of Heathron, sand spraying out around him.

"Heathron!" he cried, his voice full of concern. "Are you okay?"

Heathron lowered the stick, relief flooding him as he recognized the man before him.

"I think I will survive, if we can stop the bleeding," he said.

Then Heathron heard a scream. He looked past Dallin Sarkkand, his opponent dressed in black, to see Kathleen running down the steps closest to the arena walls. "Jared! Are you okay?" she cried loudly.

The Princess paused and looked down the twelve-foot drop to the arena floor.

Heathron raised his hands to stop her but Kathleen climbed over the rail.

"I'm coming!" she said and then leaped.

She fell to the sand and rolled up to her feet, quite gracefully in fact. Her two Imperial Guardswomen were only a step behind her. The crowd grew silent at the spectacle of the Sundiland Princess leaping to the aid of her fallen love. She ran to him, her feet pounding the sand.

She called out, "Are you okay?"

She looked at Dallin Sarkkand and hesitated, as if she had expected to see someone else. Then she turned to Heathron and shuddered at the remaining portion of the Calvaris stick protruding from his armor.

Heathron was not sure he had heard correctly until Dallin spoke.

"My name is Dallin," he said, bowing to Kathleen. "But who is Jared?" He looked around to see the other riders now coming to their aide.

"I spoke to Heathron," Kathleen said. Her face was flushed, and she wore an expression of intense concern as she examined Heathron's wound, but she would not look him in the eye.

"Call for the litter! We need the nurses too," shouted Dallin.

He began to quickly unbuckle Heathron's armor.

"What did you call me?" Heathron asked.

Kathleen looked down at the sand.

He used his gloved hand to raise her chin and look into her eyes.

"By what name did you call me?" he said again, struggling to retain his composure.

"Jared," she admitted.

"Have I not done everything in my power to please you? Have I not done my part?"

Kathleen nodded silently.

"I asked you to give us a chance. How dare you call me by the name of the usurper, the Sīhalt Guardian that stole you away while bringing you to my door?"

"I'm sorry," Kathleen whimpered as tears began to well up in her eyes.

"I am sorry, too," Heathron replied. "You have hurt me greatly this day. I do not know if you should remain in Tyath."

"I didn't mean to...," she began.

"Go back to Sundiland if you wish," Heathron snapped. "I release you from your obligations, if you will release me from mine."

"I don't want that!" Kathleen sobbed.

The nurses lifted him onto the litter and the riders of both teams removed their helmets and stood to attention as Heathron was carried out by men from the Royal Infirmary. Kathleen followed for a short distance, walking beside him as he lay bleeding on the stretcher.

"Are you in great pain?" she asked through her tears, trying to show her concern.

"You have embarrassed me and injured me more deeply than this wooden spear could ever have done," he said. "Consider your heart, Kathleen. I know mine."

She stopped and watched him be carried into the dark tunnel beneath the arena. He saw her wringing her hands as she turned away from him. The guards she had chosen escorted her back toward the arena gate.

18

MOTHERLY ADVICE

"Heathron this is serious," Empress Rema said, grabbing her son's hand. She held it firmly and looked into his handsome face. They sat in Heathron's private office. She looked around at the charts and record books that lay on his desk.

"I know, mother," he replied softly. "I am doing the best I can."

"Your father is not as healthy as he likes to tell the public he is," she explained. "You need to be ready to assume more authority."

Empress Rema poured herself a drink into a crystal goblet.

"Would you like some?" Rema offered the glass to her son.

"It's rosewater. Very refreshing," she said.

Heathron accepted the glass and raised it to his lips. The cool water did have the familiar taste of rose petals.

"What did the reports say?" Heathron asked.

"General Tigral said all of the scouts came back with the same report."

Heathron nodded, encouraging her to continue.

"The Delathranes have moved west, across the river. Not one warrior was found on the east side of the river."

"That's fantastic!" Heathron exclaimed. "Maybe they decided to flee rather than fight."

"I told the general we want to know where the barbarians are, not where they aren't," Rema said.

"Isn't that enough for now, to know that they are not surrounding the city? At least they are not killing farmers or destroying property."

"You heard the threats from the one calling himself the Serpent King," Rema said, looking at her son with encouragement. "You are a good judge of men. Do you think he intends to flee?"

The question hung in the air — as foreboding as any Heathron had considered. Heathron looked at the ceiling. He tried to put himself in the mind of his foe. He considered the rage the barbarian king must feel toward the Golden City. Empathy and understanding of the Delathrane leader swept over him.

"He will be back. I am certain of it," the Prince said.

The Empress nodded in agreement.

"I've already asked to increase the number of paid soldiers. Men from the outer villages as well as those within the city have signed up in record numbers. Here, we have the defenses of the city. If we fight here, the battle will go in our favor."

"You don't want to leave to pursue them? Fight them in their own lands?" he asked. The Empress inspected Heathron closely. "Your mind is not focused on this war, is it?"

"My mind is on Kathleen, as it should be. Wouldn't you agree?"

The Empress nodded in understanding. "I am confident you will win her over. She's a smart girl. Any young lady worth her silver would choose you."

"She didn't come with any silver or gold, remember? Father hasn't ceased to remind me of that," Heathron replied.

"The value of a bride is not in her dowry. I am proud that you see that," Rema declared.

"Do you think I made the right choice? Trying for love?"

"Acting on love is always a risk, but so is acting on any emotion — or even faulty reason for that matter. We are made to laugh and cry. What is marriage if it isn't a union in which we are willing to risk everything?"

"I think I inherited more of my emotions from you than father," he remarked.

"You might surprise yourself, my son. You're equal parts lover and fighter. That's the way I have always seen you."

"The greatest battle I'm engaged in right now has nothing to do with the barbarians and everything to do with the Sīhalt Guardian who captured Kathleen's heart during her journey."

Empress Rema looked at her goblet of rosewater and swirled it. Light danced off the carved patterns in the glass.

"You have some work to do," she admitted. "Forgive her of the mistake she made in the arena. Remember it was you, to whom she was running, not the other man."

"I have already forgiven her. I can't seem to stay angry with her."

"It is because you love her, but a dangerous man of mystery is often more tantalizing than the wealthiest, kindest suitor."

"Why do girls always go for the scoundrels?" he asked sincerely.

"It's the thrill of uncertainty and the fact they can't control them. Sometimes, to our own detriment, we women desire to control the men we love, but we end up despising them when we gain it. Kathleen is a strong girl. If you wish to keep her happy, break some of the rules. Show her not only the smitten man of wealth, but also the rogue within you."

"The rogue within me?" He said, considering the importance of the statement.

Empress Rema patted her son's hand.

"I'll be with you, to guide you and Kathleen. Even when your father can no longer rule, we will see the power of House Dol Lassimer pass to another generation."

"I would like nothing more," he replied.

"You have found the woman with which to reign successfully for many years. I was impressed by her. Now you just need to finish winning her over."

"Any other suggestions as to how best to 'win her over'?"

"Show her the rouge and shower her with gifts, but don't forget to let her see your gentle heart as well," Rema counseled.

"The yacht I have commissioned is almost ready."

"I'm sure she will love it, Heathron," she replied and kissed her favored son on his forehead.

19

THE PASSIONFLOWER

Kathleen kept to herself for the rest of the week. Melva tried to console her, but it was not until a letter came from Heathron, that she began to be cheerful again.

"He asked me to accompany him on a walk to the waters' edge. He said we would be together all day." She held the letter up for Melva to see.

"I told you that he would forgive you," the old woman chuckled.

"I should have never packed up my things," Kathleen admitted.

"He is not going to let you run away," Melva replied.

~

THE BEAUTIFUL SLEEK yacht lay at anchor in the harbor. It was painted in two tones, a deep, marine blue and alabaster white. The name *Marine Escape* adorned the boat above the water line, in bold letters. Two flags flew from the stern. One for the Golden City, and the other flag for House Turlin.

"That's Jessica's yacht," Heathron indicated. "She often is a strong contender in the regatta."

"It reminds me some of the ships I've seen from Hestin," Kathleen observed. "I've always dreamed of sailing a ship like that."

It sat lightly on the water and seemed to strain against the mooring ropes with a desire to run with the wind. Kathleen admired the lines of the watercraft. She walked around the harbor edge to be able to look at the ship from another angle. The yacht had ropes tied forward to a spar jutting out over the water. The dagger board would have to be deep to compensate for such large sails. "Everything seems so well-balanced, certainly it would not take many people to sail it," she remarked with a note of admiration.

"I love ships and the sea as much as I love horses and solid earth. The excitement on the waves is a balm to my soul. I love the solitude to be found on open water," Heathron said.

Kathleen reached for Heathron's hand. She needed to apologize and the small talk only served to cover up what she really wanted to say. He did not pull away.

"I'm sorry for hurting you, the other day, in the arena," she said.

Heathron touched his shoulder where the wood had punctured the skin. "Perhaps I was somewhat dramatic," he admitted. "The pain you caused me has healed much faster than the wound from Dallin."

"My mind has been in some turmoil, but I am trying to be honest and caring, toward you, and I am grateful for the compassion you have shown me."

"Let's put this behind us, Kathleen. Today, I look forward to making beautiful memories with you," he said.

Kathleen felt thankful that Heathron was willing to forgive. She wanted another chance with him, if only to show him how much she appreciated him. She could not have born it if that last memory he had of her was in the arena. His words had taken her aback and as much as it hurt to hear the criticism, she knew Heathron was right. She needed to consider her heart. She determined to be fairer in her consideration of him.

"I long to go sailing again," Kathleen said wistfully. "Just before I left home, I took my little sister to the barrier islands off the coast of Candoreth. They are the islands where the sea turtles spawn — it is magical. I went there almost every year when I was small."

"Is that the place where you were abducted by pirates?"

Kathleen nodded.

"I guess the ears of the Empire are keen. I did not know that word of my adventure with the Sīhalt and Girdy had come this far north," she admitted.

"I was informed. We have a network of people willing to pass along information... for the good of the Empire."

Kathleen smiled.

"Most people call them spies," she said.

"I suppose you are right. It is good you took an overland route for the Wedding Procession. I thought of sending ships to carry you to Tyath, but I heard about the pirates along the eastern coast. They are growing in numbers, are they not?"

Kathleen nodded. "It's even impacting our trade with Horming. Father said, in his letter, that our navy is struggling to maintain sovereignty over our territorial waters."

"The Straits of Windstall help to protect the Capital. The pirates have to be fully committed if they are going to sail right up to the harbor at Tyath. Our Imperial Navy would cut them off at the straits if they ever came into the Clearwater Sea.

"Candoreth is much more exposed. The pirates have plenty of hidden coves in which to anchor and wait for the perfect time to strike. I just wish we knew more about them. Why are they so numerous now?" Kathleen asked.

"They are vicious, and they operate according to their own customs and reasons," Heathron agreed.

"I wasn't harmed on the island when the pirates attacked us, but my Sīhalt Guardian was hurt badly. Girdy almost died, but Melva healed him right on the docks."

"Not even a Sīhalt Guardian was able to defend you?"

"It was my own fault. I refused to take along the additional Sīhalt Guardian you sent to protect me. Two of them would have been more than enough for our safety. I know now that you made a good choice. I would not have made it to Tyath alive if you hadn't sent the Sīhalt to protect me," Kathleen said.

"I tried to find the person most capable of bringing you here safely. Despite the dangers and ... complications."

He slowed his speech but continued.

"Watching you run for the gate with the might of a Delathrane horde behind you was almost more than I could stand."

Heathron stepped closer to Kathleen, allowing his shoulder to touch hers, but he kept looking out toward the water as he spoke, so Kathleen could not see his full expression. She imagined the Prince still felt some bitterness about Jared. She had fallen for the man he hired to protect her. The name of the Sīhalt Guardian, Jared DeTorre, was still difficult for him to hear.

Kathleen didn't know what to say to make Heathron feel better. She looked out at the waves on the Clearwater Sea and the slow rocking of the yacht anchored before them.

"I'm glad to be here with you," she finally said.

Heathron nodded and turned to her. His jaw clenched and Kathleen could see the muscles along his sharp jawline flex. He looked deeply into her eyes, searching for the truth in her words. Kathleen remained determined to hold his gaze without flinching. She was happy to be in his company. Heathron was honorable and sincere. His easy manner, thoughtfulness, and bright smile brought happiness to her. Kathleen knew that without him, her people would truly be in dire circumstances. In so many ways, her life was not her own, but in this she felt that her duty as a Princess was beginning to fall in line with the desires of her heart. Did it matter whether she had felt affection for the Sīhalt Guardian in the past or not?

Heathron certainly acted sincerely toward her. The Prince seemed to find what he was looking for in her eyes.

"I arranged for us to go out to sea today," he said. "Our vessel will be here soon. With your skill at sailing, I thought it might be fun for you."

"We're going to race in the regatta?" Kathleen grinned. "How far is the destination?"

"There are some small islands about twenty miles offshore. We will sail out leisurely, eat lunch, and then race back to the harbor."

Kathleen clapped her hands in delight.

"The entrance of the harbor is the finish line. Whoever passes the lighthouse on the peninsula first is declared the winner."

"So, it's not a race on the way out there?" she asked.

"Well, not really, but at times it becomes a race to get to the picnic grounds. The arrival at the Fingers of Flint isn't official, everyone starts from different points, but we leave at the same time. It's the return home that is the race."

"Then what are we waiting for?" Kathleen smiled wickedly. "I love a good race."

Over Heathron's shoulder, Kathleen saw a woman approaching. It looked like Jessica Turlin, dressed in white.

Heathron turned and looked in the same direction.

"There she is! She is a beauty," he said slowly with awe in his voice.

Why would Heathron be so excited to see her? Kathleen thought.

"Is that Jessica?" she squinted to get a better view of her. It was.

"Oh, I mean our boat has arrived," the Prince said.

He pointed into the distance, beyond the young woman with her seductive gait and Kathleen saw the large white triangular sail moving along the shore in their direction.

"It's brand new," he explained. "I commissioned its construction for you last year. The shipwrights just finished her."

Kathleen felt more than a little relieved when she realized that Heathron was speaking about the yacht rather than Jessica.

"She is a beauty," Kathleen marveled. "You've never sailed it?"

"I wanted it built in preparation for our marriage. I would have sent that ship to Candoreth and had you sail back to the Golden City if it had been possible."

Kathleen admired the ship as it approached. She stood with hands at her side in rapt attention as the sleek form hoved further into her view.

"In your honor, I named it the *Passionflower*," the Prince declared.

The boat swept into the harbor. The prow had the likeness of a young woman carved into the wood. Her hair was flying back and she wore an expression of supreme confidence. The scrolls of her thin dress were intricately sculpted, one breast and one shoulder bare to the wind and sunshine. Her hair was painted fire-red, her skin milk-white. Dolphins, sea turtles and seashells carved in relief, flanked her hands, which were caressing the waves that flowed around her.

"Is that supposed to be me?" Kathleen asked, her eyebrows lowered as the carving came into full view, "because we don't dress like that in Sundiland. The weather is hot, but not that hot. We are more modest than you Northerners give us credit for."

"I asked for the artists to capture the spirit of Sundiland. That is what they came up with. But now that you mention it, she does bear a striking resemblance to you," he looked Kathleen up and down. She blushed.

"Prince Heathron!" she cried with wide eyes.

He laughed heartily at her reaction. His sandy blonde hair rustled in the sea breeze.

"No need to feel objectified, Princess. I simply admire you, and I am very happy that you turned out to be as beautiful as I had always hoped."

Kathleen relented, sensing the humor of the situation, and softened at his compliment. She still blushed furiously. She shook her head and ran her fingers through her hair.

"Tell me more about this boat," she insisted, trying to change the direction of their conversation.

"The yacht has the lines of the new design, but it is slightly larger and taller than Lord Turlin's yacht. The flags on the stern have both the Fox and Acorn of House Dol Lassimer as well as the Passionflower of your own house."

Kathleen leaned over the railing to get a closer look at the stern.

"You like it?" he asked.

"It certainly is in a class all its own. This is amazing," she gushed.

"Should we go aboard? I'll show you around," Heathron offered his arm.

Kathleen placed her arm in his as they walked up the gangway.

The small team of sailors aboard were smartly dressed in blue uniforms trimmed in white. They saluted the Prince and bowed to the Princess.

"We've got her ready for you, Your Highness," the captain said.

Heathron gave Kathleen a tour of the ship. From the crow's nest high above to the teak wood decks below, the yacht was a thing of beauty.

"Had things gone differently," Heathron explained, as they looked down from above the deck, "we could have sailed this ship to visit your family already. Perhaps we will one day."

Kathleen had an image in her mind of stepping ashore in

Candoreth, the daughter of the realm, now the Empress of the Golden City. The possibility seemed more real now than ever.

"Heathron, you're so thoughtful. You invite me out to sea. You remembered the day of my birth, and now you have made my desire to sail come true. This boat is more than anyone could ever dream of! You, my Prince, are a true gentleman."

"It is not a difficult thing to reason, Kathleen. I am trying to win you over. Truly, your love is worth more than all the ships in the harbor to me. A day at sea with you is worth even more. I can't keep you trapped in the city."

Kathleen felt gratitude swelling in her heart. He truly understood her! Heathron seemed to anticipate her every need. She threw her arms around him and gave him a long embrace.

"I could stay here forever with you, Kathleen, but the other boats are getting ready to leave. You should probably be at the helm now."

"I get to be the captain?" Kathleen asked in surprise, pulling back to see if he was serious. "I didn't think highborn women were supposed to take the helm of a ship."

"If you would like to do so, the boat is yours. The crew hasn't been together long, but most of these people have years of experience. The captain is already prepared to become the first mate since you and I are on board."

He gestured to the helm.

"Kathleen, you may captain the *Passionflower* if you wish. She was made for you."

The ship's officers smiled and saluted her as they made their way toward the pier. One of the sailors stopped and bowed to Kathleen.

"We've heard of the good that your mother did for the seamen in Candoreth, Your Highness. She is a saint to weary sailors. It is an honor have the daughter of Queen Annalise aboard," he declared.

The importance of the moment, the sweetness of the Prince,

the thoughts of home, and the memory of her beloved mother combined to bring a tear to her eye. She brushed it away and nodded.

"The honor," she replied with a smile as she grasped the helm, "is all mine."

20

FINGER OF FLINT

"So, where did you learn to sail?" Lilly asked as she boarded the boat. She seemed at ease with the rolling walk common to those who lived on the water.

"I've sailed the Turtle islands near Candoreth," Kathleen replied.

"The Clearwater Sea is easier than most, but the wind does tend to change direction without warning," Lilly said. "But as long as you aren't going through the Straits, it is a great place to sail."

"What about depth? I'd like to look over some charts if possible," Kathleen inquired.

"The other yachts are pulling in their mooring lines," Heathron interjected, looking across the stern to the other Tyathian yachts as they slowly began to move past the *Passionflower*.

"Don't worry, Prince Heathron. Kathleen has this in hand," Larissa insisted.

Kathleen watched Jessica Turlin's blue yacht glide alongside the *Passionflower*.

Kathleen's vessel was taller and sleeker than Jessica's, and the newness of the paint and finish made hers look somewhat dull in comparison.

Kathleen saw Jessica Turlin look up at the yacht as she steered her own vessel. She looked disdainfully at the decorative statue that embellished the prow.

Sour grapes, Kathleen thought. She decided to stand even taller, with her chin up and chest out, mimicking the spirit of Sundiland that adorned her prow.

Jessica's feet pranced down the planks. She waved to Kathleen and Heathron.

"See you at the picnic," she called. "Don't get too seasick."

Kathleen waved back.

"What did she mean?" she asked. "I've never been seasick in my life."

Heathron pursed his lips and looked down for a moment.

"She's probably referring to a time when I got seasick. I was already feeling ill the day I was invited to go sailing with her," he said.

"You got sick on the water?" Kathleen asked.

"I sprayed vomit down the entire length of that beautiful blue boat when the sea was rough. I haven't been sick since."

"I see..." Kathleen mumbled, wondering when and why this little day trip occurred.

"My parents have not always been supportive of my keeping our contract for marriage. At one point, they encouraged me to consider...other options," Heathron said, as if he had heard her thoughts.

"The poor girl from Candoreth didn't measure up?" Kathleen asked. Anger flared within her heart, and it surprised her. Jessica Turlin and the whole Tyathian system at times felt stacked against her.

"My father thinks very politically — to a fault," Heathron replied.

"No wonder she hates me. I am an obstacle to her advancement," Kathleen observed.

"She hates everyone except herself."

Kathleen could hear Jessica laughing.

"Her crew moves efficiently. They understand how to work on the water," Kathleen remarked.

"I know these waters well. I have been sailing them with my father since before I could walk. I will guide you," Lilly said.

"We are racing to the islands called Fingers of Flint. Are you familiar with them?" Larissa asked.

"Those towers are an excellent place to fish," Lilly noted. "I have been there often."

"House Stellat claims those islands and the waters around the Fingers," Heathron added. "To my knowledge, no one is allowed to fish there."

"As I said, it is an excellent place to fish," Lilly smiled deviously.

The Prince raised his eyebrows and smiled back.

"You've chosen the right bodyguard, Kathleen. This one is willing to take risks," Larissa remarked.

"It's only a risk if they can catch you," Lilly said,

"You seem very confident," Heathron observed. "The largest island has a few trees and a clear place to relax above the water. You can see for miles if you climb to the highest point, and it is almost like a tower on the city wall but made of natural stone."

"We have been racing there each summer for years. I'd love to get there before Dallin Sarrkand and Jessica Turlin," Heathron said.

"I've never been in a race before, but I could outpace some of the larger ships when I sailed in and out of the harbor at Candoreth," Kathleen explained.

"Racing is simple," Lilly said. "Just get there before the other boats."

"Who else will be there?" Kathleen asked.

"Most of the heirs to the major houses will be there, a few of the minor ones too. Yachts will be moored all around the Flint Fingers," Heathron said.

"Aidan plans to attend," Larissa added.

Kathleen tried not to wince at the comment. The young lord made her cringe, and she wished Larissa would not spend so much time with him. Kathleen was glad to have Larissa with her today. They had spent less time together in the past few weeks and she wanted her friend close by.

"It is a great time to show off too," Larissa said. "The winters are long in Tyath. Summertime should be enjoyed."

"That is the truth!" Heathron exclaimed. "I hope you all came prepared to swim."

Lana shook her head. "I will not be getting in the water at any time today."

"Let us cast off and show the other boats how to sail!" Lilly exclaimed.

"The voyage out to the rocks is just a matter of bragging, it is the trip back that is the official race," Heathron explained.

"All the same, I look forward to seeing the *Passionflower* cut through the waves," Kathleen replied.

"I fear I may need to lash myself to the mast with you two in charge of the ship," he joked.

Bright, white sails passed close by, the falcon crest of House Sarkkand was emblazoned on the main sail.

"Ahoy, Heathron! Are you planning on racing or just taking a day trip with a couple of beauties?" Dallin shouted across to the Prince. He stood tall and his open shirt blew in the wind revealing a broad, tanned chest.

"A couple of beauties?" Lilly pouted in mock disappointment as she looked to Lana, Larissa and the Princess.

"Larissa, Lilly — Sorry he left you both out," Lana said to the surprise of everyone on board. The stoic guardswoman did not often jest. Kathleen laughed.

"We may need to embarrass Lord Sarkkand outright in this race," Lilly suggested.

"He looks happy," Larissa observed with Heathron's spyglass held to her eye, perusing the competition. Young lord Sarkkand was surrounded by a passel of beautiful girls from among the lesser houses.

"Maybe he just happened to find an exceptionally well-presented group of young ladies to crew this yacht," Lilly suggested.

"Unlike your guests, Lord Sarkkand," Heathron assured him with a shout back across the water, "these ladies sailing with me actually know how to handle a boat."

"We shall see, but just so you don't get lost, the islands are that way," Dallin pointed out to sea in the only direction they could possibly go while moored in the harbor.

"He's funny. I like him," Kathleen said as she borrowed the spyglass from Larissa and gazed across the water toward the Sarkkand boat.

"Most people do like Dallin," Heathron replied. "I wish I knew his true political loyalties though."

"An easy smile is not all that makes him attractive. I think I can see his abs from here," Larissa remarked. "I don't even need the spyglass."

Kathleen laughed and continued to look through the lens of the brass tube.

"Ahem, may I borrow my spyglass Kathleen, I'd like to umm...scan the horizon and...see if Eldin Stellat has made his way out to sea," Heathron said, reaching for the instrument.

"Just a moment, Your Highness," Kathleen said continuing to inspect the deck of the Sarkkand vessel. "There seems to be another young lord with Dallin, I have not seen him before either and...they are almost out of sight."

Larissa and the female guards laughed, and Heathron shook his head and smiled.

"Let me know what the competition may hold for me. I am sure I can handle it," Heathron said with a laugh.

"Oh no, Your Highness, let us handle the competition," Larissa replied with a little growl.

"The other two men on the deck are Dallin's friends and believe me when I say they are not the kind of young men with whom you ladies should associate."

"They seem to be having a good time," Larissa observed.

"If life were simply a day at sea in beautiful weather, they would make fine companions. Unfortunately, life is not always a sunny day trip."

"But today is!" Kathleen said and twirled around on the deck feeling the wind blow her hair about her neck. The sunlight faced off the waves and the *Passionflower* slowly eased its way forward out of the harbor.

"Girls in Tyath don't typically go sailing themselves?" Kathleen asked as Lilly held a steady course. Lilly shook her head.

"They go as passengers," Larissa explained. "Jessica Turlin is an exception though. She is highly competitive and will steer her own boat today I am sure."

"She prides herself on her ability at sea," Heathron added.

"Well, we will just have to see what she is capable of," Kathleen said with a look of determination on her face.

"That is the spirit!" Lilly replied happily. "Now, if only the wind would just begin to pick up."

They cleared the harbor and the high walls of Tyath. The winds blew northeast and the sails bent in the sweet summer breeze.

Heathron tied down a line on the windward side. They felt the boat tilt beneath them slightly.

"I love that feeling!" Kathleen exclaimed.

"I do too." Heathron ran his hands along the rail and wet his hands with the spray that drifted upward from the prow. He braced his feet, breathing in the salty air. Kathleen looked at the Prince and smiled. He was a picture of delight — the wind blew his white cotton shirt against his body and Kathleen could see that Heathron could easily compete with Dallin Sarkkand or anyone else, for that matter, where musculature was concerned. He just seemed to be more modest about it.

"Get ready to tack," he said.

"We are coming up dead into the wind," Lilly called. They turned slowly, the *Passionflower* cutting through waves as the momentum carried the sleek ship forward. Then the boat turned, and they were off and racing again, delirious with delight.

Kathleen held the wheel with both hands. The yacht responded well. In the distance Kathleen could see the sails cutting across the water making their way through the Flint Fingers. A great rock eagle, larger than any she had ever seen, flew in the clear blue sky. The metallic green feathers contrasted with the white feathers of its head and tail. The giant bird then dove, streaking through the air like a child's kite caught in a downward gust. It struck the water with great force, and just as swiftly as it had plunged, it re-emerged from the surface, its powerful wings launching the bird of prey skyward again. In its talons, the eagle held a large, rainbow hued fish, still struggling to wriggle free.

The rugged display of nature's brutality reminded Kathleen that she should not be angry at the adversity she faced.

"Strength rejoices in the challenge," her father always used to say.

"What was that, Your Highness? Should we speed up?" Lilly asked.

Not realizing she had quoted her father aloud, Kathleen waved the question away.

"I'm just getting a feel for the *Passionflower*," she said to Lilly.

The crews on some of the other ships waved and made a slight mockery of the *Passionflower's* slower pace.

"You're not used to being in anyone's wake," Heathron remarked.

"Let them enjoy it while it lasts. The return trip is going to be a different story," Kathleen replied. She could feel how the boat responded to her hands. It was a thing of true beauty. She felt at one with it.

"So, you're giving them a false sense of superiority. I like it," Heathron smiled approvingly.

"It's called 'pulling up lame'. In the Calvaris tournaments it is an honored tradition to try to make your opponent believe you are weaker or slower than you really are," Larissa explained. "Don't underestimate Katie. She will surprise you just when you think she is out of the competition for good."

"She has surprised me many times already in the short time we have been together," Heathron agreed.

"And you are full of your own tricks!" Kathleen rejoined. "This fine vessel being an excellent example."

"He didn't tell you?" Larissa asked as she pulled a length of her billowing dress to remove it from her vision.

"He wanted to surprise me."

Larissa look up and down the yacht. "This is quite a surprise. I need to find a man that would build me a pleasure boat. Did you like the figurehead mounted to the prow? It may just be a coincidence, of course, but does it not look like you?"

Heathron grinned but said nothing.

"I already reprimanded him for that. He says it's supposed to represent the spirit of Sundiland."

Kathleen eased the graceful new yacht toward the Flint Fingers. The rock pillars jutted out of the sea and were shadowed by a smaller chain of islands beyond.

"It's probably best if we anchor here. I don't want to get

tangled up in the rocks or be too close to the other boats," Kathleen said.

"Can't you get a little closer? We don't all swim as well as you," Larissa requested, peering nervously at the water between them and the rocky islands.

"It's not a problem, we can take the dinghy onto the island after I go below deck and change into my swimming dress," Kathleen advised.

They stepped into the smaller boat and Heathron rowed them to shore, where they were met by a number of other young members of the nobility.

"Feeling a little sluggish this morning, Your Highness?" Dallin Sarkkand asked. "This is by far the greatest lead I've held over you on the outbound trip."

"Just enjoying the sunshine on the Clearwater Sea. Perfect day for a picnic. Don't you think?" Heathron replied.

"Perhaps your new yacht's design is not as agile as you had hoped?"

"The *Passionflower* handles fine. Princess Kathleen took the helm this morning. She was getting her sea legs after being trapped on land for so long."

Dallin smirked.

"I don't know how you expect to win, allowing a lady to captain your boat."

"We ladies can do just fine, Lord Sarkkand," Jessica Turlin chimed in. "You only beat me by a small margin."

"I was toying with you, Lady Turlin. Didn't you know that?" Dallin said. Aidan Naystrom leered quietly from beyond.

"Why does that one remind me of a wolf?" Kathleen asked Larissa, looking over her shoulder toward Aidan.

"Doesn't he remind you of the Sīhalt Guardian with his dark hair and brooding face?"

"Not in the least," Kathleen declared emphatically.

"Sure, he does. Just look at the way he carries himself. Confident and dangerous."

"Come! I'll help you up the stairs," Heathron said, as he retrieved the picnic basket from the dinghy and offered his arms to both Kathleen and Larissa.

Lilly and Lana followed behind, carrying the blankets they would spread on the ground.

The wind blew strong into their faces when they finally rounded the spiraling steps that had been cut into the rock. The Fingers were aptly named. The spires of rock extended from a palm-like base that rose above the water. The line of young men and women made their way upward until the natural stairway opened onto a flat grassy area. The turf grew in clumps where enough soil had accumulated to allow it to root. In areas where the stone was visible, moss had covered it and given the black flint the look of green velvet. A small tree grew in the open area, its trunk twisted grotesquely by the constant battering it endured from the wind.

"Let's lay our blanket near the tree. We will have shade when the sun is at its zenith," Heathron suggested.

Lilly and Lana carefully laid the blanket out and used some stones to secure the corners to prevent the breeze from blowing it out to sea.

Taking a deep breath, Kathleen turned her face toward the wind.

"Do you like this?" Heathron smiled.

"Look at that view!" Kathleen exclaimed.

The sailboats were moored conveniently close to the largest island. The morning sun shone on the eastern face of the Flint Fingers and cast angled shadows on the water below. "From the height of our position, I can see for miles!"

"On some days you can just make out the shore to the south," Heathron said.

"The other islands remind me more of spines than fingers,"

Kathleen observed. "Can't you just imagine a dragon swimming just below the surface? Those look like the spines on its back, sticking up through the water."

"Where we are standing would be the Dragon Master's palm, releasing a fledgling for its first flight," Heathron added.

The thought made Kathleen look down into the waters below. They were a deep blue.

"Are we standing on the tip of a giant human form, holding its hand aloft?" she asked.

Heathron looked down, to where the waves crashed into the wrist of the rock.

"I suppose it could be possible. My ancestors wrote that they believed a great civilization had already flourished and died long before their ships arrived on these shores."

"Just imagine the courage it took for those adventurous people to make the voyage nowadays. All the records I have seen speak of impossible storms at the halfway point. Very few of the original pilgrims survived to colonize Desnia. Most died and although a few attempted to make the return voyage to the Old World, they were never heard from again."

Kathleen looked out as far toward the morning horizon as her eyes would allow. Beyond her sight were the Straits of Windstall, and beyond that, the great ocean. It called to her, the beauty of the waves and the feeling of the damp wind on her skin, but there was comfort for her on land — a place where she could be surrounded by a multitude of plants. She knew the waters teemed with life underneath, but above the waves, the open ocean could feel barren at times.

"They were brave to do it," she said.

"But are you brave enough to do this?" a young man ran past them at a full sprint, almost making Kathleen lose her balance. His bare feet left the grassy edge as he launched himself from the edge of the cliff. Even as he fell, Lord Dallin Sarkkand struck a pose in mid-air, flexing his biceps while smiling. Then he let out a laugh and rotated his body to enter the water headfirst in an elegant dive. Little or no splash was made as he cut vertically through the surface.

"He scared the life out of me!" Kathleen cried, looking down from the dizzying height to where the young man rose back to the surface, wiping the water from his face.

"Who's next?" he called up to the picnic-goers.

Kathleen felt sick at the thought of falling that far. The vision of Jared hanging for a moment in a dazzle of lightning came back to her mind's eye. "I'll pass," she said.

"I'd like to eat first. I'm hungry," Heathron called down to Dallin.

"You would jump from this height?" Kathleen asked Heathron.

"I'm the one that taught Dallin to do it." He smiled.

"I'm on my way!" called Aidan.

Aidan Naystrom looked toward the edge of the cliff with the same abandon as the first diver.

He, too, was wearing only his knee length swimming pants drawn tight at the waist.

"Please clear the way, Your Highness. You are standing at the diving point," he declared.

"Of course," Heathron replied, gesturing with a sweep of his arm toward the grassy runway that led to the precipice as he led Kathleen back toward the picnic blanket.

"We will eat our delicious meal and enjoy the spectacle of young noblemen trying to impress us. Who will be foolish enough to try to exceed my abilities in cliff diving?"

"Not I," said Eldin Stellat, looking through the two round pieces of glass that he claimed allowed him to see more clearly.

"That is because you are a coward," Aidan chuckled as he ran swiftly to the edge and tucked himself into a pike, his body rotated twice, then three times before he extended his hands and dove expertly into the water.

"I'm not a coward," Eldin said. "I just don't like the water all that much."

"Don't listen to them, Lord Stellat. Courage is not to be demonstrated by showing off or taking unnecessary risks. Knowing you might be harmed and going forward anyway because it is the right thing to do—that is courage. If you don't swim well, you certainly shouldn't be diving," Heathron reassured him.

"I've been practicing. I just don't want to do it right now," he said, looking toward Larissa, but her eyes were fixed on the muscular form of Aidan, as he pulled himself back onto the rocks to make his way to the stairs again.

"He's never jumped before," Heathron whispered to Kathleen.

"Come, share some cheese and new wine with us, Eldin," Kathleen offered. "We can see better from here anyway."

They ate and enjoyed pleasant conversation. Eldin's eyes seldom left the beautiful visage that was Larissa. He laughed at each of her jokes and even laughed when she wasn't trying to be funny. Kathleen felt sorry for Eldin and cringed when he would venture to share his interests with Larissa. Lord Stellat was handsome, after a manner of speaking, but he was slight of build, and Larissa had little interest in new ways to perform mathematical calculations. Kathleen could not ever see Larissa being enticed to form a serious attachment to him.

Heathron made his way to each of the blankets to offer greetings. The groups of young lords and ladies showed varying degrees of deference to the Prince. Kathleen watched as they spoke with him. Some of them smiled sincerely and showed honest respect toward the son of their ruler. Others barely hid their open disdain, preferring to engage in conversation only long enough to meet the obligations of etiquette. Nevertheless, Prince Heathron seemed to offer his friendship to each one.

How does he do it? she wondered. *I would want to wipe the smugness off their faces and throw them over the cliff on the shallow side.*

Yet he remained composed and smiling.

"Have you gathered your courage yet, Eldin?" a loud voice called. It was Aidan Naystrom, walking up the last of the steps. His deeply tanned torso was the very picture of youthful vitality — handsome and lean. His voice, however, was cutting and had an edge meant to elicit humor from those in the audience that found laughter in cruelty.

"I haven't jumped yet!" Heathron interrupted, diverting the attention away from Eldin.

"For those that would like, let's play Follow the Ruler. I will dive and swim to the next island. Those of you who would like a refreshing swim, follow me!"

Heathron peeled off his shirt, and Kathleen found her eyes drawn to his finely formed body. He had the perfect balance of strength and softness in his clear complexion. His back widened at his muscular shoulders and narrowed at his trim waist as he cinched his belt tighter in preparation for the dive. Kathleen swallowed in admiration and averted her eyes, only to see that she was not the only young lady who was enjoying the scenery.

Heathron stretched his arms wide and clapped his hands before he ran toward the edge. He appeared to fly instead of dive. He spread his arms wide and arched his back, looking toward the rising sun. For a moment, he resembled a seabird, hovering on the ocean breeze, elegant and free. Kathleen watched, spellbound.

Most of the young noblemen were lining up to join the diving procession. Heathron surfaced and began swimming out to the island closest to the Hand. Some of the younger boys were clearly nervous to make the jump but joked with each other with bravado to mask their misgivings.

When the boys had all plummeted down with whoops and

dramatic screams, chiding each other playfully, a few eyes turned to Eldin Stallat, still seated on the blanket with Kathleen.

"What about you Eldin? Are you going to join the men or stay here with the women?" Jessica Turlin asked scornfully.

"I...I am the host of this party," he stammered. "Some...someone needed to stay here to look after the ladies."

"Are you saying you saved the best for last? We would love to see your dive. We find it so exhilarating to watch the men jump," Jessica laughed viciously.

"You don't need to do it, Eldin. I am enjoying your company and would be disappointed not to have your intellect here at this picnic with me. Your conversation is so intelligent and friendly. That isn't to be found with everyone I've met in Tyath."

Kathleen gave a half-smile in Jessica's direction, trying to make it obvious that her expression was insincere. Jessica pursed her lips then forced them into a smile. Kathleen raised an eyebrow, daring her to continue.

"Lady Larissa Albodris said she didn't think you were man enough to make the jump," Jessica said.

"I said no such thing!" Larissa exclaimed.

Eldin Stellat looked hurt. He hunched over like he had been punched. Then straightened and began to remove his shirt with trembling hands.

"Don't listen to her, Eldin. I didn't say that," Larissa pleaded.

"I don't need you to protect me," Eldin said quietly.

Larissa began again but Kathleen silenced her with a touch on the arm. She shook her head subtly.

A silence descended on the noblewomen as they realized the drama that was unfolding.

Eldin Stellat was pasty white and his narrow shoulders and skinny arms were pockmarked with a scattering of acne. He seemed to shiver as he made his way slowly towards the edge of the cliff. His pants seemed too big for him as he approached the precipice.

The other young men were climbing onto the rocks of the island further out to sea and yelling encouragement to each other. None of them saw the lone figure of Eldin Stellat paused at the top of the cliff.

He turned and looked to Larissa, his eyes brimming with moisture.

"I have courage," he said, then dropped from view as he stepped over the edge.

21

ELDIN'S ANGEL

"What did you do?" the girls exclaimed as they ran to the edge.

Kathleen rushed over just in time to see the form of the young man falling face first into the water. His arms moved around like a windmill, and he didn't make any noise except for a pitiful yelp just before he slammed into the water at high speed.

"That was crazy," Jessica said. "I didn't make him fall."

"You pushed him into it," Kathleen replied accusingly.

"I didn't touch him."

"Still, you pushed."

They looked down at the water. Eldin wasn't moving.

The girls screamed for the other young men, waving frantically. Heathron and the other boys waved back. Kathleen was certain her words could not make it across the distance, but she cried out anyway.

"Help! Eldin is in the water! He's not moving," she screamed.

The other boys just waved back. Their reply was swept away by the wind. They were too far away to help Eldin.

Kathleen considered running down the steps.

She looked down the cliff. They were so high. There was little chance that anyone could run down the spiral steps fast enough to reach him in time.

"If he didn't know how to dive, he shouldn't have jumped," Jessica said defensively. "He was trying to impress you, Larissa."

"He's still not moving!" Kathleen exclaimed, ignoring Jessica.

Far below, Eldin still lay face down in the water with arms and legs spread out on the gentle waves. His body was motionless.

Kathleen quickly unbuttoned her dress.

"What are you doing, Kathleen?" Jessica demanded.

"Someone has to try to save him."

"Why are you taking off your dress?"

"I can't swim in this thing," Kathleen replied. "I have my swimming dress on underneath."

The other young ladies looked at her with astonishment.

"What is a swimming dress?" one of them asked.

"It's a dress," Kathleen snapped impatiently as she stepped out of the fabric that made up the gown she had been wearing, revealing an underdress beneath.

"Good thing none of the men are here," Jessica snorted. "That's scandalous. It barely covers your bottom!"

"It's perfectly normal where I come from," Kathleen replied as she hurriedly stripped off the outer layers.

"Girls can't jump from here. You might die if you try," Larissa cautioned.

"Eldin will certainly die if I don't," she said.

"Don't do it, Katie," Larissa pleaded.

"There's no time to waste. Abbath save me," she whispered as she jumped from the cliff's edge.

Kathleen had never dived from a cliff. Many times she had jumped into the water from the side of a ship or from a tree branch hanging over a brook, but never from a cliff. The belfries of the cathedral were small compared to the Fingers of Flint and yet she had leapt from them.

The wind screeched past her ears and the approaching water came quickly. She closed her eyes and tucked her chin in, holding her nose closed with one hand. On impact she wondered if her swimming dress would even stay in one piece. Weightless beneath the surface for a moment, she regained her bearings and kicked against the water, propelling herself upward. Kathleen broke the surface, and gasped in air as she looked around for Eldin.

She saw him floating close by and swam toward him.

She approached Eldin from behind and reached over to grab his shoulder and twist him onto his back. She hooked her elbow under his chin and began to sidestroke her way back toward the rocks. Kathleen didn't notice as her heart pounded in fear for the boy she held in the water. Her toes finally touched a solid surface, and she was able to pull him to shore.

With his body halfway in the water and his upper half on the rocks, Kathleen bent over and placed her cheek close to his mouth. She felt no air. Eldin was blue and didn't respond.

Kathleen pushed on his chest with her hands and saltwater gushed out of his mouth and nose. She pushed again, harder this time. More water came out. She could begin to hear the voices of the girls running down the steps. Kathleen leaned over Eldin and opened his mouth. She placed her lips against his and emptied her lungs into his mouth.

Eldin's chest rose slightly.

Kathleen leaned over with a second breath and sealed her lips to his mouth once more.

"What are you doing?" cried one of the girls.

Kathleen went back to pumping Eldin's chest with her palms. His head bounced against the rocks slightly as Kathleen pushed even harder and faster.

"Is he okay?" Larissa yelled. "The boys are coming!"

"Why are you doing that to him?" another girl asked.

Kathleen counted, remembering what Melva had taught her. "Make the body move to remind the soul what to do," she had said the day she rescued a child from the surf. "Sometimes the spirit will come back, and the person will live."

The child had lived that day, coughing up seawater and crying for its mother.

Kathleen had been amazed and asked Melva to teach her more. Now she attempted to apply her training to the lifeless body in her arms.

"Come on, Eldin," she cried. "Help me turn him on his side. He has too much water in his lungs!"

"This is strange, Princess Kathleen. I won't do this," one of the girls said.

"I'll help," Hannah said. She stepped forward.

"Lift his shoulder," Kathleen instructed. "We need to let the water out."

They turned the young man on his side and expelled more water.

Then they saw Eldin's muscles contract. His stomach heaved and water poured from his mouth again. Kathleen pounded his back. Eldin gasped and began to cough. He wheezed and then coughed again, this time opening his eyes.

He lay on his side as Kathleen knelt beside him.

"What strange magic is this?" one of the girls asked as they stood watching just paces away.

"It's not magic," Kathleen said. "I was just helping to get the water out and the air back in."

"I saw you giving him a kiss," the girl said.

"A witch's kiss," another one added.

"You kissed me?" Eldin looked up at Kathleen confused.

"I wasn't kissing Eldin," Kathleen said. "I blew air into his chest."

"Your lips were on his when I came around the rocks," the girl said.

"It did look like you were kissing," Hannah admitted.

"Your lips were on mine?" Eldin asked. "I can't remember anything. Did I fall?"

"You jumped. You're a fool," Jessica answered scornfully.

"I jumped?" Eldin said disbelievingly, looking up toward the towering Fingers of Flint. He was impressed with himself. "And I got a kiss from Princess Kathleen — all in the same day?" He looked bewildered. "I wish I could remember it."

"No, you don't. You landed on your face. You're going to have a terrible bruise. If Kathleen had not jumped in to save you, you would have died," Larissa said.

Eldin turned to Kathleen again, still laying his head near her lap. "Thank you, Princess," he said sincerely. "But, may I ask you a question?"

Kathleen nodded, wondering what he might ask.

"Where are your clothes?"

Kathleen looked down at Eldin.

"I'm wearing a swimming dress. In the summer months in Candoreth, this is what the young ladies wear in the water," she explained.

The fog that seemed to cloud his eyes until this moment, began to lift. His countenance brightened.

"I need to visit Candoreth in the summer," he said dreamily. "Where are all of the other boys?"

"They are swimming back," Hannah interjected. "Dallin and Heathron are racing to make it back."

The young men made it to the nearest rocks that led down to the sea and climbed back onto the land. They began to run toward the group surrounding Eldin. They leaped from stone to stone as they rushed back.

"Oh, I thought I was dreaming," said Eldin. "Why else would I be surrounded by beautiful ladies?"

"You're not dreaming. You're probably just stunned. You should take it easy for the next few days," Kathleen said. "The bruising is already starting to show."

Eldin touched his stomach gingerly. His pale skin was blotched with patches of red where his body had struck the water.

Heathron arrived with Dallin running right behind him. Their bare feet left wet footprints on the dry stones.

"I'm so glad to see you are okay," Heathron said to Kathleen. "I saw you fall from the cliff."

"She didn't fall, she jumped," Larissa corrected him.

"That's incredible," Dallin said. "How could a woman survive such a fall?"

"Eldin needed my help. He tried to follow you and was knocked unconscious when he hit the water," she replied.

"She swam out to him and pulled him to shore!" Hannah said.

"Wearing nothing but a....towel, I see," Dallin said, his eyebrow raised.

"That is an example of Candorethian swimwear, Lord Sarkkand. If you studied more, you would know that," Heathron chided him.

"Well, it is scandalous to wear something like that, and when we came down the stairs, she was kissing Eldin like a long-lost lover before he woke up," Jessica said, her hands on her hips.

"Are you just upset about being upstaged by Kathleen's swimming dress? Don't worry, Jessica. That white gown of yours leaves little to the imagination," Dallin said.

Jessica scowled at Dallin, and he threw back his head and laughed.

"Go back up to the top and gather our things," Heathron said. "We should get Eldin back to Tyath to see the physicians there. He still does not seem right."

"He can travel with us," Jessica offered. "After all, we will be the first ones back in the harbor."

"You think so?" Dallin asked. "This is a new year and a new day! Just because you won last year does not mean you are the fastest."

"He will go aboard our yacht, but I agree we have little time to lose," Heathron decided. "Will one of you captain his boat back to the city?"

None of the young men spoke up. Heathron looked around.

"Will no one agree to captain Eldin's yacht?"

"They all want to win the prize," Jessica said. "Can you blame them?"

"It is just the bragging rights! Very well, I will captain his ship," Heathron offered.

"Who will then be at the helm of your new boat, Your Highness? It would be a shame to not see what that beauty, the *Passionflower* could do," Jessica taunted.

"My beauty will do just fine as she sails my yacht. Kathleen knows what she is doing at the helm. She will get Eldin safely to the harbor and do it in record time, I am sure of it."

Jessica Turlin sneered at Kathleen with puckered lips.

"Well she's just full of surprises isn't she," Jessica all but snarled, cocking her head to one side. "If she is willing to put some clothes on, I'm happy to race the Princess back to Tyath."

Kathleen shrugged off the insult and stood tall in the brilliant blue swimming dress. She pulled her shoulders back, and raised her chin as her fiery hair still dripped water. Kathleen felt defiant in the face of the stubbornness and disregard Jessica demonstrated toward others. Kathleen surprised herself as she heard the words coming from her mouth.

"That is alright, Jessica. With hips like yours, I can understand why you would not want the idea of a swimming dress to catch on, but it makes a lot of sense instead of wearing long fabric that could pull you under the water. You should be a little more courageous. You were not willing to jump with me when Eldin needed our help. I had to wait for you and the others to come down the steps, so I don't expect you to be right there with me when we are sailing either. Don't feel too badly if you can't keep up." Then turning to Heathron she said, "Put Eldin on the *Passionflower*, Your Highness. I will see you back at the harbor. Thank you for swimming back when you saw me jump. You are a gentleman."

She stood on her tip toes and gave Heathron a small kiss on the cheek, then turned to walk back to the rowboat. Kathleen allowed her hips to sway a bit more than usual as she felt the glances of all the young lords and ladies watching her. She would not be humiliated by the likes of Jessica Turlin.

22

THE EAGLE'S EYE

Maxwell flew high above the Golden City. His large eyes were sharply scanning the small figures below. He caught the sight of Kathleen walking hand-in-hand with Heathron onto the deck of a beautifully constructed boat. Maxwell followed them out to the small islands, miles out to sea. He soared above the clouds and dived low and flew barely above water. He was enjoying himself.

Maxwell watched them for a number of hours as they played on the islands in the Clearwater Sea. He observed Kathleen and Heathron relaxing with each other, dangling their feet in the shallows, and soaking up the warm summer sun.

It appears she is doing well, he thought to himself and turned to fly back toward the western lands.

THE GREAT ROCK eagle swept down from the sky. It flapped its dark green wings and arched its neck, slowing itself before its talons finally touched the earth. The great bird let out a screech that pierced through the humid summer air. Channing winced and placed his hands over his ears.

"Do you really have to do that?" he asked.

"It never gets old to hear irritating noises, as long as you're the one making them," Jared agreed.

"Easy Max, I'm just saying your voice is loud, and high-pitched... and irritating," Channing said.

The bird stretched out its wings, blinking its enormous eyes. The eagle glared at him fiercely, as if it might attack the captain. The bird screeched again.

"Change back already!" Channing demanded. "You found out what we needed didn't you?"

The eagle stretched and chirped.

"Toss him the loincloth," Jared suggested. "He will want to take it with him when he goes to change."

"I don't want to pick it up, he's the one who stuffed it in the saddle bag," Channing replied to Jared. Then, turning to Maxwell, he said, "Why don't you swoop over here and pick it up yourself?"

The eagle cried out again.

"I've been saving this for you, too," Channing added, holding up a squirrel.

The eagle launched itself into the air. Channing threw the dead rodent and the loincloth aloft, and the rock eagle grabbed both with its talons and flew to the nearby grove of trees.

Jared and Channing sat in their saddles, arms crossed as they leaned forward.

"It really is amazing what he does, but it gives me the shivers to see a man change like that," Channing opined.

"I'm glad he came on this journey with us. Maxwell is very close to Seth. He's like a little brother to us. He'll do anything to save him."

Maxwell came walking out from the grove of trees in his natural form — a brown-haired young man with a crooked smile and intelligent eyes. His torso was heavily muscled, even though his form was lean. He swung his arms around in circles.

"That was a workout," he declared. "The wind up high is blowing strong, but it's nice to have my feet back on the ground."

"I can only imagine what it must be like to fly as a bird," Jared mused. "What did you find out?"

"Well, geese don't like it when you fly through their V and pick off the leader. That was hilarious," he grinned.

"You know what I mean, Maxwell. Did you see the Princess? What news do you have of her?"

Maxwell nodded his head.

"I flew over the city for days. I circled the royal palace and even perched on the Great Cathedral to watch the comings and goings. I finally found her far out at sea."

"Is she safe?"

"She is spending her late summer days with the young nobility of Tyath."

The Sīhalt Guardian clenched his jaw, the muscles flexing at the corners of his mandible.

"How was she?" Jared asked.

"Are you sure you want hear?" Maxwell replied reluctantly.

"I know she's not married yet. That won't happen until the next summer solstice. So, stop being coy. How was she?"

"Maybe that will give you time to wrap things up here on the frontier. I wouldn't waste any time if you have a hope of winning her over."

"Was she with the Prince?"

Maxwell nodded — eyes wide with mock alarm.

"What did you see?" Jared asked, tiring of Maxwell's antics.

"It looked like she was socializing..."

"That's good. She's making friends," Jared said. "I'm glad for her."

"They were on an island off the coast Tyath — a small island in the middle of the Clearwater Sea."

"You mean the Fingers?" Jared asked.

"She and some friends were laying around on the rocks... scantily clad," Maxwell added.

"She was sunbathing," Captain Channing added. "It's very common to do that in the summertime in the south, especially along the coast. It's very good for one's constitution!"

"So, she's healthy," Jared said. "I hoped that she would have health."

"They sunbath in their underclothes?" Maxwell asked.

He squinted and raised his eyebrows while looking at Channing.

"You shouldn't be spying on the young ladies," Channing chided him. His sense of honor was clearly offended by Maxwell's aerial report.

Maxwell rolled his eyes. "I was a bird, it's not the same," he explained.

"But, you're a man at heart," Jared countered. "Channing has a point."

"You told me to check on her! Besides, there were plenty of young noblemen with them."

"What?" Jared asked, incensed. "Those rogues!"

"They were swimming together and jumping from the rocks. The Princess did seem to be the life of the party. I don't think you need to worry about her anymore," Maxwell reassured him.

"Was she with Heathron?" Jared asked.

"Definitely. There is no doubt that they were getting along splendidly," Maxwell said.

Jared nodded.

"Why do you look so dejected, Lord Sīhalt?" Channing inquired. "She is simply enjoying the summer as any young woman of her station ought to do."

"I'm happy to hear she's doing well," Jared replied, but his words did not match his tone.

"I am, too. My nation needs that marriage to occur," Channing said.

"I fear she could never be yours, Jared," Maxwell sighed clasping his friend on the arm.

"I've heard that 'distance is to love as wind is to fire, if it's weak it blows out, if it's strong it makes it higher,'" Channing remarked.

"Well the wind should be roaring over the Clearwater Sea right now, based on the distance between us," Jared said, gazing into the east, toward Kathleen.

"It sounds as if she is kindling the flame for the man she was supposed to marry in the first place. You should celebrate that," Channing replied.

"Don't tell me what I should celebrate, Captain. You know nothing of this," Jared rejoined.

"We can sort it out next summer. We will get Seth, and then you can head back to see her next year," Maxwell offered.

"Just in time for the wedding," Jared looked dejected, his eyes fixed on the ground.

"I've never seen you like this before, Jared. What's gotten into you?" Maxwell asked.

"He's in love!" Channing exclaimed.

"I don't need to explain myself. Maybe someday you'll understand too," Jared said.

"I would not have teased so much if I knew how much she means to you," Maxwell added.

"I don't think this is a good time for you to go to battle. You are not in the right frame of mind," Channing suggested.

"Believe me, there's never been a better time for me to go into battle," Jared said through gritted teeth.

Captain Channing grinned.

"I don't envy the next warrior who is unlucky enough to face you in a fight," he laughed as they moved toward the first Delathrane encampment they had encountered after weeks of travel.

23

FIRST ENCAMPMENT

"Halt! You may go no further," a voice called out.

Jared kept walking.

"I said stop! Approaching the King's tent means death," he cried.

Jared walked up to the hidden sentry and spoke directly to him.

"I'm looking for my brother," he said.

The sentry looked awkward, feigning concealment but obvious to the eyes of the Sensor.

"What does he look like?" the Delathrane asked, standing up to his full height.

"Just like this," Jared pointed to his own face. "Except for the color of his eyes. His eyes are the color of the sky."

The warrior frowned and shook his head.

"Anyone who looked like you would not last long among our people. We would make him run the gauntlet many times. We would make him carry the piss pot and keep the fire burning like a child. That is what we do with a man that looks like you, among our people," he said derisively.

"I don't have time for this," Jared replied. He viciously

slammed his right elbow into one side of the man's face, then struck hard from the opposite direction with his left fist. The warrior dropped without another word.

Jared kept walking, intent on approaching the chief.

"How did you get past our warriors?" a surprised barbarian demanded when he saw Jared strolling toward them.

"The sentry told me I could find you here, so I walked over," Jared replied, indicating with his thumb the direction of their arrival.

"You think you are brave? *Handri* slave!"

"I am no slave, but if you have one that looks like me, I'll be very interested to know about him," Jared said calmly.

"I did have one like you, but I splayed him alive," another barbarian spoke.

Jared pointed his elegant sword at each of the warriors.

"Did you really have a slave that looked like me, or are you just running your mouth?"

He placed the tip of the sword under the chin of one warrior, and a few drops of blood sprang from his skin as the edge, sharper than a razor, pressed against it.

"Yes, I had a slave just like you, but I beat him so hard that he started crying for his mother," the man replied, showing courage in the face of danger.

With the tip of his sword, Jared cut the earrings free of the man's ears. Then he lopped off the topknot he wore. The Delathrane tried not to show his surprise at how fast the movements were made, and how effortless the sword cut.

"What was the name of his mother?" Jared asked.

"*Handri* dog! You cut my hair. I'll see you dead for that."

"What was the name of your slave's mother? Did he really look like me?" Jared asked impatiently.

"You're crazy, *Handri*!" he cried, brushing away the blood from his chin where the sword had cut him. "You must have a death wish."

"In a manner of speaking, I do," Jared replied seriously. "I'm looking for my brother, and I am willing to die to find him."

Delathrane warriors began making their way to the flank of the Sīhalt Guardian. Jared did not try to maneuver to stop them.

"We have you surrounded!" a barbarian crowed. There was a glint of victory in his eyes, as if he had accomplished a great feat.

The circle of warriors began to close in on him. They stretched out their arms holding knives and clubs. Surely, they must have heard the tales of *Der'Antha* to be so cautious when they outnumbered the Guardian so greatly.

They grinned with anticipation, expecting to find some fun at the hands of a crazy *Handri*.

"Step back or I'll gut all of you! I want to speak with your chief if you will not give me more information," Jared commanded.

"You can talk to the dirt when your face lands in it," the leader of the group said as he lunged forward, but he quickly drew back when Jared nimbly dodged his attack.

"You can't say I didn't warn you," the Sīhalt Guardian growled.

With that, Jared began to spin, leaning outward, extending the tip of the whip-like sword. He forced the Delathrane warriors to jump back as the blade whipped past them.

Of the five warriors that had encircled him, only two were untouched by the first sudden pass.

The other three bore looks of surprise and confusion. They glanced down toward their abdomens with horror, wondering why their bowels suddenly wanted to spill out. Those three clutched their stomachs and dropped their war clubs, no longer part of this fight.

One of the two remaining warriors retreated, unslinging his bow. He nocked an arrow as he ran away then turned and drew it back.

Jared stood upright, tall, and straight. He held the slender sword with the tip pointing downward toward the ground.

The barbarian let the arrow fly.

It streaked towards Jared's heart. The Sensor saw the arrow as it left the bow. He calculated the trajectory, responding instantaneously. Jared stepped to one side and used the blade of the *impla* to cut the arrow in half as it passed by him harmlessly. The heavy arrow tip struck a tree, while the lighter shaft, with fletching, spiraled ungracefully to the ground, landing in the leaves at his feet. Jared did not take his eyes off the warrior.

The barbarian warrior who was nicked on the chin ran away. He sounded the alarm, not turning back to look at Jared.

"I was just going to sit this one out and watch, but I promised to protect you," Channing said as he stepped from the trees to join Jared in the open.

"I am doing just fine," Jared replied.

"I know, but you have more coming."

They turned toward the sound of many warriors streaming from the tents further down the thoroughfare of grass and dirt that made up the central road of the Delathrane encampment.

"Did you try to negotiate?" Maxwell asked, picking up one of the war clubs the moaning Delathrane warriors had dropped.

"I think he passed on that one," Channing said, looking around at the three wounded barbarians.

"They attacked me first. I don't have time to mess around. We need to find Seth," Jared insisted.

"I know," Channing agreed, "but is this the best strategy?"

"I think I should not have told him all the details about the Princess," Maxwell observed as he reached for his daggers and scooted on his belly to see over the rise to the valley below.

"Let's get out of here and try this another way," Maxwell said.

Channing looked at Maxwell and smiled. "My thoughts exactly."

"I'm ready for a fight if need be," Jared added, still holding his bloodied blade.

"There are thousands of Delathrane warriors camped just over the hill. We need to think this through," Maxwell said.

"Even if we could win, a massacre isn't going to help us save your brother," Channing replied.

Maxwell winced as the words were spoken, and Jared looked toward the captain with eyes fiercer than those of the rock eagle.

"Am I right?" Channing asked, mystified by the reaction.

"You're right," Maxwell said and patted Jared's shoulder to calm his friend.

"Jared, he doesn't know. Channing was just offering his advice," Maxwell insisted.

The Sīhalt Guardian visibly relaxed.

"Did I say something wrong?" Channing asked.

"That's how he lost Seth in the first place," Maxwell explained.

24

RACE TO THE FINISH

Lilly and Lana helped Kathleen get Eldin into the boat. They rowed him back to the *Passionflower* in the dinghy.

"Get that anchor pulled up," Kathleen commanded, but Lilly was already doing it.

Eldin coughed a few times.

"Hang in there," Kathleen said. "I'm going to have you sit below deck. When the race is fiercest, I'd rather not have you fall out."

"Just lash me to the mast," he suggested with a weak smile. "Thank you for taking me back to Tyath. I'm really not feeling well."

"You don't look well," Lana replied as she helped Eldin into place.

Eldin looked at Lana in surprise, "That is the first time you have spoken to me today," he said.

Then he paused and thought for a second, wincing from the pain in his head. "Actually, that is the only thing you have ever said to me," he added, more certain of his recollection.

"She is a woman of few words — you should count yourself lucky. Hearing her say four words to you should be counted as a rare blessing," Lilly explained as she quickly coiled a rope and tightened a line for the canvas.

"You mean five words," Eldin corrected her. "Don't is really just two words made into one — it's a contraction."

"Like it's," Lana said flatly, unimpressed with Eldin's observation.

"Exactly!" Eldin exclaimed. "And that makes two...three more words I've heard from you!"

"Maybe he isn't too hurt after all," Lilly joked.

"Get him settled. There is a strong wind blowing from the south that should push us along nicely as we head back to the city," Kathleen said.

The *Passionflower* moved forward as the last of the young people scrambled onto their various yachts. Sails unfurled and the beauty of the scene at the Flint Fingers was now punctuated with triangular white slashes of canvas and colorful flags.

Lilly and Kathleen looked at each other in excitement. Kathleen gripped the wheel, trying to loosen the muscles in her shoulders as she shrugged them back. She remained barefoot, her wet toes making prints on the teak wood deck.

Jessica's yacht was four or five spaces away from the *Passionflower*. Kathleen looked in her direction and remembered the girl's golden hair and sneer.

"You really want to beat her," Lilly observed, looking in the same direction.

"She needs to be humbled," Kathleen replied, thrusting out her lower jaw slightly.

Lilly smiled at Kathleen.

"So now you're just a servant of Abbath? Helping to remove the hubris of one of his daughters?" Lilly asked.

"I didn't say I didn't have my own pride," Kathleen admitted. "Do you think we can win the race back to Tyath?"

"Her boat looks fast, and the *Passionflower* is new to you. I believe it will be a close race," Lilly said.

"Those are the best kind!" Kathleen remarked as she looked out over the water ahead.

THE RACE BEGAN when a stretched rope was released by the boat furthest from the Fingers. It snapped back and cleared the way for the racing boats to move forward.

Horns blew crisp and clear from halfway up the Flint Fingers. The race had begun.

Jessica's yacht, the *Marine Escape*, moved out ahead of the surrounding competitors. The sleek hull of the light blue boat cut through the water like a knife. At first it led by only a few feet. Then, because of the expertise of the crew and their adjustments to the sails, the *Marine Escape* moved up to half a length ahead. The wind blowing in from the south caught the sails more easily because the Turlin boat stood alone, allowing its canvas to make full use of the wind while the other boats struggled to catch the breeze in a more compact group.

The *Passionflower*, having arrived later than the rest, was already positioned on the southern edge of the lineup.

"You anticipated the wind would come from the south," Lilly said to Kathleen.

"You intentionally showed up late to be able to pick the best position to start the race, didn't you?"

Kathleen looked at Lilly with mocking surprise.

"Would I do such a thing?" she asked with a smile.

The *Passionflower* moved ahead of the other boats. Its larger size made it slightly slower at the beginning, but the masts were tall, despite the ornate workmanship of the decorations. It had been designed by skilled boatbuilders of Hestin.

Kathleen looked back to see Eldin's yacht moving but falling further behind.

"I hope Heathron takes good care of her," Eldin said of his boat.

"I'm sure he'll bring her back in one piece," Lilly offered.

Kathleen turned the wheel. She felt the tension as she turned the rudder, increasing the efficiency of the direction of the boat. Force against the rudder was transferred from the shaft to the wheel and then into her arms. It felt good to be a part of the Clearwater Sea.

Kathleen paid attention to the wind as it blew in short gusts that skipped across the deck. She watched the waves undulating and judged the crests of white where the wind gained speed and pushed against the waters. There were few things Kathleen enjoyed more than the freedom she felt when sailing. Only the plants on the open water served to slightly decrease her love of moving across the deep in a well-built craft.

As she sailed, her thoughts turned to Heathron in the weeks they had spent together so far. Kathleen bent her knees to absorb the shock of the yacht picking up speed and moving across the waves. She felt young, strong, and free.

Wouldn't I be happy with him? she asked herself.

He had given her so many reasons to smile — reasons that had nothing to do with all the gifts. Kathleen felt secure in knowing that the alliance with the Golden City still held despite the lack of marriage between them.

But that is all based on hope, Kathleen considered silently.

She remembered the moments when Heathron gladly accepted the ridicule and disapproval of some of the high noble families in the capital. He was a man of his word. He stood beside her in confidence, despite their disapproval.

His parents, though powerful, were also kind to Kathleen. She could picture herself building a strong relationship with both of his parents if ever they were to become her in-laws.

Kathleen tried to imagine how Heathron would interact with Elayna. She was certain in her heart that her little sister would love the Prince. She had an image in her mind of the three of them having a picnic along the shore of the Clearwater Sea.

Elayna was always cheerful and bright. Kathleen needed to marry somebody who accepted her Talent, and Heathron met that requirement.

The letter from her father alluded to the fact that Elayna was showing signs of certain abilities. It filled Kathleen's heart with joy to think that she was not the only daughter of House Dal Sundi who had inherited the Gifts. Perhaps it would be something she could share with Elayna in the future.

"Don't you think we should change direction now?" Lilly asked.

"I'm preparing to do so. Get ready, on my count. Five, four, three, two, one, now," said Kathleen as she swiftly turned the wheel. The yacht responded, nosing northward at an angle toward the city. The *Marine Escape* hadn't turned yet, and the delay on Jessica's part brought the *Passionflower* closer to the *Marine Escape*.

As the distance closed, the *Marine Escape* also turned, paralleling the *Passionflower* on this new course that had been laid out.

He's always smiling, Kathleen thought to herself. *Even when I know there are reasons for him to frown. Life throws enough challenges at each person. It's helpful if they can confront them with a smile. I do love that about him,* she thought.

Kathleen looked westward. Her thoughts turned to the Sīhalt Guardian who was so far away. She was still far enough out to sea that she couldn't see the spires of the cathedral or any of the golden walls of Tyath. She couldn't help but wonder where Jared might be.

The white seabirds flew overhead and cried with shrill voices, comforting her. Some of her earliest memories from childhood were hearing seabirds, and it made her feel that all was right with the world. She could not imagine living in a place without them.

Would Jared come back? Would he survive the dangerous mission to find his brother Seth?

The thought of him not coming back to her made Kathleen gulp. She remembered the torture Jared had endured at the hands of the Serpent King. He was a formidable enemy. Though she had great confidence in the Sīhalt Guardian, she worried about him.

Kathleen looked to her crew.

Lilly and Lana made excellent bodyguards. Their constant presence was something she was adapting to more easily than she feared. In fact, she welcomed them. They were becoming friends, especially Lilly.

"What's on your mind?" Lilly asked.

"My little sister turned seven this month."

"You miss her."

"She's a little squirrel, always getting into things. She's so happy and energetic — you'd love her."

"I look forward to meeting her someday," Lilly replied.

Kathleen nodded toward the *Marine Escape*.

"Keep it tight until we get closer," Kathleen said. "I have a few tricks under my hat."

"But you aren't wearing a hat," Lilly countered, bewildered.

"It's a figure of speech."

"It would make better sense if you were wearing a hat. Instead you should say you have a trick up your sleeve. That's what we say in the north. You have sleeves, so that makes sense," Eldin explained.

The girls rolled their eyes at each other.

"You keep holding your head. Are you okay?" Kathleen asked Eldin.

Eldin shook his head. When he removed his hands, they were trembling.

"It hurts so bad," he said. "I feel numb on my left side."

Kathleen gestured to the wheel and had Lilly take it.

She walked over to Eldin to examine him.

"It hurts right here," Eldin said, pointing to his right temple. "If I had my dagger, I would be tempted to relieve the pressure."

Kathleen recalled a thought.

"Look at me, Eldin."

She held up a few fingers.

"Can you see my fingers okay?" How many am I holding up?"

He blinked and squinted, still cringing and placing pressure on his temple.

"I don't know, Your Highness," he said. "Nothing seems right."

"It's getting worse, and he will need to see a physician immediately," Kathleen concluded.

"If it's dangerous for him, let's stop playing cat and mouse with Jessica and get this boat back into the harbor," Lilly said.

"My thoughts exactly," Kathleen replied.

Kathleen called for a change in the sail configuration. After a brief hesitation, the crew followed her commands. The added surface area pushed the *Passionflower* further to one side. The unsecured items rolled across the deck. Kathleen took it home again. The dagger board of the elegant yacht bit deeper into the water. The distance between the *Passionflower* and the *Marine Escape* closed bit by bit. When it came time to tack to the southwest, the boats were almost even.

There was no friendly waving this time. The string of competitors was far behind them. The race was really between the two of them at the lead.

Jessica cut in front of the *Passionflower*, seeking to steal the wind, and breaking the rules of racing etiquette.

"We need to get this injured man to the harbor safely. If she shoves us off course, it could mean his life. This is serious," Lilly said.

"Raise the flag to communicate that we are in an emergency," Kathleen said.

The red flag with black trim was raised. The *Marine Escape* ignored the message.

They didn't give any leeway to the *Passionflower* as they closed on the southern edge harbor entrance.

"Be careful. The water gets shallow here. You can see by the buoy that we're off course," Lilly yelled.

"Jessica is shoving me to the shallow water," Kathleen replied.

Eldin's body began to seize and he thrashed about on the deck. Lana and Lilly held him down and steadied his head in order to keep it from banging against the floor.

"Your Highness, hurry at all costs!" Lilly cried.

"At all costs!" Kathleen replied.

She turned the *Passionflower* against the *Marine Escape*.

"What are you doing?" Jessica screamed, as the boats actually began to slide against one another.

"Make way! I need to get to the harbor," Kathleen yelled back.

"I'm not falling for your trickery. Eldin isn't that bad," she said.

Full of frustration, Kathleen angled the Passionflower just inside the harbor entrance. The stone guard tower, where the beacon fires were burning at night, had a causeway leading from the guard tower to the city walls.

"If we can just make it there, the guards keep horses, and chariots in the towers. We're almost there," she said.

"The water is deep across the harbor, but it gets very shallow on the side just past the guard tower," Lilly interjected.

"I can't set another course. I am going to try to make it to the guard tower, though," Kathleen replied. "Blood and serpents!"

Lana looked down, shocked at the language the Princess used. But she was just as determined.

"He needs a surgeon," Lana yelled.

The *Passionflower* didn't change directions to circle around trying a new approach.

"I'm not going to reef the sail and make our way behind the *Marine Escape*, ending up in the middle of the harbor!"

Instead, Kathleen angled the boat forward.

"Are we going to come right alongside the guard tower?" Lilly asked.

"Get the anchors ready. We will cast them both out as soon as possible," Kathleen ordered. "Slacken the line so we can drop them and hopefully stop when we need to."

"I don't think this will work," Lilly groaned. "We are going too fast."

"I don't care. Look at him," Kathleen said pointing to Eldin.

The nose of the *Passionflower* crossed the plane of the harbor entrance before any other yacht, but that wasn't on the mind of Kathleen or the crew. Their thoughts were fixed on Eldin and what they were about to do.

"Throw the anchors now!" Kathleen yelled. The crew members threw the anchors off the sides. The guards in the tower, now visible, could be seen running away. They were certain the *Passionflower* would smash into their walls, throwing wooden debris in all directions.

The anchors lodged among the boulders at the bottom of the deep waters of the harbor. The line snapped tight and yanked the boat in an arc that was cut short as the dagger board slammed into the shallow rocks alongside the guard tower. Kathleen and Lilly were thrown forward.

Lilly tumbled like a child. Kathleen's head smashed into the helm with such force that she flipped over it and landed seated on the deck, her face against the mast. Lana secured Eldin in her arms as she braced herself with the rigging.

In a less critical moment, Eldin Stellat might have had great appreciation for being held so tightly by the guardswoman, but for now he only quivered with uncontrolled tremors, unconscious. Kathleen stood up — her adrenaline filled bloodstream ignored the pain.

"Get him into the guard tower," she cried.

The women lifted the young lord. Lana held his arms and

tried to put him on her back, but she stumbled under his weight. Eldin's slight build was deceptive. He still outweighed her.

"Let's try again. Let's lift him together," Kathleen said. She and Lilly got on one side with Lana on the other. They lifted him like a rolled carpet and managed to get him to the rail.

"Are you all right?" a man in the guard tower asked.

"We need your help! Take this man to a physician immediately! Tell them he sustained a head trauma. He fell from a great height and has pressure on his brain. He will need surgery without delay."

"Yes, Your Highness," the soldier replied as he lifted the man from the hands of the three women.

"And what about you? Do you need to be tended to as well?"

The numbness she felt from the sudden impact on her face transitioned to a throbbing pain. Kathleen reached up and felt her face to see if any blood was running. Her hand was clean, no blood.

"I'll be just fine. Take him by horse or chariot. And go quickly!" she ordered.

"Yes ma'am," He replied, rushing Eldin through the guard tower window.

The crack of a whip and the sound of horses' hooves was a relief to Kathleen. She looked up to see Eldin being carried away toward the city. Kathleen leaned against the broken rail.

"I think I've completely ruined the yacht my betrothed has given me," she remarked.

"And perhaps saved the life of his friend," Lilly added.

"Should we try to jump over to the window?" Lana asked.

"Heathron will be here soon, I can see his sail over there. He can rescue us."

"I realize there was a lot going on," Lilly said, "but you did win. You know that, right?"

Kathleen nodded and began to smirk.

"I know," she said.

25

DIPLOMACY IS BETTER

"The serpent mound we passed yesterday was a good sign, was it not?" Channing asked.

Jared nodded.

"Clan Razewell builds the mounds wherever they hold a war festival. How many effigy mounds did you see as you flew over, Maxwell?" Channing inquired.

"More than I'd like to admit, but they must have divided their forces as they sent out recruiting war bands. I couldn't follow all the trails that led away from each one."

"If we can find the encampment with the Serpent King, we could have you sneak in and kill him," Channing suggested.

"We'll be sipping cider at the Windstall Hermitage before the first leaves of autumn fall!" Maxwell said.

Jared shook his head.

"I'm not sure I want to try it that way...again," he replied.

"Again? What do you mean?" Channing asked.

"He's had an altercation before with the barbarian Snake Chief," said Maxwell.

"He goes by the name 'Serpent King'," Jared corrected him.

"Don't make the mistake of calling him 'Snake Chief' if I have a chance to talk with him again."

"Altercation? What kind of altercation?" Channing asked.

"Jared killed the Serpent King's father before Seth was taken as a slave. That's why we need to rescue him," Maxwell said.

"It wasn't that simple." Jared felt exasperated by the simplicity in which Maxwell chose to explain the dilemma.

"This ought to be fun," Channing said.

"You can always count on the DeTorre boys to show you an exciting time," Maxwell joked. "You should tell the Captain about the time we first went to Fishing Point."

"That's a story for another day," Jared replied.

"You never want me to tell that story!" Maxwell laughed.

"Why not?" asked Channing.

Jared kept a tight lip.

"He's embarrassed he actually lost a fight! I mean he loses one time in his whole life, and the man is embarrassed! What gives?"

"I didn't lose, I was helping those weaker than myself," Jared said.

"Sure, whatever you say, but don't include me in that 'weaker than myself' nonsense. I was doing just fine! I had her little brother pinned down so he wouldn't blindside you."

"You got beat up by a woman?" Channing inquired, rubbing the semi-circle scars that remained stamped on his chest from his arena duel with Jared. "I feel worse at having lost to you," he chided.

"It wasn't a woman, he lost to a girl," Maxwell chuckled.

"She was big for her age," Jared replied defensively.

"When was this, Lord Sīhalt?" Channing asked, grinning.

"It was the first time I ever miscalculated my opponent. It was a powerful lesson."

"In humility..." Maxwell said.

"And I have never forgotten it. If I ever meet her again, I will honor her in my defeat, as I failed to do that day."

"She knocked you unconscious with a bonefish!" Maxwell laughed until he almost fell from Steed's back.

"I'm so happy you are having such a great time while my brother languishes among the Delathranes," Jared snapped.

"He's still alive. I am sure of it. You would have survived, and Seth is way smarter than you," Maxwell said. He laughed and, in truth, Jared felt better for it.

"I believe he is alive," Jared agreed.

"How can we rescue him without killing anybody?" Channing asked.

"We are outnumbered. Diplomacy is better, if we can manage it. If not, perhaps we can beguile them," Jared said.

"I like the diplomacy of cold steel," Maxwell opined as he played with his dagger and twirled the knife across the knuckles of one hand.

"That's why Master Tove trained you to be an assassin instead of a Guardian," Jared said.

"People should stick with what they're good at — Master Tove always believed that, and I have special...abilities," Maxwell replied proudly.

"So, how do we plan to beguile them?" Channing asked.

"The Delathranes will do us no harm if we can convince them we've come to trade horses with them," Jared said.

Channing looked at Jared incredulously.

"Why would a savage people like the Delathranes suddenly welcome a group of *Handri* into their territory just to trade some horses?"

"I did not say welcome, I said they would not kill us," the Sīhalt Guardian explained. "It is an ancient custom honored among even the most bitter enemies. The horse trade is sacred to the barbarians."

"I hope you are right. I kind of like this animal, though," Channing said, patting the mare. "I'd rather not part with her."

"I will not be trading my horse either," Jared agreed, as Steed walked onward. Then Jared looked at Maxwell.

"You're not going to make me do that old routine are you?" Maxwell said, looking forlorn.

"It will work again," Jared insisted.

Maxwell rolled his eyes.

"You know I'd rather be a larger version of something small, than a smaller version of something large," he said.

"Just follow my lead when we enter the Delathrane encampment. Do whatever I say. Understand?" Jared said.

"As you wish, Lord Sīhalt," Captain Channing said.

"You owe me one," Maxwell murmured, walking away toward a nearby hill.

"The Delathrane encampment is just over the next rise, follow my lead," Jared reminded him.

26

DREAM POWDER

Seth looked at Cedric, searching for any sign that the barbarian king had a trick up his sleeve. He often did. Seth had lost track of how many times he had won the game. He didn't need to keep track, though. Cedric, the Serpent King, always had a running total in his mind.

"You have defeated me three times more when you were defending," he reminded Seth as he set up the *Chendris* pieces again.

The game was the only thing that kept Seth alive. He was sure of it. The Delathranes had no cultural history of cheering for the underdog. In their view, the underdog deserved to be beaten. Weakness deserved a boot in the throat. The barbarians abhorred weakness, but they never cheered for Seth during his victories at the game with Cedric — not if they valued their lives.

"I am happy to go on the attack," Seth said.

"It is my natural way to be on the attack," Cedric admitted. "Even when I was a small boy, I always preferred the position of the attacker. To die defending a wall is a shame."

"I would say I'm just the opposite, Cedric," Seth replied. "I prefer a fortified position and to hold the line."

"All you *Handri* like to build walls. You hide behind your walls and act brave."

"It is the way of our people. Every clan has its way. One is not better than the other, only different."

"The Sīhalts are different from the rest of *Handri*," Cedric said. "I am glad the *Handri* do not listen to the Sīhalt Guardians. They remain weak."

"We come from every land. It is our training that makes us Sīhalts," Seth explained.

"Where do you train?" Cedric inquired. He finished setting up the center of the board. "I will defend!" he exclaimed and clapped his hands rubbing them together in anticipation of a new battle of *Chendris*.

"We train at the Windstall Hermitage. It is built on the southern side of the Straits of Windstall, at the mouth of the Clearwater Sea. I believe your people call it the Gates of Wind."

"I have heard the stories," Cedric looked off into the distance. "It was one of the first places we lost after the founding of the Golden City."

Seth nodded. He inclined his head ever so slightly as a mark of respect to his host and the losses of his people.

"Our records say the original Sīhalt Guardians made a peaceful treaty with the Delathranes. Your people and mine made peace," Seth said. "Nevertheless, it may be as you say. It was long ago, and I only have the written records to go by."

Cedric's eyes narrowed. Seth could feel him searching his face for any challenge to the narrative he had been told.

"The *Handri* of the Golden City have dealt falsely with us from the beginning."

Seth noted the distinction. He was making progress.

"The order of the Sīhalts came to Desnia a generation before the Golden City was founded. Our very first storytellers speak of the settlement north of Adisfall. The warlike people of the land of ice came in their longboats with their sheep and vines. They built homes within the sod and tried to live through the harsh winters. Many of them died the first and second winter. A small group of boats moved south along the coast in search of warmer lands. This was the beginning of the kingdom of Sundiland."

Cedric frowned but nodded. Seth could tell that the barbarian king was fascinated by the history.

"What do your storytellers say of the earliest times?" Seth asked.

"I will bring him here," Cedric said. He waved to servants close by, commanding them to bring the old storyteller into the tent.

The wise, old man walked into the tent. His eyes were milky white, and he was missing enough teeth that his brown lips folded inward in a puckered expression, as if he had eaten something sour.

"Tell us the story of the people," Cedric commanded the old man. He held his hand up to his ear cupping it.

"What?" he asked.

"Tell us the story of the people," Cedric repeated, more loudly. "Why else would I invite your skinny gopher hide in my tent?"

"Oh yes, oh yes," the Delathrane man replied. "The story of the people!"

He began moving his jaw, evidently working his lips and tongue to moisten his mouth.

Seth leaned back from the board. He had never heard a Delathrane storyteller share his craft.

"Start from the beginning," Cedric ordered the storyteller. "From the very beginning."

The man seemed irritated at the excitement from the young Serpent King. The thought that there would be any other place to begin the story seemed offensive to the old storyteller. The old man took a deep breath and began to chant.

Seth couldn't understand all the words. The man was using an older form of the common tongue with more words that only belonged to the Delathranes. There were references to people and things Seth had never heard. But the old man chanted of the beginning of the world, how floodwaters had risen and the people of the serpent were scattered across Desnia. When those waters receded, they landed on the tallest mountains on the Spine of the Serpent far to the west. The Delathranes grew. They spread in all directions north, south, east, and west. They learned to make their homes. They learned to fish and hunt. They learned to tame the beasts and use them as their own. He spoke of crossing the great Serpent River lands eastward — all the way to the inland sea stretching out to the rising sun. The Delathranes within the tent sat in rapt attention. Respect was given to the ancient storyteller, the keeper of their ways.

He spoke of the great chieftains of the past, who had obtained a vision-quest — men who obtained a pathway for the people.

The storyteller spoke of the wars of the Delathranes and then how the Sīhalts, Tyathians, and Sundiland men arrived. They came on ships, one after the other, without stopping. They planted gardens and fields. They tamed the Auroch and put fences around the bulls and cows.

Finally, the people of the serpent were forced into the Serpent River valley. They could spread no more eastward because the powerful *Handri* had built cities with walls. Nor could they go westward for the people of the plains and their fierce chariots afflicted them. And, so, the people of the serpent lived in the river valley and waited for the day when they could once again ascend to the mountain tops and in peace look out upon the endless sea and watch the rising sun lift from the eastern waters.

The storyteller finished. The reverence of the mood was such that Seth didn't utter a word. He allowed Cedric to break the silence.

"What do you think of the song of my people?" Cedric asked

"It is a beautiful and sad song," Seth replied.

"Do you see why we must fight?" Cedric asked.

"I would do the same," Seth said. "Unless I could find another way."

Cedric tightened his pieces at the center of the board responding to the feigned attack on Seth.

"What are the other ways you can perceive?" he asked. "The Great Sickness has weakened the *Handri*. There are many fewer than there used to be. Just how many, I do not know."

"I believe that you will need to unite all of your people, perhaps joining the Delathranes of the western lands. Trying to defeat all the *Handri* will not be easy. It always requires more attackers," Seth said, as he moved two more pieces to join the first.

"My people are not as strong as they once were either. Even though the Great Sickness passed us over, we have had no innovation, only tradition. And even our traditions have been corrupted."

"How so?" Seth asked.

"I chewed the dream leaves soon after I was made King. I had no time as a young man because I grew so quickly with the Healing. It is a sacred vision quest, one that the Delathrane men hold with reverence. The images and dreams from the dream leaves are a gift from our Father Spirit. Now we must travel very far to find the plants. They no longer grow in the river valley."

"Why are they so rare?" Seth asked.

"The young men dig them wherever they can. They trade them for the powder."

"Dream powder?"

Cedric nodded. A look of disgust on his face.

"And when we do, we traded with the *Handri* merchants of the Golden City."

Seth moved pieces on the other side of the circle, flanking those of Cedric.

"The dream powder is more concentrated. It leaves a man unable to hunt, fight, or work."

Cedric spat on the floor beside him and ran three fingers across his forehead, brushing away a few wisps of his long black hair.

"Why don't you put a stop to it?" Seth asked.

"Our people would be better if they did not use the powder," Cedric said, almost to himself.

"If you unite the clans and convince the people not to trade the dream leaves, use of the dream powder will stop."

"In my vision, when I chewed leaves, I saw the Golden City burning. My people wore armor like that of the *Handri*. They rode chariots pulled by great beasts. The shining walls of the Golden City were broken. I do not know how this will happen. It is my vision, and every time I share it, it becomes more real. So, tell me, Sīhalt, how can this vision be true? What would break the great walls of Tyath?"

Seth listened intently.

"In all of my studies, I do not know what could break the golden walls. There are no war machines I know of that could destroy the work of the Talented Builders of old. The walls may be breeched but not broken," Seth said.

"Why would the people of the serpent be wearing shining armor? Where are the great beasts the storyteller spoke of? Even the oldest men have not seen them," Cedric said.

Seth saw in the great barbarian king a sincerity and a humility he had not witnessed during the months of his captivity.

"Cedric, I do not know all the answers to your questions, but I do know that your people are suffering because the men use the dream powder instead of doing their duty. I see the poorest of your people suffering most. I hear babies crying from hunger, and the strong will not help them. They have time only for the dream powder."

Cedric frowned considering this. Seth knew that in days past, a critical statement like the one he just offered would have meant his death.

"There will be chieftains who will fight me. They will not want to change," he said.

Seth shrugged.

"You knew they would fight you even if you didn't call for the end of dream powder use. Strike at their defenses before they know you're on the attack," Seth suggested.

With that he brought a *Chendris* piece forward, following the lines instead of the spaces of the game board before them and struck the very heart of Cedric's defense.

Cedric removed the piece representing his king. He smiled with a malicious grin and crushed the bone carved game piece with his massive fist. The vertical scar wrinkled in the middle as his upper lip curled.

"I like having a Sīhalt Guardian as my adviser," he said.

27

NEW RECRUITS

Cedric rode with his new adviser beside him.

A man I once hated is now my trusted counselor? Cedric wondered curiously.

He gave the Sīhalt his black cloak with the silver trim. It came into Cedric's possession when he assumed the leadership of Clan Razewell. The previous owner who had helped to capture Seth the night of the massacre, hadn't wanted to give it up, but the Serpent King had been persuasive.

"He is my advisor now. He must look the part when we visit the other clans," Cedric explained.

The young warrior bowed his head in obedience and removed the cloak without delay, handing it to his King.

Cedric noticed a light in Seth's crystal blue eyes when the long black cloak was positioned over Seth's shoulders once more. The prisoner had a long way to go before he regained the muscle and strength he had lost during his imprisonment, but he seemed to stand taller when wearing the cloak.

The Sīhalt Guardian looked gaunt. His eyes stared out from sunken sockets, and a face with hollow cheeks. His sharp jawline was even more distinct, the skin stretched tight from the hunger he had endured, but his eyes were just as bright, and Cedric knew his mind was sharp.

How many times has he bested me in the game of Chendris?

Cedric didn't want to remember the count, but he knew the number.

As emaciated as the man looked, at least Cedric had a Sīhalt Guardian, and blood-sworn no less. No other clan chief could make that claim. Cedric felt proud. The Delathrane King recognized a man of sincerity when he saw one. For all of their brutality, his people kept their word. The Guardian would do the same.

Cedric was almost prepared to give the man back his sword. Certainly, the Sīhalt Guardian would be handy in a skirmish. Cedric recalled the night his father had died. The brothers, dressed in black with whirling blades, had been astounding in their fighting abilities.

The sentries posted around Clan Ermine whistled. Cedric raised his hand for his entourage to halt. No one moved in the tall grass before them. Eventually a warrior made himself visible. He stepped out from the grass, warclub in his hand.

"A peaceful day to you and all the people of the serpent," the sentry said.

"A peaceful day to Clan Ermine," Cedric replied in his deep, guttural voice.

"What brings you to our lands?" the man asked.

"I come with news and a proposal for your King," Cedric said.

The warrior was painted with light and dark lines across his skin, a pattern that made him blend with the grass around him. He nodded, then whistled to others hidden in places beyond him.

These would be the outer ring — the watchmen tasked with sounding the first alarm.

"Why do you bring this skinny, hungry one with you?" he asked, pointing to Seth.

"Does a watchman question a King?" Cedric replied. "He is my sworn adviser."

Cedric saw the man's eyebrow raise slightly. The sentry was impressed — as rightly he should be. He had never seen a Sīhalt Guardian in the service of a Delathrane King.

Cedric had accompanied his father before on meetings like this one. He knew the basics of what he must do. He would try to use diplomacy.

As they moved toward the central encampment, Cedric noticed that the second string of watchmen was sparse, and the third ring was nonexistent.

"Where are the other watchmen?" Cedric asked.

A flicker of frustration ran across the face of the warrior that had halted them on their first approach.

"They will stand watch tomorrow," he said. "We use a rotation."

Cedric pursed his scarred lips. He frowned slightly, considering the statement.

"Does King Teisa know of their absence?"

The strong young man nodded, color rising in his cheeks. He was ashamed.

The center of the clan's encampment held most of what would be familiar to any regular visitor to a Delathrane village. There were cooking fires, tethered horses and an arrangement of black fabric tents. Their wall flaps moved gently in the late summer breeze.

Cedric and his entourage were invited to the royal tent, but the King did not come out to greet him.

Perhaps he views himself as my superior? thought Cedric.

When Cedric ducked into the tent, his eyes had not even adjusted to the dimness of the torchlight when he covered his nose. The stench of human filth blended with the haze of the dream powder smoke. Cedric didn't have a good sense of smell from the day his face was cut so deeply by the Sīhalt blade, but even he recoiled.

The throne was empty. Instead, King Teisa sat near the fire, cross-legged, on the floor. He wore a coat of white ermine skins. The black tipped tails accented the expensive coat. The man used a hand that was decorated by many rings to pinch small amounts of the dream powder and sprinkle it on the heated stone. Blue smoke rose from the dream powder as it burned. Seth coughed and brought his cloak up to cover his mouth and nose. Warriors laid scattered about the tent, their cups of liquor spilling on the hides that covered the floor, lying in their own filth.

"Welcome, brothers," King Teisa said.

Cedric pulled his dagger as he stood over the King. He reached up and instead of doing the man harm, he slashed the fabric of the roof open until sunlight spilled into the darkness of the smoky tent. As the blue haze escaped upward, the King looked up squinting, shielding his eyes from the sunlight with his hand.

"Who are you?" he asked in a feeble voice unbecoming of a Delathrane clan leader.

"I am the son of your brother in arms," Cedric said. "I call upon the right of blood-ties formed in battle between you and my father. I need your help."

The King of Clan Ermine shook his head.

"There is no more need to fight. The days pass as a dream. There is tranquility to be found in the smoke of dreams," he slurred.

Cedric grabbed the older King and raised him to his feet. Then he drew back an enormous hand and slapped him across the face.

"Awake, King Teisa!" he commanded. "You do not belong in the dust."

Cedric looked around at the group of women and children. They had gathered, watching the enormous King that had just slapped their leader.

"Your people need you," he cried.

The older man nodded slightly. Cedric released him from his shoulders, and he immediately slumped onto the ground.

Cedric turned to the gathering people.

"This is your King?"

He pointed to the pathetic figure crumpled on the ground.

"When did Clan Ermine become so weak?" he asked.

The warriors didn't reply, the shame was easy to read on their faces.

"Did the weakness not come as you increased your trade of the *Kabris* plant?" Cedric asked. "My Sīhalt Guardian has explained the process to me. We send them *Kabris*, the sacred plant of our vision quests. They have medicine men who use their craft to make the powder from it. Our Father God gave us the *Kabris* but did not intend that we abuse it."

Cedric pointed to the barbarians laying on the ground, most of them unconscious.

"How can a warrior protect his family in such a state? How can he find meat when his eyes are clouded with the blue haze?" Cedric asked, anger swelling in his breast.

"We tear it up by the roots, leaving nothing to grow for the future. Because we are paid by the weight, we give it all — leaves, twig, and root," said the warrior who acted as the first sentry. He clearly agreed with Cedric.

"The trade with the Golden City will cease today," Cedric stated. "Our young men will no longer search for the *Kabris* plants to give to the *Handri*. No more for our enemy!"

"Who are you to tell us the laws of our clan?" King Teisa rejoined, more irritated that his intoxicated stupor had been broken than by the challenge from a rival King.

"I am not dictating the laws of your clan to you. I am dictating to you what will from this day be the law of the entire Delathrane people. The People of the Serpent and Clan Ermine are now joined together," Cedric said.

"No more *Kabris* will be sent to the Golden City?" King Teisa asked, crestfallen.

"And what if we don't agree with the Serpent King?" the young, clear-minded warrior asked.

Cedric grasped his small dagger. He held it up in front of him and ran his thumb along the sharp blade.

"Anyone willing to destroy their brothers for their own pleasure has no right to life or freedom."

"I agree with you," the young warrior said passionately.

"What is your name?"

"I am Tan-Atta."

"You are chief of the Ermine Clan now," Cedric said as he stripped the armbands of rank from the biceps of King Teisa and clasped them around the strong arms of Tan-Atta.

"Go back to the old ways," the Serpent King commanded. "Send your men to hunt and gather meat. The women must plant soon to capture the second harvest. A surplus will be needed. War is coming. We cannot sit at our tents, wasting away in a smoke-filled dream."

28

DINNER WITH THE COUNCIL

"I'm almost ready," Kathleen said.

She pinched her cheeks to give them more color and noticed her freckles were a bit more prominent as the summer sun had tanned her skin to a light bronze. The tan didn't hide the new bruise on her face. Hitting the mast of the ship at the end of the race left her with another embarrassing injury that could not be easily hidden. Mara, the servant girl, held the door open for Kathleen as she left her room to join the dinner party in the formal dining hall.

Kathleen did not look forward to small-talk during dinner. She did not want to smile and curtsy or be asked a thousand questions about her adventure during the Wedding Procession that ended in failure. She did not want to explain yet again how she was injured during the race to the harbor.

In truth, at this moment Kathleen would rather have been unconscious. The blueish-black bruise on her cheek, clearly marked her as the unfortunate bride-to-be. The fact that she was visibly hurt would only serve to remind the nobility that she had a Healer in her service that was Talented. Kathleen wanted them to see her as one of their own.

They would never know what she had been through, though. They couldn't know the pain she had suffered, how close she had come to death in the mountains, or how truly powerful she could be. She had to keep her gift hidden at all costs.

Kathleen wanted sincerity, not the pity of their powdered, pinched faces. She thought she would look ridiculous if she tried to wear that kind of makeup to hide the new bruises on her face.

"I can't imagine what my father would say if he saw me wearing the powdered makeup. I'll just have to deal with a bruised face—again," she sighed, instinctively turning away from the mirror.

Mara only nodded agreement.

Each step she took brought her closer to the vaulted halls of the imperial dining room.

"Why do you not look at me?" Kathleen asked the girl who led her toward the dinner. The girl kept averting her gaze, and moved in quick, sharp movements as she scuttled ahead.

"Servants in Tyath are expected to serve, Your Highness, not befriend their superiors," she replied in a quiet voice.

Kathleen shook her head, "Well, back in Sundiland, my servant, Sam, would have carried on a pleasant conversation with me at the very least. He would not hesitate to tell me his opinion if I asked — sometimes even when I didn't." The flame of Kathleen's frustration was momentarily dimmed as she smiled at the memory.

The girl nodded, still not meeting Kathleen's gaze.

"Mara, I thought we were starting to become friends the other day," Kathleen said, "And now you've gone back to being so demure."

"The disparity between the classes in the capital is much greater than in the south?" the girl asked, deflecting the remark.

"In Candoreth, it is common for people of different classes to mingle in public, even marry each other sometimes."

The girl drew her breath quickly inward. She was shocked.

Kathleen smiled to herself. She still enjoyed shocking people with tales of camaraderie between the social classes back home. She considered all the strange customs, so different from Candoreth, that she had to get used to.

The doors to the dining hall opened. A pleasant aroma of roasted meat and baked bread enveloped Kathleen's senses. A variety of greens and flowers decorated the tables. Large candelabras flickered brightly, their flames dancing around the grand and commodious room. All the seats around the long table were filled — except one. The people around the table stood up, pushing back their chairs as Kathleen's entrance was announced.

"Princess Kathleen Delunt Dal Sundi of Candoreth, Daughter of the Realm," the herald said, tapping his staff on the marble floor. The noise echoed around the dining hall, reverberating from up and back along the high ceiling.

Only the emperor remained seated in what struck Kathleen as a curious chair, fitted with wheels. The other noble guests acknowledged her in the appropriate fashion, a curtsy by one and a nod of the head by another. One's rank and station in the hierarchy meant so much to them.

Kathleen felt a tightness gathering in her chest. Her breathing became a bit more shallow as she looked around the expansive hall. The faces were not all easy to read. Their future Empress had arrived and not all of them seemed particularly impressed.

Kathleen did at least see someone happy to receive her: standing there, smiling grandly, was Prince Heathron. Surrounding him, the men in military uniforms at the table, she noticed, did not smile at all.

The emperor stretched out his arms as if to give Kathleen a hug. Empress Rema did the same. Her frame was as slight as her husband was massive. Even in his seated position, Kathleen could see that Kade Dol Lassimer was a man of powerful and imposing stature.

"Welcome, Kathleen. What an arrival you have had to the

Golden City," he said. His voice was deep and rolled like the waves of the ocean. Kathleen was not able to tell if he was happy or displeased by her presence.

Agreement rose around the table from the well-dressed guests. Lord Stellat and his wife, Lady Kayla Stellat, bowed deeply along with Chief Magistrate Dirm Uppenslaw.

"Thank you." Lady Stellat mouthed the words to Kathleen silently from across the room. Eldin's mother was grateful to her for rescuing her son.

Kathleen curtsied and calmed her emotions. She had not expected this dinner to be in her honor. Although she had allies here, there were clearly those who resented her presence. Admiral Hale stood rigid in his deep blue uniform, ribbons adorning his broad chest. Pilus Dol Lassimer stood beside him, the second-in-command of the navy. The army General Tigral wore a uniform of deep green. His mustache accentuated his frown, the ends turning downward in a curving slope. The other Dol Lassimer son, Jason, stood by his side, just as rigid. He did not seem pleased to be attending this dinner either.

"It seems I arrived just in time," Kathleen said, moving toward the only open seat at the table.

"At least you are on your feet once again," Heathron remarked. "And Eldin is doing just fine! He is conscious and his humor has returned. He asked me to thank you most profoundly when I visited him in the infirmary earlier today."

Heathron stepped away from his chair and walked over to her. He offered her his arm, and escorted Kathleen across the room to her seat beside him near the head of the table. He addressed the guests.

"Noble Houses of Tyath, welcome my betrothed. Some of you have not had the opportunity to meet Kathleen in person. Thank you for attending this evening."

He gripped her arm tighter, then his hand drifted down her forearm and his fingers intertwined with hers.

The movement comforted Kathleen. The tightness in her chest eased somewhat and she felt that she was able to breathe again, if only slightly.

"Princess Kathleen has agreed to reside in the Golden City for the coming year, prior to our being married next summer."

Heathron lifted her hand to his lips and kissed it.

Gentle applause arose from the guests at the dinner table.

Kathleen's legs felt weak. If Heathron hadn't been holding onto her arm, she wondered if she would have collapsed to the floor. She had not gained as much strength as she believed since wrecking the yacht.

"You may all be seated," Emperor Kade declared.

"You will have to guide me," Kathleen said. She looked at her place setting with three crystal goblets of different sizes. The plate was surrounded by elaborate silverware set out for the meal. She counted two knives, three spoons, and four forks!

Kathleen took a deep breath.

Why is everything overdone in the Golden City? she wondered.

Could she possibly guess what the tiniest silver fork, with three small prongs was used for?

Oysters? she wondered.

Heathron touched her arm. "Don't worry," he said quietly. "Just follow my lead."

During the blessing of the meal, those words cleared the fog in her mind. Kathleen opened her eyes as everyone bowed their heads. Kathleen looked at Heathron, but in that instant she saw only Jared's face. She remembered Jared uttering that exact phrase during their dance in Altrastadt. She had held her own that night of the dance. Perhaps this night she could manage to do the same.

When the blessing of the meal was completed, Kathleen allowed herself to smile and picked up the tiniest fork. "I just hope this isn't for the dessert," she said and winked at Heathron.

He laughed out loud, delighted. A few of the others looked his way and smiled.

"Oh, don't worry about the silverware, Kathleen," he said. "You will use them all eventually."

Then, under his breath he explained to her. "Notice how the guests follow our every move. They listen to every word we say, even when they pretend not to do so. Every look, every laugh, every glance or question — most of it is part of the game. These people view a statement in passing as a challenge given or accepted."

"How dreadful," Kathleen sighed.

"Right now, I want to keep them off balance. I just want them to see we are actually having fun," Heathron said.

Heathron pointed to the far end of the table. "There are nine houses that make up the Imperial Council. The man dressed in scarlet at the opposite end of the table is Lord Sarkkand. You see his son Dallin beside him."

Lord Sarkkand nodded in their direction.

Jessica Turlin, dressed in white, sat beside Dallin. They made one of the most handsome couples Kathleen had ever seen. Dallin's jawline was chiseled like the Sīhalt Guardian's, but his hair was light brown and curled in large loops that framed a face that glowed with youthful strength. His shoulders were broad and when he sat upright, Kathleen realized he might be the tallest man in the room. Dallin laughed and Kathleen saw that he and Jessica had perfectly straight, white teeth.

"And you have met the Lord and Lady Turlin? Those are Jessica's parents seated beside her. White is the color of House Turlin."

Kathleen swallowed when the beautiful face of Jessica Turlin turned toward her. There was not even a hint of friendliness in her ice-filled eyes. She even traced her finger down her right cheek and wrinkled her brow ever so briefly, in mockery. Kathleen got the message.

Jessica might as well have called her a cry-baby. She was making fun of the black and blue steak that marred her face. Her amber eyes held no warmth, but rather offered an unrepentant challenge.

"I don't think Jessica approves of the way I finished the race," Kathleen said to Heathron.

"There isn't much she does approve of, my dear, but you did win," he replied quietly, and then gestured to a couple nearest the far corner of the table.

"Next, are Lord and Lady Tivius. Their house color is gray, but they think that hue is more befitting of servants. So, they wear whatever they want. Tonight, I guess it's mustard? Their heirs are too young to come to the dinner, thankfully."

"Lord Balfoest there is the skeleton wearing silver." Heathron pointed subtly with his knife and took another bite of the seasoned vegetables. "I never see him eat, even at a dinner like this. Watch him, he just plays with his food and sips his wine, never actually eating. I think he has difficulty in trusting the cooks."

Kathleen snickered. She was enjoying the jabs that Heathron was making. They lightened the otherwise oppressive atmosphere.

"Lord Balfoest doesn't have any heirs, but he is related to everyone here. His family is very old and well-connected."

"Who are the plump couple dressed in purple?" Kathleen asked.

"That is the Count and Countess Aviella, their daughter is Hannah and their house color is purple as you can see."

"She is as sweet as they come," Kathleen said.

"I won't tell the Countess you called her plump. They are one of House Dol Lassimer's strongest supporters," Heathron said with a smile. "Count Aviella served with my father in the military when they were both very young."

"And in the green? House Stellat?" Kathleen asked.

Heathron nodded.

A skinny man with a shock of straight, black hair sat across the table from Kathleen. He squinted intently at the plate in front of him as he worked efficiently to move the food from his plate to his mouth in moderate but continuous mouthfuls.

"That is Lord Stellat, one of our other powerful supporters. He just recently rose to head of his house. Their estate lies eastward from the mountain to the Clearwater Sea in the north. Eldin is their only son."

"He looks hungry," Kathleen said. "I have not seen him even look up from his plate."

"Lord Stellat is reserved. I think that is where Eldin gets it from. He is also smart and sincere. Despite his wealth, he is often treated poorly because he is socially awkward. Their house color is green."

"Larissa visited their estate this past spring. She said she and Eldin kissed."

Heathron raised his eyebrow. "Larissa?" he asked. "I'm surprised. That explains a lot of his behavior lately. Good for Eldin!"

"I believe *she* was the one who stole a kiss from him."

"That makes more sense!" Heathron laughed. "I suppose she does not want to be left without a seat when the music stops, even if that seat is beside Eldin."

"And over there?"

"That's House Kristara in light blue. They are good people. Their daughter, Jemma, recently came of age," Heathron explained.

"Who is that seated next to them?"

"Her older brother, Connor, who married a first cousin of Lord Balfoest. She was quite a bit older than him, but they seem happy. I'm not sure what to make of his politics though."

Jemma sat quietly between her mother and older brother. She looked to be about fifteen years of age. Her straight black hair hung in shining strands. She had bright blue eyes and the tips of her ears poked through her hair when she turned to speak or look down the table.

"She has a very delicate air about her," Kathleen observed.

"Jemma is Lord and Lady's Kristara's greatest treasure. She is the picture of nobility, isn't she?"

"We'll have to make sure she is invited to the next dance," Kathleen said.

"It could only help our cause in trying to gain the support of House Kristara," Heathron replied. "Next to Connor is Lord and Lady Naystrom, Aidan's parents. They are quite influential, and their house color is crimson."

Suddenly, a question came from a young man seated just on the other side of the emperor, succeeding a very awkward clearing of his throat. "Excuse me, Your Highness, is it true you won the race before you destroyed your boat?"

The young man flipped his hair out of his face and revealed a complexion that was unfortunately consistent with his age. He looked to be perhaps sixteen and spoke in a soft but confident voice. His face was inquisitive and refreshing for its lack of calculation.

"Ah yes, I'm sorry, Kathleen, this is Michael Tivius, heir to House Tivius. I didn't realize he was here. They have significant holdings in the Merchant Quarter within the city. Michael has a great interest in all things foreign if I remember correctly," Heathron said.

Michael nodded modestly, then brushed another strand from his face, this time with his hand.

"Soldiers in the Harbor Watch confirmed that we crossed the line first," she replied.

"They were in a position to see," Jessica cut in. "She almost put the front spar through their tower window."

"Are all the women in Candoreth like you?" Michael asked, a sheen of admiration glinting in his eyes.

"There are few women like Kathleen, young Lord Tivius," Heathron said.

"Father says I must learn all I can from those around me before I take charge of running our family's endeavors." Pausing, Michael leaned forward and asked very earnestly, "Is it true you were captured by the barbarians?"

"I have heard that lecture myself many times!" Heathron laughed.

"I was captured by the Delathranes, it is true," Kathleen said, not wanting to expound on a story that had so much potential to reveal so much about her. She knew a follow-up question was inevitable.

"And how did you escape, if I may ask?" Michael's curiosity seemed to radiate out from him.

A few of the guests stopped eating to listen to her reply.

"Well, Prince Heathron hired a Sīhalt Guardian to escort me from Candoreth. He came to my rescue and we escaped," Kathleen said, and flicked an awkward glance at Heathron.

Her reply sounded hollow even to her own ears. The young Michael Tivius, sensing the sudden shift in the atmosphere, seemed to recognize that she didn't want to talk any more of the topic, and was wise enough to let it go. He smiled politely and said, "I am glad you were not harmed."

"Where did you find him, this Guardian?" bellowed a rotund young nobleman from across the table.

Heathron shifted uncomfortably before answering. "I was lucky to find a Guardian at the Windstall Hermitage. There are so few of them now."

Seemingly satisfied with this answer, the man who asked the question introduced himself. "Princess Dal Sundi, my name is Simeon Carnado. Welcome to the Golden City," he said. An elderly woman was sat next to him, matching the nobleman in the shades of yellow that she wore. "This is my mother, Lady Beatrice Carnado."

"How do you do?" Kathleen said politely to the old woman dressed in a gown that was loose fitting, and a matching cap that covered her closely cropped hair.

The old woman set her glass down and squinted at Kathleen, irritated.

"What's it to you?" she asked in a voice louder than was necessary. "That is no way to speak to my son!" she said.

"No, no, mother. She said, 'How do you do?'," Simeon interjected, loudly enough to allow the old woman to hear. Unfortunately the rest of the room could too.

"Oh, oh, I'm very sorry," she apologized, "I was certain I heard you say 'what's it to you' and that would have been impolite."

"It's okay, Lady Carnado," Empress Rema cut in. "It can be difficult to hear with so many speaking."

The elderly lady shrugged and said, "After all, why wouldn't we want to know how she got her bruises? Why in my day, I would never have shown my face looking like that," she gestured at Kathleen.

Kathleen raised her hand to her face, unsure of what to say next.

"Hush now mother, your voice is very loud. We mustn't berate her," Simeon hissed.

"He beat her?" Lady Carnado asked in shock to her son's statement. "That is no way for a Prince to behave!"

"No, no mother!" Simeon cried and turned to apologize to a blushing Kathleen.

"Lady Carnado, I assure you, the Princess is safe in my presence. I would never harm her," Heathron said trying to enunciate his words clearly.

The old woman stood up and extended a shaking finger in the direction of Heathron.

"Of course it should alarm her! Take it from a woman who was struck almost daily by her intemperate husband," she said to Kathleen. "If he is hitting you now, he will do it more when you are married. It is wrong, and I won't stand for it!" she said, anger quivering in her voice.

The room was silent now. All the guests had stopped their conversations to focus on the drama unfolding near the head of the table.

"I am so sorry," Simeon said again and placed his arm around the shoulders of his widowed mother. Now he was the one who blushed most furiously. Family secrets revealed at a royal dinner were nothing to be proud of.

Then a loud piercing feminine voice broke the quiet of the room.

"He did not hit her!"

All the faces turned toward the speaker. Jessica Turlin stood with a hand on her hip and a wine glass in her other hand. She looked exasperated at the old woman.

"He did not hit her," she repeated, pointing to Heathron and Kathleen. Recognition seemed to be slowly dawning in Lady Carnado's mind. She raised her eyebrows and covered her own mouth.

"Why, Simeon? Why didn't you correct me?" the widow asked weakly. "I've made a fool of myself."

Simeon shook his head and patted his mother on the shoulder gently.

"It's okay, Mother. No one in the room would fault you for standing up for Princess Dal Sundi," he said.

"Since I am already standing, might I invite you all to join me in offering a toast to our Prince and his betrothed?" Jessica said.

There was a clamor as chair legs screeched over the flagstones as people rose to their feet. When they were all standing, Jessica Turlin raised her crystal glass high.

Kathleen braced herself for the toast, knowing it would be like a double-edged sword: glinting on one side, but cutting on the other.

"To Princess Kathleen Dal Sundi," Jessica began, "may her...

talents be of use to the Empire. And may the undying love she shares with Prince Heathron, along with the addition of her realm of Sundiland, lead us to many years of prosperity for the Tyathian Empire and all the lands of Desnia."

She didn't smile.

Around the table, toasts were offered by a representative of each house. Lord Tivius went last and raised his glass.

"To love and safety for our future Empress!" he said.

"Hear, hear!" they exclaimed. Kathleen tapped the edge of her crystal glass with Heathron's and allowed herself a tiny sip of sweet wine.

29

WHO CAN BE TRUSTED?

They resumed their seats and sought to continue with the meal, but Empress Rema began to cough right after the toasts were concluded. She set down her knife and fork and pushed back from the table. She coughed and coughed again, leaning forward.

Emperor Dol Lassimer struck her back in an attempt to help dislodge whatever obstruction there might be.

"Are you okay, my dear?" he asked.

Empress Rema continue to cough. It sounded as though something was caught in her throat.

"Oh dear, Rema, are you okay?" Kade repeated.

Kathleen got up from the table and began to walk around to the side of the Empress.

Rema wheezed and coughed again as she placed her petite hands around her own throat. When she sought to inhale, she coughed again, unable to clear the blockage.

From his seated position, the emperor struck her on the back more fiercely a few times. The Empress stood. She retreated from the table a couple of steps before coughing once more and collapsing to the floor in a panic.

"Mother!" Heathron called out. He ran to her side.

"Call a nurse and the physician!" Heathron commanded.

Rema leaned over and placed her hands on her knees. Lifting her chin, she tried to extend her neck to expand the airway. She coughed three times, but each attempt to clear her throat became weaker.

"Empress!" Lady Aviellla cried. She swept forward, placing a hand on the Empress's cheek.

"She's choking!" Kathleen said, motioning for the crowding dinner guests to move back.

Kathleen remembered a day when her father was eating an oyster, freshly caught from the sea. The air to his chest was blocked and he began to turn blue. On that day, he looked the same way Empress Rema did now.

Kathleen immediately mimicked what she'd seen Sīhalt Girdy do to her father. She encircled her arms around her, balling her fists in front of the woman's chest just beneath her breasts and thrust inward with her fists like she was plunging a dagger to the woman's heart.

Once, twice, three, and four times she quickly lunged with the woman in her arms.

"Kathleen, what are you doing?" Heathron asked, bewildered.

Kathleen swept her fingers in the woman's mouth and then pulled sharply with her arms, giving another thrust.

At last, a piece of food sprang forth out of Rema's throat, landing on the floor in front of her.

Kathleen let go as the Empress took a deep shuttering breath and began to regain her senses.

Rema placed her hands on the floor, where she knelt, gulping in the air. There was a sigh of relief in the room from the guests and a few applauded.

"Thank you," Rema gasped. "I thought I would die."

"Would a drink help?" Kade offered tenderly. "Have a sip of

wine," the Emperor offered. She took the glass and sipped, swallowing carefully.

Servants came to clean up the mess. They picked up the silverware scattered on the floor.

"I believe I'm fine now," Rema said. "Thank you," she said again as she made her way back to her chair.

"Well, that was all very shocking," Lord Turlin said.

"Yes, Princess Dal Sundi, wherever did you learn that maneuver?" General Tigral asked, his mouth fixed in a permanent frown.

"My father was once saved from choking by our Sīhalt Guardian. I mimicked what I saw that day," Kathleen explained.

"That would be Sīhalt Girdy Frast would it not?" the general remarked, "Hero of Dumal Wells?"

Kathleen nodded. "He is like a grandfather to me."

The older military man raised his glass.

"I was just a boy when I saw him fight the Delathranes at the most pivotal of battles. In all my subsequent years of service, I've never seen the like."

"It seems more than one good thing comes from Sundiland," Empress Rema said.

She took a few more sips of wine.

"That's much better. Thank you again," she said, smoothing her hair as she settled in again at the table.

"The Sundiland Princess seems to have a way of showing up just in time," Lady Stellat said with a smile.

Empress Rema suddenly dropped the wine glass she held. It broke as it hit the table and spilled the contents on the cream-colored linen, and soaked into the golden runner. She looked at her husband in fear. White foam bubbled at the corners of her mouth.

"What is happening?" she cried as more of the small white bubbles rose to her lips. Rema placed her napkin to her face and dabbed the corners of her mouth. The thick, white foam continued to seep out.

"Someone help her!" Lady Stellat cried out.

"The nurse is already on her way. Hold on, mother!" Heathron said.

Rema tried to speak again but was prevented from doing so by the foam cascading from her lips. Like the last gasp of a drowning swimmer, Empress Rema opened her mouth wide. Despite the loud calls for assistance, no one in the room knew what to do. Foam spewed from Rema's gaping jaws and nose. The nurse burst into the room and ran to the side of the Empress. She grabbed another napkin from the table and began to wipe the foam away from her mouth.

"How long has she been afflicted?" she asked in a commanding voice. "Bring me a lamp!"

The nurse knelt behind her and took a long-handled serving spoon from the table. The nurse used it to press the tongue downward, straining to see down the throat without actually touching the lips, cheek, or tongue of the Empress. Heathron held his mother under the arms to support her as she lost consciousness.

"If I can't get her some air..." the nurse said, clearly struggling. Depressing the tongue only made the foam bubble out more quickly.

"Remove the lamplight. There is no blockage," she said, careful to avoid touching the foam still exuding from the ashen lips of Empress Rema.

Minutes passed like an eternity. Finally, the nurse looked at the Emperor and shook her head.

Kade looked on with an expression of disbelief. He rolled his wheelchair closer to his wife, then looked at the petite woman slouched on the marble floor. He gripped both arms of his chair, his knuckles turning white from the force. He turned to look at the dinner guests with tears streaming down his cheeks.

"Go home," he said in a voice full of grief. "Today we have lost the Lady of the City."

The nobility began to file out of the dining hall. Pilus and Jason Dol Lassimer went over toward their mother. One by one the guests moved toward the door. Kathleen moved to the door along with the rest. Unsure if she should comfort Heathron or allow him to grieve with his family alone.

"Stop," Heathron commanded, as he knelt beside his mother.

Everyone stopped.

He walked over to the door of the dining room.

"Come back in," he commanded. "Everyone who is in the hallway, come back in this room, immediately," he commanded.

The nobility began to stream back into the dining room, standing along the walls, facing the Prince.

"Guards, close the door," Heathron commanded. "No one leaves until they are dismissed."

The guards swiftly obeyed him, standing at attention in front of the closed doors, hands on the hilts of their swords.

"My mother..." he said with his back to the audience.

His words were ice.

"...was not supposed to die tonight."

Heathron turned to face the small audience. He looked older, less innocent, and his face was that of a man determined to regain a precious treasure he had lost.

"Allow House Dol Lassimer the dignity of announcing her passing to the city she loved," he said.

The gathered heads of the high houses of Tyath nodded in understanding.

"I also expect you to keep your tongue from wagging about how her death was...most unnatural."

The tension in the room increased as Heathron's tone transitioned from one of pain to one of anger.

"I'm putting you on notice now." He inspected each of their faces slowly, searching their features. "If one of you is responsible for the death of my mother, I will be merciless in my revenge. I don't know what evil was used to take her life. If I knew what I was looking for, I would have you all strip-searched before you left the room."

At this, there rose gasps of indignation.

"Ask yourselves if you would do the same in my position," Heathron added.

"Who touched her during dinner?" the nurse asked, her hands on her hips. "Who had contact with the Empress?"

Many of the faces turned toward Kathleen and Lady Aviella.

"She was choking, and I helped her," Kathleen said.

"You put your fingers in her mouth," Jessica Turlin added.

"Just to get the blockage clear," Kathleen replied.

"Mother took a sip of wine after Kathleen helped her. In the commotion, I didn't see who might've touched the wine glass, but it wasn't Kathleen."

Everyone's eyes turned to the shards of the goblet glistening on the table.

"Your Highness, we don't even know if this was a poison of the delayed sort. Empress Rema could have fallen ill or had a reaction to the food somehow. It seems strange, but we do not know," the nurse said.

"Where is the physician? Was he not called for?" Emperor Dol Lassimer cried. "What good is a doctor if they are nowhere to be found in a time of need?"

"We will get to the truth of this before the night is over," Heathron said.

"You plan to keep us prisoners?" Admiral Hale asked.

"Let them go, Heathron," Pilus Dol Lassimer said. "You cannot keep members of the military or the Council of Nine as hostages no matter how aggrieved you are right now."

Heathron looked at his brother. His jaw flexed as he clenched his teeth. Then he nodded to the guards, and they moved aside to allow the guests to depart.

Kathleen decided she would allow Heathron some time with his family after all.

30

APOTHECARY

The next day, Kathleen sought out Heathron. She wanted him to know that she was there for him. She arrived late in the morning and found the Prince sitting at his desk with his head in his hands.

"Come in," he said and offered her a weak smile when he saw it was her.

Lilly and Lana waited by the door as Kathleen entered Heathron's study.

"How are you feeling this morning?" she inquired.

Heathron looked at her and nodded unconvincingly.

"I am managing," he replied. He didn't rise to stand as he normally would have when she entered, but Kathleen wasn't offended. She knew the pain of losing a loved one.

"I remember the morning after my mother died. I felt lost and very alone."

"We know our parents won't live forever, but it is a shock to feel the loss nonetheless," Heathron agreed.

Kathleen looked at him. He wore the crown as usual, the polished metal band with its intricate pattern positioned over his forehead. Heathron's sandy blonde hair curled out around the edges. The summer sun had lightened parts of his locks. Kathleen noticed he had not shaved. A light stubble grew along his jawline and accented his well-formed lips and chin. He looked up at her with his brown eyes and Kathleen saw the sadness again. She wanted to hold him, to comfort him.

She took a couple of steps closer and leaned over to wrap her arms around his shoulders. Heathron straightened and turned toward her while he was still seated. He encircled her waist and pulled her closer. Heathron rested his head against her body.

"I'm so sorry," she whispered.

Heathron didn't reply but held her close for a moment of silence. Then he spread his hands wide across her back until she was sure he could hear the increase in her heartbeats. Kathleen resisted the impulse to kiss the top of his golden hair. The Prince was grieving and she wanted to comfort him in whatever way she could.

Heathron looked up at Kathleen.

"In school, there was a priest who I always liked. He was an excellent teacher. We should visit him," Heathron said. "He can tell us what this is."

The Prince held up a folded napkin.

There was a hardness in Heathron's voice as he spoke. Kathleen rarely saw this side of him.

"Is he someone we can trust?" she asked.

"Father Wittenbrook always keeps to his word. He is not involved in politics. He always made comments in class that were critical of the way things are done in the city today. He is not the most celebrated clergyman because, for all his friendliness, he is relentless in his search for the truth, despite the consequences. That's who we need right now."

"Where can we find him?" Kathleen asked.

"He has offices beneath the great library. I haven't seen him for years though."

The Prince looked at the cloth in his hand. "We should go

quickly, this poison, or whatever it is, may degrade with the passage of time."

Heathron folded the cloth, carefully wrapping it.

"Are you feeling sick at all?" Kathleen asked.

"Last night I wondered if I might meet the same end as my mother, but I don't think I got any on my skin. I don't feel sick, I feel angry," he admitted.

He did look sick, but from the poison of grief. Kathleen remembered the look in her own eyes when her mother had died.

"I need to know if this is poison. I need to know who made it. We need to speak with Father Wittenbrook privately," the Prince declared.

∿

"HOW MANY FLOORS GO UNDERGROUND?" Kathleen asked. "It seems like we have been descending as far down as the towers are tall."

Kathleen lost count of the number of steps they had traversed as they descended.

"I used to explore these levels when I was a boy, but I never reached the bottom. Some doors are locked, and other passage-ways are so dusty it is clear that no one has used them in many years." Heathron pointed to the layers of dust coating the shelves.

The lower levels of the library were replete with stacks of books jostling each other for shelf space, like the rookery islands with their countless bird nests. White stone arches formed the foundations supporting the upper level of the main library. The ceilings below ground were lower and the flared pillars of stone were thick and strong so that the soaring ceilings of the library's main floors above could be lit by colossal windows of colored glass -windows rivaled only by those of the Cathedral itself.

"Some of these books haven't been used very often either," he said, dragging his finger across the spine of an ancient volume.

"Do not touch the archives with your bare hands!"

The suddenness of the authoritative command made Heathron jump. Kathleen squeaked, and quickly raised a hand to her mouth.

They turned to see an older man in a white robe walking toward them. His gray beard was neatly trimmed, and his pale complexion was set off by kind brown eyes. A curly mat of brown hair peeked out from beneath a white, priestly cap.

"We are looking for Father Wittenbrook," Kathleen said, holding her hands behind her back to show she had no intention of touching the dusty old books.

"Well, you have found him," the priest replied, "but my office hours are over at noon."

As he made his way closer, the priest squinted and looked down his nose at Kathleen.

"You are not one of my students, are you?"

"Father Wittenbrook," Heathron interrupted, stepping forward, "we need your help."

"Heathron!" he cried with recognition. "I'm glad to see you are well. I won't ask what you are doing with a Sundiland maiden deep in the archives of the library...a Prince can do as he wishes, I suppose." Father Wittenbrook smiled and squinted at Kathleen.

"This is Kathleen Dal Sundi, my betrothed," Heathron explained.

"Oh yes! I do remember hearing something about that. I don't come out of my burrow enough to keep abreast of such things. But I offer you my congratulations, nevertheless. Yes, yes, marriage is a good institution, if done correctly. Fortunately, Abbath gave me a wife who helps me to tread the path of light."

He motioned for them to follow him through an open door. It swung on well-oiled hinges and did not look abandoned the way most of the doors in the long hallway appeared.

In the room, lit by faint candlelight, a petite woman stirred a glass bowl set over a flame. Her long brown hair had wisps of grey and a natural curl. It was pulled back away from her delicate face and tied at the nape of her neck. She looked up and smiled.

"Hello, Heathron. It has been too long," she said.

"Mother Wittenbrook!" he cried, crossing the room to embrace the small priestess.

Kathleen noted that neither of these two called the Prince by his title. They were completely at ease in his presence.

"This is Princess Kathleen Dal Sundi of Candoreth. We are to be married on the next Longest Day."

"It is a pleasure to meet you, Kathleen," Mother Wittenbrook said. "I heard of the difficulties of your arrival. Welcome to Tyath."

"Why have I heard nothing of this?" Father Wittenbrook asked. "Lift my face from the books when I need it, Mother."

Mother Wittenbrook looked at him ruefully. "I try," she said with a smile.

"I have never seen a place such as this!" Kathleen mused, amazed. "What kind of magic is done here?"

"The natural kind!" the older woman exclaimed, as she continued to stir the contents in the bowl. "Welcome to my kitchen, Kathleen. It is called a laboratory."

Kathleen walked over to the bowl and looked at the flame that burned beneath it. The fire was blue and seemed to appear as if coming out of the metal beneath the glass. Kathleen could see no wood or other kind of fuel for the flame. She leaned over the bowl to peer inside.

"Careful! This kitchen is full of recipes that can cause harm. You must tie your beautiful red hair back if you are going to be an assistant of mine."

Heathron held up the leather pouch he carried.

"That is why we have come. I think my mother has been

poisoned. We came to see if you might help us discover by what means."

"Oh, my! Then we have no time to lose," Father Wittenbrook said. "Why didn't you say this sooner?"

"It is not as urgent as you might think," Heathron said sadly. "No antidote can save her now. My mother died this past night. I only bring you what I believe to be the residue of the substance that killed her."

A sadness passed over the faces of both Father and Mother Wittenbrook.

"I am sorry, Heathron. I knew your mother to be a generous ruler. She strove to serve the people. How is your father?"

"He suffered some sort of paralysis that night. Although, I do not believe it was the poison."

Heathron's eyes were no longer red, although a sadness glistened in them. "He can only move half of his face and has lost the use of an arm as well."

Father Wittenbrook nodded gravely. "I am familiar with such things."

"Father will not allow the physicians to examine him. He doesn't trust them anymore."

"Most of the physicians are priests of the Luzian order. I would not trust any of the younger ones either. Politics have no business in medicine, or the Church. I will gladly examine your father, if that is your wish?"

"I will arrange it," Heathron said gratefully. "Could you help me discover the nature of this poison?"

Mother Wittenbrook nodded and drew in a deep breath. Her face was one of determination.

"I will, Your Highness," she replied.

31

DEADLY RECIPE

"As we work to extract the compounds, tell me exactly what happened," Father Wittenbrook said as he poured a light-yellow liquid into a glass vessel. "I want to know it all. Forgive me if the details are painful for you to recount."

Heathron shook his head.

"I know that you must gather the facts quickly. My mother's passing will not be undone by the retelling."

"How long did the poison show its effects?" Mother Wittenbrook asked.

"My mother began choking during the evening meal. I thought it was simply the effect of food having gone down the wrong pipe. Anyone can choke on food. Kathleen helped her remove the blockage."

"How did you do it?" the priest asked.

"I embraced her from behind and pulled forcefully under her ribs. She coughed up a piece of food that was lodged in her throat."

"How long did she choke for?"

"She was turning a shade of blue and was unconscious before

we were able to revive her," Heathron said.

The priestess swirled a clear liquid with an acrid scent in the vessel, before crushing a fine white powder into it and mixing vigorously.

"She regained her senses again — back to normal?"

"The coughing was horrible, but after a few gasps she regained her composure and returned to sit back at the table."

"Did she drink anything afterward?"

"Father gave her a sip of wine."

"I see," Father Wittnebrook murmured.

"It was my father's own glass. He drank from it only moments before my mother collapsed. It was not poisoned then."

"Was she touched by anyone else in all of this?"

"I swept her mouth with my fingers to remove any blockage."

"I see," said Father Wittenbrook, nodding pensively.

"You think I did this?" Kathleen asked, thinking back to the moments before Rema began to choke.

The priest shook his head.

"I am only trying to reconstruct what happened. I do not have any inkling as to the identity of the assassin," he replied.

"Empress Rema seemed fine when she sat down again at the table. Other than some mild embarrassment at her choking spell, she was fine."

"Some poisons contain compounds that are delayed in their effects. Until we know what was used, we can only guess when the poison was administered."

Mother Wittenbrook placed the soiled napkin into the clear solution using a pair of tongs to avoid touching the fabric.

"When she collapsed, the second time, she began foaming at the mouth. Small white bubbles flowed from her lips." Heathron's voice cracked as he struggled to contain his emotions. "Then I think her throat closed, because the bubbles stopped, and she went rigid and turned ashen."

"I am sorry, Heathron," Father Wittenbrook consoled him.

"She walked the path of light. You will see her again. I am sure of it."

"There were only so many people in that room that night. One of them killed my mother," he said, his eyes hardening again.

"I am getting some color here," Mother Wittenbrook said as she continued to swirl the cloth napkin in the fluid. Faint streaks of red began to drift outward from the soaked napkin, like blood worms leaving a corpse. They wiggled as the fluid churned and then dissipated leaving the glass a faint pink color.

The priest and his wife looked at each other, eyes wide.

"You said your father gave the Empress a drink from his own glass of wine?"

Heathron nodded.

"Did he drink from it again that night?"

"I do not remember. We were all distraught. Father went back to his chambers alone. Not even a servant accompanied him. He didn't even want to see me," Heathron said.

"His loss of speech and movement happened that night too?"

"What was on the napkin?" Heathron interjected.

The priestess wrung her hands and wiped them on her apron.

"I did not want to believe it, but you both saw the red streaks in the glass," she replied. "Had it been a more common poison, we could have helped."

Kathleen and Heathron nodded and looked at the older woman. She paused, as if she did not want to reveal the answer.

"The poison used was *Blood Cutter*," she finally said.

Kathleen wrinkled her brow. "I don't know what that is," she said.

"Where would someone get poison made with *Blood Cutter*?" Heathron gasped.

"It was outlawed long ago. I thought we saw the last of the *Blood Cutter* vines in Desnia during the Plague."

"Who would make such a horrible poison?" Kathleen wondered aloud.

"It was used as a medicine during the Great Plague, harvested from the imperial gardens, but the side effects on those who survived its use made it illegal. All the herbalists and Healers swore it off, as well as the nurses and physicians in the Imperial Infirmary. Finally, the High Luzian order pulled the vines up by their roots and salted the ground where they had grown for centuries," Mother Wittenbrook explained.

"I can only think of a couple of people alive today who might know anything about *Blood Cutter*," Father Wittenbrook said.

"I imagine they used to work at the Talented Academy?" Heathron said.

"It was not their fault for being trained as they were. Their traditions are older than the current ones, by a long shot," Father Wittenbrook replied. "They never called themselves witches, it was the High Luzians who began that rubbish."

Kathleen shrank back. Hearing Heathron speak of the Talented with a tone of skepticism made her wonder.

Would he ever truly be able to accept me as a Green Grower? she thought.

"Do I need to worry about contamination for myself?" Heathron asked, looking at his hands both font and back.

"The poison is dangerous, even on your skin. If taken orally it is fatal," the priestess replied.

"That is the reason father is paralyzed on one side?" Heathron asked.

"The poison was likely meant for him," Father Wittenbrook said.

"The servants that night would have cleared the table after the meal. We need to find out if any of them suffered paralysis after cleaning up last night," Mother Wittenbrook insisted.

"I want the names of the people with special knowledge of

Blood Cutter," Heathron commanded. "I will have a word with each of them."

"We need to be discreet. These folks live in danger," the priest warned.

"They will be in danger if I determine that they had anything to do with murdering my mother." Heathron frowned deeply, and Kathleen realized it was the first time she had seen him look like this. Heathron normally smiled.

"The vine is very difficult to cultivate. There cannot be many to speak with," Mother Wittenbrook said. "Any person capable of growing *Blood Cutter* probably has at least a little of the Talent."

"No one, except Kathleen, knows I came to see you about this," Heathron replied.

"We'll be discreet," the old priest reassured him. "And I request the same of you. I've known men to lose their lives for less in Tyath."

"We need to speak with them," Heathron said.

"They can be found in the Smuggler's Quarter," Father Wittenbrook replied, as he passed a folded paper to Heathron. "Just follow the avenue to the end nearest the outer wall and turn right. After you have spoken to the gardeners, go speak with the kitchen staff."

Heathron grasped the priest's hand in gratitude, but the older man pulled him closer into a hug. Mother Wittenbrook joined them, and Heathron returned the embrace with tenderness.

"We believe in you, Heathron," Father Wittenbrook said. "You will make a great ruler one day."

32

THE PRANCING PONY

"**S**houldn't we be in disguise or something?" Channing asked, looking around at the empty grasslands. Maxwell had just disappeared over the gently rolling hills behind them.

"Are you kidding me? Look at you! Many a court jester would be dressed less audaciously than you," Jared replied, gazing at Channing's brilliant red jacket, and his hat, its side adorned with a large, white feather plume.

"Is that a compliment?" Channing asked. "It's the hat, isn't it? You don't like my plume?"

"It might be seen as an ostentatious display of our confidence," Jared said without cracking a smile.

Channing raised his eyebrows, considering the notion.

Jared stared into the far distance and cocked his head to listen.

"The Delathranes are coming," he said.

As the barbarians approached, Jared and Channing rode forward to meet them. Jared raised his hand in friendship.

"Greetings!," he cried. "We come in peace."

The two young warriors were surprised by the flashy Captain

of Candoreth and the black-clad Sīhalt Guardian. The sentries were young and seemed cautious of foreigners.

"Stop!" they shouted, ignoring the hand raised in friendship. They galloped to see the newcomers, their weapons raised.

"Be calm," Jared told Channing as the two warriors on horseback bore down on them. "They are testing our resolve."

The warriors yelled loudly and turned their horses aside just before they were in range with their weapons and rode past Jared and Channing. They encircled them, checking to see how many others were in their company. When they were satisfied that the two men were alone, the young Delathrane warriors drew back to talk.

"What is your purpose here?" one of them asked warily.

"We come to trade a horse with your chief," Jared said.

The warriors looked at Steed. Even with their relative inexperience, the two could recognize a good horse.

Excellent, they will escort us to the Chief, Jared thought.

The two young men gestured for the visitors to follow.

"King Wrangell will want to trade with you," the warrior in front stated. The other rode silently behind them toward the central field of the Delathrane encampment.

Little children and adults ran out to meet them along with younger warriors on horseback. They whooped and hollered, kicking up clouds of dust as they rode their horses in circles threatening with bows. A few had swords.

Channing removed his hat and lowered it to sweep it reverently before the chief. Jared rode tall in his saddle.

"We come in peace," he repeated, holding out an open hand toward the Delathrane King.

They were escorted into the center of the crowd in front of the chieftain's dwelling. Men dressed in leather leggings and women wearing beaded, leather dresses poured from the tents around the central pasture.

"*Handri* strangers," the chief said. "My name is Chief

Wrangell. I hear you would like to trade horses, although I believe you did not need to come this far west to find someone to trade with."

"It is true, chief. I've lost my brother. I am looking for him. Some say he was rescued by the Serpent King. Do you know him?"

A general murmur could be heard in the crowd at the mention of the Serpent King.

"Cedric of Clan Razewell is growing in power," the chief replied. "He asked for my young men as warriors. Many have already joined his ranks. He gives great hope to the people of the serpent, I believe such hope is well founded."

Jared nodded. "He is a man of great power. I wish to find him."

"Why should I help a *Handri*? Do you have anything to trade for the knowledge I have of his encampment?

"I am willing to trade a horse," Jared said.

The chief looked at Steed approvingly. "Surely this animal is worth more than I can tell you," he said.

"I have another horse unlike any you have ever seen," Jared replied. "He is just beyond your encampment. I will call for him, but if you desire this horse, you must tell me where I may find the Serpent King, and perhaps share a meal with me and my friend. We are hungry and tired from our travels."

The Chief was intrigued.

"I've seen many horses, but never one like the one you ride. How much better can this other horse be?" the Delathrane asked.

"The horse I wish to trade is wise beyond measure. He is fierce. He is rebellious and headstrong. Some say he is...unbreakable," Jared said dramatically.

"There is no horse I cannot break," the barbarian scoffed. "We have tactics unlike those of the *Handri*. The animal will take the bridle, I am not worried about that," he added.

"This horse will bring you much notoriety. There's not a King among all the clans that has one like him."

The people stood in rapt attention. Jared continued, building the suspense.

"My home is on the eastern shore, looking out over the endless waves of the great ocean. I've traveled north to the mountains where the valleys of snow never melt. I've seen the south, where the sweltering heat of the sun can be felt all year and still, I have never seen a horse that is his equal. This stallion is truly fearless and more intelligent than any horse I have known."

Steed snorted and pawed the earth with his front hoof. Jared laid a hand on the great horse's neck. "No disrespect," he said to the Windstall stallion.

The Delathranes wanted to know more. Their interest was piqued.

"If the horse is truly as amazing as you say, I will give you the information you seek, *Handri*."

Jared got down from his saddle and extended a hand to seal the deal. The chief hesitated. "I will only agree if this horse is truly what you say. If you are trying to trick me, I will cut your throat, *Handri*."

Jared kept his hand extended.

"I speak the truth. You will see," Jared said.

The chieftain grasped his forearm and the warriors crowded around them, nodding their approval. They all wanted to see this amazing beast, this horse the *Handri* had come to trade for information.

Jared placed his fingers to his lips and whistled loud and long.

The high-pitched sound echoed over the hills and soon a sharp whinny responded. The grass waved in the wind, and the sunlight shone down on the healthy earth. Two of the sentries closest to the hill began to point and call out. Others could not see the object of their attention. Then the animal appeared, standing proudly on the grassy plain.

A little stallion galloped with his head up. He raced right and left, showing off his glistening flanks. He spun around, then he charged towards one of the sentry's horses, bearing his equine teeth. The larger horse reared up, shying away from the aggressive, diminutive stallion. This brought laughter from the Delathranes as they saw the little horse buck and kick, now charging at the other horse from another direction, almost causing the warrior to be thrown from his mount.

The little stallion ran down the embankment, locked his forelimbs and slid on his back hooves to a halt. He shook his mane and whinnied loudly, raising his upper lip in front of the chieftain.

The serious Delathrane leader looked at Jared, then back at the horse, and began to roar with laughter.

He slapped his thigh and pointed at the little horse.

"You are entertainers! I did not expect it. This is very funny, very funny indeed," he said.

The little horse looked at the Delathrane chief savagely.

"Papa, can I ride him?" a little Delathrane girl asked, standing beside the chief.

"I would not recommend it. This little horse has the heart of a killer. He must be trained before you can ride him," he said.

The little girl stood close to her father, spellbound by the stallion that was perfect for her size.

"I cannot ride a little horse like this, *Handri*. I admit this is funny, but what is your game?"

"I did not say you could ride him. In fact, I said he might be unbreakable. Everything else I said is true. This horse is very smart. He will follow any commands you give him, but will not suffer a saddle," Jared replied.

"He seems to understand the human tongue," Channing offered.

One side of the chieftain's lip rose, and an incredulous grin spread across his face.

"He will do anything you tell him to do?"

Jared and Channing both nodded.

"Show us what you can do," the captain said.

The miniature horse ran in a circle, pounding his hooves into the sod and flinging clumps of earth as he turned in tight cicles. The Delathrane audience gathered into a tighter group around the scene.

"Now the other direction," Jared yelled.

The little horse swerved and ran the other direction as fast as he could. His head was down, and his mane whipped in the wind like a flag at the farmer's fair.

"Halt," Jared called.

The little horse suddenly stopped, dead in his tracks, heaving from the exertion.

"Walk on your hind legs," Jared commanded.

The little horse rose and began to take steps, one after the other, walking forward with his front hooves and nose held out in front of him. The crowd of Delathranes began to cheer.

"Now, lay down," Jared commanded.

The little horse laid down on his side.

"Roll over," Jared said.

The stallion rolled over, kicking his hooves in the air, enthusiastically rubbing his back in the dust.

"Now stand up, and shake off the dirt," the Sīhalt Guardian demanded.

As the horse rose, shaking off the dust, the chieftain tucked his thumbs inside his belt.

"I see what you mean, *Handri*. I have never seen a horse that can do this."

A Delathrane boy of about eleven years stepped forward.

"I can ride him, Father. He's only little. Allow me to jump on his back. I can ride him," he insisted.

"I would not advise it," Jared said. "This horse is very dangerous."

"He looks like a baby," the boy remarked in a high-pitched voice.

The little stallion snorted menacingly.

"That being said, I promise you there's not a more dangerous horse to be found among all the Delathranes," Jared said seriously.

"I don't believe you," the boy replied.

Jared shrugged.

"Climb on if you think you are man enough for him. His name is Maxwell."

The older warriors hooted and encouraged the boy. He sauntered over to the little horse and placed a hand on its back. The small stallion did nothing. He seemed to be ignoring the boy.

"Maxwell likes me," the lad said and promptly climbed onto Maxwell's bare back. The boy touched his heels to the little horse's belly and the horse flinched and began to move. The Delathrane boy grabbed a handful of Maxwell's mane in his hand and twisted it to hang on.

The little horse stopped and bowed its head. Reaching back toward the young rider's foot, Maxwell clapped his teeth down on the boy's toes and yanked.

The boy let out a shriek as he was quickly unhorsed and dragged to the ground. The little stallion began to run, but kept his teeth firmly clamped on the boy's foot as he dragged the boy and shook his head for effect. Some Delathranes laughed heartily while others cried out in defense of the boy.

"Release him!" Jared called, and the little horse complied. The boy got to his feet and half scampered, half limped back to the safety of his father.

"He refuses to be ridden, but he can be trained," Jared promised. "Captain Channing, get down and show the Chieftain's son what the horse will do while you lie on the ground."

Channing stared at Jared with wide eyes. "You mean as I'm laying in the grass?" he asked.

"Lay down on your back in the grass like you've done before. Look up at the sky. I'll tell the horse what to do," Jared said.

Channing dismounted reluctantly and lay down in the grass. He lay his hat beside him. Jared moved his fingers in quick succession as the little stallion watched. Jared formed the words of the Sīhalt sign language.

"I've trained this little horse to do the Delathrane stick-dance over the body of a man," he explained.

Channing's eyes opened wider, but the chieftain narrowed his in disbelief.

"Surely you jest," the barbarian scoffed.

Channing closed his eyes tight and clenched his jaw, as if he expected something to land on his face.

The pony pranced carefully to the captain, stepping high with his gleaming elegant hooves.

"Hold very still, captain," Jared said to the amusement of the crowd.

The pony began to step on either side of the captain, trotting back and forth faster and faster. He imitated the movements of the Delathrane stick dance. The people clapped and laughed, cheering for the horse when he finished by smashing the captain's fancy hat into the grass and crushing the large plume that adorned it.

The captain grabbed his defiled hat, and dusted it off, glaring at the pony while he tried to straighten the feather.

"Miserable beast!" Channing said.

"He does make mistakes...sometimes," Jared admitted. "But, as you can see, he is one of a kind!"

"Tonight, you will dine with me," Chief Wrangell said. "Put the little horse in the paddock with the other horses. You can feast tonight and leave at daybreak."

"You should not put him in with the other stallions," Jared warned.

"Is the little horse afraid of the others?" he asked as the bigger horses laid their ears back and began to approach the newcomer. The little horse snorted, and kicked. His small hooves connected with the head of the larger horse. The bigger horse bit the back of the little pony's neck. It lifted the little horse off the ground and shook him slightly. The little horse squealed in pain and was dropped back to the ground.

Jared and Seth winced as the little horse shook off the saliva clinging to its neck.

The Delathranes laughed at the antics of the horses as they sought to establish the hierarchy in the paddock. The chief clapped the Sīhalt Guardian and the Captain of Candoreth on the shoulder.

33

MORNING OF BLOOD

The evening hours approached, and darkness descended on the grasslands. Jared tired of the conversation in the tent. He wanted to know which way to ride so he could be on his way to find Seth at first light.

"Which way is the Razewell Encampment?" Jared finally asked.

Chief Wrangell stretched and rubbed his swollen belly. The food had been plentiful.

"The Razewell Clan is down south, past the canyons," he replied. "But I heard the Serpent King plans to head north and gather all the clans, even as far as the mountains."

"Can we cross the canyons by going around the western edge?"

Chief Wrangell nodded. "That is the fastest way."

His answer was interrupted by the sound of horses fighting.

"It is probably your little horse," the chieftain said. "That little stallion needs to be taught a lesson. His confidence is too big for such a small body."

Jared looked knowingly at Channing.

"He sure is," Channing agreed.

"Should I go check on him?" Jared asked.

"He is my horse now, *Handri*. Enjoy the food and drink. There will be plenty of time in the morning," he replied.

The tent was comfortable, and the food had been satisfying. Jared's eyes felt heavy. He began to doze in front of the flickering flames of the cooking fire.

Jared sat upright at the sound of an unearthly growl. He looked around the tent at Channing and the sleeping Delathranes. Jared realized that no one else had heard the sound.

Was I imagining it? he wondered.

Then it came again, a primal growl that rumbled like a demon's discontent.

Suddenly the flap of the tent burst open. A Delathrane boy with a torch cried out in fear.

"The horses! Many have fallen and others broke free of the fence. They are stampeding to the south!"

The warriors poured from the council tent and ran to secure what horses remained. In the darkness, all the commotion and the screams of terrified animals echoed in the night.

Most could not see in the darkness, but Jared saw the form of a beast no larger than a man. It lunged at the neck of a stallion then reared up in anger. The animal had thick fur and long claws. The ears were laid back against the wide skull. The Windstall horses were still in the enclosure, running in a tight circle, avoiding the carnivore as it raged, running and growling, its yellow eyes gleaming in the torch light.

"A wolvermink!" a Delathrane warrior shouted and knocked an arrow to shoot at the beast.

The animal leaped up and clamped its powerful jaws onto the hindquarters of the vicious horse. It let out a whinny and tried to kick the wolvermink free from its rump but the powerful jaws of the beast held fast. It brought its claws into play and held onto the bucking backside of the horse as it ran terrified into the night.

"I have never seen one so big!" the chief gasped.

"I have," Jared said stoically.

Steed made his way to Jared and nuzzled him with his nose. Channing's horse followed with ears flicking warily in every direction.

"You should go, *Handri*. This has been a bad omen tonight."

"Thank you for your hospitality. We will leave now. Good luck gathering your horses."

Channing and Jared gathered their few items, mounted their horses, and headed south.

No sooner had they passed beyond the sight of the Delathrane campfires, Maxwell came walking into the path in front of them.

"What was that all about?" Jared said.

Maxwell had blood on his lips and hands. He stooped to wash his face and hands in a puddle of water, then shook them dry.

"You mean that was...?" Channing began.

"The wolvermink. Maxwell loves the wolvermink," Jared said.

"You made quite a racket!" Channing exclaimed, "why did you attack their horses?"

"Didn't you notice when Maxwell was a little horse how he squealed when that stallion latched ahold of him?" Jared said, beginning to laugh. "I knew he wouldn't put up with that for long."

Maxwell drew himself up in indignation.

"I showed him who was boss in the end!" he exclaimed.

"Truth is, I liked you better as a pony. You're cute like that," Channing said, chuckling.

Jared snickered and shook his head. "You better watch it, remember what he did to the Delathrane horse," Jared said.

"It was gruesome," Channing said.

"Those horses were acting like jackasses, you have no idea what it was like being around them," Maxwell touched his ribs and the back of his neck, where large, dark bruises colored his skin.

"You owe me for that one," Maxwell winced, touching the tender spots.

Jared tossed a shirt and pants to Maxwell.

"Get dressed and rest up for awhile, Max. Don't try to fly for a few days, at least we know the way we are supposed to go now," Jared said.

34

SMUGGLER'S QUARTERS

"I'm going with you," Kathleen said, her smile melting his resistance. To Heathron, each smile from her was a treasure.

She had already gathered a convincing disguise — the dirty dress and matching bonnet hid her blazing red hair.

"We cannot be seen in the Smugglers' Quarter of the city without causing rumors and worse. There are elements within Tyath that are unsavory," Heathron said. "That is why I am going like this."

He gestured to his own peasant clothing.

Kathleen nodded.

"Lead the way. I will be fine," she said. "I already told Lana and Lilly that they can't come. They wanted to follow us at a distance, but I think that would increase the risk of our being discovered."

Heathron touched her on the shoulder protectively.

"Kathleen, I am touched by your willingness to accompany me."

She tucked the scarf around his neck adjusting his disguise.

"It won't do for criminals within the city to know the Prince is walking about in the Smugglers' Quarter," she said.

"Are you sure you want to do this?" he asked.

"You need a partner in this. I'm going with you."

Heathron smiled.

My mother would be proud of her, he thought.

HEATHRON WRINKLED his nose as he walked through the unkempt streets of the deepest part of the Smugglers' Quarter. It smelled of rancid fish, human waste, and rotting produce. There were flies too.

Some things cannot be delegated, he thought to himself. I will make sure to clean this quarter of the city...someday.

He needed to find out exactly where the *Blood Cutter* poison was obtained and whom was responsible. When Kathleen insisted on coming, he had at first resisted, but the woman had a way of chipping away at him. He found himself always wanting to see her face brighten with a smile.

He looked over his shoulder at the shuffling form of Princess Kathleen. He felt amazed by her resourcefulness. Who would have guessed the Princess could adopt such a convincing disguise? She would make an excellent spy.

Perhaps she is a spy, he thought, then brushed the idea from his mind. What would it matter? He had nothing to hide from Kathleen.

He glanced back at her, a few paces behind him. It was good that she had covered her hair. She would've stood out for sure if she hadn't. The crowds in the streets of Tyath were mostly dark-haired, especially in the Smugglers' Quarter.

Kathleen didn't seem to have trouble mimicking the dejected walk of the poorest people in society. She even managed to walk right by when she saw a street urchin begging for food. The look in her eyes made Heathron cringe, though.

He felt embarrassed for this part of his city. It represented the failings of his people — and his House, as the rulers. Heathron considered that history seemed to show there were always poor people in every society, no matter what the government was like, but that was little comfort to him. No matter how devoted the Church remained in assuaging the desolation of the desperate, there always seemed to be those who, even in times of plenty, were impoverished.

Maybe it was just the nature of society that some rose to the top, while others sank to the bottom. Through a combination of traditions, values, and work ethic, or lack thereof, some people seemed to thrive while others seemed to make destructive choices at every turn.

Heathron inclined his head, indicating his desire to turn left into an alleyway. There were no clear signs marking the names of the streets, but he didn't dare stop to ask. It would've looked odd to do so and drawn unwanted attention.

He was close to his destination, so instead he tried a different approach. A small boy walked by, carrying sticks on his back.

"Is the medicine lady in today? I've heard she was sick," Heathron asked.

The boy turned and looked over his shoulder across the street.

"No, she's there," he replied. "I saw her sweeping the front steps this morning."

Heathron thanked him, patting the lad on his shoulder. He walked up the steps that led to a green door.

Kathleen stopped to examine some produce being sold by a woman in the alley when Heathron angled back in her direction.

She's a natural, he thought as he stood on the narrow porch.

The old woman opened the door a crack.

"What do you want?" she croaked in a raspy voice.

"Medicine for my sister," Heathron replied.

The old woman squinted at him. "Medicine?" she echoed. "You don't sound like a customer of mine."

"She is very sick," the Prince said.

"I don't have time for more customers, not this morning."

Prince Heathron shoved the toe of his boot between the door and its frame. He moved closer and spoke to the old woman in hushed tones.

"Actually, it is my mother who is sick," he said. "She choked at dinnertime, with white foam rising from her mouth. I have it on good authority she was given *Blood Cutter*."

She tried to close the door but Heathron would not allow it.

"We are not criminals," the woman wailed.

"And I am not the police," Heathron replied. "I need your help."

"We've had enough unwanted visitors. Harold still hasn't recuperated," she said.

"Open the door. Allow me to speak with you!" he hissed.

"I won't do it," she cried.

From a distant room within the house, Heathron heard the voice of a little man.

"Bernita, who is it? I'm coming, Bernita."

"It's nothing. Stay in bed, Harold. You haven't the strength."

The old woman threw her frail body again the door in a futile effort to close it in Heathron's face.

Heathron took off a battered leather glove he wore to reveal the imperial insignia on his finger — a golden ring bearing the Fox and the Acorn.

"I am your Prince, woman," he said, showing her the ring. "Open this door and allow me to speak with you and your husband."

"If those ruffians want to fight, I'll give them a fight!" the old man said from within the house.

Heathron rolled his eyes and shook his head.

"Now he's saying he's the Prince of the city. These people must take us for complete fools," the old woman cackled.

Heathron tried to be quiet and discreet, but the clamor the old man and woman were raising would alert the neighbors, so he threw his shoulder into the door, thrusting with his legs, and drove the woman backwards.

She tottered and fell, landing in the middle of the room. Heathron quickly closed the door as Kathleen made her way inside. He turned to the elderly couple.

The old man named Harold stood with a sword leveled at the Prince. He puckered his lips and appeared to have missing teeth, because his mouth appeared drawn, and his bottom lip protruded more than it should have.

"Don't touch my wife, young man. You need to learn your manners, forcing your way into our home like this!"

Heathron pulled off his hood and removed the disguise exposing the silk jacket and gilt-threaded embroidery of his royal regalia underneath.

"I am Prince Heathron Dol Lassimer, and I came for your help."

"Run him through, Harold!" the old woman yelled. "These ruffians need to be taught a lesson. They think they can walk all over us in this quarter of the city. He's delusional. He's probably been sniffing dream powder like all the rest."

She turned to Kathleen and gave further advice. "I'd not get tangled up with this one, Missy. He's no good. Take it from a woman who has known some bad men in her day. This one is no good."

Heathron looked shocked at her words. Harold dropped the sword and begin to kneel.

"I fought with your father years ago. You have his brow and his eyes. Please accept our apologies, Your Highness. We've been mistreated by our neighbors lately."

Bernita looked from her husband to the young man standing before them.

"Oh piss-ant," she said and began to kneel slowly, placing one hand on her right hip, the pain evident in the movement.

"There's no need to kneel, good woman. We came here in disguise."

"I have little to offer you except herbal tea," Bernita said. "We just finished our breakfast and we weren't sure where lunch was going to come from. So few of our customers are paying these days."

"Does the Church not bring food to the poor? Are the sisters of the Welfare Society not still active in this quarter of the city?" Heathron asked.

"It's gotten bad, Your Highness. The bread wagons are no longer seen every day. We have to walk to meet them, when they do show, and we don't always know what time they will arrive. There are ruffians willing to steal anything including a free loaf of bread. Now that dream powder has become commonplace, they all just want their next dose. It isn't safe for us."

Heathron nodded gravely.

"Even near the Golden City it seems the order is under assault."

Heathron offered a bag of coins to the old woman.

"Buy food for the next month," he said.

The woman opened the bag and pulled out a large, heavy coin.

"And where am I going to spend a Gold Crown like this in the Smugglers' Quarter?" she cackled.

"Just put the purse away and be grateful," Harold chided her. "House Dol Lassimer has come to the rescue."

"Unless you can help me, my House may not stand firm. We are under attack and do not know the face of our enemy."

"We are at your service," Harold said.

"Do you still grow the *Blood Cutter* vine," the Prince asked.

There was a moment of silence, before Bernita answered.

"I do," she finally admitted. "It is an old-world plant. My family brought it across the ocean generations ago."

"It is illegal," Kathleen said.

"When used properly, it will cure what other medicines cannot. Only when it's misused does it become the horror it's made out to be."

"My mother was killed by it, just days ago."

The old woman swallowed. "I am sorry," she said.

"She succumbed to the effects of drinking it. My father was half paralyzed. He got the poison on his skin. I understand there's no remedy."

"I am sorry, dear boy. There is not," she confirmed.

"I am coming to terms with the attack on my parents," Heathron continued, "but as I rise to sit on the throne as ruler of Tyath, I need to know whom I can trust. I cannot have an assassin in my inner circle."

"I can tell you who took the *Blood Cutter* from me," the old woman said.

"The tax collector forced his way in here and demanded I give him some *Blood Cutter*. He told me it was illegal and if I didn't give it to him, he would have me arrested. I'm not sure which is worse, his demand for my property as a criminal or a tax man. It felt the same."

"What was his name?" Kathleen asked.

"He goes by the name Sorrento. I think his first name is Bartholomew," Harold said.

"You must not tell anyone that we came to visit. Your lives depend on it," Heathron said.

"My Prince," Harold replied, "we will join you in this fight."

The old man's eyes gleamed with a newfound vigor.

35

TAX COLLECTORS

Heathron entered the local tax house. His dark brown hood covered his head. He stood with shoulders hunched and his head down in a submissive posture.

"What can I do for you?" the man at the counter asked, but his tone was one that suggested he would offer no help at all. Clearly, he was irritated at the interruption during his afternoon cup of tea.

"I've come to pay my taxes," he said in a voice that mimicked the voice of a poor citizen.

"Drop off your coins as you like," the tax collector replied. "Set them on the counter, and I'll mark it in the books when I'm done."

"You haven't even asked my name. The Missus and I, we worked hard together to pay our taxes and although we're late, we want to make sure they're marked off correctly. Can I see Sorrento the tax collector?"

"He's off relieving himself. Just put it on the counter. I'll mark it down."

"My name is Heath..."

"Okay, I've got it. Now be gone with you!"

"I want to see Sorrento."

"Where do you live? Eighth ward?"

"Not far from here, but I ain't leaving until I see my payment marked in the book," Heathron said in his best peasant vernacular.

"I'm not inclined to write it down at the moment," the man replied haughtily.

"The Missus and I don't mind waiting," Heathron offered humbly.

"Have it your way," he said, sipping his cup of tea. "But don't say I didn't warn you."

Bartholomew Sorrento walked into the room hitching up his pants.

"What seems to be the problem?" he asked.

"This man and his wife said they will not leave until you mark down that he has finally paid his taxes."

"I don't believe we've ever met. Are you paying for yourself or someone else?"

"For myself."

"What is your trade?"

"I don't have a trade, per se," Heathron said.

"Per se, huh? Sounding kind of high and mighty for a man that relies on the missus to bring the food home. If that's true, maybe we can work something out."

He laughed irreverently.

"What's your trade, Missy? What do you do for money seeing as your man has got no trade 'per se'?"

He sneered and looked at Kathleen. She drew back reflexively.

"We have our money. Mark my name in the book," the disguised Prince said.

The tax collector opened the big book and ran down the columns. "Where do you live?"

He glanced back up at Heathron.

"We live on Hart Street with my grandmother. She's the medicine woman," he said.

The tax collector's finger paused as he slid down the page. His eyes rose slowly until they were level with Heathron's. The Prince detected a flicker of thought in his eyes at the mention of the medicine woman's home.

"Well, it's about time they paid," he said. "We will mark it down with you living in the house also. Any children yet?"

"Not yet," Heathron said. "Perhaps someday."

He grinned at Kathleen, and she made a look of intensity for the seriousness of the situation.

"What is your full name? First, middle, and last."

"Heath."

"And your middle name?"

"Rhondol."

"And you last name," the tax collector demanded impatiently.

"Assimer."

The tax collector began to write the name and then stopped.

"Heath Rhondol Assimer? So, you want to be cute and make fun of our Prince, huh? That'll cost you," he said.

The tax collector grabbed the bag of coins and slid them into his own pocket.

"Pretending to be the Prince can get you hanged. It looks like you still need to pay your taxes."

Sorrento smiled smugly in the knowledge that a young couple had no recourse for his ill-treatment of them.

Heathron reached across the counter and grabbed the tax collector by the golden chain about his neck. He yanked him forward, twisting the chain, with a bundle of clothing in the mix.

"It would be a crime," he said, "if I were pretending to be the Prince. But my name *is* Heathron Dol Lassimer. And you are in violation of imperial law."

The guards stationed outside made their way inside the tax

collector station, hearing the exchange. Heathron torn off the disguise and pointed to the tax collectors.

"Take them into custody," the Prince commanded. "I will question the fat one."

The tax collector sputtered, unable to believe what was happening as the guards sat him down and placed irons on his wrists and ankles.

"Who told you to get the *Blood Cutter*?" Heathron demanded.

"It was one of the cooks in the royal kitchen. I don't keep track of who has a grudge against whom. She offered me money, if I would get it from the medicine woman. That's the only reason why I was involved."

"What was the name of the cook?" Heathron demanded.

"Melrose, I think. I'd never seen her before she came in and spoke with me. She said she lived in the Clothing District but worked in the kitchens at the palace. I had never seen her before, I swear. She came to pick up the *Blood Cutter* just a few days ago. I have no idea what she did with it. Some say it's a medicine."

BACK AT THE PALACE, Heathron stormed down the hallway with his Imperial Guards and Kathleen in tow. He was no longer in disguise. Neither was she. He burst through the main doors of the royal kitchen. The Master Chef was conducting the cooking like a maestro would an orchestra.

His wooden spoon punctuated the air as he called out to his sous-chefs, who were baking, brazing, and dicing.

When the Prince slammed both doors wide open, a few of the cooks attempted to bow or kneel when they recognized him.

"Your Highness!" the chef exclaimed. "To what do we owe the honor of your presence in this humble kitchen?"

Everyone from the Master Chef to the scullery maids stood wide eyed. The clanking of pans stopped almost completely.

"Do you have a cook by the name of Melrose?" Heathron said.

The Master Chef shook his head.

"Poor Melrose was killed by cutthroats as she made her way to work yesterday morning. She was a good girl and well liked."

"Master Chef, you know of my mother's passing and have been sworn to silence. Answer me this — are there any more people of your staff who have become sick since my mother's passing?"

The Master Chef hesitated, clearly afraid of the consequences of his answer.

"Answer me, man!" Heathron yelled.

"There is a serving girl that worked the tables that night. Her name is Elsa. She is sick and has not returned to work since."

"Heathron scanned the faces of the kitchen staff. Many stood with eyes downcast in shame.

They know they have let me down, Heathron thought.

"Stir that pot," Heathron commanded to a cook nearest a bubbling stove top. "I wouldn't want your glaze to burn."

He looked up, nodded, and immediately turned back toward the stove, stirring slowly.

"Does anyone know where Elsa lives? Does she reside within the palace or in a residence outside?"

"I know where she lives, Your Highness. She's the eldest daughter of the baker named List just outside the Commerce Gate," a scullery maid interjected.

"Will you take us there?"

The girl curtsied and the Master Chef waved her onward.

JUST OUTSIDE OF the Commerce Gate, a clean bakery had been built in the traditional Tyathian style. The roof had a steep pitch, and timbers framed the outline of the structure. Inside lay the girl named Elsa.

The man and woman of the house were distraught at the arrival of Prince Heathron and his betrothed. On this day, they found no reason to celebrate the arrival of such a vaunted guest.

"How long has she been sick?" Kathleen asked.

"She came home after her work and has not risen since. She's half-paralyzed, Your Highness, and we don't know what to do. No remedies seem to work."

Heathron nodded gravely at the girl, sweating in a stupor on her little bed.

"Can she speak?"

"Very little," the mother replied.

"May I ask her a few questions?" the Prince asked.

Both the father and the mother agreed. They stood beside her bed. The small window allowed daylight to bathe their faces.

"Elsa, Prince Dol Lassimer is here to speak with you," the mother said.

Elsa opened one eye and turned toward the Prince.

"He is so beautiful, Mother. Am I dreaming?"

Elsa reached out with one hand as if testing the truth of the apparition. Her fingers brushed Heathron's golden hair.

"He seems so real."

"She must have some of her wits about her," Kathleen said quietly to the Prince. She winked, but did so discreetly so as to show no disrespect to Elsa, or the family.

"I am sorry about your mother," Elsa said to Heathron.

He put his hand on hers.

"Have no worries," he said, "but I am trying to find the people responsible for her death and your sickness."

The girl lifted one side of her lips in a half-paralyzed smile.

"I'm willing to help."

"Did you hear that Melrose is dead?" Heathron inquired.

"One of my friends told me. She always acted so kindly, but Melrose was bad."

"What do you mean?"

"I think she brought the poison. I saw her give a packet to one of the guests that night — a man in rich robes that talked through his nose."

"Magistrate Uppenslaw," Heathron said to Kathleen.

"When I was serving and the Empress choked, I thought I saw that man put something in the emperor's wine. In the commotion, I wasn't sure. When I cleared the table, I tried to see what it was, but the glass was broken so I picked up the pieces carefully and threw them away...I got sick that night."

"I promise to bring the guilty people to justice," he said.

"Will my baby walk again?" the mother asked.

Kathleen shook her head, "We are not sure. Elsa is young and so she may yet recover, but the poison used was very dangerous."

Tears fell as Heathron and Kathleen bid goodbye to the baker's family.

36

FUNERAL AT TYATH

Musicians played the funeral dirge for the Empress of Tyath. Kathleen sat with Larissa Albodris in the sedan chair carried by the Imperial Guards. An empty chair was carried beside them representing the lost Empress. The Prince, Heathron Dol Lassimer, walked tall and proud, dismounted from his horse, holding the reins in his hand. Emperor Kade Dol Lassimer would have walked beside his son, but he had lost the use of his legs many years before. Only days ago, he lost the use of his left arm and hand. Now his speech was slurred, and his face drooped on one side.

The Blood Cutter potion did its work, Kathleen reflected.

Ingested by the Empress, she died. At least the emperor only touched it.

Father Wittenbrook pushed the wheelchair that carried the emperor. Mother Wittenbrook walked with him, a white cowl over her face, her hands were clasped in prayer.

The funeral procession used the long winding ramp, instead of the stairs, that led to the front doors of the Great Cathedral. The doors were flung open and light streamed through the colored glass windows. Rays of light illuminated the space with heaven's blessing. Crowds of people gathered in the streets to mourn Rema's passing. Others looked out from windows high above the scene.

"This reminds me of Candoreth on the day you left," Larissa said in the privacy of the sedan chair.

"I was thinking the same thing. It was supposed to be a happy day for me, but I died a little bit that day, too."

Larissa nodded solemnly.

"Empress Rema was a good woman," she opined.

"In the short time I knew her, I could actually picture her being my mother-in-law and getting along nicely with her," Kathleen said.

"I think she is a significant reason why Heathron is so loved by the people," Larissa observed.

Kathleen agreed. She looked at the tall form of the handsome Prince as he walked in front of his horse. His lips were set firmly together, the muscles in his jaw tightly clenched.

"If you were already married to him, you would be the Empress of Tyath," Larissa remarked.

"I had not thought of it, but you are right. Hopefully, the Emperor will get better, though," Kathleen replied.

"He is in no shape to rule," Larissa said with such certitude and lack of empathy that Kathleen recoiled inside.

Will the capital city finally get to me too? she wondered. *Is that my future as the wife of an emperor — antipathy?*

"I know little of such things. He just looks poorly," Larissa explained. She peered through the curtains toward the emperor as he rolled along in his chair. "He looks so sad."

"We found out what killed her," Kathleen declared.

Larissa turned to her with wide eyes.

"What kind of poison was it?" she asked.

"The same kind that caused the emperor to be paralyzed." Kathleen replied. "It's called *Blood Cutter*, and it's illegal."

"Is that why I haven't seen you lately? You and the Prince have been investigating this together?"

"You have been off with Aidan every day, it seems. I didn't know you missed me," Kathleen said.

"You're my best friend, Kathleen. Why would you say that?"

"Aidan just isn't the kind of man I pictured you with," Kathleen replied.

"I suppose you think Eldin Stellat would make a better match?" Larissa rolled her eyes.

"I don't want to fight with you, especially not now," Kathleen said as she nodded to the throngs of people standing in silence or singing hymns, in reverence.

"Seriously though, I have so much fun with Aidan," Larissa continued. "He's exciting in a way that is different from any boy I've ever known."

"He's definitely different... I can't stand to be around him," Kathleen declared.

"I'm finding my way the best way I can," Larissa replied. "You have a Prince who wants to marry you and still you hold yourself aloof. I can't afford to do that. I don't come from a high, noble house. Every year there's a new crop of girls that come of age. Some of them may be prettier and more capable than we are." She flipped her hair as though she thought that was possible, but unlikely. "The competition is only going to increase, the longer I wait. I don't want to end up like Lady Aviella with a husband three times my age."

"I'm just saying, I don't think Aidan is good for you. You don't act the same when you're around him," Kathleen said.

Larissa sighed.

"I'm through talking about this. Maybe if you devoted a little more time to your dear old friends, they wouldn't have a need to find new ones."

"I've been helping Heathron try to find out what's going on," Kathleen said.

"Then don't complain to me when the two of you are always running off alone together. What does it matter to you who I spend my time with anyway?"

"I care about you, Larissa," Kathleen said.

"Now you sound like my mother."

Larissa gazed out of the opposite window.

As the funeral procession moved forward, Kathleen felt the tension in the air between them. This argument was different from the silly ones of their childhood. The dynamic was changing. Was Larissa jealous of her?

"If you decide to pursue a relationship with Lord Naystrom, I wish you well, but be careful," Kathleen said.

"He's the one that needs to be careful, Kathleen. You know me," Larissa replied and flashed her overly-devious smile. But this time, it failed to bring the usual mirth to Kathleen's heart and she didn't know why.

37

THE AUROCH CLAN WELCOME

Seth felt the wind blow against his face as he rode beside Cedric, and listened.

"They are more numerous than Clan Razewell. I will ride with only our finest warriors, so that they know we are unafraid," the Serpent King explained.

Seth nodded. "We cannot match their might, but they do not need to know that. We will see if the rumors of your prowess have spread beyond the western bank of the river."

Kalt, fidgeting a little, looked troubled. "What will you do if the Aurochs do not believe in you?"

Next to Kalt, Tan-Atta seemed to mirror his unease.

"Calm yourselves. It's simple. I will request a marriage to Chief Lystern's daughter," Cedric said, and paused to gauge their reactions. "Chief Lystern knew my father well."

"Who would not want you as a son-in-law?" Seth said with only a hint of sarcasm.

It was lost on Cedric.

"I would make a very good husband to his daughter," the barbarian chief said, frowning and nodding at the thought.

The Auroch clan warriors met the party of the Serpent King

in silence. They raised their hands in greeting but held spears in the other hand.

Cedric grinned at Seth with his split face.

"See, I told you they would welcome us, as long as we do not bring numbers and display our strength," Cedric said.

"Drop your weapons," commanded the Auroch war band leader.

Cedric looked surprised.

"Is this how Clan Auroch treats the Serpent King who comes to speak with your chief?" Cedric made no move to drop his weapons.

"You are not our King. We have heard of the troubles you have caused."

Cedric growled and spat out a chain of profanities. The war band leader reached out and gently struck Cedric on the shoulder with the side of his spear. It surprised Seth and Cedric both.

"Be silent," the Auroch man said, and fixed him with a look of contempt.

Cedric towered over the man. In hand to hand combat, Seth was certain Cedric would destroy him, and yet the Auroch clansman treated Cedric with derision. He seemed unafraid to start an altercation. He had dozens of men beside him. Cedric remained silent.

Seth caught Cedric's glance that seemed to say, "I will wring his neck when I have the chance."

Seth did not doubt he would.

As expected, they were brought to the central tent of the encampment. It stood taller and broader than all the others. Inside, the Auroch Clan chieftain sat comfortably on his throne, and ran his finger through his long black hair. The throne was made of enormous horns of the great wild cattle of the plains, with leather stretched tightly over the seat.

Chief Lystern leaned forward to have a closer look at the two men approaching. He wore a blue leather wrap around his waist, decorated with a pattern of horned animals in various postures: running, leaping, and falling. His sinewy chest was bare except for a strap of leather that looped over one shoulder and held a knife in a sheath and elongated beads of alternating colors. In one hand he held a short spear like a scepter.

His old, heavy eyes studied Cedric, unimpressed. Seth felt Cedric's presence harden. He seemed to bristle with barely restrained rage, just waiting to be unleashed. His hands were interlinked behind his back, one palm grasping the hard, balled fist of the other.

"We come in peace," Cedric began.

The Auroch war band leader, who had been leading them toward Chief Lystern, turned and struck the Serpent King's face with the side of his broad spear tip. A triangular welt rose on Cedric's cheek.

"I told you to have some respect."

Knowing the history of abuse that Cedric had endured as a child, Seth wondered if he would be able to restrain himself. Since becoming the Serpent King, the little boy within the giant was unwilling to suffer abuse. His pride could only endure so much. Seth prayed that Cedric's strategic mind would win the day.

May he swallow his pride and negotiate rather than fight when we are so greatly outnumbered, Seth thought.

"You were told to remain silent," the Auroch chief said from his throne. "I am Chief Lystern, I have questions for you. If you answer truthfully, you may live."

Cedric gritted his teeth while Seth nodded his assent.

"You carry a load of *Kabris.* Why?"

"We gathered it from the Raven Clan and others to keep it from the *Handri* in the Golden City. They turn it into poison and our people are suffering," Cedric explained.

"If you were more disciplined as a people, your clan would

not suffer so. I will not stand for a river rat to disrupt my trade networks. We seek the *Kabris* and travel far to find it. When we send it eastward to the Golden City, we expect to receive payment."

"The *Handri* dream powder destroys our men and women," Cedric protested. "Mothers no longer wish to care for their infants after they use it. Fathers will not hunt when the blue smoke rises from their tents," Cedric's scarred lips rolled the words out with conviction. Seth saw a number of the Auroch clansman listening intently.

The Auroch chief sneered.

"It is not our fault that Clan Razewell and the other river clans are weak and have forgotten the Delathrane ways. What do you plan to do with the *Kabris* you have stolen from your brothers?"

"We will cultivate it. We will guard it for the sacred vision quests of our young men. We will-".

"You do not fool me, Fork Tongue!" Chief Lystern snapped, cutting him off. "You plan to keep the dream plants and enrich your clan at the expense of others. We will not allow it. Guards, bring the *Kabris* to me."

He turned to his warriors, ordering them to retrieve the plants that had been carefully wrapped and moistened so they survived the journey.

He fixed Cedric with a look beyond contempt. "At least we know what to do with it," he added. Then he draped his glowing eyes over the pile of enormous treasure his warriors placed before him.

Cedric instinctively began to lunge, but held himself back. Sensing his bristling tension, multiple spear points of the warriors were leveled at him.

"Why would we trust you? You enjoy the company of the *Handri*," the Auroch chieftain scoffed, as he looked at Seth.

"He is not *Handri*. He is a Sīhalt Guardian. He is my advisor."

"You need a *Handri* guardian? I would have thought you could have taken care of yourself..."

A few of the warriors chuckled at the comment, sneering at Seth. Chief Lystern waved his hand toward Cedric and the others as if they were the leftover bones from his meal.

"Throw them into the pit and call all the people to watch. We will see if Cedric of Clan Razewell is truly the King of Serpents. If he survives this test, perhaps we will discuss his plans to destroy the Golden City."

The spear tips were leveled at the small group. Seth, Tan-Atta, and Kalt followed the Serpent King as they walked from the tent and were led across the field of the encampment. Families of the clan streamed out from their tents. Others drove horse-drawn chariots and called out for all to come see the Serpent King die.

The gathering mass of people mocked them as they walked.

"Take that!" a youth shouted as he threw manure in their direction. His friends laughed and the encouragement guaranteed further taunts.

Others threw food scraps in their direction and the captives raised their hands to ward off the debris that rained down on them.

"Well, that did not go as well as we hoped," Cedric said.

"They are very disrespectful," Tan-Atta agreed.

Seth could not help but smile at the understatement. Here they were, about to be thrown into a pit of some unknown terror, and they were nonchalantly discussing the meeting.

Disrespectful?

"Tan-Atta, I'm trying to think of any positives to a pit. It is all negative in my mind," Kalt said stoically.

"It is likely a mass grave," Seth said.

"A pit could be a good thing," Tan-Atta said. "Like a salt dig. That's a good pit. Sometimes we dig pits to catch large animals, too."

"Large animals caught in a pit? That still doesn't sound very promising," Seth shook his head.

As they approached the huge hole, a pungent reptilian smell arose in the wind. It made Seth want to vomit. Tan-Atta wrinkled his nose. "That is not good," he said.

Cedric frowned and spat. "He mocks me. He plans to feed the Serpent King to snakes."

The Auroch chief stood at the edge of the pit, his arms folded, a sneer on his lips.

Rows of spears moved quickly in short jabs, forcing the men forward toward the edge of the pit. When Seth looked over the rim, he saw the rock-strewn floor of the pit far below. The depth was easily fifty feet. In some spaces the ground seemed to have sunken out of sight and boulders filled one side of the hole, piled haphazardly against one wall. It reminded Seth of the opening of the cave network beneath the Windstall Hermitage, and for a moment he was taken back there. He pictured his training, when he was first dressed in the white robes of the initiates. His brother had helped him to tie the white belt around his waist and had been there every time they had reached a new level of advancement. The quest to become a Sīhalt Guardian was not an easy one. Grueling mornings of systematic combat, drills, routine, would be followed with endless afternoons of study in the classroom. Their academic pursuits always circled back to the training grounds at sundown, however. Seth remembered those moments most clearly: when would-be Guardians drew brotherly blood as the dying sun to the west painted its own across the darkening, Desnian sky.

"You are not going easy on me are you, Seth?" Jared had demanded.

Seth remembered hearing Master Tove congratulate him on defeating his brother in hand-to-hand combat.

"I think he is the better grappler," the old Sīhalt observed.

Seth felt proud of his small victory, but somehow ashamed at having defeated his older brother.

Jared wiped his bleeding nose on the sleeve of his white robe. "I'm not done yet," he growled, resuming his stance, ready for another bout.

"You are done," Master Tove insisted. "Now show the proper respect to the victor."

Seth remembered how reluctantly Jared knelt in the sand and recited the words of the defeated.

"I kneel before you in gratitude for my life. Thank you for the mercy you have extended to me. You fought valiantly, and bested me in honest combat."

Seth saw how bitter the words were in his brother's mouth, and he was grateful that Master Tove had called an end to their training for the day. Seth was not sure he could have held off Jared's next attack, even if it was without weapons.

Seth looked back at the many warriors advancing with spears. There would be no honest combat today. Hoping for mercy would be futile.

The Delathranes laughed at their predicament. Seth chose to make a decision himself, rather than have it thrust upon him. The reptilian stench, coming from the pit, was overpowering, but he turned himself around and slid his legs over the rim of the pit. If he was going in, he wanted to land feet first, and possibly hit the ground, not be tossed headlong into an abyss.

The rest of his party began climbing over the rim. Cedric resisted. His hulking form stood at the edge of the pit. He roared at the men who advanced with spears.

"I am the Serpent King. I will rise! I have seen it in a vision. Your wheeled chariots will follow my command. The Delathranes will sack the Golden City."

Chief Lystern waved a couple of fingers, gesturing for the spearmen to advance. Cedric turned and leaped from the rim to the darkness below. Seth heard a grunt as the barbarian King landed and rolled up to his feet.

"You will pay for this, Chief Lystern," Cedric yelled from the darkness below.

The Auroch chief laughed. "Whatever I must pay will be covered with the fortune you have brought me, river rat" the Auroch chief leaned over the rim of the pit. "We will soon see if you are truly a King of Serpents."

A warrior with a long spear made Seth lose the small grip he had on the stone walls. He tumbled down the steep slope, banging his knees and shins on the way down. Tan-Atta and Kalt landed close by, grunting with the impact.

"Gather rocks that can be thrown. We don't have any other weapons," Seth said.

Tan-Atta picked up a tree branch, but it was decayed and broke easily in his hands as he lifted it.

Cedric ran toward the group of friends. He looked up in anger and saw the Aurochs peering over the edge. They rimmed the pit in every direction. Some began chanting.

"Oh snake. Oh snake, where are you?"

Their voices rose in a cadence, the men and women singing together.

"This is not good," Tan-Atta said.

"You already said that," Seth reminded him.

Cedric raised his fist toward his adversaries.

"I am the Serpent King!" Cedric bellowed. "Do you call for me?"

Clods of grass and dirt rained down over them in response.

Then, cutting through the noise of the rabble, a loud quivering whisper could be heard coming from the pile of boulders.

"Erm, what is that?" Seth said.

Cedric's eyes stayed fixed on the rocks.

"Whatever it is, it doesn't sound friendly."

38

MOTHER OF SNAKES

Seth stepped closer to get a better look, but as he did, the beast emerged. With glowing eyes, the thing approached from a gap in the rocks. Then there was a hiss, the sound of something guttural, powerful, and raw. Then a long, forked tongue began flicking in and out as the monster's spade-like face was revealed.

"I think we should move back..." Kalt said, ominously, and as he did, he threw rocks at the gleaming eyes. "Get back!"

The people at the top of the pit were now bloodthirsty with excitement. The giant, snake-like creature finally pushed its way forward, coming into full view. The rays of the sun illuminated the metallic sheen of its scales. The color was a deep blue at first, until the serpent began to turn, winding its way forward. Then the scales shimmered a bluish-purple, then a purplish-red.

The monster paused, but not for long.

"I have a plan," Cedric said, and before anyone could answer he flicked his own forked tongue out and called for the serpent.

"Come and get me," he beckoned defiantly, his rage chasing away any hint of fear.

A few of Kalt's rocks struck its back, but the enormous serpent treated them as if they were raindrops. The Sīhalt Guardian led Tan-Atta and Kalt as they climbed up a small pile of rubble trying to reach the available high ground within the pit. Cedric decided to stand his ground.

The snake's head was as thick as Cedric's thigh. The tongue that flicked out was a deep purple, and it turned from side to side, tasting the air for the scent of blood. The eyes looked out from a white film that covered lenses that had rarely seen the sunlight.

As a child, Cedric had never feared snakes, but this monster was bigger than any he had ever encountered. Kalt had a horrified look on his face, and the young chief, Tan-Atta, was wheeling backwards to stay out of its range. Cedric and Seth stood alone.

"Looks at the eyes. Is that thing shedding or is it blind?" Seth asked.

"I don't know. Maybe it can't see us?" the Serpent King replied.

The snake dodged away from some of the larger rocks thrown by Kalt.

"Guess it can see just fine," Seth shrugged.

Cedric roared with anger as the snake came forward.

The snake gathered its length in a coil, pausing momentarily to check for their scent — even the roar of the crowd failed to disturb the snake.

It's probably used to this sort of feeding, Seth thought. *We are just more poor souls thrown down to nourish it. It looks hungry!*

As he thought this, the snake suddenly launched itself at Cedric. Sharp teeth closed over his elbow as Cedric threw his arm up for protection. The snake knocked the barbarian off his feet, quickly wrapping its coils around his body.

In response, the Serpent King smashed his fist into the snake's nose, and with his free hand, grabbed it by the corner of its mouth and ripped three teeth away from the flesh of his arm.

The coils of the snake cinched tighter, and Cedric could see his rib cage straining against the compression. The barbarian warrior dug his fingers deeper along the upper and lower jaws of the snake and began to pry it open. He pulled the snake's face close to his chest so he could use the muscles of his shoulders to generate the required force. He grabbed the other side of the snake's mouth too, and although he was being squeezed at his torso, with tremendous effort, Cedric pried the jaws further apart. The mouth opened wider than Cedric thought possible, but Cedric kept stretching the jaws apart.

The snake's mouth began to rip at the corners, and the tearing worked its way downward. The snake flailed and twisted, some of the coils coming loose from Cedric's body. The barbarian continued to rip the jaws apart. Once the tear began, Cedric gained even more control. He shrugged his shoulders back and with a great effort, his rippling muscles tore the bottom jaw free from the enormous serpent.

The injury would be fatal, but for now, the serpent unwound its coils. The other three men began to pry the snake loose from around his torso and Cedric shouted in exultation. The wounded snake sought cover in the rock pile, but there wasn't enough room for it to hide completely.

Cedric picked up a large stone and threw it at the snake. He just missed. Then he hoisted up an even larger stone to the height of his waist. Holding the stone close to him, Cedric staggered under the weight as he crossed the empty space where the serpent lay coiled beneath the rock. The Serpent King smashed the rock down on its head as the people of the clan watched from above and went wild with delight. Cedric grabbed the midsection of the snake and pulled the serpent's body out. It was easily seventeen feet in length. He swung the snake around over his head, bellowing, "Chief Lystern! I am the King of Serpents!"

Cedric looked up at the Auroch chief, standing at the rim of the pit.

"We have defeated your monster. Now free us from the pit!"

"We are having fun watching you fight, but you have proven nothing," Chief Lystern replied. "What talisman do you have that compels us to follow you?"

Cedric tore a tooth out of the jaw of the snake. "This is the symbol of my power!"

He held it up — a shard of ivory with a bloody stump.

The words echoed off the walls of the pit. The man seemed to consider them for a moment.

"You're nothing but a half-breed," he said as he shouted down to Cedric. "I was there when your father captured your mother. I told him not to keep the *Handri* slave girl, but he would not listen."

"You knew my mother?" Cedric said, all rage melting from his face. The little boy within rose to the surface.

"Look at you, pale as a *Handri* child. You were an embarrassment to your father."

"I killed the mother of serpents. You will release us," Cedric demanded.

"That," Chief Lystern said, "was not the mother." The crowd roared with more excitement, and the chanting began again.

"The mother lives deeper in the caves," the prideful chief continued. "She will join you at any moment."

And then the head of what appeared to be a dragon forced its way out of the largest openings beneath the boulders. Cedric could have walked into the cave with arms stretched out overhead and still not touched the stones above, but this snake filled the entire void.

Raw fear filled his heart, but he fought it down and closed his eyes momentarily to remember the vision he had seen. He would not die this day. He had a destiny to fulfill.

The Serpent King stepped forward. A rage glowed in Cedric's eyes.

"My father was proud of me," he shouted at the form of the

Auroch chief above him. "I will gut your snake from the inside if need be," Cedric said. He held the fang of the slain serpent like a dagger.

"It may swallow me whole, but I will return from the underworld. I saw the vision, and I am not meant to die. I will rise!"

39

SNAKE CHARMER

Seth stepped close to Cedric and placed his hand on the barbarian's shoulder.

Cedric whipped his head around to see that is was the Sīhalt Guardian standing beside him.

The dragon-like head of the mother of snakes swayed back and forth. Her eyes were not milky white, but clear as a ruby on fire. When she opened her mouth, Seth saw a row of ancient teeth that were broken but worn smooth. The teeth were set in a backward slant, better to grip prey and swallow it whole. Seth could sense she was old, a creature from a bygone era.

"I may be able to help you," Seth said.

"You have more courage than I imagined," Cedric said, keeping an eye on the enormous snake before them. "Surely if you will stand with me now, there is no foe in the world that would deter you."

"I never liked snakes. Beasts with warm blood are easier for me to understand, but I will do my best."

"What can you possibly do against a viper such as this?" Cedric said. "You do not even have your sword."

"I need you to distract the snake long enough so I can get

behind it. I need to touch it without being bitten, crushed or swallowed."

"I will attack its belly," Cedric said, holding up the sharp tooth. "I will stab this mother of snakes with the tooth of her offspring!"

A gleam shone in Cedric's eye, and Seth knew he was witnessing undaunted courage.

"I just need a moment," Seth said over the shouts of the Auroch Clan above them.

Cedric began his attack. He took a few steps forward as the mother continued to push her body through the rocks into the open ground of the pit. She raised her head and looked down at the small barbarian before her. Cedric ran at her, trying to reach the horizontal white scales of her belly, but the snake struck violently and seized Cedric around the torso.

The snake held him in her mouth, dangling Cedric above the ground. She worked her mouth, positioning the man in order to swallow him more easily.

When the snake lifted Cedric skyward, Seth made his move. He ran to the snake and laid both hands on the undulating body. Gathering all the force of his Talent, he reached out with his mind and felt it meld with that of the serpent. Seth's consciousness encircled the snake's mind as tightly as its coils held Cedric. The monster tried to twist its mind free, but the Talented Tamer of the Windstall Hermitage held her fast. Seth commanded the snake in a forceful thought — *Stop.*

The serpent froze. Seth struggled mightily to maintain a connection with the animal. He had flashes of imagery where it seemed he was looking through the serpent's eyes and could smell Cedric's blood. The snake froze with the single command, but the ancient mother was willful and resisted his Taming. Seth closed his eyes and arched his fingers where they touched the metallic scales.

"Release him," Seth said in both verbal and mental commands.

The jaws of the mother of serpents opened and Cedric fell to the ground with a jolt. Cedric rolled to his feet and regained a fighting stance.

Again, the snake was poised as a statue, perfectly unmoving.

"Hold it still so I can slay it," Cedric said, wiping his own blood in a smear across his chest.

Seth shook his head.

"Seek no more to harm her, Cedric. She is under my control," Seth said.

Cedric looked at the iridescent snake standing at least three times his height.

"That is impossible," Tan-Atta said from the rock pile.

The Auroch Clan had grown silent, watching the drama unfold.

"Lie low to the dust," Seth commanded.

The purple tongue flicked the air and the gigantic snake's head descended until the beast rested its lower jaw on the ground again. Seth swung a leg over the snake and held on the edge of one of the enormous scales.

"Come, climb on her back," Seth said to his companions. "She will lift us from the pit."

Tan-Atta complied, joining Seth on the back of the serpent, but the warrior Kalt stood shaking his head in disbelief.

"I cannot do it," he said.

Cedric slapped the warrior on his back and pushed him forward.

"Of course, you can. We are People of the Serpent, and she has come to help us."

"She wasn't helping us a bit ago when she was going to eat you," Kalt said with uncertainty as he climbed onto the snake. Cedric sat right behind her head and placed his legs along the grooves that lined the edge of the skull.

Rise out of the pit, Seth commanded with his thoughts as the effect of the Taming settled into the creature's mind. She probed the bond, but found not a sliver of weakness as Seth calmed himself and deepened the mastery he had over her.

She lifted them up, following the rocks that made up the walls of the pit. The men leaned forward and held on tightly as they rode the giant snake to the surface. Seth expected the warriors of the Auroch Clan to throw spears and shoot arrows as they rose from the pit. No rocks were thrown, no insults were hurled at them as they ascended.

They rose out of the pit. The wind that swept across the grasslands once again blew in their faces, and Seth was grateful that the worst of the reptilian stench was swept away.

Chief Lystern knelt in the grass before the oncoming snake. The giant serpent rose up to a height of thirty feet and swayed menacingly while the companions rode her forward. She hissed and the sound reminded Seth of the beginnings of an avalanche, like those that threatened Adisfall when snow was heavy in the spring. The many layers of the sound seemed to speak of ancient hunger when the world was still young.

"Truly you are the Serpent King," Chief Lystern said as he knelt and then bowed his head to the earth. "Our people ask your forgiveness. We have dishonored you and wish to make amends."

Seth whispered in Cedric's ear, and Cedric nodded as the giant snake undulated beneath them.

"Bring an offering to the Serpent King," Cedric said. "I desire a bullock as a sacrifice to your new King."

Chief Lystern motioned to a young cattle herder to do as he was commanded, and the boy began to run back toward encampment.

"No, you will go and bring the sacrifice," Cedric said to Lystern. "You led these people in their derision of my right to rule, and now you will lead them in the expiation of their transgression. Go and get the bullock yourself and go quickly."

The Delathrane chief leapt to his feet and ran past the boy on his way to the cattle enclosure.

"I am the Serpent King," Cedric said to the people of Clan Auroch. The people of the serpent are now your masters. You will join us in the fight against the Golden City. We will not be stopped!"

The Delathranes prostrated themselves on the ground. They chanted to Cedric and the snake.

Lystern returned with a young Auroch bull. Its coat was the color of cream and red clay bricks. It bellowed and tossed its head, resisting the lead rope when it caught the scent of the giant snake.

"The serpent mother is hungry," Cedric said as he dismounted the snake. Seth, Kalt, and Tan-Atta slid back to the ground behind him.

Seth walked over to the struggling bull. He placed his hand on the shoulders of the animal as it strained, wide-eyed against the rope.

"Be still," he said and gave a Taming impulse to the bovine. It ceased to struggle and stood still, its heaving sides calming like a flag in the dying breathe of a storm.

Now eat, Seth commanded the snake as he stepped away from the bull.

The enormous ancient serpent slid through the grass and struck the bullock. She wrapped her body around the animal and cinched the coils tighter, then positioned her mouth around its head. The unhinged jaws spread wide, and she began to swallow the beast.

The Auroch Clan saw the symbolism as the giant snake devoured the bull. The awe they demonstrated for Cedric only grew.

"The Serpent King," they murmured one to another.

"We should bring her with us," Cedric said to Seth as a fierce grin spread across his face.

"She could be helpful," agreed Tan-Atta.

"She is not made for the cold that is coming. I will release her back to the pit."

"Or we could kill her," Kalt said. "As long as you made her hold still like that bull."

"Her kind is very rare," Seth said with a faraway look in his eyes. "She should not be killed."

Cedric glared at Kalt, offended at the suggestion.

"Wild beasts will obey your command?" Tan-Atta asked, shaking his head in amazement.

Seth nodded.

"I am a Tamer, and with that Talent comes the ability to speak with beasts of every kind. I do not like reptiles, but she is different. I am glad that I have looked through her eyes, but I was not sure when I first touched her if she would harken to my voice."

"I am glad she listened," Tan-Atta said.

"What should we call her, this mother of snakes?" Cedric asked, taking a deep breath and swelling with pride at the effect the giant serpent was having on the powerful Auroch Clan.

"She calls herself Desnia," Seth said.

Kalt frowned. "Like the land?"

Seth nodded again, watching the snake.

"Yes, Desnia just like the name of our continent...perhaps she came first, and it was named after her kind?" he wondered aloud.

"What were you planning to do if Desnia didn't listen to you?" Kalt asked.

Seth looked at the snake and it wiggled its body over the muscular hump of the Auroch bull, only the hindquarters remaining visible.

"I was hoping Cedric was right. He maintains that he saw a vision of his eventual triumph. If that is true, what do I have to worry about?"

Tan-Atta and Kalt both considered this thought with furrowed brows.

"Guardian," Cedric said, slapping Seth on the shoulder. "You are now my Tamer and my advisor. Together we will gather all of the people west of the great river."

Chief Lystern stood and came forward.

"I can take you to the clan chiefs beyond the hills. I will help you gather the people," he said.

Cedric smiled. His plan was coming together.

40

SURROUNDED

"Quiet down!" Jared raised his hand. "I can hear riders in the distance."

"How many?" asked Maxwell.

Jared climbed down and placed his palm on the ground. Then he put his ear to the earth.

"What direction are they coming from?" Channing asked, scanning the horizon.

"There's a lot of them, coming fast," Jared said. "They are coming from every direction."

"Maxwell looked around, his nose to the air, as if the scent of the coming threat hung there. How much time have we got, Jared?" Maxwell asked.

"Just a few minutes. They must've been waiting for us." Jared rose from the ground and scanned the distance. "This is the first I heard them."

"Okay boys, I'll see you later," Maxwell said. "He swung down from Jared's horse and began running away."

Channing sneered. "So now you decide to run away, just when things are about to get interesting!"

"I don't like that kind of interesting," Maxwell said over his shoulder as he ran, tossing his clothes back toward Channing "I'll take a look from above."

"No problem. I'll throw your clothes in my saddle bags as we prepare to fight five hundred barbarians!" Channing replied.

Maxwell leapt into the air and before his feet could touch the ground again, his arms shot out creating wings of feathered metallic green. His bare toes curled into the talons of a giant rock eagle as he sprang into the air.

At first Maxwell flew low over the grass. Then, beating his wings, he rose upward turning and rising further into the air. The bird let out a long screech and soared overhead.

"What did he say?" Channing asked.

"He was laughing."

Jared shook his head watching his friend circle high above in an avian form.

Channing began to draw his sword and stretch his arms and shoulders, twirling the blade.

"Put it away, Channing. We are not going to do it that way. There's too many of them."

"You're not even going to fight?" he asked in surprise.

"We aren't going to run away either," Jared stated, looking toward the rising dust of approaching riders.

"I swore to defend you to my death," Channing said, still stretching.

"Well, don't make it today. Die for me when I have a better chance of escaping," Jared said.

"Whatever you say, Lord Sīhalt. But if that was meant to be a joke, I prefer Maxwell's sense of humor to yours." He sheathed his sword.

～

CEDRIC FELT a stab of anger as he approached the large black horse and its rider.

"*Der'Antha*," he growled.

Now he had a host large enough the killer could not possibly get away or fight his way to freedom. Cedric wanted to throttle the man, to crush his throat with his fingers. Images of his father dying on the Razewell throne swept thorough Cedric's mind.

"That is my brother!" Seth said, the joy clear on his face.

Cedric scowled and held up a fist so that the riders behind him would stop.

The hated Sīhalt Guardian sat tall in the saddle. Cedric was reminded of how similar the brothers looked, but the rider of the black horse was somewhat broader at the shoulders than his brother.

The last time Cedric laid eyes on this enemy, the man looked like a porcupine with arrows filling his back like quills. Cedric could see that *Der'Antha* was older than Seth by a number of years. He had gray in his hair at the temples.

He was saved by a Meat Witch like me, Cedric thought.

JARED SAT WATCHING the barbarians approach. His eyes scanned the approaching riders, and he immediately saw the hulking Serpent King. Jared's heart began to beat faster when his eyes fell upon his brother.

"Seth," he said, almost in a whisper.

Thank Abbath you are still alive, Jared signed.

Seth's demeanor was that of an advisor, not a slave. Jared could see there were no chains that bound him, and his visage was clear, no bruises on his cheeks. He was not broken or mangled as Jared feared he might be. He was alive!

Seth's fingers discreetly signed a message:

Walk softly brother. Cedric can be reasoned with. I have made progress with him, but he still holds a grudge against you.

Riders many ranks deep surrounded them on all sides. It was

the largest host of Delathranes Jared had ever seen. The Serpent King rode forward and positioned himself directly in front of Jared. He made a motion for his officers and Seth to remain a short distance from them.

Jared did the same with Channing.

"Stay here for a moment," he said.

"Well, I can't easily go elsewhere," Channing replied, looking at the hordes of barbarians staring at him.

Steed walked forward but his ears were alert. The Windstall stallion was tamed for Jared, but the horse knew danger when he smelled it.

"Easy boy," Jared said to the great black horse.

"*Der'Antha*," the barbarian King shouted so that as many might hear as possible. "Have you come here to our lands to finally die?"

"I have come to aid my brother," Jared replied.

The Serpent King sat quiet for a moment. Jared listened for the heartbeats of the man. He was breathing somewhat faster, and the rapid pounding in the man's chest told Jared that the threat of an attack could be imminent.

"He said you would come for him."

"He is my brother. I had no other choice," Jared replied.

"I swore to drink from your skull *Der'Antha*," Cedric said.

Jared nodded.

"And I swore to rescue my brother...if possible."

Cedric yanked his broad sword from its sheath and held it high above his head.

Jared heard the pounding of the Delathrane's heart. If the Sīhalt Guardian was going to die today, it would not be without making a good show of himself or being able to embrace his brother once more.

"Tell me, Guardian, why should you keep your head while my father lies moldering in the earth?"

"If I had that day to do over again, I would do it differently, Serpent King."

Jared saw the first bit of tension relax as he used the title Cedric had chosen for himself.

"You regret killing my father?"

"I regret many decisions we made that day. I was sent to negotiate with your father but on the way, I found my sister dying and her child taken."

Jared swallowed, remembering the bitterness of that day.

"When your father offered me a drink in a cup made from the bones of my nephew, instinct took over. Rage, Serpent King, and justice. I'm sure you of all people can understand that. I killed him for what he had done."

"I offered you that drink," Cedric said, remembering the moment that now seemed so long ago.

"We were not authorized to be the arbiters of justice on that day. Nor was it the desire of our master at Windstall Hermitage that we be used as instruments of destruction. Many of your clan died that day. There is nothing I can do to bring them, or your father, back and for that I am deeply sorry. I have sought forgiveness from our god Abbath but I cannot make restitution for what I have done and I am tortured by it. I understand if you cannot forgive me."

Cedric was shocked by the apology. Never in his life had he seen a great warrior display regret for the lives he had taken in battle. Here the great *Der'Antha* looked at him sincerely and said he was...sorry? The weakness Cedric would have expected from such a display was absent. The Sīhalt Guardian looked him in the eye without fear and without guile.

"You made me, *Der'Antha*. I am the Serpent King because of you."

"I had never struck a child before that day and will never do so again," *Der'Antha* said with emotion in his voice.

Cedric believed him but did not know how to respond. No man of authority had ever offered an apology to him. Those that did so were usually groveling and pleading for their lives. This was new to Cedric and he did not know how to respond.

"Your brother is blood-sworn to me. You cannot take him," Cedric managed.

Jared steered his gaze to his brother and spoke. "I understand. And I thank you for keeping him alive."

"He has become my..." Cedric paused, considering the reality and strangeness of this conversation with his sworn enemy.

"He has become my friend," Cedric said finally, his voice dropping lower so that only *Der'Antha* might hear.

The Sīhalt Guardian smiled.

"Seth can be very handy to have around. I have missed him greatly," *Der'Antha* said.

❧

CEDRIC WAVED for Seth to come forward and meet his brother.

Jared dismounted quickly and Seth did as well. They ran to each other. The brothers embraced and wiped tears from their eyes at the joy of being reunited.

"I'm sorry I took so long," Jared said.

"It is good you came when you did. Any earlier and it would not have turned out so happily for us I think," Seth replied.

"Serpent King, I thank you," Jared said to Cedric still seated in his saddle. Jared thought he caught the slightest softening of his expression and moisture at the corner of the barbarian King's eye.

"You may call me Cedric," he said in his guttural voice.

"Then refer to me no more as *Der'Antha*. I am Jared," the

Sīhalt Guardian said, reaching a hand up in friendship to the barbarian.

Cedric nodded and grasped the hand of the man he had sworn to kill.

"Join us as we unite the Delathrane people," Cedric said.

Jared looked back at Channing and then to the horde of warriors that surrounded them. The captain nodded his agreement vigorously.

"We will," Jared said with a smile.

41

LITTLE TIME TO SPARE

"Look at her," Heathron said. "She must have the scent of a mouse or something."

Kendra the fox crept silently forward on soft paws. Her nose sniffed the leaves that had fallen the night before in the formal palace gardens.

"She is growing so fast. She's not a pup anymore," Kathleen said.

The fox gathered her body and remained with eyes fixed at the base of the shrubs.

"What is it, girl?" Heathron asked.

Kendra didn't respond but rather jumped into the air, pouncing on the leaves. A small mouse began to run between the shrubs but the fox was faster. Kendra snapped her jaws and tossed the little mouse into the air, spinning the small rodent end over end. She then leapt and caught the thing in her mouth, crunching down voraciously.

Kathleen winced at the sounds the fox made as she chewed.

"Oh Kendra!" she said.

Heathron furrowed his brows.

"Sometimes I feel like that little mouse, running for cover amongst all the forces that would eat me alive."

The brisk wind of autumn blew across the gardens and stirred the fallen leaves into a whirlwind of color.

"I've noticed it is getting colder," Kathleen remarked, gazing outward.

"Heathron smiled gently. "Your first year in Tyath is bound to be memorable for the weather alone, I've asked the clothiers to make you some warmer attire for the fall and winter."

"Kendra will change her coat. I suppose I should do the same." Kathleen said.

Heathron slid his arm into hers and turned to face her.

"I can't have my southern beauty freezing in the cold north, can I?" he said with a smile.

"You are so thoughtful."

"And handsome?"

"And handsome," Kathleen agreed.

Heathron grabbed her hands in his and gazed down at her face. The brilliant green of her eyes, set off by her red hair and white skin — it was a blaze of beauty to him. He was feverish with it. He looked at her lips, how her soft, full upper lip rested so softly on the lower. And then at her eyes — how perfect they were! Another gust of wind tossed a lock of her hair into a rebellious wisp and then it settled again on her shoulder.

Heathron smoothed it back. He felt the delicate strength of her body beneath the jacket she wore. He fought with the desire to sweep her into his arms.

"Can I kiss you?" he asked finally.

"If you have to ask, maybe you shouldn't," Kathleen replied.

At that the Prince grabbed her again by the shoulders and pulled her close to him. He pressed his lips firmly against hers and was delighted to feel her respond to him. She raised her chin, looking up at him with a softness that made him want her even more.

"What made you do that?" Kathleen asked when they had finally brought their kiss to a lingering close.

"I'm being the rogue," he said.

"The what?" Kathleen smiled and squinted at him.

"Just something my mother said."

Heathron winked and smiled, showing his perfect teeth.

Kathleen stood on her tip toes and laced her fingers through his hair and kissed him again.

"I love you, Kathleen."

"I know. You have shown me in so many ways," she said, her eyes falling from his gaze momentarily.

Heathron stiffened a little, and then allowed his embrace to soften. "I can tell your heart is still divided," he said tenderly, turning to lead her to a wooden bench at the edge of the path. "I can tell at times you are thinking of him."

"I do wonder if he's okay," Kathleen admitted.

"Jared DeTorre seems to be an honorable man and a dedicated Sīhalt Guardian. I do not wish ill on him, but if he never returned to Tyath, I would be okay with that."

"He said he would return," Kathleen replied.

The look on her face was one of concern mixed with hopefulness. Heathron's heart sank like a stone in the Clearwater Sea.

"To come for you?" he asked.

"Only if I wanted him to... he told me that I must give him a sign that I wanted him otherwise he would just wish us well and never seek contact again."

"I wondered what his last words to you might have been," Heathron said. "But his request is fair." He shifted his weight on the bench, turning to face her fully now. "That is all I am asking for, Kathleen, for you to give me a sign that you accept me."

Maybe a minute passed in silence after that. Both Heathron and Kathleen sank into the silence between them. They watched the birds, traced the wind along the boughs through their rippling leaves. It was Kathleen who broke the spell.

"He promised to watch us walk up the steps of the Great Cathedral on our wedding day – if I chose you."

"And have you decided your desire?" the Prince said. He could not look into her eyes as he asked the question — afraid of what the answer might be.

"I don't know," Kathleen said. "It is hard for me to see a way forward. Things seem so tumultuous here."

"It is true that I need you. I need you to be my queen and Empress of the Realm."

Kathleen nodded in understanding, but Heathron still felt her hesitation like a shield between him and his desires.

He took her hands and held them tight. "I need you to be my wife, my helper, and confidant. Kathleen, I need you to bear our children, I want House Dol Lassimer to continue, but most of all, I simply want you."

"Everything seems so political, Heathron. I wish it were not so, but I suppose this is the existence of a woman in my station."

She said it with some resignation, just the sort of sentiment the Heathron abhorred when it came to matters of love.

"Then forget the necessities of the Empire, Kathleen. Just know that I need the woman you already are. You don't need to be something else for me." He leaned in, kissing her, holding her face close to his.

"I need your lips close to mine. I need to be able to walk hand-in-hand with you," he stroked her fingers. "I need to be able to caress your neck and smell your hair and feel your warmth against mine. I want to hear all about your dreams and desires, to know all of your hopes and aspirations. What I desire most has nothing to do with the Empire and everything to do with the man in love with you. I will not give up on you, Kathleen."

He spoke with sincerity and hoped she could feel it. The fact that she did not simply toss aside her true emotions in favor of the wealth and power he offered was one of the reasons he loved her so much.

"I don't know a man more deserving than you of my love, but I am not sure that I can give you what you ask," she said.

"Have you learned anything during our months together?" Heathron asked. "Please tell me our time has not been wasted."

"I've learned that you deserve to be the ruler of the Empire. You are just and kind."

"What have you learned about yourself, Kathleen?"

"I believe that I could find happiness here in this city with you," she said.

Heathron's heart leapt to highest heights at her words.

"What can I do to make you certain of it?" he asked, he held her hands in his like the practiced touch of a master jeweler, examining the finest gem. He held her fingertips to his lips and leveled his eyes at her.

"I just need more time," she said.

"If you would ask for gold or silver or a thousand luxurious dresses, I would gladly give them to you. You have my devotion. To my eyes, there is no other woman but you. Time is the one thing I have very little to spare."

He took a deep breath before going on.

"Kathleen, I cannot afford to arrive at the Longest Day this summer, only to realize that you do not desire me — that the love you allowed to begin in your heart for the Sīhalt Guardian will keep you from being my wife."

"Are you giving me an ultimatum?" she asked.

There was no anger in her voice, nor bitterness. She asked simply and seemed to consider his words with care.

"If it is time you need, then it is time you will have, until the very last second when I can wait no longer."

He let go of her hand and tightened his fists.

"I must fight for my position as ruler of the Golden City. There is no one who can take my place."

"I will give you an answer by the winter solstice. During Winterfest you will know my heart. I agree it isn't fair to make you wait. You'll need time to find another bride if I am not to be the one," Kathleen said.

Heathron could hear the pain in her voice as she agreed to his request. He hoped the pain was for her own conflict and not for the pain she knew she might cause him.

"I hesitate to accept your offer," he said, "because I want the dream to continue even if the reality doesn't. The belief that you could be my wife and that we could share our lives together holds more for me than all my other dreams combined. I would gladly grow old with you, Kathleen, sitting by the fire."

"I suspect I will soon find out, how much a fire can be a comfort," Kathleen shivered as the autumn sunset no longer cast the warm rays of the sun in their direction.

"Let's walk to the water's edge," Heathron suggested. "The sun is still warm there."

They walked together in silence, each considering the words they had shared.

Heathron and Kathleen stopped at the water's edge, and he picked a small flower and tossed it in the wishing fountain. The delicate petals swirled in the clear water before being washed out to the reflection pool basin. The branches of the bald cypress growing beside the pool spread wide over the water. The soft needles were just turning a copper-gold. Kendra came quietly back to them. She pushed her head between their legs, and looked up inquisitively at them with intelligent eyes. Kathleen laid a hand on the fox's head.

"I accept your offer of a Winterfest response. I pray to Abboth that between now and then, his guidance will lead you to me," Heathron said.

42

STRIKEN RULER

"Father, we have information that you will want to know," Heathron said.

The emperor sat still and looked at the wall. He blinked slowly and his eyes sagged. It had been weeks since he was coherent enough to understand the words of others. His eyelids seemed too heavy to be lifted. Heathron knelt at his father's feet.

"I know you are hurting, Father. So am I. But if you can hear me, I want you to know that the assassin used *Blood Cutter*. I went to see the Wittenbrooks. They pointed us in the direction of possible suppliers."

"Do you think he can hear you?" Kathleen asked.

"I don't know."

"Can you hear me, Father?" Heathron asked in a louder voice.

The old man sat still except for the slightest tremble of movement from his right hand. Kathleen looked at his fingers.

"Move your finger if you can hear us," Kathleen said more quietly.

Kade tapped his index finger once on the armrest under his hand.

"He moved!" Heathron said.

"Do it again, Your Majesty, if you truly can hear us."

Both Heathron and Kathleen waited for a moment in expectant silence.

The emperor tapped his finger ever-so-softly again.

"There it is!" Heathron said.

"Now do it twice in a row," Kathleen encouraged him.

Kade's slack face seemed to take on an air of determination. The drool running down his lip dripped onto the cloth tied about his neck. His breathing was almost imperceptible, but then the response came.

Two taps.

A sudden thought came to Kathleen. "Use two taps for yes and one tap for no," she said to the emperor, who appeared to understand.

Two taps.

Heathron turned to Kathleen, his eyes brightening.

"We can communicate after all?" he asked. He turned to his father.

"The navy refuses to obey my commands, father. Admiral Hale will harken only to Pilus and finds reasons to delay his obedience to me." Kade Dol Lassimer sat trembling but silent. "The army is also less than compliant. General Tigral and Jason are increasing conscription from the entire Empire. I think it wise given the Delathrane threat. The army needs to be increased. Would you keep Jason as second in command?"

Emperor Dol Lassimer tapped once on his arm rest.

"Then I will seek to replace him," Heathron said.

"Will you tell him what else we have learned?" Kathleen asked.

"We cannot act yet. I doubt that the assassin acted alone in this," Heathron said.

"If you try to seek revenge, we may destroy all chances to discover the other conspirators," Kathleen agreed.

A slight but rapid tapping could be heard as they spoke. Heathron looked over to see his father, still facing the wall, his right finger tapped again and again on the wicker arm rest of his chair.

In his condition, it is the equivalent of screaming, Heathron thought.

He knelt down again before his father.

"We traced the trail of guilt back to a man within our own circle," Heathron said. "Do you want to know the name?"

Two taps.

Heathron looked around the room, ensuring they were alone.

"A serving girl confirmed that Magistrate Dirm Uppenslaw put *Blood Cutter* in your cup during the feast. He meant it for you."

Heathron didn't need to remind his father that he had given that poisoned cup to his wife. The pain was enough already.

"What shall I do? I desire to see justice done, but you always taught me to be thoughtful in anger and to not allow rage to rule me. Should I call him out? Should I bring him before the judges of the city?"

They waited.

One tap.

Then the old ruler strained forward in his chair. Veins stood out on his neck as he struggled to make words form in his mouth.

"Not yet," he managed to say in an airy, barely audible voice.

"That is very good!" Kathleen said. "Perhaps you will get better."

Heathron watched as Kade slumped back into the chair. His father was not encouraged by the ability to say a few words, even if it did represent an improvement in his condition.

"I didn't think so either," Heathron said. "We will wait and learn. We will build our case and take the lot of them down when the time is ripe."

Kade Dol Lassimer trembled and Heathron knew it was not

only from the paralysis. Rage infused the crippled man. Heathron imagined how his father might react to the news in his younger years, before the accident and before the poison. The thought was terrifying.

His fingers trembled more than they had before. A tear welled up in Kade's right eye, it filled the rim of the eyelid and watered the bloodshot sclera. Then a single tear rolled down the sagging skin.

"I promise to make it right, father," Heathron said.

43

COUNCIL OF NINE

"Welcome to another meeting with the Council of Nine," Lord Lars Balfoest said.

Light danced around the table in the flickering candlelight. The guests nodded their heads, the golden gleam of their masks reflecting the firelight.

Lars really didn't care who the houses sent to represent them. He was in control now. If they were willing to come to an unofficial, secret meeting of the Council, they were clearly in his hand.

"You all realize that I control the flow of dream powder within the city and into the kingdoms beyond. Illicit trade needs to be controlled and taxed. It's a new source of revenue for the city and the council...if you will join me."

His audience remained silent. Lars thought he detected hesitancy from the woman wearing the cat mask. He leaned close and touched her on the arm.

Ah yes, definitely reticent in her desire to join, he thought, *what else do I detect... fear?*

He smiled to himself. Some Talents were more subtle than others.

Lars positioned himself in the middle of the domed room — the place where he could more easily hear the richness of his own voice.

The man disguised in a stag mask seem to be nodding his head approvingly as he listened, but Lars still had his work cut out for him.

"House Dol Lassimer will fail. This we all know. The only question is, how soon?" The young man in the golden sparrow mask tilted his head to one side, considering.

Lars wished he were not positioned so far away. If he could just touch the man, he'd know for sure if he was bluffing.

"I suggest we remain as a Council of Nine. There is no need for one house to rule over the others," he declared airily.

"How do you propose to split the power?"

Balfoest turned and looked at the man wearing the pig mask.

How appropriate, he thought. The man came from House Aviella.

"I have no heirs. I have no wife. Although I am related to most of you, what I care about most is maintaining the order once the emperor and his spoiled son are deposed."

A small gasp rose from a woman wearing a swan mask.

"Does it surprise you that I speak so openly? Remember, I am the only one not wearing a mask. I am at your mercy," he reminded them.

His voice sounded reasonable and wise. Just as he desired. Lars Balfoest didn't realize he was Talented until an old priest that died in the Great Sickness had complimented him on his oratory skills in school. He called it Oration, but Lars knew it to be the power of Persuasion. He remembered the day he realized that others could not discern his emotions. Yet, at the slightest touch, he was able to know exactly how a colleague felt while they all remained blind to his emotions.

My mask is one they cannot see, he thought deliciously.

"I come before you with an honest solution. I have plans to

neutralize the barbarian threat before they return. I am willing to share power and execute a transition unlike anything that has happened for centuries. Because I have no heirs, you needn't worry about my desire to pass authority to my offspring. I only want Tyath to attain her former glory. We should be planting crops, not headstones in the fields beyond the walls. We should be ascendant. Why haven't, for example, the dominions of Adisfall been brought within the Empire? Hasn't it been long enough?"

"Joining the Empire has always been voluntary, has it not?" sparrow mask said.

"They benefit from our labors, and yet they charge a high price for their trade goods. The merchants at Horming could also do more to show proper respect to the Golden City."

There was a general murmur of agreement. He had struck a chord.

"Of course, my leadership of the council would expire once we are sure the barbarian threat is neutralized. If we choose to return to one house rule, you people, or the ones you represent, will have a voice as to whom will be charged with the responsibility as the new imperial family."

Even without a physical touch, Lars Balfoest could feel the greed emanating from some within his view. Only a few remained stoic, their faces tight with expressions behind the masks. Had he won them over? He couldn't be sure. He would risk the vote once he knew more.

Balfoest walked to one end of the table and in a moment of elocution, he placed his hands gently over the shoulders of his target. He resisted the urge to close his eyes as the emotion of the man flowed through his hands and arms. Lars could feel the man's emotion. He could not read his mind, but with his gift of Empathy, Lars knew what he was feeling — could infer what the man was thinking.

"Two Talents are extremely rare," the old priest was surprised at his pupil, but that was a number of years before the Luzian sect began its rise to power within the Church of Tyath. Lars had eliminated the old man with knowledge of his Talents when he realized it would be a danger to his advancement. Lars concealed his guilt for the murder of the old priest, until he finally felt it disappear.

Time heals all wounds, he thought.

"The decision for us is as follows — if you wish to continue to support House Dol Lassimer, with its invalid emperor, and spoiled Prince who is rumored to be engaged to a Plant Witch, you will be held in contempt when others take their places.

Alternatively, you could lend me your support as an arbitrator of our combined power and as a leader willing to lay down his own desires for the benefit of this city, our people, and our way of life."

"Give us time to consider," the man in the golden stag mask enjoined. "There is no reason to hold a vote this night."

"I told your masters to come prepared. There is no time to waste." Lars passed a hand over the arm of the woman in the swan mask. He held her hand and pleaded with her. He allowed her emotions to flow into him.

She is recalcitrant, he thought, *no matter... she is outnumbered.*

"Our Empire grows weaker by the day while the barbarian threat grows stronger. We must make a decision and stand united."

Balfoest knew the risk he had taken. If the numbers went against him, he would likely need to flee the city. However, if they were in his favor....

"I agree that we need to make a decision." A butterfly-masked woman sauntered to the table, the golden voting rod clinked as she placed it in the crystal vase in favor of Balfoest.

How very brave of House Turlin to send their only daughter, he thought.

"Thank you," Lord Balfoest declared.

Three more golden rods made their way into the crystal vase. Including his own, he was within two votes.

But then the ox, the sparrow, and the cat placed voting rods for Kade Dol Lassimer and his sons. If you included the vote from the current ruling house, the vote was tied.

The man dressed as a stag stood silent, looking at the table. He was the last of them all. Lars resisted an urge to grab the man's wrist and shake loose the golden rod. He wanted it for his own.

So close!

The tension in the room increased, and the others waited to see what he would do.

"I abstain," he said. "I was not given authority by my master to make this decision. I propose a meeting in three days to hold the final vote."

The other representatives and their golden masks exchanged glances.

"Will your master not be disappointed that you kept the Empire waiting?" Lord Balfoest asked pointedly in his persuasive tone.

"Before I vote to depose a sitting emperor, I politely request three days' time to weigh the matter sincerely," stag mask said. "The emperor you are speaking of has been sitting for decades. The man cannot stand nor even speak these past few days."

"It is not an unreasonable request given that we are changing over six centuries of tradition," pig mask said.

Oh shut up! Balfoest thought.

What could he do to force the issue this night? He used his velvet voice like a weapon.

"I am sure you have all been told that Emperor Dol Lassimer is very ill. The physicians intend to treat him experimentally in the hope of his improvement. They are...not confident," he said.

"Heathron is the rightful heir should something unexpected happen," Cat mask declared.

A man with the golden horse mask snorted. "He's not ready to rule." They were the first words he had spoken.

"He is already betrothed. He will soon be ready to take the reins."

"It's not the wife that makes the ruler," another said.

"But she can often enough unmake him. I see no reason to be confident in this Sundiland girl. Her nation brings little to the Empire as it is," Lars observed.

"Swear to me that you will vote tomorrow night," the swan mask said.

The Stag shook his head.

"We shouldn't even be meeting like this — in secret, no minutes taken of our deliberations."

"I feel the same way," the cat-masked woman said, "this isn't right."

Lars noted that she didn't reveal herself despite her protestations.

"Dark clouds are gathering and our Emperor is doing nothing to prepare us for the Delathrane storms that will surely lash our faces within the year," Lars said.

He felt the turmoil of emotions swirling in the room. He was on the precipice but had not been able to tip the stone to start the avalanche. It would be better to wait for another day.

"We will meet again," he said, "Next time, be ready to cast your votes for the future of Desnia,"

The representatives filed out silently, one by one they returned to their houses to report the proceedings.

After all of the guests left, a hidden wooden panel slid open in one corner of the council room.

"Dirm, I have work for you to do."

Lars Balfoest pressed the handle of a small dagger into the soft hands of the chief magistrate.

"Take this and make sure the physicians were...overly ambitious in their medicinal bloodletting of our invalid ruler."

Dirm sniffed and handed the dagger back to Lord Balfoest.

"Keep it," he replied in his nasal tone. "I have one of my own."

44

A GOOD HAND

"Come closer," Emperor Kade Dol Lassimer leaning forward in his wheelchair, whispered ever so softly.

"What is it, Your Majesty," Dirm said, leaning in to hear what the old man might say before he did what needed to be done.

The emperor moved his lips but didn't speak. The smacking sound they seemed to make caused Dirm to cringe.

Thankfully, I no longer must endure this man as my liege, he thought.

Out of curiosity, Dirm leaned even closer to hear what the emperor was trying to say. The words came out in a faint whisper. Dirm wrinkled his nose as he brought his cheek near to the dry lips that struggled to form the words.

"You and I share a love for Tyath, how may I assist," Dirm said, trying to make out the faint words of the once proud ruler.

"The only thing we share in common are the pock marks from the Plague. I wish you would have died then," Kade said, as he fingers of his paralyzed left hand trembling involuntarily.

Dirm drew back.

Is the emperor really trying to put me in my place? Is this drooling old man still trying to rule me?

Dirm looked him in the eye. The patriarch of House Dol Lassimer no longer had the coordination to roll his own wheel-chair from the room. He smelled of stale urine and dried saliva.

How dare he make a remark like that.

"We both could have been easily taken by the sickness," Dirm said. "But we survived. We even prospered after... in a manner of speaking." He gestured to the wheelchair.

"You...should...have been taken," Kade spoke quietly, looking up with his one decent eye, his lips and hand trembling all the more. His right hand clenched the armrest, knuckles white.

"Are you angry with me, Emperor?" Dirm asked, then laughed aloud.

"I have only... ever... served... you faithfully!" Kade managed to sputter.

Dirm stood upright and waved his arms, taunting the enraged invalid.

"Even now as I leaned over you and noticed the stench of piss upon your imperial clothes, I felt sorry for you. A once proud man brought low by time and fate. You no longer rule. Heathron is a clueless boy," Dirm spoke to the quivering form before him. "If there was any hope you would improve, I would remain subor-dinate, but House Dol Lassimer will probably fail before your impotent body even sees the grave."

"Where did you get the poison?" Kade said in a whisper.

"What was that? I saw your lip tremble like you are going to cry. I guess I would, too, if I were in such a pathetic state as you."

Dirm turned his back to the emperor. The feeling of power it gave him made him smile.

"I do not know what you speak," Dirm said.

He thought of a dozen reasons why he was innocent. Lies came easily to the magistrate.

"Thank you," the emperor whispered again.

Surprised by the relief that flooded him, Dirm turned back to his liege.

Had he wanted her dead? Ah yes, no chance to remarry...

How could he not have realized that the emperor wanted his wife dead? He had unknowingly served the emperor's desires. Dirm stroked his chin, trying to work out these new details.

"Rema's death left you solely in charge. Heathron has not yet consolidated the high houses behind him," Dirm said, putting the pieces together.

Kade shook his head almost imperceptibly. He agreed!

"Your Majesty, you are paralyzed on one side of your body. You are not likely to gain their support either," Dirm said.

The emperor shook his head.

"She threatened your authority, Your Majesty. We couldn't have that, could we?" Dirm said, he loved the intrigue of this final view into the heart of the man who had ruled the Golden City for a generation.

The old man shook his head gravely, his left eye sagged the way it had drooped since the dinner. His right eye seemed to be moistened with emotion. The man wanted to say something more. His lips shivered and he leaned forward.

Dirm offered his ear again to the old man seated in the center of the room.

Kade Dol Lassimer shook his head. He looked grieved but this was to be expected. The man had to see little chance of regaining his former glory.

"For giving me a chance to..." he said softly.

A heavy rattle could be heard in the old man's chest. It was louder than the low whisper he used to speak. Dirm leaned even closer, his clean-shaven cheek almost touching the whiskers of the man who used to hold him spellbound with his might and authority. Kade seemed to strain against gravity, pulling himself more upright in the chair.

"For what, Your Majesty? For giving you the chance to what?"

Dirm asked as he reached into his pocket for the small blade he carried there.

"To avenge my love," Kade said with more strength than Dirm thought possible.

The words came out quickly and with a force the old man hadn't used in weeks. The words were crisp and sharp, almost as if they issued forth from the mouth of a younger man. Dirm's eyes widened at the vice-like grip that clamped down upon his throat.

Kade's fingers had gained their strength. Fingers that had been weakened by the Plague and almost extinguished by a stroke, now gained a portion of their old glory.

Dirm tried to pull away. The fingernails dug deeply on either side of his neck, working their way along the side between the muscle and the cartilage of his windpipe.

His scream came out like the squawk of a goose just before its neck is wrung. Dirm even flapped his arms, struggling in panic.

He could not think. He lunged and the wheelchair toppled over backwards taking the old man and his lap blanket with it. Both men landed on the rug spread over the stone floor. Dirm raked his fingernails over the face of his enemy. He tried to shove himself away with all his strength, but the iron grip on his airway did not relent. The hand pulled him closer. Dirm kicked his legs and struck the emperor again and again, straining against the dead weight of the body attached to the arm that held him. Dirm grabbed Kade's head in his hands and smashed it into the floor. As a young man, on the field of battle, Kade Dol Lassimer withstood the war clubs of the Delathranes. A smash to his head did not make him lose his grip then, nor did the impact do so now. Three quarters of his body was limp, only one hand and one arm had movement. But this man did not shrink away from a battle.

Dirm felt the fear of a creature that knows it's dying. He struggled like a maniac, raining blows on the emperor. He grabbed the imperial crown from Kade's head and smashed it into the old man's face. Still, the grip remained. Darkness threatened the edge of Dirm's vision. It gave him a glimpse of clarity through the panic. He reached again for the knife that he kept hidden.

Dirm went for the eyes. He used his knife to rake the skin on the face, neck, and brow of the old man. A saber-toothed cat could not have done worse. The emperor tucked his chin to protect his face, and his iron grip cinched tighter. Dirm struggled, trying to shift his angle so that he could slash the wrist of the emperor as they flailed on the floor. The darkness began to close in on the chief magistrate's mind as he struggled.

Dirm recalled the image of Empress Rema kneeling by the table, white foam bubbling from her throat and panic in her eyes. The panic that had delighted Dirm when he saw it that night was now reflected in his own eyes.

His body began to lose strength. His muscles twitched and his vision narrowed. Dirm kept plunging the small knife into the emperor's chest until he no longer had the strength to push the slim blade forward again. As his vision collapsed into a single point of focus, Dirm looked into the fiery eye of Kade Dol Lassimer, Emperor of Tyath.

He thought he heard the emperor's battle cry whispered into his dying ears — "Wise as the fox, strong as the oak, Dol Lassimer forever!"

***

"Tell me about this Sīhalt Guardian. I've heard all the rumors," Dallin Sarkkand said.

"What have you heard?" Kathleen asked, her mind immediately going to the most private conversations she and Jared had ever shared.

"He was arrested, banished from the city, was he not?" Dallin said.

"It is a long story," she said.

"But he was banished? I mean we've got all night. You don't seem too enamored by the company this evening," Dallin said.

"You don't seem like the others. Why do you spend so much of your time with Aidan?" Kathleen said, avoiding the question again.

"We've been friends since childhood," he stated.

"He and his father have turned against House Dol Lassimer," Kathleen replied, knowing the young lord would understand exactly where she stood on the issue.

Dallin nodded and chewed a bite of bread as he chased his vegetables with a fork.

"Where do your loyalties lie?" she asked.

Dallin looked at her. He leveled his eyes with the seriousness that she often had seen in him.

"My loyalty lies with Tyath," he said.

They looked across the room, scanning the crowd of young nobles.

"It seems as if they do not even believe that war will soon be upon us," Dallin observed.

Larissa laughed loudly and spilled her drink as she shied away from Aidan Naystrom, as he held her by the waist.

"Larissa seems to be enjoying the evening," Kathleen noted, her eyebrows raising a little.

Dallin followed her gaze. "Ah yes, Aidan is corrupting her."

Kathleen nodded but she couldn't tell if he thought it was humorous or not. He really was good at masking his opinions — a useful ability in a place such as this.

"She's not the same girl I used to know," Kathleen went on.

"There is much you do not know...I think," Dallin said cryptically.

"Then tell me what you know, Lord Sarkkand. You wouldn't leave a damsel in distress, would you?"

There was a little pause.

What is he getting at? she thought.

"Someone is trying to get you in trouble with the Council of Nine," Dallin said quietly.

Kathleen allowed herself the time to absorb this, and to study Dallin after he had said it. "You have a talent for politicking, I've noticed," she replied when she was ready.

"I'm not the talented one, Your Highness," he said smiling and looking out across the dance floor again as he sipped from the goblet.

He said talented. Did he mean Talented?

The thought that Dallin Sarkkand might know about her Talent made Kathleen's heart suddenly snap into action — she felt it pull down at her chest, her throat dry. Despite this, she kept her expression smooth.

"Are you going to believe all the rumors in the Golden City? I expected more from you, Dallin," she added skillfully. Out of the corner of her eye she gauged if he was in turn studying her.

"Shall we continue our conversation on the dance floor Princess Dal Sundi? It might be more private as we swirl amongst the throng."

The young Lord Sarkkand set down his drink as he said this, as if answering the question for her.

Kathleen held out her white-gloved hand and allowed him to escort her to the dance floor. The music was light-hearted, and she soon was able to follow the steps that led them in an octagonal shape. The movements reminded Kathleen of the carved wooden ponies that spun around and around at the spring fair when the traveling families of entertainers set up the carnival on the beach. She remembered holding onto the pole that secured the horse as it rose and fell to her childish delight. There was little delight in the precise movements of their dance when Dallin whispered in her ear.

"It's spreading like wildfire among the nobility. The rumor is that Prince Heathron tried to hide the fact that you are Talented," he warned.

Kathleen felt her palms begin to sweat. She could not pull away. She needed to know if Dallin was a friend or foe. Her mind raced. He smiled to a passing couple as they twirled past, then leaned in and whispered again.

"Is it true that he made you a private garden within the city?" Dallin said.

Kathleen hesitated.

"He did, didn't he?"

Kathleen's guilty expression was a wordless answer.

Dallin whistled softly and looked around to see who might have heard.

"It was an act of love, Dallin. He knew I would greatly miss my home and did it out of a gesture of kindness. The garden holds many of my favorite plants that would not grow here otherwise."

"Do you practice your magic there?"

Kathleen pretended the question was just a tease. She hoped that is all he meant by it.

Dallin looked across the room to where Larissa lounged with Aidan.

"Three months ago, would you have said she would ever use dream powder?" Dallin asked.

Kathleen shook her head.

"She needs help," Kathleen said.

"Kathleen, you need help," Dallin stated seriously.

Dallin's use of her given name made her pull back. She would have let go of his hands and walked away from the dance floor if he had not held on. His grip was like iron, but his face remained calm and noble.

"How dare you threaten me," Kathleen said, looking over his shoulder to see where Heathron might be. She caught his eye and in an instant was able to communicate all she needed to the Prince.

"I'm not threatening you. I'm offering you my assistance!" Dallin said it earnestly, under his breath, still holding her firmly.

Kathleen saw Heathron excuse himself from his current company and walk toward them quickly.

"Young Lord Sarkkand, I believe I'd like to have this dance with my betrothed," The Prince's tone was hard and threatening.

Heathron held out his hand to Kathleen and bowed properly as Dallin released her.

Kathleen turned to the Prince, placing a hand on his chest to calm him.

"It's okay, he is not our enemy. I'm afraid that we have others, though."

"Is there a place we might speak privately?" Dallin asked. His expression was urgent in a way Kathleen had not expected.

"We can get a drink and speak on the veranda," Kathleen suggested, her voice was once again its usual smooth, pleasant note-consistent with the Autumn celebration.

The three exchanged pleasantries with those around the punch bowl. Filling their crystal goblets, they glided toward the large open doors, and out into the cool night air.

"Why do you think I would trust you?" Heathron said to Dallin when they had the privacy of the night around them.

"Your Highness, if I could kneel before you without drawing attention from the crowds and thus endangering our endeavors, I would swear my loyalty before you with pride," he said.

"What game are you playing?" Heathron asked, looking directly at Dallin.

"It is no game, My Liege. House Sarkkand has ever been faithful to House Dol Lassimer. I have been your friend within the enemy camp all these years. My parents are of the same heart.

As we saw the rebellion develop, we got to the inside, and so I tell you this night, they will seek to slay your father if they have not done so already." The words peeled from him with emotion he was not completely able to hide.

"And then they plan to move against the two of you before your wedding can be performed. I fear for the future of our city. I fear for the future of the Empire," he said.

"How can I be sure that what you tell me is true? How can I trust you?" Heathron asked, his eyes narrowed.

"Take off your father's ring with the imperial seal."

Heathron blinked several times, absorbing the command. Then did as Dallin said. He slid the ring from his finger and held it in his fist.

"Hand it to me for a moment if you have any hope that I am being true," the young nobleman said.

Heathron held up his fist. "What would you do with the imperial seal, Lord Sarkkand?"

"I would humbly kiss the ring of my Crown Prince," he said. "Not all of Tyath has turned from the old ways. House Sarkkand will continue to serve you."

Heathron's fingers slowly opened, and Dallin Sarkkand picked up the heavy golden ring: the emblem of imperial might and the rightful seat of House Dol Lassimer.

He brought it to his lips and kissed it. Then bowed his head.

"It is not to you but the office that I swear my allegiance," he said. "But you, as a leader, are deserving of it. That is all I can do for now, but in my heart, I gladly bend the knee."

A few people noticed when Heathron slipped the ring off of his finger. Some of the nobility began looking in their direction.

Dallin raised his voice and assumed his haughty air.

"If you think you can keep it, so be it! But I believe House Dol Lassimer may be finished," he said loudly as he handed the ring back to the Prince.

Dallin winked at Kathleen, then spoke under his breath to

Heathron again.

"I will stay faithful to you, my friend. Be safe and well. May the Fox and Acorn rule during the lives of my children as well."

Heathron stood dumbfounded.

Dallin Sarkkand nonchalantly took another sip of his autumn wine and walked away.

Kathleen and the prince watched him leave, waiting for the sound of his boots to fade away.

"What do you make of it?" Kathleen asked.

"He's telling the truth. Dallin would never kiss the ring or swear to bend his knee if he did not mean it."

"So what do we do now?"

"I will go to my father."

"I'm coming," Kathleen began.

"You are coming with me. I know that much by now — and thank you," Heathron said.

He escorted Kathleen across the ballroom, making their way to the exit.

Hannah Aviella glided over, attempting to learn of the nature of the curious conversation she had been spying on.

"Kathleen, I wanted to tell you..."

Kathleen curtsied and nodded sweetly. "Hannah, I cannot speak with you now," she said. "Heathron would like to see me alone."

Hannah giggled and covered her mouth. She waved goodbye while Lilly and Lana made their way smoothly through the door behind Kathleen. Heathron sprinted down the hall, Kathleen close on his heels. He turned the corner running towards his father's chambers.

"Is my father inside?" Heathron asked between deep breaths as Kathleen came running up beside him.

"His Majesty has been speaking with Chief Magistrate Uppenslaw," the larger of the two guards said, motioning them toward the entrance of the emperor's abode.

They pushed past. Just inside the door, Heathron saw his father laying on the floor. The smell of death filled the air. His chair was tipped over. There was a pool of blood surrounding the bodies of both the Emperor and the Chief Magistrate.

"Father!" Heathron called loudly. He ran a few steps forward and knelt beside the figure on the floor.

"I'll call Melva," Kathleen said, turning to Lana, but Heathron shook his head slowly. The fingers of the Emperor still clutched the throat of the Magistrate. Dirm's knife was buried in the neck of the Emperor and many bloodied punctures could be seen in his chest.

"He is beyond her help," Heathron said.

"I am so sorry."

She laid a hand on his back to comfort him. He looked up at her.

"My father fought to the death, and so will I, if I must," Heathron said as his lower lip trembled with emotion.

45

LONGEST NIGHT

Kendra's coat changed slowly. At first Kathleen only noticed a few hairs that were white along the ridge of her back. As the days and weeks passed, her scarlet fur was replaced, ever so slowly, by white. When the bald cypress tree by the reflecting pool finally lost its coppery needles, Kendra's coat was mottled. Patches of her fur remained red while other areas were as white as a cloud. When a heavy frost came one autumn morning and coated her windows with a layer of ice in geometric patterns, the fox had made her transition to white. Only the black on her nose, the tip of her tail, and her stockings contrasted with the white fur. She was bigger, too. She loved to hunt in the palace gardens, or in the fields as Kathleen and Heathron took their morning horseback rides together.

Kathleen promised herself she would always remember the first time she saw a snowflake or a puddle of water covered in ice.

Heathron laughed at her antics as she reached out with her tongue in the cold air to catch a delicate six-sided flake.

"It tastes sweet!" she insisted.

He laughed again.

"I think you are imagining things. Snowflakes don't have a taste," he said.

"Well they do to me," she said, and stuck out her tongue again to catch another.

Heathron looked around at the empty fields lightly covered with a dusting of snow.

"The harvest was good this year," he said, almost to himself.

"Has it taken the pressure off at all?" Kathleen asked.

"Not really, I still need the support of the council and the army, as well as the navy. My father's death gave me a groundswell of support from the common people, but that will not last forever."

"You still need the high noble houses, don't you?" she asked.

Heathron nodded.

"If I cannot bring enough of them to my side, to reaffirm their support, I am not sure what will happen. Suffering a crisis of leadership with a war to be fought is hard to consider."

"Will your brothers remain obstinate? Why will they not help you?"

"Pilus and Jason feel no obligation to support me. I am their younger brother and not of full-blood to them. My betrothal to you, a Daughter of the Realm, does give me some standing. My father made it known that I, not my brothers, was to take his seat on the imperial throne."

"I am sorry that things did not go...as planned...over the summer," Kathleen said.

Heathron stretched his arms out and inhaled the crisp air. The fur lining around the collar of his coat danced in the breeze.

Kathleen noticed his face did not look as boyish as when she first saw him. He appeared more manly, and not just in a physical sense. Heathron was building himself as a leader and a ruler. The trials of the year weighed heavily on his well-formed shoulders, and she wished she could help lighten his load.

"We needed the time Kathleen...didn't we?" he said.

"I will always be grateful that you did not push me too hard in this," Kathleen said.

"That sounds promising," he replied with a smile.

Kathleen, for the first time since late summer, hesitated to grasp his hand. It wasn't him, but the fact that she knew she must answer him. The decision remained a tight knot of tangled, conflicting emotions. She loved Heathron, in many ways, but Jared... He still possessed a part of her. Somewhere deep and untouchable. The Sīhalt Guardian owned a shred of her soul, and she knew it. The thought of him still made her heart pound, and she wondered if it was normal to feel this way. Could she accept that her desire for Heathron was real and would grow to be as strong as those first feelings of passion the Guardian had stirred in her heart? Might the admiration, friendship, and comfort she felt with Heathron grow to even eclipse the whirl-wind of emotions she was swept into during her journey alone with Jared?

Why couldn't it have been simple? She and Heathron devel-oped a friendship that made her laugh, and she found herself wanting to be with him almost every day. They shared similar interests such as sailing and riding in the fields and forests. They had been promised to each other from childhood. Why did this have to be so difficult?

"It is wonderful tonight," she said from the fur-lined hood she wore to cover her ears and the back of her neck.

"How do you manage to look so stunning all the time?" he asked softly.

Kathleen blushed a little. "Now you know that isn't true," she said.

Heathron never hesitated to offer compliments or share his mind with her. Heathron was open and true.

"No carriage tonight?" Kathleen asked.

"We go by sleigh," Heathron said as he assisted her walking from the doorway.

The snow was piled high along the path, but it had been packed down on the roads. The horses stamped their hooves, blowing clouds of moisture into the cold evening air. The bells on their harnesses were polished brightly and shone under the flicker of the lamp light.

"I didn't know the world could be so cold and so beautiful at the same time," Kathleen said. She thought briefly how magnificent the waterfalls in Altrastadt must look now.

Jared said the city became encrusted in ice crystals.

Now Kathleen had an idea of how that was possible.

"There is fun to be had in winter too," Heathron assured her. "The wind will be very cold as we travel to Eldin's home. I am glad that you bundled up!"

"Is it a long ride to his home?" Kathleen asked.

"In summer it would take us all night, but we will cross a portion of the Clearwater Sea because it is frozen solid."

"The horses can walk on it?"

"Oh yes, the ice is as thick as the horse is tall in winters like this," he said as he helped her step into the sleigh.

Lana sat beside the driver and Lilly climbed onto the back of the sleigh where a foot servant could easily ride.

They set off, swishing through the snow that covered the streets and out the harbor gate toward the Stellat Estate. The wind was very cold, and Kathleen found the need to bring the scarf that covered her neck up to cover her mouth as well. The sound of the horses' bells rang into the winter night, their hoof beats muted by the new-fallen snow outside the city walls.

A number of other partygoers were traveling the same road as Kathleen and Heathron. They waved gloved hands and greeted them as they passed, slicing smoothly through powdery drifts.

Kathleen leaned forward and found that Heathron had brought a thick blanket to share. He threw it over her shoulders and pulled the ends close, holding in the warmth. Kathleen shivered and drew closer to him.

"This is like a dream. Look at it coming down through the night sky," she said.

"Did you know each one is unique? No two snowflakes are the same."

"Have you seen them all?" Kathleen asked as one landed on her nose and began to melt as tendrils of her breath rose upward.

"In school, we were taught that each snowflake forms a six-sided shape, and as the water freezes in the sky, it crystallizes into its own special shape."

"They are like people. Each one is unique and beautiful, but only lasts a little while before it is gone," she said.

"I had not thought of it that way, but yes, their beauty and form is to be enjoyed while they last and not mourned for long when they are gone, for they have fulfilled their purpose."

Kathleen removed a glove from her hand and slid her fingers inside Heathron's glove, her hand against his.

"Thank you for being there for me, to comfort me when each of my parents died. You being with me has brought so much..." - he hesitated - "protection."

"I'm glad I could be here with you," she said, leaning her head onto his shoulder, watching the snow fly up from the skids of the sleigh.

"Tonight, is Winterfest," he said.

Kathleen knew what he meant. This was the night she had agreed to give him an answer. Her heart thumped at the thought. When should she tell him her decision? Now? She couldn't do it now. She wanted to be alone with him — without bells ringing in the background. She wanted her face uncovered when she told him, so that he might read her emotions as she explained to him her choice. It wasn't fair to make it last any longer — he needed an answer. He deserved an answer.

Heathron squinted his eyes against the cold wind of the night. He seemed to be smiling, too. He flexed his fingers against hers and leaned down to kiss the hair of her head and he wrapped a strong arm more tightly around her.

They rode like this in silence, slicing across the level ice of the Clearwater Sea, then back on shore where they followed the King's Highway until they drew up to the entrance of House Stellat. Eldin waved from the front where he stood warming his hands next to the enormous braziers burning for the comfort of the guests on the front patio. Eldin pulled his green jacket down at his waist and shivered despite the firewood burning in front of him.

"Happy Winterfest! Great night for a party!" he said, pushing his eyewear further onto the bridge of his nose.

"I've never seen anything like it!" Kathleen said, twirling to catch another snowflake.

"You'll get used to it quick. Right about now is when I am done with winter, but we will have much more of this before the spring is here."

"Speak not of next year until the stroke of midnight, Eldin. You know it is bad luck to do otherwise," Heathron said.

"I'm not superstitious, Your Highness, and it's true. Princess Kathleen will be pining for the warm waters of Candoreth before the first icicles melt in Tyath. Why our ancestors chose to anchor the Empire here instead of further south is beyond me. Do you have your speech all prepared?"

"I plan to give a rousing tribute to the Empire and House Dol Lassimer," Heathron said.

"That's the spirit!" Then turning to Kathleen, Eldin said, "Happy Winterfest, Princess. Let's get you in from the cold."

"And a very Merry Winterfest to you, Eldin," she said as they crossed the foyer and entered a spacious ballroom. Her heart beat faster and her palms began to sweat as the evening wore on.

46

WINTERFEST ADDRESS

"Eldin, thank you for allowing us to join together at your beautiful home," Heathron said. "House Stellat always knows how to show us a good time."

"Yeah, like cliff diving from the Fingers!" Aidan Naystrom said to a round of laughter. Eldin looked irritated as he tilted his head to one side to wait until the irreverent comment's supporters quieted once more.

"It is my pleasure, Your Highness. We have been looking forward to your speech tonight," Eldin said.

"I suppose during this festival of the Longest Night it is appropriate for me to share with you the State of the Empire. I am happy to share with you how the Empire has stabilized recently," he said.

"You mean, since the crisis of leadership?" a voice called out.

A few of the noblemen scoffed and rolled their eyes. Others looked at him steadfastly. Kathleen saw some holding their gaze and their attention in the hope it was true. Perhaps Heathron had stabilized the Empire.

"Many of you have heard about the unusual circumstances of my father's death..."

There was a murmur among the guests — a few nodded heads. They had heard the death of the emperor had spread as only gossip can, including the gruesome scene that Heathron had stumbled upon that night.

Heathron's words came in a solemn note. "My father left very specific instructions for me to follow — guidance for the coming few years. His policies and contracts were renewed before his passing. They are still in place."

Some of the high nobility nodded, while others remained expressionless, their arms folded across their chests tightly. They were, it seemed, unconvinced.

"The flow of goods and services will continue just as all of you would like. I will maintain order during the transition," he said.

Finally, after fidgeting for a short while, it was Dallin Sarkkand who spoke next: "By what right do you have any say in what happens for the new year?" Another murmur rippled through the crowd. "Your mother and father are dead!"

Before Heathron could react – his eyes filling with blank rage – Hannah Aviella interrupted. "Thank you for informing us of the clear circumstances of this situation," she began, before turning to Heathron. "But as much as you may not like it, he *will* be our Emperor."

A few called out angrily from the back of the crowd not happy with the idea of Heathron's continued rule.

"You're not even married. Your brother at least has a child. Perhaps he should sit on the throne."

"His brother is as dull as a broken arrow shaft. He has neither the intellect nor the commanding personal presence to lead us," Michael Tivius said. "No offense, Your Highness."

"None taken," Heathron assured him. "There is a reason my father chose me."

"You still are not married. Are you even betrothed anymore?" Aidan Naystrom asked.

The question hung in the air quiet and cold like the weather outside.

Heathron turned to look at Kathleen.

He stood like a buck surrounded by wolves with no ability to run. His escape was closed because Kathleen remained silent.

"The Princess Dal Sundi and I have..." he stammered.

"...have played all summer long, and even into the harvest season, with no formal announcement," Aidan said. "Some say that you don't want her because she is tainted goods. Others whisper she is a witch, unworthy of Abboth's grace. What do you say Heathron, isn't it high time you chose a girl from among our ranks if Princess Kathleen isn't cut out for it? We wouldn't hold that against you."

The young man sneered and the room grew even more tense as the crowd waited for his response.

"You will address me as your liege. You may not like it, but your house is sworn to mine."

"If the strength was there in reality, you would never need to say it. True leadership relies on a foundation of confidence it has built. I invoke the right to challenge my obligation to your house. You have offended me, and I demand satisfaction."

"I will have the loyalty of your blade or show you the edge of mine," Heathron said as his hand went to the hilt at his side.

"A duel then?" Aidan replied. It was not really a question. The consequences of the words spoken could mean only one thing.

Tension filled the room. No one spoke. The only whisper uttered was that of fine steel being drawn from the wool-lined scabbard at his hip.

"My friends, clear the ballroom, we need the space for a different kind of dance," Heathron declared, his lip trembling with fear or rage, it was hard to distinguish.

The people separated according to their desires to show to what degree they supported the ruling house. Some moved behind Heathron, others walked to where Jessica, Dallin, and

Larissa stood. A quick tally showed Kathleen that Heathron's supporters, even in the house of his friend, was lacking.

She stepped forward and cleared her throat. "Excuse me," she said loud and clear, "before we begin the next dance, there is an announcement I would like to make."

Chairs ceased to shuffle and murmurs died down.

"It is true, what they say about me."

Heathron looked at her wide-eyed, shaking his head slightly to say, "Do not reveal this, Kathleen."

"I was hesitant to marry Heathron."

The crowd quieted. She had their attention.

"You see, when I left my home in Candoreth, I was like many of you. I was a just a girl hoping for a chance to improve my family's lot and perhaps to gain a handsome husband in the process. I had been warned about the politics in the city. But I couldn't have comprehended, nor do I fully comprehend now, how one decision fully affects another," she said.

"But before my journey began, violent men attempted to kidnap me. Those men were hired by someone here in the city. I was able to escape. During my royal procession, we were attacked by the barbarians, and I was taken. Savages guarded me and at one point, I heard them speak of how they would trade my weight in gold. Someone in Tyath hired them. Perhaps it was someone in this room.

"But I escaped again, with the help of my Sīhalt Guardian. We fled to the mountain forests until we finally saw the gleaming walls of the Golden City. This place represented, for me, salvation. Because of my injuries, I don't remember the dramatic circumstances of my arrival, but I know many of you were there. Some of you were right in hesitating to believe that I would make the kind of queen the Capital City deserves. Some of you would like nothing more than to see me leave — another house to assume the role of leadership in the capital."

She looked at Aidan with her chin lifted in a challenge to him.

"However, in the time I have been here, I've become more familiar with the character of your Prince. His parents were wise — they believed in us. Heathron loves the people of the Empire. He was born to lead and I stand beside him. Pirates may have pursued us, barbarians may have attacked, poison may stain the lips of our loved ones, or a dagger be thrust into the father we love, but we will not bend. We will not step down. His royal Highness, Prince Lassimer, and I will be married. Although we might be tempted to accelerate the nuptials due to political realities, we will wait till Midsummer's day because we honor the law and tradition laid down by our ancestors. House Dol Lassimer will endure. The seed of your late Emperor Kade will not be extinguished."

A murmur ran through the crowd. A scattering of applause accented the gathering. Toasts of health were offered.

Heathron was speechless.

Kathleen found herself short of breath too.

"Perhaps we have been too hasty. We would very much like to see House Dol Lassimer strong and vibrant," one nobleman said.

Aidan's hand dropped away from the sword, and Kathleen let out a breath she didn't know she had been holding.

"Congratulations!" another one said and moved forward to shake Heathron's hand.

"A catastrophe avoided?" Kathleen asked him quietly between those greeting them.

"I could have handled him. Don't mistake my native cheery temperament for weakness," he said.

"I did not doubt your martial skill for a moment. I just consider it bad form to get blood on the floor of a guest's home, especially if that blood belongs to another of the guests," she said.

"Eldin would have forgiven me."

"It would have made you look small and foolish."

"He does need to be taught a lesson!" Heathron said.

"Do it in the privacy of a quiet wood. If he wishes to challenge you, take him up on it if you must, but I do not want to see a duel where the father of my future children could be killed," Kathleen said.

"Thank you, my darling for saying yes," the Prince said.

"It was 'yes' from my earliest memory," Kathleen replied.

"But now as you are here with me, as I breathe in your breath, I thank the blessing of my departed parents for the blessing of you as my bride."

He leveled his eyes at her and blinked slowly. His brown eyes flicked a quick view of her lips and then back at her gaze. Kathleen knew what that meant. He wanted to kiss her. She realized she wanted to kiss him too.

"Will you take me for a stroll?" she asked.

"Outside? In the cold?"

"I don't plan to be cold," Kathleen said and looked at him through her lowered eye lashes.

She saw him swallow and she laughed softly.

"I would be happy to walk along the patio with you, even on this, the Longest Night," he said with a broad smile as he bowed to offer his arm.

They came to the full-length windows that could be opened like doors. A few forms stood outside in the falling snow. They tossed split logs onto the fires burning in the great basins of stone. The servants paused momentarily to warm their hands before they noticed Heathron and Kathleen approaching the stone archway.

They bowed and one of the men pointed to a small bundle of green wrapped in red above their heads.

"Beware the mistletoe," he said. "Tis an ancient custom but one to be honored, nevertheless. Abboth wouldn't mind an expression of love even if the tradition started before the people of Desnia knew of him."

Heathron looked up through the lightly falling snow and smiled. Kathleen wrinkled her brow and squinted up at the small sprig of green.

"What is that?" she asked.

"Mistletoe is a reminder of life during the long cold of winter. It is used as decoration for parties like this."

"Do you eat it?" Kathleen asked.

"No, it's poisonous, but it is designed for you to enjoy!" the servant said, smiling as he tossed another log on the blazing fire. He turned to leave them alone in the Winterfest night.

"That is strange," Kathleen said, still looking up at the small piece of greenery attached to the stone arches of the patio. "If we can't eat it because it's poisonous, and it has no flowers or alluring scent, then how in the world are we supposed to enjoy the little thing?"

She turned to Heathron but did not get another word in before his lips were on hers, and he pulled her closely into him.

The suddenness of the intimacy seemed right to Kathleen. The comfort of his kiss, and the strength she felt in his hands upon her waist, made her ignore the concerns that would have made her pull away. Instead, she felt for his neck. With her eyes closed and their lips responding to each other's, Kathleen reached up to slide her hands inside the high collar Heathron wore. She ran her fingers through his curly hair and allowed her fingernails to gently caress the back of his scalp. His neck, like his mouth, was warm and strong. She found herself wishing he was not wearing the heavy jacket as she leaned further into his chest. She wanted to feel his body closer to hers, and wished there were not so many layers between them.

Prince Heathron pulled her close and gave her another small kiss on her cheek. He spoke softly into her ear, and the feel of it made her giggle and tuck her head to the side.

"It is considered proper to kiss beneath the mistletoe on a

night like this," he said, pushing his nose closer to her ear as he spoke despite her playful resistance.

"We shall decorate our entire home with it if this is the effect it has on you!" she said.

"You asked how we were supposed to enjoy it, if we can't...eat it," Heathron said as he nibbled on Kathleen's earlobe.

That was too much for Kathleen. She pulled away and ran to the far side of the stone fire pit. She extended her hands and laughed into the night.

"You are not entirely how I imagined you!" she said, looking up at flakes of snow falling down like a million troubled stars falling to the earth.

Heathron laughed and extended his hands toward the fire on the opposite side.

"Did you think I would only be stuffy and proper — pursuing you as a matter of state? I am in love with you, Kathleen! And tonight, you have given me a reason to sing."

He ran to the edge of the patio foundation that looked over the expanse of fields covered in new-fallen snow. He almost slipped in the white fluff but righted himself and placed one foot on the decorative railing. He spread his arms wide and began to sing;

"How is it that the wind doth sing,
Thy name as it passes every bow and bud of spring?
Can thy presence cheer the very atmosphere,
With a song so sweet I feel my knees go weak?"

"Be careful. If you slip over the edge, you may never see a new spring," Kathleen warned with a smiling shake of her head.

His singing gathered the attention of other guests who looked out the windows at the couple.

"Are you getting cold? We can go in?" she said.

A scowling Lord Aidan Naystrom looked out from among the faces.

"I am as warm as a fox in its den, Kathleen!" Heathron said, "Thanks to you."

With a sweep of his hand across the railing, he gathered a large handful of snow and packed it into a ball.

"Well, we have gained an audience tonight, not all of them approving," she said, looking at the bitterness Aidan showed on his face.

"He will simply need to deal with it or...get out of the way!" Heathron said as he wound up and launched the snowball across the patio at the scowling face of Aidan. The haughty young lord's eyes widened as he saw the ball of white come hurling toward him. He let out a sharp yelp and jumped to get out of the way. Just as the snowball thumped heavily against the thick glass of the window. Aidan crashed into one of the servants holding a silver tray of lightly bubbling champagne. The goblets shattered against the floor and the liquid spilled down the front of the nobleman and the servant.

Heathron laughed loudly and said, "Leave off with the blades tonight, Aidan. Let us duel with snow!"

The crowd of young people laughed as couples began spilling out of the ballroom, scooping up handfuls of snow and throwing them at one another. There were delighted screams, and when any of them passed beneath the stone arches, they kissed beneath the mistletoe.

Heathron grabbed Kathleen's hands and pulled her into an embrace from behind.

"See what we have started?" he said.

"I'm afraid the consequences of this night might not all be happy," Kathleen said. "Aidan looked ready for blood."

"It will all work out my dearest - as long as we are together, it will all work out."

47

DUEL OF HONOR

The wheels of the carriage rolled through mud puddles of the overgrown forest road just north of the city. Patches of snow remained scattered among the trees on the ground. The horses strained in their harnesses and Heathron looked out the window. He could barely see through the cold fog of the early morning. The air felt heavy but warmer than usual for this time of year. The morning was unseasonably warm for late winter. The cold of winter had not served to cool young Lord Naystrom's anger. Aidan's red carriage was parked on one side of the clearing — the horses stamped impatiently.

I feel impatient myself, thought Heathron. He needed to finally be done with this and bring Aidan to heel. He did not want to kill the rebellious lord, but he couldn't have him disrupting the willingness of the other lords to follow him.

"I wish I didn't have to do this," Heathron said as he took a deep breath and patted Eldin's knee. "Thank you for being my second."

Eldin tilted his head back on his skinny neck. He looked at Heathron through thick glasses.

"I hope you don't need me for anything more than a witness. I'm as talented with the blade as I am at cliff diving," he said.

"Hopefully this won't take very long. If I could have turned him down, I would have, but he does have the right to challenge," Heathron said.

"There is Dallin Sarkkand — of course he would stand as Aidan's second!" Eldin said.

"Go over to the middle of the clearing and speak with him. I will prepare myself for the duel."

Heathron wasted no time, unsheathing his sword and limbering his arms and legs. His heart felt heavy, and yet, he also held an edge of anger that fueled his willingness to win.

"If he had not behaved so much like a stubborn mule, we would not be here this morning. Now he's gotten himself to the point where his pride won't allow him to back down. Men will die for stupid pride," he muttered to himself.

Eldin walked into the clearing, leaving footsteps in the damp fallen leaves. He met Dallin Sarkkand and, not for the first time, Heathron felt thankful it was Aidan and not Dallin who was fighting the duel. The young Lord Sarkkand was a terror with the sword, and Heathron had no desire to be dead at the end of it. Dallin towered over Eldin. He looked down at the smaller man then leaned in to say something quiet. Heathron considered what it might be. Could it be possible that Aidan had come to his senses? Was he negotiating another way? Heathron hoped so. Eldin gestured emphatically and raised his voice a bit. Heathron caught the words.

"No, we will not leave without satisfaction," Eldin said and turned back, walking in Heathron's direction.

"What did he say?" Heathron asked.

"Those two are full of tricks. Lord Sarkkand told me Aidan is ready to fight, but then grabbed me by the arm and spoke seriously. He said we should return to the city immediately. He said the Princess is in danger, and that this duel is only a ruse to remove her from your protection."

Heathron's heart jolted at the words. Could they stoop so low?

"What are the chances he is lying?" Heathron said.

"They cannot be trusted. I can hear them now, 'They ran away from the duel because they were afraid to fight.' If you don't fight, and win, Aidan no longer must support you. You can't afford to lose the soldiers of House Naystrom from your service."

"An unwilling servant is sometimes more dangerous than an enemy," Heathron observed. "Did he say anything else?"

"He started to say you needed to watch your back, but I cut him off. Let's do this," Eldin said.

"You keep saying 'we'. I am the one holding a sword," Heathron smiled.

"I can enjoy a victory vicariously, can't I?"

"Do you think he will yield once I've bested him?"

"Aidan is cocky, but he's not a fool. I'm sure he wants to live."

"I will do my best to give him a way out," Heathron said. "Although, I don't believe he would offer me the same grace."

"That is why you deserve to be the Emperor, and he must be brought in line," Eldin said.

Heathron walked to the center of the clearing and motioned for Aidan to join him.

"It's a fine morning, Lord Nystrom, don't you think?"

"I'm glad you think so, Heathron. A fine day for you to die as any," he said.

"Expecting such finality?" Heathron smiled. "No one has to die today. I am here because of your challenge and my unwillingness to allow your ungentlemanly behavior in the presence of my betrothed."

"You caused me public humiliation. I demand satisfaction!" Aidan said.

"I am sorry your honor was bruised, but let the record show I did not want to fight you."

"That's because you are a coward and so is your little friend." He sneered at Eldin Stellat.

"This fight is between you and I. Today you will learn the difference between courage and cowardice. Turning away from a fight does not make me a coward. Just as demanding a duel does not make you courageous. Why would you risk your life when all it would take for us to make amends is an apology?"

"Remove your jacket and draw your sword. I am tired of your lecture."

"I prefer to keep my jacket on. This morning is chilly, and I do not intend to work up a sweat."

"So prideful, so self-assured," Aidan said, swinging his blade back and forth gracefully.

"Your public humiliation was justified. You saw fit to demean Kathleen in front of everyone," Heathron said.

"If only your mother and father could see you now, Heathron. I'm sure they would be so proud of you," Aidan said sarcastically. "How would you like to do this, my Prince?"

"Will you only be satisfied when my blood is on your hands? Very well, then. If I cannot get my point across through your ears, I will endeavor to drive it home through your skin. On guard!"

Heathron brought the tip of his sword upward and felt the strike of his blade against Aidan's. His opponent moved quickly, shuffling his feet with a wide stance. They had trained under the same master. Heathron did not expect to be surprised during the fight. He had spent countless hours practicing since childhood. He knew there were only a few men that could match him one-on-one.

"I am stronger and faster than you, Aidan," Heathron said. "Why do you persist in this madness?"

Steel rang against steel, as they parried, thrusted, and deflected each other's swords.

"Don't underestimate me," Aidan said, kicking debris from the forest floor up at Heathron. The Prince evaded the clod of half frozen vegetation and closed the distance, easily working his way further past Aidan's defenses. Their warm breath condensed like clouds of smoke rising up in the icy forest.

"You can't win, Aidan. I am better than you."

Young Lord Naystrom swung his sword with all the more vigor.

"I don't need to beat you, Heathron. I've already won." He smiled and Dallin Sarkkand called out from the perimeter.

"Look out!"

A bolt from a crossbow slammed into the tree nearest Heathron.

"Get down, Aidan!" Heathron yelled and tackled the young man to the ground. Aidan began to fight him. His size was smaller, but he was no weakling. Heathron abandoned his sword and began to grapple with Aidan. They were being attacked and still Aidan struggled with him.

"Stop it, man!" Heathron said and slammed a fist into Aidan's face. The blow stunned him, and Heathron pointed in the direction from which the crossbow bolt had come.

"We are being hunted!" Heathron hissed while clamping his hand over Aidan's mouth to silence him.

Three men in dark helmets closed in on them as they lay on the forest floor. The men with crossbows and swords wore clothing familiar to Heathron. Their gauntlets held the crimson wolf of House Naystrom emblazoned on each hand.

"Release our master," one of them said as he aimed the crossbow at Heathron's chest. "Heathron Dol Lassimer, by the authority of the Council of Nine Houses, you are being arrested for treason against the Empire.

48

ARRESTED

"**K**eep close to me," Lilly said as they entered the chamber of the Council of Nine Houses.

"Why would they demand I come here? Perhaps it has to do with our announcement," Kathleen said.

The noble families of the Council of Nine Houses were seated in a semi-circle. They stared down from their high seats. The design of the room reminded Kathleen of the arena in Candoreth. She stood on the circular floor and looked up. *Were these council members judges, vicious spectators, or both?* she wondered.

Kathleen nodded to each one individually. There was clearly uneasiness in the room. Lady Aviella shifted uncomfortably.

"Why did you call us here, Lord Balfoest?" she asked. "This meeting was a surprise."

"This is an emergency meeting. Details have come before the council that must be rectified immediately," he replied. A number of the nobleman nodded their heads gravely. Lord Stellat refused to meet her eye.

Kathleen looked around trying to make sense of the nonverbal cues. In the months she had lived in the Golden City, she had learned to take no subtle gesture for granted. Every glance had a meaning. Every offhanded comment could be a threat. She struggled to make sense of what this was about, but she, like her guards, sensed danger.

"My betrothed, Prince Dol Lassimer, is unavailable at this time. I would prefer to wait for his presence before we continue a meeting," Kathleen said.

"That is right. We want to congratulate you on your formal announcement for the coming Wedding Day. Some of us were beginning to wonder if you would really go through with it," Lord Sarkkand said.

His tone was neutral, and Kathleen was not able to see whether he was a friend or foe in this meeting. Like his son, Lord Sarkkand played it safe. It was always hard to tell whose side that house was on.

"I don't trust him," Lana whispered.

The dome of the ceiling magnified what she had said.

"The architecture of this room is designed so that we may hear the person before us. If your statement was meant for Kathleen's ears only, please know that it can be heard by every member of the Council of Nine Houses," Lord Balfoest said smiling.

"I am sorry, Your Highness. I spoke out of turn," Lana said more softly than before.

"You may dismiss your guards, Princess Dal Sundi. It is not customary to bring them along when you address the Council of Nine Houses," Lord Naystrom said. His dark eyes and thick black hair held the same intensity as his son.

"Is it customary to bring the daughter of an independent King to be interrogated in this manner?" Kathleen asked sharply.

"You have been a guest in our city since the summer solstice. Have you not been treated with dignity?" Lord Balfoest asked. "Why would you feel... uncomfortable now?"

Lilly stood closer to Kathleen, her arm brushing her shoulder.

It was as if she was saying, *I will not leave you.* Lana and Lilly both seemed to sense the danger. Kathleen wasn't about to second-guess them.

"I will keep my guards. Emperor Kade Dol Lassimer gave them to me as gift. They have become my friends. Surely you wouldn't deprive me of their company if I wish for them to remain at my side?"

"Of course not, Kathleen!" Lady Aviella said. "Whatever the council needs to talk with you about is fine to discuss in the presence of imperial protectors." She looked around, trying to catch the eye of the other counselors.

Lord Stellat spoke up. "You have no reason to be concerned, Your Highness," he said to Kathleen. Then he turned to Lord Belfoest. "The doors are shut and bolted properly. Now what is this about?"

The question hung in the air. Lars Balfoest sat with his fingers laced together, pressing his extended index fingers against his thin lips.

"Princess Kathleen, do you know why the Empress died?"

"She was poisoned," Kathleen replied.

"Yes, we all know that," Balfoest said slowly. "But, do you know *why?*"

Kathleen shook her head. She didn't know where he was going with this.

"I was warned the city is dangerous," Kathleen replied. "I do not know the reason behind the assassination of Empress Rema."

"The whole world is dangerous, my girl," Lord Balfoest said. His voice was dark. Kathleen thought she could see Lilly move her fingers slightly towards her sword.

"Recently I have been made aware that you were the target of the poison, not the Empress. The chandelier that fell from the ceiling of the cathedral was another attempt on your life."

Kathleen swallowed and nodded.

"I feel very fortunate to be alive today."

"Why would there be such a great effort to end your life?" he asked.

Kathleen looked from one side of the room the other. Two of the lords looked down at their hands, almost embarrassed it seemed. Lady Aviella furrowed her brow and looked disbelievingly at Lord Balfoest. Lord Sarkkand looked as if he was considering the gravity of the words. He frowned and pursed his lips. Lord Stellat shook his head subtly. He did not agree.

"This is not the first time in history that unsavory factions would try to eliminate the possibility of an heir to the throne," he said.

"This is, however, the first time since the Great Sickness, that a known witch has been allowed to walk the halls freely of the Golden City, let alone inside the Imperial Palace," Balfoest said with a finger stabbing in Kathleen's direction.

"What proof do you have of this?" Lady Aviella said. "Kathleen is innocent!"

"I've heard the rumors, but if there was any truth to it, she would never be allowed to sit on our throne. Am I right?" Lord Naystrom said.

"I'm no devotee of the Luzian Church, but the people would rise up against it, I am sure," Lord Sarkkand said.

Kathleen took a step back. She remained silent as her pulse pounded in her ears. Why would they bring this up now? She had been discreet and very careful not to show her Talent.

"I wish to leave now," she said. "We may resume this discussion...this interrogation, when Heathron is back."

"I have it on good authority that he will return to the city in chains. Our Prince has been aiding and abetting sorcery within the walls of the Golden City. Perhaps because of his youth he isn't able to recall the bodies stacked in piles when the Plague struck. Perhaps he cannot remember the cries of the children without a mother or a father. Perhaps, due to his inexperience, he cannot know of the curse that was brought to this land by the workings of those who call themselves 'Talented'. But we remember, and we uphold the law. Sorcery will not be tolerated."

"What evidence do you have besides scurrilous accusations?" Lord Stellat said.

Kathleen put her hand to her forehead. Despite her demand to leave, the guards who stood at the door made no move to unbolt the entrance to the chamber. She tried to think of any situation where she had given the wrong impression. Kathleen tried to remember if there was ever a time in the past months when she used her power unintentionally. She hadn't. Only in the privacy of her secret garden, built within her private chambers, had she ever used the Gift that flowed within her. A small blossom of Gardenia. That was it, and that could only have been witnessed by Melva or...Larissa.

"Bring in the witness," Lord Balfoest sneered as he spoke.

The guards moved to open a small doorway on the side of the chamber. From the adjacent room stepped Larissa Albodris. Her expression was flat. She looked at Kathleen as she entered the room and stepped up the few stairs that led to the stand where the council sat. Her expression was one of pity mixed with resignation. Her eyes still held the dark circles beneath them that had appeared since she began using the dream powder so often.

"State your name," one of the guards said.

"I am Larissa Albodris."

"State your relation to the accused," he continued.

"I'm the accused now?" Kathleen said indignantly. "I demand you open these doors at once!"

"Order!"

"Why are you doing this, Larissa?"

"Because I'm not going to be left without a chair when the music stops."

"This isn't a game, Larissa. People's lives are on the line."

"No, it's not a game, and my life is on the line. My future and my happiness are on the line. If you don't want to take what's offered to you, I'll take it."

"How do you see this ending?" Kathleen asked.

"I get what I want."

"That's so selfish," Kathleen replied. "I loved you like a sister."

"Silence, witch!" Lord Balfoest shouted. "Now speak up, Lady Albodris! What have you seen?"

"She's a Plant Witch. So was her mother. There are people down in Candoreth who still think it's okay. Prince Heathron knows. I was there when they undressed her after she fell coming in the gate."

Larissa turned back to Kathleen.

"Do you still wear the necklace, Katie? The one made for witches?"

Kathleen stammered. She opened her mouth and closed it again, not knowing what to say next.

"Why are you doing this?" she managed to ask.

Larissa ignored her and turned back to the council.

"Prince Heathron made her a beautiful private garden next to her bed chambers. It has a glass ceiling, a water source, and rich soil. All of it is so she can enjoy her 'Green Growing' sorcery right in the midst of the Imperial Palace," Larissa said.

There was a gasp from Lady Aviella. The woman covered her mouth in horror and looked to Kathleen for some evidence to the contrary.

"My mother helped our people..." Kathleen began, struggling to organize her thoughts in the face of the onslaught.

"Seek not to justify the wickedness with which you have infected our Golden City," Lord Balfoest said.

Kathleen was sure his carefully selecting his words brought images in the minds of the other councilors of the destruction brought by the Plague.

"Did Heathron know you had this...ability?" Lord Sarkkand asked.

"He knew it was a possibility," Kathleen admitted.

"Do you know what we call these now, Princess?" Lord Naystrom asked, lifting up a necklace identical to the one given to Kathleen by her father.

"I want to leave," Kathleen said.

"It is called a Locket of the Damned," he said as he held the silver chain with a stout dagger, not allowing it to touch his skin. He dropped it back into the black velvet bag he held in his other hand.

"I don't wear it," Kathleen protested.

"You tell the truth, Princess Kathleen, because this necklace is the one I retrieved from your chambers. You don't wear it because you are trying to hide what you really are."

He held the black bag up and dangled it for all in the room to see.

"You stole it from my room?" Kathleen said. "You had no right, Lord Naystrom!"

"I serve the Imperial City! The private residence you have enjoyed thus far is not yours. Nor is it Prince Heathron's to give you! He cannot harbor a witch as his soon-to-be-bride and expect the people of Tyath to just go along with it!"

Kathleen was afraid, but also angry. Larissa smirked at her from the upper level and shook her head.

"I warned you, Kathleen," she said.

Kathleen turned sharply to leave but the guards at the door stood with their arms crossed over their chests-unmoving.

Lilly and Lana flanked her. They did not say a word but stood on their toes ready for action.

"Seize her!" Lord Balfoest said.

The guards came alive and moved toward Kathleen.

"Easy now," one of them said.

Lana and Lilly drew their swords and stood between Kathleen and the oncoming men.

"Do you consent to be taken?" Lana asked, holding her sword high, pommel oriented toward the guards.

"I do not consent to this injustice," Kathleen said. "I wish to leave at once!"

"You don't have a chance," the largest of the men said. "Tell your girls to put away their blades. We wouldn't want them to get their pretty faces hurt."

"Stop this foolishness and arrest her!" Lord Balfoest commanded.

The big man lunged for Kathleen without drawing his own sword. His meaty hand closed on her shoulder but was immediately severed from the wrist. Lilly's sword swung expertly in a downward stroke, and the hand lay twitching on the polished marble floor.

The guard screamed and grabbed the stub that remained.

Lana and Lilly remained ready.

"Open the door!" Lana roared, but the remaining guards drew their swords and advanced toward the three women.

"Go out the other way!" Kathleen shouted. She sprinted toward the small door Larissa had used to enter the council room.

In the confusion, Lilly and Lana slid over the wooden bar that separated the floor from the podium and ran for the smaller doorway. None of the nobility tried to stop them, but Larissa extended her foot as Kathleen ran by. She struck Kathleen's ankle, sending her sprawling onto the floor.

Guards were almost upon her when Lana came leaping back through the door. The first man struck his sword against Lana's. Sparks showered at the doorway, and Lana gritted her teeth against the shattering blow.

Lana, with her athletic build and muscular arms, was able to deflect the man's sword for three more combinations of strikes. Kathleen was lifted to her feet by Lilly, and they ran through the small room to a hallway that led toward a vacant dining hall filled with tables and tall windows along one side.

Lana tipped over chairs and tables as they tried to make their escape. Kathleen picked up her skirt and ran as fast as she could to keep up with Lilly, but the guards pursued them, and the men were faster.

"I'll slow them down," Lana said. "Keep running and turn right at the end of the hall!"

Lana turned and yelled a battle cry as she attacked the first man who entered the narrowed hallway. He took a defensive stance, waiting for the remaining guards. The second one to arrive threw a chair at Lana and attacked her as she tried to dodge the flying furniture. He closed the distance and, despite all her training as an imperial protector, Lana's slighter build was no match for the brute force of the man's attack. She lashed out with a kick that caught his shins, but he stomped a kick toward her knee. He swung his sword low, and as Lana blocked it, he smashed his fist into her nose. Kathleen saw Lana crumple to the floor — the guard stabbing her through the heart as she and Lilly rounded the corner.

"They killed her!" Kathleen screamed to Lilly as they ran through another door that led to the kitchen.

More guards poured out from the gates across the courtyard. Guards on top of the walls directed them toward the fleeing women. Cooks and servants leaped out of the way of the fleeing Princess and the imperial protector with a bloody sword.

"We cannot fight them all!" Kathleen said. She thought for a moment about using her powers, but there was only grass and a few shrubs in the courtyard where they stood. This was nothing like the ancient forest near the mountains, where tree after tree stood like sentinels of freedom. She could not save Lilly here.

"Run to get help. Find Heathron if you can!" Kathleen said.

Lilly nodded, eyes wide.

The guards were coming.

"I will hide in the Smuggler's Quarters until I can find help," Lilly said. "I will not abandon you!"

"Go!" Kathleen replied, "warn Melva and set Kendra free."

Lilly quickly scaled the corner of the wall before the guards could follow. They surrounded Kathleen as she held her wrists out in front of her in defeat.

"We're putting you in irons," a guard said as they clamped them on her wrists and made her walk chained, at the point of the sword.

The gathering crowd parted when Lord Balfoest walked into the courtyard, breathing heavily.

He walked up to Kathleen, drew back his arm, and swung his open palm in a powerful arc. He slapped her across the face, and the force of the blow almost turned her in the opposite direction.

She held her arms up waiting for another blow.

"Drag the witch to her room," Balfoest said. "I will be there shortly."

As Kathleen was roughly handled by her captors, she heard Lord Balfoest say to the leaders of his guardsmen, "Unfortunately, no one in the kitchens or courtyard who witnessed this attempted escape can be left alive. Blame it on the witch. It is her fault after all."

49

TURNCOAT

The skeletal figure of Lars Balfoest slowly penned a letter while sitting at Kathleen's own writing table. That made Kathleen seethe.

"My father will come looking for me," Kathleen insisted with more certainty than she actually felt.

"No one will even suspect you are missing," he replied. "Everyone believes that you are sick. Evidently, you couldn't stand the cold and caught the consumption. It is rumored that you dallied in sorcery and became ill as a result."

The man stood and stretched and handed the letter he had written to a servant waiting quietly in the corner. Then Lord Balfoest walked across her bed chamber and stood in the corner looking closely at the wall.

"It should be here somewhere," he muttered.

"His long fingers found their way into a crack and with a click, Kathleen saw the corner widen as a hidden door opened in the wall. Lars pushed the door open further. No windows illuminated the narrow spiral stairs that led downward to the darkness.

"Heathron made it convenient for me to use your rooms. Lord

Balfoest gestured into the darkness of the secret door. "After you, Princess," he said.

Kathleen resisted.

"Where does this lead?" she demanded.

"Carry her, if you must," Lord Balfoest said impatiently.

One of the guards came forward and grabbed the chain that connected her wrists. He yanked her wrists over his right shoulder as he stooped to pick her up, heaving her onto his shoulder like a sack of meal.

Kathleen began to scream.

"Somebody help me!" she shouted in a shrill voice, but as the darkness enfolded them, and the heavy steps of her captor drummed on the spiral stairs, she realized no one could hear her scream.

Kathleen turned to sobs when she realized, with a sinking heart, that only her enemies might know her location.

Lord Balfoest began speaking again, as if he had not heard her crying for help.

"I haven't decided what to say for sure, but I suppose telling the city that you are now confined to your apartments, would work. I could say the Prince is so in love with you that he is staying by your side, day and night, unwilling to leave. He refuses food even, he is so lovestruck with your beauty. The Empire must be run by the Council of Nine."

His evil smile, with receding gums, matched his eyes in the darkness.

"We will deal with Heathron in due time," he continued. "You will stay here tonight. We have work for you to do in the morning."

The heavy iron door slammed shut.

"Can anyone hear me?" Kathleen called out.

There was no answer but her own echo. The room felt wet, and there was a chill in the air. Kathleen shivered with cold and walked the perimeter of the room, trying to keep herself from panicking.

As her eyes adjusted to the darkness she began to see a faint circle of light, only slightly different from the surrounding black shadows.

The room was five steps wide at the door and eight steps by the wall. Kathleen looked out a small opening in the wall and saw faint stars in the night sky. She could tell the walls were thick because the slightest movement from one side or the other obscured the tiny twinkling dots of light.

"Help!" she yelled, trying to see if there was any response.

There was nothing but the sound of her own breathing. She felt along the ground to see if there was anything on the floor. She could feel the edges of the stones. Her fingers searched in the darkness and a few large, hairy spiders scampered over them. She drew her hand back with a sharp breath, then gingerly felt her way forward along the floor again.

She found a piece of rock that seemed to be loose. Kathleen picked at it with her fingernails. The small stone came free, and she tapped the rock against the dungeon door again and again, calling for help. After hours of trying, she finally stopped. Her voice was hoarse from the effort. Kathleen sat with her back against the wall, facing the door. She pulled her knees to her chest, circling her arms around them — she sat shivering.

Kathleen remained like that all night. Her mind ran over the events that led to her captivity. Her best friend turned out to be an enemy, and that tore her heart most deeply.

"How could she do it?" Kathleen asked herself again and again. "We were friends."

Kathleen felt haggard but could not sleep. Hours passed in the darkness and the small circle of light began to brighten.

"Now it's time to see if Larissa was telling the truth," a voice outside the cell called. The door swung open and a helmeted guard grabbed Kathleen by the arm. He yanked her to her feet so quickly that Kathleen lost one shoe. Then he pulled her violently toward the door.

In the torchlight of the hallway Kathleen could see the mud on her knees and feet. She was still shaking from the cold. She ascended the circular steps, back to the beautiful private rooms Heathron had made for her.

"How was your rest, Plant Witch?" Lord Balfoest asked. "Are you prepared to work today?"

"I demand to speak to the Council of Nine. I am Princess Kathleen Dal Sundi of Candoreth, Daughter of the Realm. What you're doing is a crime. I demand justice," Kathleen said.

"You're in no condition to demand anything. You illegally entered our city under the pretense of marrying into the royal family. You knowingly violated our traditions by keeping secret what you really are."

Balfoest paused and cocked his head, looking at her like a bird examining a worm.

"Bring her to the garden," he commanded.

"I will walk. You do not need to drag me," Kathleen said with as much imperiousness as she could muster. Would that save her? It would at least preserve her dignity — her pride. Wearing only one shoe on her foot, they crossed the flagstones of the floor in her bedroom.

"Make it grow," Lord Balfoest said, pointing to a small vine at the edge of the garden.

Kathleen hesitated. "I..."

"Do it. Make it grow."

"I don't know what you're talking about."

Balfoest sighed. "I don't know exactly how it works because I've never seen it before," he said. "But I understand the general idea. Make it grow."

"I haven't had breakfast," she said. "I'm hungry, and these manacles are hurting me."

The guard behind her slammed a spear handle into her side. She cried out in pain and clutched her side, falling to the floor.

"Don't hurt her," Balfoest said. "She needs to be able to work. Take the chains off of her."

"My father will come for me," she said. "You will pay the price for this treatment with your life."

"I sent a letter telling your father of your delicate condition. We control the communication. He won't come looking for you or we will stop the food shipments if he does."

"I sent Melva in a ship to bring the news," Kathleen said, hoping to bluff her way to freedom.

"No, you didn't Princess," Balfoest smiled. "We gathered Eldin's ship up neatly at the harbor's mouth. The only news leaving Tyath is the news I send. Bring the Meat Witch in so Princess Dal Sundi knows I'm telling the truth. I have a feeling we'll need the old hag shortly," he said.

The door opened. Melva came in, her eyes were downcast and her wrists were bound together.

"Make the vine grow," Lord Balfoest said again.

"Don't you dare hurt her!" Kathleen said.

"Oh, I wouldn't dream of hurting my witches. How else do you expect me to keep you healthy?" he said with a smile.

Another guard came in with Larissa standing beside him.

"You said we would share in the power! I would have a place in the palace. You lied to me!" Larissa said tossing her golden curls angrily.

"If you have no loyalty to your best friend, how can I ever expect loyalty from you?" Balfoest asked. "Last night Kathleen said she loved you like a sister. If that's true, you may still be useful to me."

Kathleen remained looking at the stones. She did not look at Larissa.

The foolish girl.

"If you don't make the vine grow, I'm going to hurt Larissa,"

Lord Balfoest said.

"You're a monster," Kathleen cried.

"You will find out how much of a monster I can be if you do not do as you're told," he replied.

Kathleen wasn't sure if she had the strength. The space from where the vines sprouted along the edge of the garden to where she stood was quite a distance. She wondered if she could make the plant grow fast enough to do any good. Adrenaline pumped in her veins. She decided to try.

She knelt down and placed her hands along the vine's roots. The guard leaned forward, still keeping his distance. He had no desire to be too close to a demonstration of sorcery.

She placed her hands on the gentle petals. Then she squeezed her eyes shut and acted as if she was straining herself greatly. She opened her eyes.

"I don't know if I can do it," she said softly.

Balfoest grabbed Larissa by the wrist and held her hand, palm outward. He closed his hand over her first two fingers and bent them backwards. A loud snap was followed by a scream.

Larissa held her hand in front of her face. Her two fingers were bent at an odd angle.

"Leave her alone!" Kathleen cried.

"Make the vine grow!" Lord Balfoest shouted over the sound of Larissa screaming.

The guard stepped forward to land another blow with his spear, but as he drew back and thrust forward, Kathleen dove flat on her stomach and closed her hands firmly around the base of the vine. With every ounce of Talent, she willed it to grow.

Kathleen conducted the vine's growth in the direction of the guard that was recovering from his misplaced strike. She could feel the vine thickening in her hand immediately. It twisted around his legs, knocking his helmet off and spiraling up his neck and across his face.

Kathleen guided the plant, cinching it tighter and tighter

around the guard. She squeezed the base of the plant and it coiled even more tightly around his body. The vine continued to respond, crushing the guard.

Kathleen looked up to see Lord Balfoest laughing. The image shocked her. As she released the hold on the vine, Balfoest held a knife to Melva's throat while Larissa continued to weep over her broken fingers.

"I don't need the Meat Witch after all," he threatened. "I'll kill her now, if you don't back away from the guard."

Kathleen let go of the vine and took a few steps back. The gurgles of the guard on the floor finally subsided.

"I knew you had it in you," he said. "And for Abboth's sake, stop your whining! Heal her," Lord Balfoest said to Melva, while pointing his knife to Larissa.

Melva knelt and within moments Larissa had stopped sobbing. Her fingers appeared like new.

"Put them back in chains, I think we have a clear understanding of their Talents," Lord Balfoest said.

He walked to the table and picked up a small potted plant.

"Do you know what this is, Princess?" he said.

Kathleen looked at the small plant with broad, flat leaves and blue veins running vertical on the leaves of the stem.

She shook her head.

"I have never seen the plant before," she admitted.

"This is the dream powder plant. It's called *Kabris* by some. It's very difficult to grow and even more difficult to find," Balfoest said. "The Delathranes warriors harvest it in the wild. They chew the leaves and use it for their visions when they become a man. But we have developed ways of concentrating the *Kabris* extract. We make it into a powder — much more potent and much more...enjoyable."

Balfoest smiled proudly.

"But my supplies have been dwindling. The barbarians have only been able to supply me intermittently with the plants I need to satisfy the market we've created. That's where you come in. You will use your Talent to grow a crop for me each day."

"I would rather die than help you corrupt other people," Kathleen said.

"I'm sure you would, but I promise you will not die. Instead, your friends here will wish they had. I will carve them up slowly, bit by bit, on any day that you refuse to do as you're told. Thankfully Prince Heathron constructed the garden so that you could practice your dark art secretly. Now we will put it to use. With enough of these plants, we can pay off our enemy. The barbarians will be so needy for dream powder, they'll have no desire to fight."

Balfoest laughed.

"Don't you find it ironic that they give us the raw materials to create the products that will destroy them? Only now, because of you, I don't need to wait on their bundles of dried leaves. I can buy them off in no time, along with half of the people in Tyath. So, what I need you to do is to make this plant grow. The barbarians say when it is mature it will send forth flowers that each contain a seed. That is what I want."

Kathleen didn't see a way out. The man would torture her friends if she didn't comply.

Balfoest forced the plant toward Kathleen.

"Now make this grow nice and slowly," he said.

Kathleen touched the potted plant. She's focused her Talent slowly, watching as the plant grew. She could feel it become stronger as it grew, pulling nutrients from the soil in the pot. Finally, just as Balfoest had predicted, blue flowers bloomed on the tall stock and then became swollen with pods full of sprouts coming out of each one.

"Very nice," Balfoest said. "Now, you will plant the seeds," he said to Melva and Larissa. "And in the morning my Plant Witch will make them grow again. Put them back in their cells, remove every living thing from that soil. All will be prepared in the morning."

50

PAINFUL LIES

"I am sorry to inform you that there has been a case of the sickness within the city," the Luzian priest declared to the congregation. A murmur of concern swept over the faithful gathered in the pews. "Two cases in fact," he added.

Voices rose, unbidden in the stillness of the Great Cathedral.

"Fear not," he said. "All of the proper remedies were followed to make sure the sickness did not spread. The personal items of the victims were burned. Their clothing, bedding, and blankets were consumed by Abboth's fire. 'How?' You might ask, 'and who?'"

The priest raised his hands and gestured for the people to quiet down.

They finally complied.

"Are you wondering if Abboth will ever accept our sacrifice? Haven't enough of our loved ones died? To what do we own such harshness from our God?" the priest said.

Lars Balfoest leaned over to Lord Naystrom.

"Now it will get interesting," he remarked.

They sat in the high seats reserved for the Council of Nine in a balcony overlooking the congregation, projecting an image of strength and stability.

"What is about to be announced might shake the city to its core," Lord Balfoest said, smiling.

The pieces are fitting together nicely, he thought.

"Our very own Prince Heathron Dol Lassimer, Heir to the throne here in the Golden City, has been taken by the Sickness." A few cries could be heard from the people. "He planned to marry the Princess from Candoreth, and it has been discovered that she is a Plant Witch! She belongs to the Cursed Ones and tried to use her sorcery to lull the Prince into a marriage that would give her the throne! As a result, they both were smitten by the Sickness and died!"

The people gasped.

"Liar!"

A single voice rang out under the dome of the Great Cathedral.

Followed by the clip clip clip of a cane being used to walk on the vast marble.

"Do not lie to the people while standing at the altar in Abbath's house," the voice said. "You will stand before God to answer for what you are doing."

"Who is that?" Lord Naystrom said, looking down at the old priest making his way toward the front.

"That is Father Wittenbrook. He is a bit eccentric. He has been in the service of the Church my whole life, and never risen above the level of a simple priest. I don't expect him to make much trouble," Lord Balfoest said.

"I am the Prince's Confessor," Father Wittenbrook continued. "I should have been called to his bedside to give him and his betrothed their final rites."

The priest at the altar hesitated. "Their bodies have been burned along with all of their belongings. It would have been dangerous to go near them," he said.

"I was administering to the sick long before you were born," Father Wittenbrook said. "I was there when the fields of Tyath were churned to dig the multitude of graves for our people during the Great Sickness. I did not shrink then, nor do I shrink now, when I am called...but I was never called," he said.

"We have all heard of your wondrous acts of yesteryear, Father Wittenbrook," the young priest said, trying to silence the old man, "but each of us must serve Abboth in our own way. Abboth does not give us all miracles. We cannot count on a miracle when our lives are on the line," he said.

"You see, that is exactly when you must count on it!" the old priest said, leaning on his cane. "Faith precedes the miracle."

"I only wanted to inform the people to warn them of the dangers we face from Abboth's wrath if we allow the Cursed Ones in our midst."

"What about Abbath's grace? You Luzians love to focus on the righteous anger of our God, but what of his love? Why do you never speak of that anymore? Abbath is love," the old priest said as he looked around at the people and the expansive ceiling overhead.

"That is what this Great Cathedral was meant to inspire: awe at the grace he gives, not fear."

The younger priest stepped back allowing Father Wittenbrook to climb the steps to the raised rostrum. He pointed to the brilliant windows of colored light.

"Do you think this holy edifice was built by stone cutters on scaffolding? No!" he said his voice quivering.

"It was built by the Builders guild within the first century of our people settling in Desnia. They used their Talent to lift the stones directly from the earth at our feet and stack them to such great heights! This cathedral in which you worship was built by Talented priests who used the Talent in service to Abbath."

"Blasphemy!" the younger priest said angrily.

"Read the ancient texts! They are available to you all," pleaded the old priest.

"We are the arbiters of God's word," the younger man said. "If you continue in this madness, Father Wittenbrook, I will have you removed from the service."

Father Wittenbrook ignored the younger priest.

"You do not need the Luzian priests to tell you how to believe," he said to the congregation. "We have each been given Talents by Abbath to share and bless the lives of others. Kathleen Dal Sundi was not a witch, hungry for power. She was a sweet soul who I am proud to have met, if only briefly."

The Luzian priest motioned for those who provided security for the holy space. The brothers in brown robes quickly began to climb the steps to the raised rostrum where Father Wittenbrook spoke with outstretched arms.

"Those with the Talents are not cursed. They are blessed. I'll show you," he said and reached into his pocket to retrieve a few sheets of wrinkled parchment.

"That is enough, Father Wittenbrook. You must leave at once!" one of the brothers said.

Father Wittenbrook cleared his throat and began to read,

"'And now in the fifth month of our arrival, thanks be to Abbath, we have finished the Great Cathedral and held our first official service in this new colony of Desnia.' How did they build it in five months? Did the masons quarry the stone and cut it with such intricate details? Allow me to continue..."

"Come with us Father," the guard said as he grasped the old man's arm and began to forcibly remove him from the great hall.

"The walls have been built," Father Wittenbrook continued as he was being led away, "...and they have the appearance of gold. Green Growers are planting crops in the fertile land toward the Clearwater Sea, surely we are a blessed people in a blessed land."

"False teachings will not be tolerated," the younger priest said.

"He is right, you know," Lord Naystrom said to Lord Balfoest.

"All the evidence I have been able to see indicates that the old priest is correct. The Talented people were not hated by the Church, and they were welcomed not only by the academy, but by the military and priesthood also."

"Times change," Lord Balfoest said.

They could hear the elevated voice of Father Wittenbrook as he was led away into the recesses of the rooms beneath the main sanctuary.

"I don't believe the Prince is dead. I want to see him with my own eyes," the priest could be heard to say.

"Yes, times change," agreed Lord Naystrom.

51

LUKALD'S LETTER

"We got another letter from Katie!" Elayna said as she burst through the door of her father's office. Queen Renata huffed and moved toward the window seat as the little girl ran into the arms of her father.

King Lukald Dal Sundi swept the little Princess up into a powerful embrace and swung her around as she laughed with glee.

"Let me see it, Elayna!" he said.

"It's got the big castle on it but not the fox," Elayna said, holding the folded paper up in front of her father's face. The letter was sealed with blue wax. It was clearly from Tyath. The handsome paper featured the embossed outline of the Golden City with the towers and skyline punctuated by the cathedral and the royal palace, but the heraldry of the fox and acorn were absent.

"Let me look at it, my little darling," King Lukald said as he playfully reached for the letter.

Elayna pulled it away from her father's grasp, giggling.

"Promise me you will read it to me!" Elayna said, squirming in his arms.

"Of course, I'll read it to you! We all want to hear news of what Katie is doing in the capital," Lukald agreed.

Renata sighed. "I just want to hear when she gets married. I don't care what summer or winter outings she is involved in."

The servant Sam approached the King.

"Princess Elayna wanted to bring you the letter, Your Majesty. I hope I have not ruined your concentration," he said.

"Nonsense! My mornings are always better when Elayna visits with me."

"It gives him a reason to avoid what he should be doing," Queen Renata said in a snide voice as she filed the nails of her left hand. "He hasn't been able to clear the pirates from the trade lanes for a month. If House Dol Lassimer wasn't sending grain and gold, we would truly be in dire straits."

King Lukald ignored the comment.

"Let me open the letter, then we can read it, Elayna," the King said as he set the letter on the desk.

Lukald looked at the letter. The writing did not look like Kathleen's. It was a more angular script than that of his daughter's. He frowned and turned the letter over. It was clearly an official letter from Tyath, although he did not recognize the seal stamped with blue wax.

Could it be from Heathron? he wondered.

Lukald lifted the daub of blue wax and unfolded the letter. He loved to read of the many activities Kathleen had shared with them. He suspected that she was not completely truthful about the ease with which she had become friends with so many of the young nobility, but then again, she could not have made up every detail. King Lukald's heart swelled with pride each time he read a letter from Kathleen. It was an escape from the challenges he faced every day to maintain his own realm. He thought this as he steered a quick glance at Queen Renata.

"Well, let's see what Katie and the Prince have gotten themselves into this time!" he smiled, and Elayna snuggled into her father's chest as they sat at his desk.

His eyes found the heading of the letter, and he immediately realized it was not a letter at all like the others.

"Read it, father!" Elayna cried with excitement.

"Very well, he placed his large finger at the beginning and started to read out loud;

"King Lukald Dal Sundi
Monarch of Candoreth and Liege of Sundiland,"

"That's you, right?" Elayna interrupted, knowing the answer.

"That's me," Lukald said, but as his eyes slid further down the page he stopped reading aloud. His eyes scanned ahead, and his vision seemed to blur.

Your Majesty.
It is with our deepest condolences that we must write to you.
The Capital City is in mourning for both our own Prince Heathron Dol Lassimer and your daughter, Kathleen Dal Sundi. He stopped.

"Is everything alright, Your Majesty?" Sam asked, noting the sudden change in the King's demeanor.

"Take Princess Elayna and get her some breakfast. I'll be along shortly," he said. His voice trembled slightly as he spoke.

"But I want to read the letter with you, father!" Elayna said.

"Lukald, what is it?" Renata said, standing suddenly as she sensed a change of the mood in the room.

Sam nodded seriously and obediently placed his hands on Elayna's shoulders to escort her from the office.

The little girl protested, but King Lukald didn't hear it. He remained seated. He felt numb.

"Why is Father crying?" Elayna said, fear rising in her voice as she was led toward the hallway.

Sam responded with words designed to distract the child.

"What has happened?" Renata demanded.

Through force of will alone, Lukald continued to read silently. Queen Renata stood behind him now and read over his shoulder.

"They swiftly contracted and succumbed to the ravages of the Sickness that has plagued our lands for a generation.

Despite the ministrations of our best physicians, they were not able to regain their health. Even the woman Melva, the Red Grower, was not able to save Princess Kathleen.

After months together this beautiful couple, in the flower of their youth, was found deceased. They passed in a last embrace, looking over the eastern wall, taking in the beauty of the Clearwater Sea.

May Abboth bless them in their journey to the next life.

With our deepest sympathy,

The Council of Nine

Capital City of Tyath"

Nine signatures followed.

"Oh dear Abbath," the Queen said.

Lukald heard a moan that rose into a wail of pain. He recognized his own voice. He crumpled the letter in his fists and threw his head back in agony. He wanted to tear the letter into pieces, rejecting the bitter words that spoke of his daughter's demise. It could not be!

Renata quickly closed the door of the office and turned back toward the King.

"Get ahold of yourself, Lukald! The servants will hear you," she said when the door was shut.

The big man shook with tremors of grief.

"My little girl!" he cried. Sobs racked his chest and when his hands passed over his face, the queen took a step back. Lukald finally stood and went to the window. He looked out at the stretch of beach where he had ridden so many times with Kathleen. He felt the pain return that he had subdued from the loss of his wife. "Annalise!" he cried to the blue sky outside.

Renata stood with her hands on her hips watching him.

"Do you think they will still send us supplies?" she said.

King Lukald blinked amidst the tears.

"Is that all you can say right now, Renata?" he asked.

"Well you are obviously unmanned — someone needs to think of the consequences to Candoreth if the marriage is not ever going to take place..."

· "Get out!" Lukald said.

The tone was the one he used in battle — the same voice belonged to the beast within him that yelled a battle cry, swung the axe, and reveled in blood. If she did not leave immediately, he was unsure of what he might do next.

The queen shook her head in disappointment and then grabbed her skirts and stepped quickly into the hall. She left the door of the office open and King Lukald roared again, uncaring if the entire kingdom heard his pain.

52

DUNGEON SLAVES

The days seemed to blend one to the next. Kathleen lost count as she waited, shivering each night until the dungeon door would open again. Every morning she was made to climb the narrow spiral stairs to her secret garden where she could feel the sunlight again. The bright light made her squint, and she reached her hands up to block it until her eyes became accustomed. The beautiful room Heathron had built for her had become part of her prison. The guards dragged her from her cell and led her to the edge of the enclosure under glass. New *Kabris* shoots were set in neat rows.

"Good morning, Princess Kathleen," Lord Balfoest said. "The planters have done their work, and now it's time to make it grow again."

Kathleen exhaled in dejection. She didn't think she could do it again. She moved slowly, unwilling to bend her back to touch the small plants.

"Do it!" Balfoest commanded.

"I can only grow so much. I only have so much strength," Kathleen protested.

"You're more powerful than you lead me to believe," Lord Balfoest said.

Kathleen shook her head defiantly. "I need time to rest. Look at me!"

She held up her arms. They were thinner and her dress clung to her body, now soiled with the dirt of the many days of labor.

"We need more food than what you give us. We'll all starve if you're treating the others any worse than me."

"You will do as I command," he said.

Kathleen kept her hands clenched.

"You're using the *Kabris* to make dream powder. I won't be a part of it," she said.

"You don't have a choice, Princess. A Plant Witch like yourself is only valuable as a slave."

Kathleen told herself she wouldn't cry again, not in front of him.

"Allow Melva and Larissa to stay with me. There is enough room in my cell. At least let us huddle together for warmth. What harm could come of it?"

The guard used his spear shaft to crack Kathleen across the back. "Bend down and do your job," he said, impatient with her negotiating.

Kathleen's face was only inches from the *Kabris* plants. She felt rage. She shook her head, kneeling in the dirt.

"I won't do it, not until you let us be together and rest for a day," she insisted.

"You will do it today and any day I tell you that you must," Lord Balfoest said.

The guard rained another blow on her back, pushing her to crouch on all fours. Kathleen cried out from the pain and tears began to flow. Her lips shook.

"I would rather die than bend anymore to your tyranny."

Lord Balfoest squatted down in front of her.

"It looks like our red-haired beauty still has some fight left in her," he said with a sneer.

He grabbed Kathleen by the hair and pulled her head back, looking into her eyes. His skeletal face cast a shadow over her cheek. "There is nothing you can do, Princess. You belong to me and me alone. You will do as I say, or you will suffer."

"You won't get away with this."

Lord Balfoest looked around at the emptiness of the courtyard and laughed. His guards joined him in malicious mirth.

"And who is here to stop me, my dear? Who would hear you scream? Who would care? No one."

The words threatened to crush any hope Kathleen felt.

"Heathron cares," she said softly.

"What was that?"

"Heathron still cares. I don't know what you've done to him, but he would use his influence to help me if he could."

"Who do you think is helping to plant the *Kabris* every night?" Lord Balfoest laughed.

"Then let him stay with me," Kathleen insisted.

"Your rebelliousness is going to cause you to suffer," he said slowly.

He grabbed her hand and placed it on the plant.

"Now grow the crops or I'll have my guardsman Karl set his dogs on all three of your friends."

Kathleen grabbed the small plant in her hand, crushing it and yanking it from the ground.

"I won't do it. I'll die before you put me back in that prison alone."

Lord Balfoest slapped her across her face. "Grow it!" he commanded.

"You have nothing that I need. You have no leverage on me except the pain you can inflict," she said.

"That may be true, but you have not yet experienced even a small part of the pain that I can inflict," he said slowly.

He stood and kicked Kathleen in the gut. She fell onto the dirt grabbing her stomach and curling into a ball.

"Your friends will pay the price for your insolence," he said. "Bring them in."

Karl nodded and walked briskly from the enclosed garden. The younger guard watched with a stoic expression. A few minutes later, he brought Larissa, Melva and Prince Heathron into the courtyard. Larissa walked quietly with her head down. Melva looked only briefly to catch Kathleen's eye. There was a fire there still! Kathleen was sure of it. Heathron saw her and called out.

"Kathleen!"

He was only able to say her name before Karl knocked him to the floor. Heathron's ankles were chained together and he was not able to catch himself. The remorse in Larissa's expression was beyond compare.

"I'm sorry, Kathleen," she mouthed when Karl was not looking.

"You are an animal," Kathleen cried.

He smiled. "No, I am the steward of the empire, and you are a witch, and have no rights. Make the plants grow," he commanded.

Kathleen shook her head. "Give us food and clean water. No chains. Let us all share my cell," she said.

Balfoest turned to the guard. "Get the dogs," he said.

Karl returned with two massive animals on a leash. The dogs growled low and raised their lips revealing sharp canines. Their hackles raised when they saw Kathleen and the others. The smaller guard flinched at the sight of the dogs but remained silent.

"These are a couple of my Horming Mastiffs," Lord Balfoest said. "They have been trained by Karl and myself. We like to keep the dogs of our kennel...service ready," he said ominously.

Lord Balfoest approached the dogs and touched each one on the neck. He closed his eyes and seemed to savor the viciousness they exuded. Larissa huddled close to Melva and Heathron. She shook her head and shrank behind the other two.

"You must stop this, Lord Balfoest!" Kathleen said.

"Make the *Kabris* grow," he replied slowly. His voice sounding like a demon.

"Not today," Kathleen replied, "I told you my demands."

Lord Balfoest released the dogs. "Attack!" he said, pointing at the group of prisoners.

The sound of their nails clawing stone as they ran was terrifying. They growled as they ran toward the huddled mass of her friends.

Kathleen threw her hands to her face, not wanting to witness the savagery. Nothing could stop the mastiffs now except a command from Lars Balfoest. Heathron bravely tried to step forward, shackled as he was, but the Prince was outnumbered and outweighed by the dogs. They took him down and immediately began to rip his arms and back with sharp teeth. The women cried out for him. Their screams rose up to the highest arches of the vaulted ceiling and Karl encouraged the dogs while Kathleen screamed in horror at the attack.

"Release!" Lord Balfoest shouted to the dogs.

The attack stopped immediately. The bloodied jaws and snout of the Horming Mastiffs were set on powerful necks and shoulders. A few more seconds of the attack and the victims surely would have been dead. The dogs stood quivering in anticipation, excited for the next command. Larissa's sobs rose and fell with the panting of the dogs.

"Look what you have done," Lord Balfoest said to Kathleen.

Kathleen met the gaze of the young guard that held her. She thought she saw a flicker of regret in his eyes.

"Let me go to them," she pleaded.

Lord Balfoest nodded to the guard and called the massive dogs to his side.

Kathleen ran to the edge of the garden and collapsed beside

Heathron. His shoulder was shredded and his thigh was torn deeply. He groaned in pain, afraid to look up for fear of another attack. Larissa held pressure on her forehead where the dogs had slashed her scalp.

"Allow the Princess to discuss the situation with her friends tonight. You may give them better food and clean water as she requested. Take off the chains and make sure they are ready to work tomorrow."

"Tomorrow?" the young guard asked, looking at the wounded and bleeding prisoners.

"The Meat Witch will need to have them ready," Balfoest said.

Melva rolled to her side and sat up, dazed. She was bleeding profusely. "I used to own a Horming Mastiff once, but mine was gentle," she said, before collapsing to the floor.

53

FORGIVENESS

D rops of blood stained the narrow spiral stairwell. Red droplets fell from the fingertips and soaked the feet of the prisoners as they hobbled toward their shared confinement. The guards escorted them down to Kathleen's deep cell, tucked against the thick outer walls of Tyath. When the heavy door slammed shut, the finality of the sound was softened by the fact that they were no longer alone.

Kathleen helped to prop Melva against the wall. Food and water were delivered as agreed. Multiple bowls of food including roasted meat, bread and broth were placed inside the cell.

Kathleen's trembling hand touched the face of her betrothed as Heathron took a labored draught of water and tore a few pieces of bread to feed Melva.

"We need her," Kathleen said, "soak the bread in broth. That might help."

Heathron used his uninjured hand to carefully place the softened food into Melva's mouth. Kathleen knelt beside him and helped to move her jaw a bit.

"Hopefully she can swallow a small amount," Heathron said.

The Red Grower began to stir and move her lips. Her eyes

opened slowly and she looked at her surroundings in the dim cell. She swallowed and took a deep breath.

"I was having the most wonderful dream," she said, in her ancient voice, "I thought I smelled roasted duck."

"I'm not sure what this is," Larissa said, still wincing every time she moved, "but it tastes like chicken to me."

Melva reached a hand out toward the girl and was rewarded with a meaty leg-bone of some fowl. The old woman weakly accepted the food and took a bite on her own, chewing the meat purposefully.

"Thank you for the bread and broth, Heathron, but the meat is what will allow me to Heal again," she said.

To the surprise of everyone the old woman stood up.

"I would be dead long ago if I had not learned to infuse my body with power from the essence of life. Hand me another piece of that duck," she said as she placed a hand on Larissa's head.

The old woman began chanting and Larissa gasped. When Melva stopped, the young woman removed her hand without fear of her scalp coming with it.

"I'm healed," she said in surprise looking up at Melva.

"And you are no more likely to suffer the Great Sickness than you were before," Melva said.

Larissa held out her arm where the dogs had bitten her. She wiped away the blood from her arm and felt for the puncture wounds that had been there. Melva went on to administer to Heathron with soft chanting.

Kathleen watched Larissa. A cold knot of anger still festered within her whenever she looked at her.

"I don't deserve this," Larissa said. "I am the reason we are all here. I betrayed all of you."

"You have been used, Larissa," Kathleen replied. "You care more about your own comfort than those that love you. Renata acts the same way, and I hate it."

"You could have helped us. Instead..." Heathron swallowed

and didn't finish what he was going to say, but Larissa understood the meaning.

"I'm so very sorry," she said, looking at both of them.

"'Sorry' doesn't help us regain our freedom. You tripped me when I tried to get away! You don't deserve to be Healed or free," Kathleen said.

Heathron looked at Larissa with horror. "You tripped her?"

"I know!" Larissa said with a shudder.

"She still must stand trial for what she has done. Lana died the day she accused me," Kathleen said angrily.

Heathron placed a comforting arm around Kathleen's shoulder as Larissa sobbed.

"Do you think it would have been otherwise if Larissa had been loyal to you? Was she the catalyst for this overthrow of House Dol Lassimer?" Melva asked.

"No," Heathron said. "She was a puppet like so many others, dancing to Lord Balfoest's manipulations."

"There are only four of us here to help one another. Thanks to Kathleen, we are together now, and better fed. There is no good in tearing Larissa apart. The dogs did enough of that for all of us," Melva said.

"Her strings are cut now," Heathron said, "the poor puppet no longer dances to Balfoest's tune."

"I am not ready to forgive you," Kathleen said.

Larissa looked up at the girl who had been her friend since childhood and nodded.

"I'm not ready to forgive myself either, but I have nowhere else to go."

Kathleen got up and walked to the door, looking through the iron bars toward the darkened hallway.

"Why do you resist?" a voice said.

Kathleen turned her head to see the younger guard who brought the food still standing in the hall, listening to them.

"Wouldn't you resist?" she asked, "I am not a slave. Are you?"

The young man winced. He didn't like the question.

"Don't you know there's no way to escape?" he said and walked away.

54

A LONELY LITTLE GIRL

"Your Majesty, we need you to lead the men," Sīhalt Girdy Frast said, with a voice full of concern for his King.

King Lukald Dal Sundi looked out the window, opposite the chambers to the harbor and blue ocean beyond.

"The men of the navy are doing what they can to repair or salvage the ships that had been damaged in the battles among the turtle Islands," the Guardian reported.

Evidence of the violence remained in the charred timbers of one ship, and the broken masts of another.

"I've lost the fight already," the King said, "what would I be fighting for anyway? First Annalise died, and now Kathleen, how can I possibly go on?"

"There is still Elayna," Girdy said earnestly.

They looked down toward the little red-haired girl playing on the beach. Her singing could be heard from the doorway. The servant, Sam, watched close by from the shade of the palms.

"She never tires," Lukald said. "I wish I had even an ounce of her energy."

"Put down the bottle, and you may find you have more strength and courage then you remember," Girdy replied.

"Old friend," King Lukald said, "I don't even have the courage to tell my baby girl that her big sister will never be coming home."

"Children can bounce back quickly from tragedy. I thought she knew."

The King shook his head. "I couldn't bring myself to do it."

Tears welled up in his eyes. "I can barely say it to myself, let alone to little Elayna," he added.

"Death, like birth, is natural," Girdy said. "She will come to understand someday."

"You must tell her, not me," King Lukald insisted.

Girdy began to protest; "I have no right..."

"You were closer to Kathleen than any of us. I know you love my daughters, Girdy. You loved them when I was unable to love them. You've been the stable foundation in their lives that I could only hope to be. So please, I ask you as a friend, take this burden from me and tell Princess Elayna the truth about Kathleen."

Girdy nodded solemnly.

"Yes, Your Majesty," he said with the formality that came from a lifetime of training.

Girdy was sworn to protect. He was sworn to defend. He was sworn to serve, and he would not begin to shirk his duty this late in life.

He turned to go, and paused in the arched doorway. In front of him stretched the beach where Princess Elayna was playing. Girdy placed his hand on the stone column and looked back at his liege.

"Thank you," King Lukald said.

The pain and frank sincerity of his expression made the Sīhalt Guardian accept his assignment with less hesitation.

The Sīhalt nodded.

No father wants to share a thing like this with his child, he thought.

The wind blew his white beard, and caused his thin black cape to dance.

Despite his age, the Guardian walked down the numerous steps leading to the beach with grace and agility. A number of sailors and shipwrights saluted him as he passed.

Girdy saw Sam wave as he approached. The servant sat in the shade — his broad-brimmed hat frayed at the edge.

"Where is Princess Elayna?" Girdy asked.

"Just beyond those palms. She said she's building a sand castle," Sam said.

The Guardian walked in the girl's direction.

"I'll join you," the servant offered, "she's been working on this thing for hours, and keeps asking me to come and see. I suppose I should humor the girl, after all she's been through."

"She doesn't know. The King has not told her," Girdy said.

Sam put his hand over his mouth his eyes grew wider. "Oh no," he said slowly, "you're not going to..."

The Sīhalt Guardian nodded. "It's time she knows. It's only fair," he said.

As they rounded the small grove of palm trees and looked out where the beach gently met the water, the two men were astounded to see the little girl, of no more than eight, putting the final touches on an elaborate sand castle. It mimicked, in perfect detail, the actual Castle of Candoreth, complete with towers, gates, and keep.

"Look what I did!" Elayna said with a cheerful smile, and dropped the wet sand she still held in her hands to run towards Sam and Girdy.

Elayna placed her hands in theirs and led the men toward the Castle.

"Can you see the main hall, and the rooftop?" She asked excitedly.

"There's my room, and there's the window and the balconies for Kathleen's room."

The men looked at each other. A wave of empathy passed over their faces. Sam closed his eyes briefly as if to ward off the sadness.

"It's beautiful, Laynie," the Sīhalt Guardian said.

Girdy got down on one knee and cited along the Sandcastle toward the royal buildings behind it. The little girl had captured every detail, right down to the landscaping. The amount of sand the little girl had moved was impressive and the detail she rendered was gorgeous.

"You're an Artist Laynie." Girdy said with a smile as he placed a hand on Elayna's shoulder.

Elayna beamed. "I've been working on it since breakfast," she said.

"How did you get all the sand here, Elayna," Sam asked. "You piled the sand high to make this castle and I don't even see a hole in the sand. Where is your bucket? Do you have a shovel?"

The little girl giggled. "That's silly, Sam. I didn't use a bucket or a shovel, I used my hands!"

She held up her small hands, sprinkled with sand, and looked at them cross-eyed with her bright green eyes. Then she pranced around the backside of the sand castle, laughing as she did so.

Her cheeks and arms we're lightly dusted with freckles, and Girdy could easily imagine that he was watching her older sister Kathleen, just a few years before.

"The time passes so quickly," Girdy said to the servant. "Elayna is about the same age Kathleen was...when I shared the news of her mother's passing."

"That was a painful day too," Sam said, "the whole kingdom was in mourning."

"I'd rather see a thousand people cry, than that little girl," Girdy said, as he steeled himself to tell Elayna the truth.

Sam turned to look at the harbor, and to hide his emotions from Elayna.

Girdy knelt in the sand and patted his knee.

"Come sit with me Elayna," he said, when the little girl finished skipping around the sandcastle. She ran to him and threw her arms around his neck.

"Do you like it?" she asked in a small, energetic voice.

"I do, Laynie, but I have some sad news to tell you," he said, choking back emotion.

"I already know," Elayna said with a sad face, "some of the sailors died when the pirates burned their ship." The little girl patted Girdy's cheek in an effort to console him. The Sīhalt Guardian gently reached up and took her hand in his.

"That is sad, Laynie, but my news, it's not about the sailors."

"What's making you so sad?" she asked.

Girdy swallowed, he realized his mouth was dry. He could hear the shouts of men working in the distance. The pounding of hammers and the movement of ropes in pulleys was muted by the wind and surf in his ears. He pursed his lips and then begin slowly.

"Do you remember when you got sick and had to stay inside for a long time?"

She nodded.

"The doctor said she had to give you medicine so you would get better."

Again, she nodded her understanding.

"Elayna, when your sister Kathleen went to the Golden City, she became sick. There was no medicine for her, and so she died."

Girdy pulled Elayna close for an embrace.

"I'm sorry," he said.

Princess Elayna wiggled her way out of his grasp and stood up in front of him on the sand. She waved her finger at the Guardian.

"You're teasing me," she said, "Katie isn't dead."

Tears began to roll down Girdy's cheeks despite his attempt at composure.

"It's true, Laynie, your father got a letter from the capital and they said she died. So did Prince Heathron. She will not come home again. I am so sorry."

Elayna furrowed her brow and now stood with arms folded in defiance. Then she leaned in to look Girdy directly in the eyes. With all the certainty of child-like faith Elayna spoke with confidence.

"Katie is not dead," she insisted.

With that, she smiled and turned around and began to work on her sand castle once again.

"She died," Girdy said again, his voice catching in his throat as he spoke.

Elayna looked at him and cocked her head, considering his words.

"My sister will come back. I know it."

"Why don't you believe me?" Girdy asked, wishing in his heart that he too could believe Kathleen would return.

"Because mother died when I was born, so I see her all the time, but I have not seen Katie since she left. So she must be alive," she said happily.

55

FRUITS OF FRIENDSHIP

Kathleen lay with her head on Heathron's chest. She drew closer to him in the chill air of the night. With no blanket to cover them, Kathleen sought the curve of his body for warmth. While she lay on the cold stone floor, Kathleen worked ideas through her mind, considering another plan.

I need to stay a step ahead of Lord Balfoest, she thought.

"Are you still awake?" Heathron whispered.

"Yes. I'm trying to think of a way out of here," Kathleen said quietly. "What about you?"

"I was just thinking how unique our first few nights together have been. This isn't what I pictured," he said, and laughed weakly, which brought with it a short stabbing of pain.

In the stark confines of the cell, they both began to giggle quietly so as not to wake Melva or Larissa. Heathron pulled Kathleen close to less injured side of him, and whispered in her ear.

"I love you, Kathleen."

She wiggled closer to him.

"These nights don't count," she said.

THE NEXT MORNING, she didn't eat the food that was placed before her. Nor did she eat the meals after that. The next day's Growing had been exhausting, and still she did not eat. When she collapsed the second time, next to the garden plot, Lord Balfoest was summoned. The Growing she had been able to complete was meager. Her heart hadn't been in it and her strength was failing.

"Why didn't you feed her?" Lord Balfoest snapped, admonishing the guards as he stormed into the room.

"We did, My Lord," one of the guards replied in a cracked voice. "She refuses to eat."

"She must eat in order to have the power to Grow," Lord Balfoest complained. "Bring me meat. Now."

Within a few seconds, the guard had disappeared and returned with a nervous-looking servant who placed a silver tray before Lord Balfoest. He glanced at the slices of pinkish meat, then he glanced at Kathleen.

"Eat," he commanded.

Kathleen again shook her head. She felt about as ravenous as she did dizzy and faint. She wanted to stuff the food down her throat by the handful, but her will was stronger than her hunger.

"Karl," Balfoest said. "Open her mouth, please."

Kathleen shivered. The guard placed a firm hand on the back of her neck, his fingertips wrapped around her throat.

"Open her mouth and feed her," the man said.

The guard stabbed a silver fork into a few slices of meat and brought it closer to her mouth. Clenching her teeth, Kathleen tried to resist — so the guard stuck his fingers inside her cheek, ramming his finger to the back of her mouth. He pried against her jaw with his thumb, so she could fight him no longer, and stuffed the meat in her mouth. She swallowed and soon felt the strength of a Talented Green Grower returning to her.

Each day Kathleen was forced to grow a new crop of *Kabris*.

Every night the plants were harvested and new sprouts were put into the soil.

Larissa seemed broken. The brightness in her eyes that had once illuminated her smile was gone. A couple of weeks into their captivity, the withdrawal symptoms of the Dream powder hit Larissa. Kathleen considered trying to comfort her as she lay doubled over in agony, writhing on the floor of the dungeon. When Kathleen asked Melva to help, the old woman shook her head.

"I cannot fix this," Melva explained. "It is a different kind of wound to have your freedom supplanted by a potion this strong."

Later that night, Kathleen dreamed of the little blonde-haired girl named Larissa who brought joy into her life after the recent death of her mother.

The next day, Larissa's screams echoed off the stone walls as she pleaded for anything to stop the pain, even just a single *Kabris* leaf to tuck inside her cheek. Her torturous withdrawal began to soften Kathleen's heart.

No one deserves this, she thought.

Kathleen remembered the fun she had with Larissa prior to leaving Candoreth. She had been so helpful and fun. Kathleen actually smiled at the memory of her and Larissa tangled up in a mess on the floor. The Sīhalt Guardian was certain their lives were in danger when he heard the peals of laughter and thought they were screaming.

Finally, the agony subsided and Kathleen lifted Larissa's head from the stone floor. When it seemed Heathron and Melva were asleep, a slender moon beam entered the small hole in the wall, high above their heads. Kathleen tightened her grip on Larissa's hands and whispered in her ear.

"I forgive you," she said to the girl that had betrayed her. A ragged breath and a repentant embrace followed by muted sobbing was Larissa's only reply.

56

NICH

When the dungeon door opened again, Kathleen had already decided to comply. She would grow the plants in order to survive—for now.

Kathleen remembered the younger guard asking the question: 'Why do you resist?'

Why did he ask it of her? Only a person who felt some care would ask such a question.

In the moments before Karl arrived, she asked the younger man, "What is your name?"

"My name is Nich," he replied.

"It is nice to meet you, Nich. My name is Kathleen."

He bobbed his head, almost as if he wanted to bow.

"How long have you lived in Tyath, Nich?" she asked.

"I've lived here all my life."

"Well I've been here less than a year, and I must say it has exceeded all my expectations."

Nich kept looking at her. He glanced down the hallway to see if anyone else was there.

"I remember when you arrived," he said.

"I was knocked unconscious when we came through the gates," Kathleen recalled.

His eyes widened at the memory and he nodded.

"That was a terrifying day with the Delathranes at the gate."

Then his face softened. "I wish you could be free."

Heavy footsteps came as the other guard arrived. Kathleen was yanked roughly into the corridor. She went willingly and Karl was somewhat surprised. He watched her warily, wondering what new tricks the Plant Witch might spring on him.

Over the course of many days, Kathleen cultivated a relationship with Nich. She came to know that he was eighteen years old. He had a little sister, just like her, and he was fascinated with the Southern Realms.

"Do oranges really grow on trees there?" he asked one day.

"I had a whole orchard of them," Kathleen said. "The smell of their blossoms is unlike anything you have ever experienced. The taste of an orange that is fresh from the tree is an experience everyone should have."

Nich's eyes remained bright in the torchlight as Kathleen described her home.

"Mother gives us each an orange on Winterfest," Nich said. "I wait to eat mine so I can have something to look forward to during the long winter."

"Oh, how I would love to taste an orange now," Kathleen said.

Nich looked around.

"I'd share a piece with you Kathleen," Nich said with a smile.

"I wouldn't want to take away your Winterfest gift," Kathleen said, but her heart leapt at his suggestion.

"I've learned more about the Southern Realms from you than I ever learned in school. I'd like to share. Just keep it a secret between us," he said with a flick of his eyes toward the sleeping form of Karl.

Kathleen slept that night with the brightest hope she had in months.

NICH PASSED the slice of the orange to Kathleen the next morning when she was brought from her cell. She slipped it into her mouth before Karl had a chance to see it in her hand. It really was a pitiful segment compared to the large sweet oranges she was used to, but for a moment, she was taken back to Candoreth — a girl in her own private garden.

Citrus oils and sugars burst forth from the fruit. She could almost forget that she lived in a dark, cold, stone cavern. Kathleen tasted the juice and the sweetness within.

"What are you smiling about?" Karl said, as he escorted her up the stairs to the garden above. "You look like a grinning wolvermink if I ever saw one," he added.

Kathleen bowed her head in feigned submission. She didn't want him to see her smile grow wider.

As she used her tongue to separate the flesh of the fruit in her mouth, her lips and teeth slid across a small hard object within the segment of orange.

Her eyes widened and her whole body was filled with the hopefulness of spirit that made her want to sing. She could feel it in her mouth — a seed!

Kathleen went about her duties almost cheerfully and resisted the impulse to hum loudly as she used her Talent to grow the *Kabris* crop for the day. She kept the seed tucked in her cheek, and the feeling of that small, hard knot against her gums comforted her as much as any blanket when she was a child.

When the guards returned Kathleen to her cell, she wanted to hug Nich and even felt no desire to destroy Karl.

"Thank you for everything," she said to both of them.

The guards looked at each other, but only Nich knew of what she spoke.

"I think the Plant Witch is going crazy," Karl said as he closed the door and locked it.

Melva looked up at Kathleen and nodded.

"So, you are making a friend?" she said. "Be careful."

Kathleen ran to Melva's side and showed her the seed.

"Look what I have!" she exclaimed.

The old woman squinted and reached out to touch the seed.

"There are plenty of small pebbles in this room, Kathleen. If I'd know one would make you so happy, I could have given you one sooner."

"No Melva, it's a seed...to an orange tree!"

"Child, I'm glad it gives you hope." She patted Kathleen on the shoulder and nodded in understanding.

"Balfoest has stripped the garden room of everything but *Kabris*. I have not felt the life of any other plant since he began making me grow the miserable crops."

Kathleen walked to the wall and looked up at the small hole cut into the rock above.

"Can you help me up, Heathron? I want to look out if I can."

"I can," he said, as he offered his knee to Kathleen.

She climbed up as far as she could and found a slight toe hold in the rocks to push herself even higher. She stretched for the opening and was able to just get her fingers into the hole. By scrambling up a bit, Kathleen looked out the small opening that was no bigger in diameter than her fist.

She slid her arm along the stone shaft as far she could reach. She pushed the seed into the wall as far as it would go, pushing the seed down into a crack that she could feel with her fingers. "It wouldn't do for Lord Balfoest to find my little seed," she said.

"I don't know what your plan is, child, but I would love to eat a sweet orange if you can manage it," she said.

"I think I will be able to manage a little more than that," Kathleen replied. "I just need to wait until the time is right."

57

PROPHET OF THE RIVER

G rawn Verda looked eastward. His scouts had been making a fuss for days. He controlled the loyalty of all the clans west of the ranges and still they acted like scared children. It was about time he saw the reason for himself. He expected to see the Serpent King at some point. A young chief, full of himself, so drunk with recent victories might have weaknesses. They were all predictable. He had been there himself, years ago.

I'm the oldest warrior on the battlefield, he thought, *and I intend to keep it that way.*

Grawn had some surprises for Cedric of Clan Razewell if it came to that, but the old chieftain did not want to fight the People of the Serpent. None of his scouts had found his daughter and Grawn was beginning to worry that he would not get her back. Ever since he had banished the families who used the *Handri* dream powder, his daughter had been missing. Grawn suspected they had stolen her when she went to the river to fetch water.

"I have little time to waste with this chieftain from the river valley," he said to his first warrior. "The exiled families are to blame for Iskabel's disappearance, and I will not be held up by them."

"Yes, my King," the warrior said as he looked toward the oncoming guests.

The Serpent King rode into the valley. He did so slowly, with only a few of his advisors. He left the remainder of his following at the border.

At least he has some manners, that's one less thing I'll have to teach him, Grawn thought.

Grawn Verda was not surprised by the paleness of the Serpent King. He was not even surprised by the wide, vertical scar running down the young chieftain's face. He had heard the reports. What did surprise him was the size of the man.

Cedric of Clan Razewell was enormous in a way that made the corners of Grawn's mouth turn slightly downward. The Serpent King's shoulders were rounded with ropes of muscle. There was little indication of where his neck finished and his head began. Grawn tried not to swallow, then stopped resisting and swallowed hard.

"You see, it is just as we told you, King Verda. He is a monster," the first warrior said to Grawn.

He waved his hand in a gesture to silence the man at his side.

I am a fool for not calling my riders back earlier, Grawn thought, *They must be three days' ride. I cannot let the Serpent King know that.*

The enormous chieftain dismounted from a very stout horse and sauntered his way to the blanket that Grawn sat upon. He carried a thick ceremonial spear with a cross bar eight inches from the tip. Grawn decided to let the man keep this thing in his hand. He would be wary though.

"King Grawn, I thank you for your hospitality while we pass through your lands. Our horses have eaten your grass, and my men have feasted on your wild game. For this, I am grateful," Cedric said.

Pass through my lands? Grawn thought. *Does he plan to leave or fight?*

"We have plenty of grass and game. But it is only called hospitality if it is offered willingly. Why are you here, Cedric, Serpent King of Clan Razewell?"

"I am gathering the clans of the Delathranes. The time has come for us to reclaim our lands from the great river to the ocean. The Golden City is a harlot that steals from us in the night. She must be removed."

Grawn nodded thoughtfully.

"I see that you believe what you are saying. You have courage to make Tyath your starting point, instead of a smaller town or village, or perhaps you are mad."

"I am mad but not with the effects of drink or dream leaves. I have seen a vision. The Delathranes will run through the streets of the Golden City. Their mighty walls will fall. Of this I am certain."

"You do not have enough men to break the Golden City," Grawn said.

"That is why I have come to collect the warriors of your clans," Cedric said.

"Collect? You say it like they're berries to be harvested in summer. The *Handri* are not my enemy. I have very little to do with them on the western ranges."

"I notice the breastplate and sword you are wearing. Did you obtain this *Handri* armor by poisoning your people through trade with the *Handri*?" Cedric retorted. "The dream powder of the Golden City is harming us all. Even the *Handri* metal is not worth the harm it does."

"This is not *Handri* steel," Grawn said proudly, "but Delathrane. It was made by a smith of the clans from the hills."

"Do our people make metal armor now?" Cedric asked in surprise.

Grawn nodded. "And knives and arrow tips. We are wealthy beyond measure."

"How do you explain this?" Cedric asked.

"We have found those with the ability to pull metal from the earth, without fire."

"The ancient songs speak of it," Cedric said in awe.

"Even the wheels of my chariots are bound in metal now and our beasts wear armor like men," Grawn said proudly.

Cedric's eyes grew bright.

"Join us," Cedric said emphatically.

"We avoid the *Handri*. We do not take them as advisers," Grawn said, gesturing to the foreign men at Cedric's side.

"This is my blood-sworn," Cedric explained, pointing to Seth, "and this is his brother."

"Who is that in the white plumed hat?" Grawn said.

He liked the way the hat looked. It gave the man a flair of energy that commanded respect.

"He represents the military of the kingdom on the sea, the one called Candoreth," Cedric said.

"He must be a brave warrior to wear a hat such as that," Grawn said, nodding approvingly.

"Thank you," the man in the hat said, as he looked at two of his companions raising his eyebrows. The two others smirked at him. Grawn did not understand the dynamic between them.

"Matched against any of your greatest warriors on horseback, he will not back down. I have seen him fight," the Serpent King said.

"You want my warriors to join you in this fight against the Golden City?"

"Your warriors will join me in this fight. What I want is for you to join me as well," Cedric said.

"What if I tell them to stand down?"

Cedric wiped the dust away from one of his eyes with his finger, looking impatient.

"Then we will kill you and any of your men who try to stop us."

"You will try," Grawn said.

A great rock eagle cried overhead. It swooped down and landed on the large spear carried by the Serpent King. One end of the spear was planted into the ground as the great bird settled. Grawn watched as the Serpent King peeled a strip of meat from the bag at his belt and fed it to the bird. The bird screeched and looked fiercely at Grawn who had never seen a rock eagle of such magnitude.

The *Handri* made hand signals to the bird, and it screeched again.

"My other counselor says that your riders are at least three days from here. Do you really want to battle?"

"You have the counsel of eagles?" Grawn said, in surprise.

"I have the counsel of the wind and the rock. I hold talks with the sun and the moon. The stars are my audience. The heavens have spoken, I am not mistaken. We will destroy the Golden City, and you will join us or die standing in our way."

Grawn nodded and swallowed again, thinking of his little girl somewhere in the vast grasslands spread out before him.

"I have a personal matter that must be settled before I go to war," he said.

"I know of your quest," Cedric said and held out his hand.

In his palm he held the ivory comb that Iskabel wore in her hair.

"Where did you get that?" Grawn growled, anger rising in his heart. No matter the size of the warrior before him, if his little girl was harmed by him or one of his men...

"I took it from the people who sold your daughter to the Golden City," Cedric said. "We made them speak the truth before we ended them. They were like ghouls when we found them, but they admitted what they had done."

"She is still alive?" Grawn asked hopefully.

"The hunger for the dream powder is very great. Many will sell their own family to obtain it. They said she was traded to the *Handri* of the Golden City," Jared explained.

"Why would they seek my daughter. There are many girls much closer to enslave."

"Did she not have a Gift? Cedric asked.

Grawn nodded.

"Iskabel is a Plant Witch," he confirmed, then his fists tightened in understanding. He went quiet then, as if watching and reading the now tumbling thoughts fall and scatter. This news had changed everything. This Chief has changed everything. He knew what he had to do. He looked up at Cedric now, almost in awe.

"If she is within those walls, I will help you tear them down, stone by stone. I give you my precious blade as my oath," Grawn said.

Cedric's shoulders relaxed and his broad chest seemed to widen in response. He took a deep breath and smiled.

"I accept your Delathrane blade," Cedric said. "And we will surely use it. If you will honor your vow, wear the sign of the Serpent and Egg from this day on until the walls are broken, and we destroy the blight of the Golden City. I will use your sword to water their stone streets with blood."

Grawn Verda smote his fist against his chest while his best warriors witnessed this act of allegiance.

"I will join you, Cedric, Serpent King of Razewell," he swore.

58

GUARDIAN OF DREAMS

Heathron held Kathleen's head in his lap. The delirium was back. She tossed and turned as she lay on the hard floor. Heathron wished there was something more he could do. They all had been abused for months. He had tried to think of a way to escape, and he was beginning to lose hope.

"I wish I could Heal her, but there is no wound," Melva said.

"She is drawn and stressed from the crucible of this we are enduring," Heathron said.

"Some pains, like those of the mind, cannot be mended by the Talented touch of a Red Grower," Melva said.

Heathron smoothed Kathleen's hair, her forehead was slick with sweat.

"Don't worry. Everything is going to be okay," he whispered to her.

The Prince was by no means certain he spoke the truth.

He hoped Kathleen's value to Lord Balfoest was significant enough to keep them all alive.

Lars Balfoest must have bales of the Kabris leaves by now, he thought.

Kathleen had been working every day to grow a new crop of the *Kabris* leaves. When she was exhausted, he would demand more from her. If she refused, the others were tortured.

He saw the look on Kathleen's face the first day the dogs were set upon them. Something changed within her that day. It was as if she became familiar with the depths of human depravity. She had been so innocent before...

What have I brought her to? he thought.

Heathron tried to sing her to sleep. He struggled to remember a nursery rhyme his mother had sung to him as a child.

Go to sleep my little darling,
When you wake,
You'll patty-patty cake,
And ride a pretty pony,
So, go to sleep my little darling...

He wished there was a better way to comfort her. The weather was even colder now, but Kathleen burned with a fever. He lifted water in his hand and held it to her mouth. Kathleen licked her lips when the water touched them.

"Jared!" she cried out in anguish. "Save me."

The words burned in Heathron's chest. When Melva looked at him, he could not hide the pain in his countenance.

"She is ill Heathron," the old woman said.

"Yet in her darkest hours, it is the Sīhalt Guardian she cries out for, not me. Despite all my efforts to win her love, Kathleen's heart calls out to another, and now I am powerless to protect even her freedom."

"She is delirious, don't hold it against her. The fever will break soon," Melva said.

"I do feel powerless in this! I am a Prince without a throne, and a groom without a home for his bride."

He leaned over her, stroked her cheek softly and whispered—

"What more can I offer you?" he asked.

"Nothing," came the voice like tearing silk. "You cannot offer the girl anything. I own you outright — bridle, rein, and saddle."

Lord Balfoest peered through the narrow bars of the door.

"Can you convince her to work a little harder?" he asked in a mocking tone. "That might help. Like the poor farmers of Tyath, I have crops to grow and harvest. If you can convince her to give me her best effort, I could make all of your lives easier."

"She will continue to grow the plants," Heathron promised.

"Looking out for your own skin, I see. You are a talented politician, Heathron. It is a shame we couldn't have been allies. None of this had to happen."

He indicated the dungeon and the darkness where the prisoners slept each night.

"I suppose I should have more fully considered my options," Heathron said.

Lord Balfoest smiled without kindness.

"Don't punish yourself over it. It was never a sure bet either way. You are not equipped to rule over people like me. Your father —now that was a man to put the fear of Abboth into folks. You didn't see that side of him, but he could be vicious," Lord Balfoest said with a gleam of admiration in his eyes.

"You haven't seen that side of me either, Lord Balfoest," Heathron said.

Balfoest smiled again. "Nor do I intend to."

"My father warned me of the dangers to each generation that spends its days in wealth and luxury. He told me that as an imperial Prince I ran the risk of thinking that all of my wealth was the natural way of things. I could start to believe and act as if I deserved it, and was owed the riches that were mine. He said if I didn't learn from the lessons of those who had ruled before me, I could easily lose the blessings of power and prosperity. I would be forced to learn through my own experiences the lessons that imbued my forefathers. I just didn't expect it to happen so quickly. I've tried to follow his advice and yet here I am."

"Once I have fully consolidated the power at the council, you will have no further value to me. Your friends in the city, and in this cell, grow weaker by the day. Consider well how you would like to spend your last days."

"Just allow Kathleen to rest. She is suffering."

"Very well," Lord Balfoest said, "Work begins in the morning."

Heathron lifted Kathleen carefully by placing one hand behind her knees and sliding the other beneath her back. He noticed how frail she had become. Her body burned with an intense heat. The constant whipsaw of emotions and grueling work of Growing every day, was taking its toll. The Sundiland Princess no longer seemed as full of life and energy. Her face was tired and smeared with the grime of the enclosed quarters.

Heathron didn't feel strong either. Even though he tried to keep his stamina up with personal exercises, he wondered how much longer he could live if circumstances did not change soon. His facial hair had grown, and he was sure his beard looked scraggly. Heathron was glad he couldn't see himself in a mirror. It would have been even more disheartening.

Heathron looked to Melva and Larissa. The Healer was obviously not well. Her body was so thin. Heathron was reminded of a standing frame of the cloth merchants. The racks, made to approximate a human form, would be draped in cloth to display them along the Market Street. Melva looked like she was made of sticks, barely human at all. Larissa remained physically strong but emotionally broken. The mended friendship between her and Kathleen had helped, but their freedom still seemed impossible.

Kathleen mumbled some unintelligible thing.

"What is it, child?" Melva said.

At the sound of her voice, Kathleen stirred again.

Kathleen tried to sit up as Heathron held her.

"Melva," she said softly, "Jared is coming for me. I can feel it. He will come for me."

Heathron's face winced as Kathleen spoke the words. He turned to Melva. "The Sīhalt Guardian planned to return by mid-summer. Kathleen told me this."

The Prince felt his pride being crushed. The way she clung to Jared's memory made him want to give up.

"Hush now, Kathleen," Melva said rising to stand beside Heathron.

"Lay her down gently," Melva said.

"I won't do it," Kathleen protested as the delirium raged. "Please don't Heal me. It will kill you. Jared is coming, and he will save us. He loves me, Melva. You know that! Save your strength. My Sīhalt Guardian will come for us."

Heathron swallowed back the lump growing in his throat at Kathleen's protestations. He laid her softly on the cold floor and moved back a half step.

"No one is coming for us, Kathleen," he said. "I wish it were otherwise. I wish I could have protected you and gained your love, but no one is coming to save us. If we survive it will be because Lord Balfoest decides to have mercy. So, you must be strong enough to make the *Kabris* plants grow, although I hate to ask it of you," Heathron said.

"And death is not the worst thing that can happen to us, child. What is a Talent for, if not to serve the ones you love?" Melva said kindly.

Kathleen seemed to wince as she tried to sit up. She propped herself up on one elbow.

"I think my headache is subsiding. I can see more clearly now," she said.

"I have been trying to convince Lord Balfoest we are useful in other ways. He might allow us to live once he has secured his power in the city," Heathron explained.

"We cannot go on much longer," Larissa said as she looked to Kathleen slumped in the corner. "We must find a way to escape."

59

SENSING DANGER

Jared felt a twinge deep in the recesses of his mind. It was painful and bore down like the pressure of a rock drill. He felt a deep sadness, a melancholy that was not his own. He winced and suppressed a groan as he placed his hand against his right temple.

"What is it, brother?" Seth asked, waking from Jared's disturbance.

Jared leveled his eyes at Seth.

"If I was not here resting beside you, I might've thought it was you, brother. There were times over the past year when I felt your presence. I knew you were alive. There were times I Sensed your pain, even from a great distance."

"For whom do you feel empathy?" Seth asked. "There are so few left who would have a bond with you."

Jared took a deep breath and let it out slowly.

"It is Kathleen," Jared said. "I fell in love as I escorted the Princess to the Golden City."

Seth sat upright-earnestly attentive.

"How can this be?" Seth asked.

Jared heard the multitude of layers within the question.

Jared shook his head. "I was weak. I opened my heart to her without even realizing it," he admitted.

Seth placed a hand on Jared's shoulder, the gesture of compassion comforting him.

"Does she know?" Seth asked.

"She offered me her love, but I couldn't accept. Our lives were in serious danger, and I swore an oath to protect her, not steal her away from the life she was destined to live."

Jared bowed his head in shame.

"Arabella always said love can come rapidly, like a summer thunderstorm, or build ever so slowly, like the natural pillars in a cave — layer upon layer."

"She was always thinking of love!" Jared said with a laugh at the memory of their sister. "My love for Kathleen Dal Sundi grew like a small stream. I accepted a few drops of rain without notice, but suddenly found the banks overflowing with a torrent of water. When the rain shower passed, the little stream was changed forever. My heart is changed forever."

"And she is in danger now?" Seth asked.

"I believe so. I Sense that all is not well with her. I fear she is in great pain."

"She is waiting for you to return?"

"I hope so. I planned to be in Tyath by the summer solstice to see what might be between us."

Seth nodded in understanding. "She may choose the Prince after all."

"I cannot say I would blame her. What do I have to offer her? The wilds of the road? A life of danger and loneliness? What kind of comfort and security can a woman such as she expect from the stark life of a Sīhalt Guardian?"

"You love her. What will you do?" Seth asked.

"I do yearn to see her again. She is in my thoughts every day. I cannot see the red in the morning sunrise without thinking of her hair. Even the wind I feel on my face reminds me of her touch. I was privileged to see the beauty of her soul, Seth. I am a changed man."

"Then you must go to her. Leave tonight! Under the cover of darkness no one will see you escape. Ride to Tyath and discover what danger has befallen Kathleen," Seth urged.

"I will not leave you again, brother. At dawn we will speak to the Serpent King and receive his blessing to be released from his service. We will go to the Golden City together."

"OUT OF THE QUESTION!" Cedric barked loudly in his guttural voice. "I need you to help me recruit the Sky Clan. They will not listen to me without you, and I will need their help when I march upon the Golden City."

"If we are able to help you recruit the Sky Clan, will you release us then?" Seth asked.

Cedric considered the question. He looked around at the vast group of barbarians he had gathered to his service. Razewell, Ermines, Aurochs, Grawn Verda's people and now the Sky Clan?

He nodded slowly.

"I will release you Guardians after the chief of the Sky Clan has sworn his service to me," Cedric said.

"Well, we have gathered everybody else on this forsaken grassland. How hard can it be?" Maxwell said.

The Delathrane chiefs that surrounded Cedric began to laugh. They looked at each other knowingly, and Cedric wrinkled his scarred nose.

"They do not live in the grasslands, these people. The Sky Clan lives in the mountains," Cedric explained. "We should leave our masses here on the plain and take a small group to negotiate with their King."

"We've tried that before. It doesn't always work so well," Channing said.

"I say we approach with a big army. That'll be more impressive," Maxwell offered.

"If we arrive with any army, they will just flee from us," Chief Lystern said.

"Well, if they don't have any courage to stand and fight, why do we want them on your team?" Maxwell asked.

"Because they can fly," Cedric said as he interlocked his thumbs and made his fingers flap like wings.

Seth frowned at the comment.

"I thought those histories were embellishments. I've read stories from the early explorers who said they witnessed men flying from the mountain tops, but few scholars believe it."

Chief Lystern nodded vigorously.

"They do fly. They wear wings like a great crane and ride the thermals of air that rises from the mountains," he said.

Jared and the others looked around at the Delathrane leaders. They all nodded solemnly.

Jared looked toward the mountains. "I haven't seen any men flying? Will they show themselves?"

"They are among the peaks. Probably watching us now. I once shot one down with my bow when I was hunting in the foothills. I barely escaped with my life. If I had not made it to the trees, I would've been a dead man. They shoot arrows from above!" Chief Lystern said.

Maxwell grinned broadly.

"Sounds like my kind of people! Let's go invite them to join us," he said.

"You will go with me," Cedric said to Maxwell. "The Guardians and the Captain will come too. The rest of you will set up an encampment for the clans. Lay the tents out broadly, and keep the horses dispersed so they cannot be spooked into a stampede. Make the encampment look impressive from above."

"Then let us climb the mountains," Jared said. "I wish to be on my way to Tyath as soon as possible."

. . .

***

THE FIVE MEN had not climbed very far up the mountain before they realized they were being watched. Once they made their way into an internal valley, the wind seemed constant. It swirled around the stones in gusts and lifted from the face of the stone when they reached new heights. They heard shrill calls from above once they were high enough to look down on a sweeping valley of green. They were able to make out a lake in the large, deep valley.

"See what I mean, Guardian," Cedric said. "They fly."

Jared looked up to see the form of a man suspended above him in the air. The shadow of the expansive wings remained rigid even as he hovered over them like a bird.

"We have come to speak with your King!" Cedric called out to the man above them.

He was answered with an arrow shot from a short bow. As Cedric turned to dodge the attack, a small shaft struck him in the back.

"Aauuugh!" he cried loudly as the group scrambled for what little cover there was to be had. "That really hurts!" the Serpent King bellowed.

The shaft was thin, and the fletching was unlike anything Jared had seen before. The flights were large for the size of the arrow as if it was meant to straighten the shaft quickly or slow it down.

Cedric tried to reach for the shaft to pull it out as he writhed on the ground between two outcroppings of stone. Jared called out to the man above them, but even a Sensor struggled to hear because of all the noise Cedric was making, thrashing about.

"I was struck with a number of arrows from your warriors,

Cedric, and I didn't moan like you are doing now. He cannot hear me if you do not be silent!"

Cedric gritted his teeth, breathing rapidly through them. "I'm dying," he said angrily. His face began to twitch on one side.

"We come in peace!" Jared yelled up to the flier. The man had another arrow knocked, and he seemed to be adjusting his feet to compensate for the wind beneath the wings. He shifted with the wind and looked down at them curiously.

"The big man will go to sleep soon. If you wish to live, pile your weapons on the ground near his side. Then follow me down to the valley floor."

Channing immediately limbered his sword and dropped it beside Cedric, holding his hands clearly before him. Maxwell dropped his daggers on the ground. Seth and Jared placed their *impla* swords and knives beside them.

"Will he live?" Jared called out as he knelt beside Cedric.

The giant of a man was rigid now, the left side of his ugly face screwed into a visage of frozen horror. He no longer clawed at the small arrow in his back.

"That depends on why you have come," the man in the sky yelled back. "Follow me."

The warriors walked carefully down the stone steps that led to the valley floor. A few shaggy white goats with black eyes and curved black horns bounded out of their way as they approached. More men with fabricated, triangular wings could be seen on the wind above them.

As Jared looked up to the highest peaks around them, he could see in the distance men running and jumping from the ledges. Some of them left a trail of yellow smoke from their feet as they seemed to fall. Jared thought they would surely be dashed against the mountain, but instead they began to fly at a downward angle. One zoomed overhead, flying faster than an avalanche of snow down a mountainside. His arms and legs were spread wide, and he had a membrane of some material between his body and his limbs. He was no more than the height of a man off the ground, at times. The mountain dropped away, and the flying warrior soared out over the rim of the valley toward the sparkling waters of the lake below.

"How is he going to stop when he reaches the bottom?" Channing asked.

"It is always the landing," Maxwell said knowingly. "I'd never thought to do it in the form of a man." He looked intrigued.

The flying man that hovered above them blew a horn and yelled to the people who gathered on the lakeshore. An answering tone came in return.

The diver leveled out his approach and touched down on the water of the lake. He skipped like a stone a couple of times and finally settled into a gradual drift. Near the shore he stood up and began wading toward the edifice built along the rocky edge.

"They weren't embellishing after all. The Sky Clan rightly deserves their name!" Seth said.

"No one is going to sneak into this mountain fortress," Channing said looking around.

"The question is, after having seen all of this, will anyone be allowed to ever get out?" Jared said.

Jared could see in the distance that the women and children were scattering. Some of the elderly did too. They took refuge in the many openings in the stone walls that lined the path they walked on. Some holes emitted smoke where cooking fires must have burned within. He could smell food and suddenly felt a pang of hunger.

"Seems like they know how to cook, too. Do you smell that?" Maxwell asked.

"Smell what?" Channing replied. "I only smell mountain goat."

"If that is mountain goat, I want some," Maxwell said as he licked his lips. Channing shuddered at the thought.

"I'm worried about Cedric," Seth said. "I hope there is an antidote to whatever poison they used on the arrow."

"I don't want to go back out to the encampment without the Serpent King. That could get ugly in a hurry!" Maxwell stated.

The glider above them slowly settled onto the grass a short distance ahead of them. He removed his wings and anchored them to the ground. He kept the small quiver on his thigh and kept an arrow at the ready. His movements as he walked seemed almost as graceful as he had moved in the air. He wore a brown leather cap on his head that had a short bill that shaded his eyes. A strap ran beneath his chin to secure the headgear in place.

His jacket was also made of leather. Some white fur reminiscent of the mountain goat poked out around his collar.

"They must use those goats for everything," Maxwell said to Channing. The captain wrinkled his nose.

"We don't eat goats on the Isle of Marth," he said. "They are considered unclean servants of the Dark One."

"Well that roasting meat smells heavenly to me," Maxwell said.

The Sky Clan flyer motioned for them to follow him. The group descended the rest of the way into the valley floor.

When they reached the central building, they were welcomed by a lone man. His hair was long and streaked with grey. His eyes were hooded by a brow, and the skin of his face, except for the areas immediately around his eyes, looked windburned.

"Why have you invaded the Forbidden Valley?" he said in a sing-song like manner. His voice was soft yet confident.

"WE ARE from the lands on the distant ocean. We did not know it was forbidden to pass here. We wish to seek your assistance."

The man looked at them without responding. The glider approached him and whispered into his ear.

"The one who was felled at the peak is of our blood, although a low-lander. He would have known. He did not tell you?" he asked.

"The man who was struck so suddenly by your arrow is the great chief of Clan Razewell. He is the Serpent King and now commands almost all the clans of the Delathranes from the foothills to the great river. A great army is gathering to fight the men of the Golden City," Seth said.

"You are *Handri* and yet you serve a Delathrane?

"We are Sīhalt Guardians, and we have sworn an oath to serve the Serpent King for some time. These men," Seth said, gesturing to Channing and Maxwell, "are our brothers."

"You have eyes the color of the mother sky and your hair is like clouds of rain. I will hear your words. Come into the temple of the Sky God. If he wishes you to live, I will hear your request."

They entered the building made of cut stone. No other structure appeared so well-crafted. The people had dwellings made with mortar and stone, but the domed building they entered was of a different style.

Inside the temple, the domed roof had openings. Characters were scrawled on the walls in columns not rows. Jared looked closely and saw charts of stars that represented the night sky.

"It is an observatory of the ancients," he said to Seth as they walked inside.

A ray of light shone down to on a relief carved into the wall. The image was of a man wearing sandals that laced up the calves of his legs contorted in pain. His arms were outstretched toward the sun above him and his face was filled with agony.

"This is Falcon the Sky God. He is the one who demands that we take to the sky and defend the temple in the mountains."

"May I touch it?" Maxwell asked.

Taken by the reverence with which Maxwell approached the wall, Jared remained silent. He had rarely seen his friend from childhood look so serious.

The chieftain nodded, and Maxwell stepped forward to place

his hand against the ancient carving. The image of Falcon was almost naked because he wore only a small cloth around his loins. It had arms spread wide and feathers covering them from wrist to torso. Tail feathers were visible. Maxwell traced the outline of the half-man, half-bird-of-prey image with his finger. Falcon seemed to be crying out in pain as drops of liquid fell from his fingertips.

"Is this meant to be blood?" Maxwell asked.

"The Sky God gave himself for us. Falcon flew to the sun to gain the knowledge for the people of earth. It is recorded here." He swept his arm around the room indicating the walls covered in ancient writing.

"But, alas, we are not as wise as our fathers. We lost the meaning of the pictures, and we are left only with the wind on our faces, as we seek to emulate him, and awe in our hearts for what was once known, and now is lost."

Maxwell turned. Tears were streaming down his face.

Jared could not remember ever seeing Maxwell cry. Even during the most grueling training at Windstall Hermitage, the little boy never shed a tear. He stood spell bound, wondering what Maxwell would say.

"I am his son," Maxwell said to the chief. He spread his arms wide in emulation of the image on the wall. "I am the son of Falcon," Maxwell said more loudly. The warriors gathered near the door shifted uncomfortably at his words.

Jared always wondered about Maxwell's family. It was rumored that he was left on the steps of the Windstall Hermitage as an infant — unwanted by his parents. Jared didn't know if that was just the story started by some of the mean-spirited apprentices teasing him as a child, or if there was truth in the rumor. Jared had avoided the subject of Maxwell's origin, but he often wondered where his friend had come from. Even now Jared thought that perhaps Maxwell was just acting out a game — another joke to laugh at later.

"We have no tradition of Falcon having a son," the chieftain said quietly, but there was an edge to his voice. "And we do not kill within the walls of the temple. But tell me, stranger, how will you give me proof that you are not speaking blasphemy?" He fingered the hilt of his knife, and Jared had no doubt that the man knew how to use it.

"We have come to ask you to join in the fight for the Golden City on the Amaranth Plain. They corrupt the *Kabris* dream plants and weaken your brothers. Soon they will spread beyond the great river. They will reach these mountains. They must be stopped. I command you to wake up the Serpent King and join him in his battle to cleanse the Golden City."

The chieftain's eyes were wide. His nostrils flared, and he grasped the hilt of the knife at his waist.

"You will not command me stranger. You are a low-lander without a clue. We watch from the heights of the clouds and see how the people of the plains behave. We want nothing to do with them, and you will not live to walk back down the mountain!"

He said it slowly in a sing-song tone, but the threat was palpable in the quiet of the observatory.

"You are my people," Maxwell said as he began to remove his shirt. He took off his leggings and stood in his loincloth with the ray of midday sun shining down in a pillar of light. His muscles rippled as he moved. The image of Falcon behind him mirrored his body in stone. The priest chieftain hesitated, confused by the response he was given.

Maxwell leveled his eyes at the priest. "Follow the Serpent King to the Golden City, and the secrets written on these walls will be revealed once more to your people."

Maxwell stretched out his arms, and Channing averted his eyes. Jared knew what was coming. Feathers began to sprout from his arms, and his eyes grew large and bright like a bird of prey. A look of agony did indeed cross Maxwell's face as he Shifted to the form of a bird. The screech that Maxwell released in the confines of the stone room would have shattered crystal if there had been any. He leaped into the air with a powerful thrust, and with flaps of his great wings, the enormous eagle flew out of the observatory and over the rim of the mountains toward the east.

Jared, Seth, and Channing mimicked the priest as he fell to his knees in devotion. The man called out to Maxwell as he flew away, then turned to the remaining three in shock.

"Did you witness that?" he asked reverently.

They all nodded solemnly, and the warriors assembled beside the door began to shout and gather the people. A great miracle had been witnessed!

The priest offered Seth a small, white, pebble-like substance.

"Put this under the tongue of the Serpent King. He will awaken after it dissolves. There is no time to waste. I must tell the Sky Clan that our prayers have been answered!"

Seth accepted the medicine, and Channing gathered Maxwell's clothes. "I'm starting to feel like his mother," he muttered, but there was a smile on his face. "I wondered how that was going to go."

"I couldn't tell if he was serious or not. I've never seen him like that," Jared said.

"It got the job done. Cedric will release us from his service now," Seth said.

"Then we ride for Tyath this evening!" Jared said, "I am eager to travel east."

60

LOYAL GUARD

"**P**ssst!"

The noise caught Dallin Sarkkand's attention. He laid the reins softly over the neck of his horse and looked around the stable. Some servants were leading horses back from the pasture now that the stalls were cleaned. Dallin stood up and looked over the gate leading to the back of the barn.

A girl, dressed in gray, stood with her back pressed against the wall and held a finger to her lips. Dallin nodded to her discreetly, acknowledging her desire for secrecy.

"Where will you be hunting today, Lord Sarkkand?" a servant asked. "You haven't been up to the Copper Hills lately, have you?"

"Aidan said he wanted to bring the hounds. So, I imagine we'll hunt there," he said, resting his arms on the gate gazing out to the distant trees nonchalantly. "But nature calls first," he added, and stepped through the gate to go behind the barn.

"I'll have your gear ready in a moment, and the pack horse is loaded already with enough supplies for a week or more," the servant called.

Dallin rounded the corner of the barn.

"Do you know who I am?" the dark-haired girl asked him as he approached. Her green eyes flashed intensely.

"You are one of the former Imperial Guards of the late Princess Dal Sundi," he said.

"My name is Lilly. I escaped when they took her captive, and some of my contacts in the city said I might be able to trust you."

"I am sorry for your loss," Dallin said.

"She isn't dead!" Lilly said, her voice strained to be quiet as Dallin looked around to make sure they were alone.

"Lord Balfoest had her arrested for being a Plant Witch, but she was not executed. He has her imprisoned," she said.

"Why would Lars Balfoest keep her alive?"

"I think he's making her grow the *Kabris*. All the dealers in the city are amazed at the surplus of the dream powder in Tyath. The traders say the Delathranes are not even sending their leaves eastward anymore, and yet, the city is awash in it."

Dallin nodded as he considered this.

"He's making her grow the plants," Lilly said.

"But where? That would never be allowed, not even by House Naystrom. The Luzian priests would burn down a place where that kind of thing was being done," Dallin said.

"Kathleen has a secret garden built in the midst of her quarters near the western wall of the city. Heathron made it for her as a gift. The ceiling is made of glass. It's planted with all manner of beautiful things. The Princess's private quarters are surrounded by a parapet wall above and few know of the garden's existence. As her guard, I am very familiar with the layout."

Dallin looked around again. His servant called, "Lord Sarkkand, are you alright?"

"I'll be right there!" Dallin replied, then whispered to Lilly. "If what you say is true, we must speak more. Meet me by the old stone bridge. Do you know the place?"

Lilly nodded.

"I will be there shortly," Dallin said.

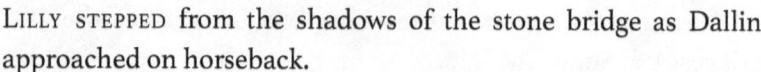

LILLY STEPPED from the shadows of the stone bridge as Dallin approached on horseback.

"Let's talk beneath the bridge," Lilly suggested.

Dallin dismounted and led his mount and the pack horse beneath the large stone arch that spanned the river.

"You are very trusting of me," Dallin said. "What makes you so sure I am your ally?"

"I am not sure, but I don't have many options. Some of my friends say you can be trusted if the fate of the Empire was in danger, and its laws were being flaunted. They say you and your father are patriots."

"How do you know I won't just slit your throat and leave you under this bridge and go on my merry way?" Dallin asked seriously. "I hail from one of the evil houses, remember?"

"Two reasons," Lilly replied. "I feel safe under this bridge, the sound of the water is obscuring our voices, and I believe you are a decent man. Besides, I am no wilting flower."

Dallin considered this and was impressed with the girl's confidence. He was fairly sure he could beat her in a fair fight, but she was an Imperial Guard and probably had some dangerous tricks up her sleeve.

"Lord Balfoest has used his leadership of the Council of Nine Houses to have himself installed as the interim steward of the city and thus the whole Empire. What are the chances he will give up that power for one of the high noble houses to take the throne?" she said.

"Not likely, but what are we to do? Heathron is the only one with the authority to lawfully lead right now. And he is dead. Even my father's hands are tied," Dallin said.

"Did you see the body?" Lilly asked.

"My father said both Lord Balfoest and his servant gave a witness to it."

"I don't know much about the Talent of a Green Grower, but I doubt Kathleen Dal Sundi would willingly do anything for Lord Balfoest after he arrested her. He must have some leverage over her," Lilly said.

"The old woman, Lady Albodris, and Prince Heathron are all missing. All of them are loved by the Princess, are they not?"

Lilly nodded.

"We need to get help," Dallin said, his brow furrowed in concern.

"The military is loyal to the throne, and the throne is empty right now. I'm afraid we cannot count on General Tigral or Admiral Hale in this. They would likely side with Lord Balfoest and the Council of Nine Houses."

"Candoreth doesn't have the strength to fight Tyath. They have been told Kathleen died of the Plague. King Lukald is in mourning for his daughter, not marching for war."

"But she isn't dead. I am sure of it," Lilly said.

"Would the military leaders listen to the counsel of a Sīhalt Guardian?"

"They might. General Tigral has great respect for the Sīhalt Order. Many within the army do."

"Princess Kathleen once said the Guardian who brought her to Tyath planned to return before the Marriage Day. He is in the contested lands dealing with the barbarian threat. He might help us."

"How long do you think it would take us to find him?" Lilly said.

"I have more than a week's worth of supplies with me, and everyone expects me to be gone on an extended hunting trip. I'll have a servant send a message to house Naystrom to have Aidan meet me at the Copper Hills. He will be looking for a while before he realizes I'm not there."

"So, we head west to look for the Sīhalt?"

"How can I be sure I can trust you? How do I know you are not in the employ of my enemies?" Dallin asked.

"Because I would not show you this if I did not trust you," Lilly said.

She walked to the river's edge and placed her hand into the swiftly running river. A small mound of water began to rise out of the flowing water. It grew slowly and began to take the shape of a reptilian-like creature. The head, formed of water, had scales with spikes that grew from its spine. It rose up and began to take shape. When the chest of the creature was revealed. It spread wings made of water and threw its head back as if to roar. Instead, a bubbling fountain of water shot out of the image's mouth and cascaded back to the river in a shower of misty spray. The droplets of water cast a reflection on the underside of the bridge, specks of light danced before Dallin's eyes.

He stood in shock at the creature that rose from the water and now looked at him with menacing watery eyes. His horses laid their ears back and moved further from the water's edge.

"I'm a Water Witch or a Sea Witch — whatever you please to call us, but I prefer the term Douser," Lilly said as she knelt by the riverbank beneath the ancient stone bridge. As soon as Lilly removed her hand from the river, the form of a dragon, made of water, slid back under the churning surface of the river.

"Is that thing dangerous?" Dallin asked, still spellbound by the magic he had witnessed.

"Water is only dangerous if you don't respect it," Lilly said. "But now you know I am serious about helping Kathleen. She doesn't deserve to be in prison for having a Talent. None of us do."

Dallin thought hard considering what he would do next.

"No wonder you were not afraid of me," he said.

"And you don't need to be afraid of me either. We are on the same team, Dallin. Help me find the Sīhalt Guardian."

61

A NEW WITCH

"I found your replacement," Lord Balfoest said.

Kathleen cringed in the darkness — a ray of sunlight cut across the dark prison cell.

Even as she shielded her eyes from the bright light, Kathleen breathed in a breath of fresh air. The air inside the darkness had grown stale.

It had been perhaps seven months since midsummer. Kathleen had watched the phases of the moon through the round hole, cut through eight feet of rock. She could barely see the tips of the trees in the distance, but their branches were outlined in the snow.

Rough hands grabbed her and pulled her from the cell. The front of her dress was matted to her body, evidence of the filth in which she lay day after day.

"Say hello to my newest witch," Balfoest said. "She isn't nearly as powerful as you, but I've already broken her will. It took me less than two days."

"What do you mean?" Kathleen tried to say.

"We finally bartered for a Delathrane girl. She may not be as strong as you, but she is less of a liability, so to speak."

"What about Larissa and Heathron?" Kathleen asked.

"Once they are forgotten, they will be eliminated, like you."

"My father will come," Kathleen said. "Will you risk that?"

"Candoreth is in shambles. The city will fall, House Dal Sundi will, too, my dear." He laughed wickedly. "The same goes for House Dol Lassimer. Now take her upstairs and get her to work again," Lord Balfoest said.

Karl and Nich obeyed and led Kathleen up the narrow stairwell.

Kathleen looked up to see ice and snow on the windows above her head. She was once again in her private garden, warm soil under her feet. She curled her toes into the dirt, feeling for the lives of the dream plant.

"Quit leaning on me, witch. You'll stand on your own two feet, or I will throw you to the dirt," Karl said.

Lord Balfoest walked up and down the aisles of plants, swinging his long walking cane. He brushed the rod gently on the leaves of the tender plants.

"You will show the savage girl how you do it. Train her," he commanded.

Kathleen hadn't noticed anyone else in the walled garden. She turned around, her eyes following the cane that Lord Balfoest pointed toward in the shadows. A frail girl with a dirty face walked forward. Her hands were bound at the wrists, and her hair was matted with twigs and burs.

"Come forward, little one," Lord Balfoest said, his voice like that of a frustrated farmer, coaxing a wounded calf to the butcher's knife.

Deep sadness welled up in Kathleen's heart.

How did this man feel no mercy for this little girl?

The girl looked up at him with pleading eyes, she couldn't have been more than eleven or twelve years old.

Kathleen wondered what happened to take this girl away from her family. She looked like she wanted to shrink down and hide herself, but she stood alone in the openness of the garden room with her hands bound.

She nodded her head and took a few limited steps forward. Kathleen saw that her ankles were bound.

"What do you want me to grow?" she asked in a soft voice.

Lord Balfoest's voice was annoyed. "You're standing in a small field of *Kabris* plants. What do you think I want you to grow, my little witch?" he said derisively. "Make the *Kabris* grow."

She felt the *Kabris* plant's texture with her hand and traced the veins in the leaves.

It was a different approach than Kathleen would use, but every person felt their Talents differently. Kathleen wanted to run to her. She saw something of her younger self within the girl. She wanted to put her arms around her and tell her that everything would be okay, but she knew better.

"She's a slippery little devil. When I traded for her among the clans, she tried to escape the first day — then the second and the third. We found her rotting under a cockle bush, so I stuffed her in a barrel so she wouldn't know where we were going. That way, I didn't have to worry about her running off again. Now she needs to learn her lesson."

"How do you know she has the Talent?" Kathleen asked.

"I know she's cursed because I watched her playing along the river. She made the water lilies bloom by barely touching the blossoms. She can't hide what she is," Balfoest said.

"Hello, little one," Kathleen said, as she knelt on the freshly tilled soil. "If you grow the plants, he will feed you. Are you hungry?"

The little girl frowned probably having difficulty with Kathleen's accent. Then a light of understanding arose in her eyes.

"I cannot eat the dream plant, it will make me sick," she said softly.

Kathleen shook her head.

"The bad man will give you bread," Kathleen said.

"You will give her bread, won't you?" Kathleen demanded, glaring at Balfoest.

"I must protect my investment," he said, nodding.

Turning back to the little girl, Kathleen placed her hands on her shoulders.

"You must do as he asks, or he will harm you," Kathleen said.

"I am not afraid of the *Handri*," she said.

Kathleen shook her head. She blinked and looked into the little girl's eyes.

"The daughters of the Delathranes are brave," Kathleen said. "But you must grow and live to tell the truth to your people about Lord Balfoest."

The little girl looked around the garden.

"Is there a way to escape?" she asked quietly.

A tear began to make its way down Kathleen's right cheek.

"I have not found one," she said.

The little girl nodded curtly.

"Enough already," Balfoest said. "Get on with it."

"She looks to be only a child. She is not experienced," Kathleen protested.

The guard grabbed Kathleen by her dirty dress and yanked her toward the nearest line of plants. The fabric cut into the thin skin that covered her windpipe. She coughed and turned her head to look up at him.

"I need to test her. I need to see if she is ready to do it," Kathleen pleaded.

"Ready or not, she will do it," Balfoest declared.

Kathleen ran her fingers through her hair.

"Come closer," she said to the little girl, motioning with her hand.

"Lord Balfoest wants each plant to grow until it drops new shoots."

Kathleen had to reach deep to find the Talent hidden within

her, past the hollowness that threatened to swallow her whole. The little girl watched intently with her dark eyes.

Kathleen began to hum. She kept her hands around the four leaves at the crown of the plant. Her volume slowly increased. She closed her hands around the plant until she held it like a captured firefly in midsummer. Her bent back displayed ribs pushing through the skin, outlining her skeletal frame. The simple dress hung loose about her shoulders.

Now standing upright, Kathleen slowly lifted her hands as they encircled the plant. It grew until Kathleen was standing with her hands above her head. Vines flowed from the top and small flowers and leaves sprouted from the stems — the offspring of the dream plant.

Kathleen turned to the little girl.

"Can you do that?" she asked.

"I am not as tall as you," the Delathrane girl said. "But I will try."

The little girl mimicked the movements Kathleen had shown her. She kept her small delicate hands around the base of the next plant. It began to grow just as Kathleen had instructed. The little girl also raised her arms as high above her head as her small stature would allow until the flowery vines drooped from the crown of the newly grown dream plant.

It was half as tall as the one Kathleen had grown.

Lord Balfoest frowned, disappointed. He clutched his walking cane more tightly.

"Just make them as tall as you can. Lord Balfoest will be angry if you make them short," Kathleen explained.

The little girl looked at Kathleen and then toward Lord Balfoest in fear.

"She's not as strong as me, don't make her do what you need me to do," Kathleen said.

"You could willingly help her. You could work together," he

said as he laughed at the suggestion. "Yes, I'm building a stable of witches."

He laughed but there was no humor in it. The man really would build a stable of witches if he could, but it would not include her. Kathleen was sure of that.

"She is only a child. She needs some experience first," Kathleen said.

"I'll take care of that," Lord Balfoest said.

He stepped forward quickly with his heavy walking cane and smashed the girl on the side of the head. She fell to the dirt without making a sound, blood poured from her ear. He leaned forward and peered down at the unconscious little girl.

"What are you doing?" Kathleen yelled. Despite her weakness, she jumped on his back trying to restrain the arm that held the cane.

She was yanked backward by Karl. She fell gasping in the dirt, panting for the air that had been knocked from her upon the impact with the ground. The guard sneered, shaking his head and clicking his tongue. Nich stood silently watching, his jaw clenched, but said nothing.

"Naughty witch," Karl said.

"Call for the Meat Witch to Heal the little one. If I haven't given her enough of a beating to ensure the Healing adds another five inches to her height, let me know. I'll be happy to finish the job."

The guard nodded. "Yes, my Lord," he said with a grin.

"I want these plants grown to full height. I have orders to fill," Lord Balfoest said.

"What about the other one?" the guard said, pointing to Kathleen.

"Take her back to her cell," he said. "If the old woman has a few more Healings left in her. I'd rather save them for the Delathrane girl."

Kathleen knew that she had seen too much. Balfoest would

never let her live to see freedom, and he had no reason to keep her as long as this other girl's Talents could be abused and exploited. As soon as the girl demonstrated her ability to grow the daily crop, Kathleen knew she would be eliminated.

Her time was growing very short. They needed a way out of the dungeon.

62

WAIT FOR OUR CALL

"I will miss having my Sīhalt Guardian," Cedric said.

He clasped Seth by the forearm, and shook vigorously. Then he placed his enormous hand at the back of Seth's head, pulling him forward until their foreheads touched. It happened so quickly Jared almost reached for his *impla*.

"You are no longer my slave. You are my brother," the barbarian said.

"If I am your brother, then he is your brother," Seth said pointing to Jared.

The Serpent King nodded slowly.

"Our shared father is Pain. We were all sired by him," Cedric said.

"Forgiveness must be our Mother, if we will ever find rest," Seth replied.

Jared nodded in agreement and whispered the word, "Amen."

"I will not show forgiveness to those in the Golden City. Our people will overrun it like stampeding bulls whose horns are sharp and wide," King Lystern said.

"My vision will be fulfilled," Cedric said. "The great city will fall, and the walls will be broken. I know this."

"I do not doubt the truth in your words. Although I do not know how it will come to pass. Who am I to say your dreams are false? You have gathered the clans, just as you foretold. Perhaps the time of the great battle has arrived. We are like sticks of wood floating on the river. We can only ride the current on our way to the sea," Seth said.

"You no longer try to dissuade me. You no longer speak of the goodness of the *Handri* or the Golden City. Why?" Cedric asked.

Seth took a moment and looked at Maxwell. Then he looked at Jared and Channing. He frowned and moved his head with uncertainty.

"Good people can be led by evil men. When those evil men are in power, many people die defending them. But they must be brought down. We fear the Golden City is in the hands of an evil man. We will go to speak with our friends there. Wait for our call. We will share with you what we discover."

Cedric nodded his enormous head. His shaggy mane shook, his face divided by the wide scar smiled an ugly grin.

"Not just the clans have joined me," Cedric said, "but the vaunted Sīhalt Guardians as well. I cannot lose."

"Do not be too quick to declare your victory. You have no machines with which to smash the walls of Tyath. When you stood at the gate, you surprised the people of the Golden City. That will not happen again. You have yet to see the might of the Tyathian Empire, gathering strength for war."

Cedric took a deep breath, nostrils flaring as if trying to smell his enemy across the great distance that separated them.

"We will have armor and chariots," he said. "We will ride the great beasts from beyond the mountains. Some are taller than trees, with horns on their faces like the spikes of dragons."

"You will need all of that and more," Jared promised.

"We will send you word by way of the eagle," Seth said as he pointed to Maxwell who nodded as he continued to eat an apple.

"Indeed, and don't do anything stupid until we talk to you first," Maxwell said between chewing and swallowing.

"And what of you, Fancy Man? Do you have advice for me, too?" the Serpent King asked as he looked at Channing.

"Did he just call me 'fancy man'?" Channing asked. "Where on earth did you get that nickname?"

The gaudy plume swayed on his hat as he shook his head.

"I have no idea," Maxwell said as he rolled his eyes and gestured with his chin toward the hat.

"It is what the women of the Delathrane people call you," Cedric explained.

A few of the barbarian women giggled and waved.

"Well, it appears we men of Marth have charms not even the Delathrane women can resist!" Channing said proudly.

"They are all very old," Jared noted. "Few of your admirers have any teeth remaining. I'm not sure how proud you should be of your gifts," Jared said with a smile.

Channing furrowed his brow and looked toward his devotees. It was true. The only ones especially enamored with the Captain of Candoreth seemed to be in the winter of their lives. Not a young, nor even middle-aged woman, stood among them.

Channing waved to them, and the women reacted with smiles and laughter.

"That's quite the fan club you've got there," Maxwell said.

"It takes a woman of maturity: one who's known love and loss and who has the experiences of life behind her, to truly appreciate a man," Channing said.

One of the one women seemed to gain courage and came forward. She held something in her hands wrapped in leather and tied with string. She approached the Captain on his horse and offered him the gift. Channing unwrapped it, finding inside the leather a string of smoked sausages. He smelled it, cut a small piece and tasted it.

"This is delicious," he said, chewing the meat. Channing

winked at his companions. "It's the older women who can cook. Don't forget that either," he said.

"Maybe their eyes are not very good," Cedric commented.

"Now you're piling on too?" Channing said to the Serpent King.

The Delathrane opened his hands and spread them wide.

"It was only a suggestion."

"Thank you, dear Woman," Channing said.

The old Delathrane woman patted his thigh as he sat in the saddle, much to the enjoyment of her friends.

The Sīhalt Guardians and Maxwell smiled.

"Let's get out of here before any more of these ladies feel the need to show their appreciation to the good Captain of Candoreth," Seth said.

"If I do not hear from you by the Longest Day, we will march on the Golden City regardless."

"Wait for the message we will send," Seth said. "'Know your enemy', remember?"

"Goodbye, Seth," Cedric said.

Then, turning to Jared he said, "Goodbye *Der'Antha*."

When the Serpent King used the title given to Jared by the barbarians, this time it sounded like a compliment.

63

HER TIME IS OVER

Colvin Mador, the assassin, entered the ornate steam baths of the palace's west wing. He didn't look dangerous. The short, pudgy young man had a face that seemed almost childlike. But Lars could feel the absence of emotion in the man. He was like a pastry puff — open to be filled with whatever needed to be stuffed inside. For Colvin, that usually meant money, which suited Lars just fine. It was cleaner that way.

Only immodesty seemed to make Colvin feel uncomfortable. It made Lars Balfoest wonder about his past. Had he worked in the Church perhaps, before the bakery? People were simple creatures, he reminded himself. They responded to subtle pressure at the right moment, in the right place.

At this moment, Lars wanted Colvin to feel uncomfortable. If a dangerous animal was to be tamed, the master needed a strong hand, and Colvin certainly was a surprisingly dangerous kind of animal. Lars wanted to show the assassin how comfortable he was in his presence. He wanted to prove that he felt no vulnerability, despite the setting of the luxurious bath.

"Must we speak here?" Colvin said ruefully as he looked away from Lars who was swimming nude in the water.

"No one else is around. It's the perfect place for privacy."

"What do you want?" the assassin said.

Clearly Colvin wanted to leave.

Good, Lars thought. *I've got him right where I want him.*

"I've written a list. It's over there on the table in the envelope."

Colvin used the ornate letter opener to break the wax seal and retrieve the list inside while Lars swam in the steaming pool.

He climbed the steps leisurely, then slowly reached for a towel to cover his skinny, wrinkled frame. He saw Colvin's eyes glance toward him but nothing played across his pudgy face.

"Most of these are nobles," the young man said scanning the list. "Some are even on the council."

"Of course I'll pay the higher rate," Lars said as he dried himself off and wrapped a thick, red towel around his waist.

"Do you need it to look like an accident?"

"That would be one spectacular coincidence, if you could manage it," Lars said, smirking to himself. "There are names on the other side too."

Colvin turned the paper over.

"What's my timeframe? Am I allowed to subcontract?"

"Working your way through the list over the next month or so should suffice. Get help if you need it."

"They will start to be defensive if their peers begin to die over the coming weeks. They will avoid going out and increase their security," the assassin observed.

"True, perhaps you should act more quickly."

The pudgy killer wrinkled his nose as if he smelled something distasteful.

"The Sundiland girl is still alive?" he said as he looked up from the paper.

"I don't need her anymore, or Heathron either. Dispatch them both along with my niece Larissa and the old woman."

The assassin nodded silently. He continued to gaze over the list.

"The Stellat family as well," he said without emotion.

Lars made his way toward the young man and put his arm around his shoulders. Unlike the other times he had managed to make contact with the killer, this time he felt an emotion within him.

Regret?

"Why do you hesitate, Colvin?" Balfoest asked softly, he used his Voice.

"I never hesitate," Colvin said.

He's lying to me! Lars thought.

Lars was intrigued. To his knowledge, the baker had never lied to him before. There was no complexity in the boy that had become a man under his tutelage. Colvin was completely transaction based. He was like an empty ledger. A dozen gold coins would buy a death at dawn. His methods were as varied as the cakes in the windows of his bakery. Colvin wasn't afraid to use poison, a knife, an intricate trap, or the strength of his own doughy hands to fulfill his end of the bargain.

This was new to Lord Balfoest. This was interesting.

"How long have we worked together?"

"I did my first work for you five years ago," Colvin recalled.

"In all that time, I've never known you to feel regret. Why do you feel it now?" he asked.

Colvin shook his head but said nothing.

"Don't you want the money?"

Colvin looked back at him though thickly-lidded eyes. His rosy cheeks and soft skin belied the hardened interior of the man.

"When is it enough for you?" Colvin asked as he looked around the room.

Gilded paint decorated the walls with geometric patterns that accented the bath. The blue and gold tiles extending downward along the edge of the pool were obscured by the steam that rose from the heated water.

"What do you mean?" Lars said.

"This room is truly luxurious," Colvin began. "Years ago you told me that by removing just three people ahead of you, you could climb to a point and have enough power to make a difference."

"Haven't I made a difference? Has your life improved since working with me? Now you needn't just rise before the sun to make dough, slaving away at your master's bakery."

"That's true," Colvin said.

"Now you have the largest chain of bakeries in the city. I don't even know why you get up before the sun to start the fires in the ovens or knead the dough."

"It provides me a good cover and a reason to travel to any place in the city at any hour."

"I suppose that's true, but I'm feeling that you also love your trade."

"You mean the killing?" Colvin asked without emotion.

"I mean the baking. You love the bread and the cookies, don't you?"

Lars smiled. He still couldn't imagine why Colvin was feeling regret.

"I love it when other people enjoy them," Colvin said.

Lars felt a flood of sweet emotion sweep downward through the man as he confessed his true joy and recalled a memory.

"Tell me what you were thinking of just now, when you said that," Lars said.

He paused and waited for an answer from Colvin. He almost had it.

Colvin didn't immediately respond. Lars could feel that his emotions had leveled again. The fat young man was empty just like before.

Then he began to speak.

"He's the reason I'm a baker," Colvin said.

"Go on," Lars said, shifting his Voice into a tone that impelled the speaker to unburden themselves.

"We lived on the Stellat estate when I was a child. I used to help in the kitchen, and Lady Stellat had high demands. One day I helped to make some rolls and delivered them at breakfast. Eldin Stellat and I are the same age."

Lars could feel a building in the emotions. He circled around and stood in front of Colvin, grabbing him by the shoulders so that he could see his face.

"What happened at breakfast?" he asked in a voice devoid of judgement.

"His mother wasn't there, and so perhaps that is why he wasn't so proper," Colvin said.

Lars felt a flood of gratitude fill the baker who also dealt in blood. Lars wrinkled his brow in consternation, trying to piece together the hesitation, regret, and now gratitude, the assassin displayed.

Colvin Mador is a puzzle after all, he thought.

"That day, Eldin Stellat said 'Good Morning, these rolls are delicious, Colvin!'"

The corners of the baker's mouth pulled into a straight line and then relaxed. It was the closest thing to a smile Lars had ever seen him make.

Colvin's face held no other emotions. If it wasn't for the Talent of Empathy Lars possessed, he wouldn't have known the depth of intensity with which the assassin held this simple memory.

Lars blinked, waiting for more, but nothing else came except the waves of profound goodwill that washed over Colvin as he considered Eldin Stellat.

That's why he felt regret. He doesn't want to kill him, Lars thought. This would not do. He had seen the list. Certainly, Colvin knew the rules.

"Have you ever worked for Eldin?" Lars asked, desiring to understand the relationship.

Colvin pulled his hand away from Lars as if he had touched a hot oven door.

"Eldin wouldn't ask me to do these things," he said, holding up the list. "But every now and again he stops in my original bakery. One day, he even brought the Prince and the Princess to try some of my rolls."

Lars no longer needed physical touch to understand exactly where the conversation was headed. He would need to find a different assassin. Although Colvin's cherubic face was a blank slate, he might as well have been beaming with pride. His simple statement was just as much a declaration of friendship, even love, as the worshipful sonnets written on the walls of the cathedral.

Now it was Lars's turn to feel emotion that was unexpected.

Jealousy.

His eyes narrowed and he allowed the towel to drop while reaching for his robe. Knowing that in that moment Colvin would avert his eyes, Lord Balfoest's nimble hands reached for the letter opener resting on the small table. He turned and struck forcefully with the sharpened metal implement. Once was not enough. He advanced as the pudgy baker retreated, reaching up to cover the hole in his neck.

Lars struck Colvin twice more, high up on his chest, the weapon plunging downward at a steep angle because of his greater height. The baker tried to take another step back but lost his footing as he toppled into the pool.

Lars noted the blank expression Colvin maintained through it all. The assassin splashed in the water, trying to cover his wounds and swim at the same time, but never made a call for help. Balfoest wasted no time jumping into the water after him. He approached the struggling wounded man from behind and slashed again, his long arms reached out and encircled Colvin's fat neck and Lord Balfoest pulled him closer. Lars whispered in his Voice, "Relax, settle down now. Breathe deeply," he said and the assassin complied as Lars lowered the man's mouth beneath the surface of the bloodied water. As the last of Colvin's life escaped him, Lars Balfoest used his Talent to reach into the mind and heart of the assassin and was surprised to feel another emotion welling up in the dying man — a profound sense of relief.

64

CHANGES IN TYATH

Jared stopped at the enormous gates of Tyath and prepared to speak quickly in his own defense.

"What is your business here?" the thick-jawed city guardsman said.

"Political," Jared said, seeing his demeanor and register consistent with a man who was used to working for the elite.

The guardsman waved all four of them through without a further comment.

None of the other soldiers who provided security at the gates hesitated to allow the Sīhalt Guardian or his companions through.

"Is there some kind of festival going on? Look at the banners," Maxwell said. "I enjoyed a nice Wedding Day festival when I was here last. Unlimited ale!"

Golden flags flew over the main thoroughfares. They were strung between the buildings of the narrower side street as well, showing a circle of nine triangles with their tips pointed inward.

"Those flags held the Fox and Acorn of House Dol Lassimer last summer," Jared noted. "I wonder what has changed in Tyath."

Jared felt a sense of foreboding. Even as the people of the Golden City went about their day, selling their wares, cleaning their homes, and doing their trade work, the mood within the city was somber. The earliest flowers of spring were in bloom, and winter had begun its retreat, yet there seemed to be a melancholy that clung to every street. The bright yellow flowers poised their golden heads to reach for the sunlight, and seemed to mock the patches of melting snow visible in the shaded corners along the streets. Jared thought of Kathleen and her blessed way of bringing sunshine to the darkest moments. She lived up to the other title she bore: Sunshine Bride of Candoreth. The citizens of Tyath should have felt joy at a new spring. Instead they seemed sad.

Jared led the way directly to the palace and was met by some of the same servants he had seen when he first encountered Prince Heathron to accept his commission to escort Kathleen. This time, no one came down the steps to greet him as had happened on that day. Instead, the four sojourners dismounted and climbed the steep steps leading to the throne rooms.

Lord Balfoest stood before the two brothers, studying their expressions, absorbing every little flicker, so that he might devour the delicious change of their spirits after he spoke. Breathing in, he spread his hands.

"She is no longer living."

The men were taken aback, especially the older Sīhalt. He looked as if he had been stabbed.

"I am sorry. She was dear to many," Lars Balfoest said. "We are currently in a crisis of royal authority."

The storm clouds of emotions that gathered on the gray-eyed Guardian's face made Lars wish that he had already killed the girl and her companions.

For Abboth's sake, why would two Sīhalt Guardians come looking for her! Lukald did not have that kind of influence, did he? Lars thought.

"When did she die?" the man dressed in black asked. His voice was shaking and Lars could sense the melancholy mixed with anger in the question.

This is personal for him. He might be in love with the girl, Lars realized.

"Months ago, we held a funeral for both Prince Heathron and Princess Kathleen in the Great Cathedral." Lars said carefully.

"I wish to visit her grave," the man stated. He looked pale despite the road's steady companions — sun and wind.

"They contracted the Great Sickness, and their bodies were burned," Lars explained. "There is a display, in the Great Cathedral, memorializing the life and love that was denied them. Two urns contain their remains. You will find the Princess there."

Lord Balfoest hadn't finished his sentence when the thought struck him that the Sīhalt Guardian might fall to the floor. The man took a few wavering steps as if his knees might give way.

"She would have made a perfect Empress," Lars said. "We plan to send her remains south now that the weather has improved. King Lukald is aware of the tragedy."

His companions looked one to another.

"Don't worry," Lars said. "We believe it was contained. We quarantined them and made sure no one visited her chambers. It appears that only those who spent significant time with the Princess died."

"In her chambers?"

"I feel your pain," Lars said from the steward's chair a few steps below the empty imperial throne. "My niece Larissa Albodris was a good friend of hers. But Prince Heathron violated the law and encouraged the Dal Sundi Princess to use her sorcery within the very walls of the Golden City. That is believed to be what brought the Plague upon them. So sad."

"You won't speak ill of Kathleen Dal Sundi," Captain Channing said. "I won't allow it."

"Calm down, southerner. This is neither the time nor the place for your honorable antics. Your visit here in the capital is at my allowance," Lars said.

~

JARED WAS SHAKING. He felt weak in the knees and almost collapsed to the floor.

"She called for me in my dreams," he said.

"There's no way we could've made it here that many weeks ago," Seth said in an effort to comfort his brother.

"But she called for me-last night," Jared said.

"Did you hear her in the night wind?" Seth asked for clarification.

"It was in my dreams as I slept," Jared explained.

"I am so very sorry for your loss. Please know the Golden City suffers too. We do not have our royal family and are trying to resolve the issue so daily life may go on as before," Lars said.

"Does that explain the rampant use of dream powder?" Maxwell asked.

"The emperor left the throne to Heathron. He intended to crown the boy, but was delayed. Now decisions will have to be made by the Council of Nine before one of his half-brothers possibly takes the golden scepter," Lars said, ignoring the question.

"That explains the funny looking flags," Maxwell said.

"Thank you, Lord Balfoest. We will visit the Great Cathedral and take our leave of your city," Seth said.

"Why do you think the flags look funny?" Lars asked.

All four men turned to look back at the steward. The man had not deigned to rise to his feet or approach them, but instead saw fit to ask a question such as that.

"I don't know," Maxwell said. "If the Council of Nine, or whatever your group is called, plans to do decent work for the capital, I'd have thought your flags would have the triangles so their tips looked outward, as an Empire should, instead of pointing inward, at yourselves."

"I see," Lord Balfoest said, clearly not liking the answer he had received.

"Come Jared, Master Tove awaits us at the Windstall Hermitage," Seth said.

"Seth, I cannot accept this!" Jared shook his head. It was all wrong. Nowhere in his mind was he able to reason that Kathleen could truly be gone. Images of the girl exploded in his mind — memories of their journey together from Candoreth. The pictures filled his eyes, and he felt his whole world collapsing. He had his brother by his side, but what was left of Kathleen was supposed to be found in a stone jar.

"Why must I always be asked to sacrifice one person I love for another?" he said.

65

GREAT REMORSE

The Steward of Tyath descended from his seat. He approached Jared with the most empathetic expression. The Sīhalt felt himself breathing quickly. He tried to calm himself. Lord Balfoest placed an understanding hand on Jared's shoulder and looked into his gray eyes.

"You feel great remorse. You loved her," Lord Balfoest said.

Jared exhaled sharply, surprised to feel an overwhelming sense of compassion from the man. He felt he was understood by the Steward. Even as he recoiled at the news the man delivered, a part of him wanted to curl close to him as a lonely child might in the arms of a caring older sibling. Instead, Jared brought his hand to his face, his fingers pressing against the bridge of his nose as he fought to keep back the tears.

"I can't believe I've lost her."

"She was a very special girl — one that could capture any man's heart," Lord Balfoest said in a comforting voice. "It is healthy to express your pain, Guardian. You're not a creature made of cast metal or carved stone."

His voice encouraged the warrior to unburden himself. Jared

resisted the comforting impulse encouraging him to surrender to his emotions.

"I need to go there," Jared said.

Then he turned and walked out of the throne room. He was silent as he mounted Steed and took the broad thoroughfare that led directly to the Great Cathedral. Seth signaled for the other companions to follow.

This is no time to leave him alone, Seth signed to Maxwell.

The normally fun-loving Shifter acknowledged the message gravely. When they arrived at the cathedral, Jared ran up the steps and something in his demeanor, or the fire in his eyes, made the Luzian priests stand back. They did not even ask him to remove the thin sword strapped to his hip or the dagger in his belt.

Jared threw open the heavy, richly decorated doors. The darkness of the cathedral invited him inside. None of the large chandeliers were lit this day. Only the light passing through the stained-glass window illuminated the ornate funeral urns along the front wall beyond the altar.

The cut stone urn, with its swirling pattern of golden Tyathian stone sat polished on a shelf. Jared stepped over the wooden barrier and approached the vessel in sadness. He reached out with his hand to touch the smooth lines of the inscription that read;

Daughter of House Dal Sundi,
Princess of Candoreth,
Kathleen Delunt Dal Sundi

Jared traced the outline of those words with his finger.

"You can't be mine, Kathleen. I thought for sure I would see you here. I left you to be protected by the strong walls of the capital, but nothing could've saved you from the Great Sickness. I've seen its work before, and I am so sad this is your end."

The Sīhalt Guardian placed his forehead against the cold, stone urn.

"I would have taken your place if I could have," he whispered.

Then he walked slowly toward the altar of the cathedral and picked up two long white candles. He placed them on the candlesticks after lighting them from the common flame burning near the altar and sat down in the nearest seat.

While the candles burned, Jared heard the footsteps of Seth approaching. His brother sat down beside him in the pew, placing an arm of comfort around his shoulder.

"I wish I could have met her-this woman that you love," Seth said.

"She wanted to come with me when I left to search for you," Jared said quietly, "but it was not possible."

"You traded her for me," Seth observed with understanding.

"I feel so empty and angry, but I have no one to blame. With Arabella I focused my anger on the barbarians, but this is like when mother and father died. There was no beast or villain on which to place our revenge — just the sickness."

"What made you love her?" Seth asked.

Jared's eyes seemed to look into the far distance.

"She was never mine, and I shouldn't have fallen for her as I have."

Seth nodded in understanding.

"Our mother would often say, 'The heart is a willful part of man and cannot easily be controlled'..."

"'...but for the tongue, there's no excuse,'" Jared smiled through his misty eyes and finished the statement their mother had always used when they were young.

"Kathleen demonstrated the best there was to be found in the human heart. I watched her as she struggled to balance the demands on her young life. She embodied womanly beauty unlike any person I have ever known. She was beautiful, Seth. She had the kind of beauty that burns from within, not superficial beauty bound only to the hair or a smooth complexion, but she had strength and grace that made me want to be a better man. I misjudged her at first. I thought she was just a spoiled girl. I imagined her as a powdered Princess who filled her days with frivolity, but she wasn't."

"Brother, your description of Kathleen Dal Sundi is most poetic," Seth said.

"She was an amazing young woman," Jared replied. "She saved the old Sīhalt Girdy Frast when he was overwhelmed by pirates on the southern coast. I watched her stand up to her step-mother, a foreign queen from Hestin. She loved her little sister and honored and respected her father, even when he didn't deserve it. She embraced the role of a leader when the barbarians first attacked us on the procession."

Seth listened with an expression of compassion settling on his face.

"She helped me regain my dignity and honor...to see the light within myself," Jared finally said.

"That alone is reason enough to love a woman," Seth replied.

"And, yet, fate has seen fit to keep us apart. I wish I could have met her long before the day I first set eyes upon her. Perhaps then, we could have been together."

"The Prince died also," Seth observed, looking at the urn inscribed with the Dol Lassimer name.

"She was supposed to decide if she would marry him while I was gone. I promised her I wouldn't interfere. I was afraid to come back to this place," he said, looking up at the cathedral. "I thought I might see her marry him when I returned. Heathron deserved a chance at love, but now a greater tragedy has befallen me. It seems she has accompanied Prince Heathron beyond my reach after all!"

"We cannot say what would have happened had she lived," Seth replied.

Jared shook his head. He walked to the urn and stood before

the silent stone memorial that encased the remains of the girl he loved.

"Kathleen," he said, "In my dreams when you called to me, I was certain you would wait for me to return. Arabella was my inspiration to live and serve as a Sīhalt Guardian. It was her loss that brought me to you. I remember the interest you had in her life and the smile it brought to your face when I told you of my sister and her child. Take this ring of mine, Kathleen. Accept my gratitude, even in my despair at your death. I know that I will try to be the kind of man worthy of a woman such as you. I love you, Kathleen. I will always love you."

Jared removed the silver ring from the forefinger of his right hand and placed it on the edge of the shelf near the urn.

"So may it be," Seth said softly in reverence for the prayer Jared offered to the dead. The brothers began to walk toward the door. Their black boots padded softly over the polished marble floors of the Great Cathedral. When they had reached the door, Jared turned and looked back at the urn. He paused and, holding the handle of the door, began to shake his head.

"Something isn't right, Seth. I just... I just cannot believe she's dead. It doesn't feel right"

"It never feels right when we lose a loved one," Seth replied empathetically. "But now it is time for us to leave and make our way back to Master Tove."

Jared shook his head. Something in his expression was more strained, more distant than Seth had ever seen in his brother before.

"I'm going back to speak with Lord Balfoest."

"Jared," Seth said, taking his brother by the shoulders. "Do you expect a different answer from him the second time? Look, I know it's hard-"

"I expect the truth." Jared interrupted, and then pushed his brother away and retraced his steps back through the doors into the sunlight.

66

GOLDEN LIES

"What is the meaning of this? You cannot barge in here!" Lord Balfoest said as his guards sought to impede the entrance of the Sīhalt Guardian.

The man dressed in black moved like angry smoke. He seemed to drift wherever he wanted in the fray, avoiding the grasps of the guards as he flanked them. The Sīhalt used the momentum of the men against them. They stumbled onto one another as the Sīhalt Guardian gave measured kicks with his boots and strikes with his fists. He didn't draw his sword. The three companions behind him had looks of mortified embarrassment.

"They should have just let him in to talk," the smallest one said through a grin.

"Stand down!" the Steward shouted so that all the guards could hear him.

They finally slowed their advance and stood still, breathing heavily. The Sīhalt Guardian looked determined. His lips were drawn tight and he seemed unfazed by his exertions.

"Who saw the Princess die? I want to speak with them," the Sīhalt Guardian demanded.

The people in the throne room remained silent. They looked from one to another and then at Lars where he sat on the high seat.

"I, for one, saw her die," Lord Balfoest said calmly, but loudly.

The statement hung in the room and the Sīhalt Guardian looked around, waiting for someone else to offer a statement.

"Where is another witness? Should I take the word of one man?" the Sīhalt Guardian said.

Lars knew this behavior was unconventional for a Sīhalt Guardian. The man was clearly at the mercy of his grief, but this was unexpected - it was dangerous.

"Do the esteemed Sīhalt Guardians now behave as common ruffians, threatening the leaders of law-abiding cities, hm? If so, your Order has fallen very far indeed."

Lord Balfoest stood at his full height, his arms folded and his features drawn as tightly into disappointment as he could muster.

"Let's get out of here, Jared. We have over-stayed our welcome," Channing said, coming into the court.

"I demand to speak with others who can confirm the death of Princess Dal Sundi."

"Would you like to speak with the nurses who gave her broth? The servants who changed her bed linens as she lay sweating and writhing in pain? Perhaps you would like to speak to the wood-cutters who stacked the funeral pyre and the priests who lit the flame? We did not try to make it a spectacle. If you ever have the misfortune of seeing someone die of that disease, you will under-stand for yourself."

"I know very well the disfiguring effect of those boils," the warrior said, approaching Lars with a savage severity that made the Steward retreat further into the cushions of his chair, "but I don't believe you are telling me the truth."

A hush fell over the court as the lords and ladies waited for Lord Balfoest to reply.

"You want proof?" the Steward said with a sneer.

"I will not leave until I speak to other people who can verify the truth of what you say."

"I owe you nothing, but I will have our nurses and priests swear to you what they saw. Would that be enough?"

The Sīhalt Guardian nodded.

"Princess Kathleen, Prince Heathron, the old witch woman, and even my niece were consumed by the Plague before they were consumed by the funeral fire," Lars said, addressing the court now more than just the Guardian. He paused then, turning his cold glare back on Jared. "Follow my guards to the infirmary, and they will tell you what you desire to know," Lars said.

Lars motioned one of his officers closer and placed a hand on his shoulder as he leaned in to whisper another command.

"Gather the Imperial Guards, as well as those of the city detachment. When you are close to the southeastern gate, force this rabble out of Tyath. I am tired of them," he said.

"The captain at that gate may not like it. He's enamored by the Sīhalt Guardians and House Dol Lassimer."

"Then we will deal with him forthwith," Lars said.

The older Sīhalt Guardian watched him from across the throne room. His eyes hardened as he turned to leave.

That one is dangerous, Lars reminded himself.

67

EXPELLED FOR THE TRUTH

"He's ordered his guards to call for reinforcements and throw us out of the city," Jared said under his breath so that their military escort could not hear.

The Candorethian Captain whistled softly. "That's not going to be pretty."

"It will be entertaining to see them try," Maxwell said with a smile.

The palace guards marched in front and back of the companions. Their faces were grim and told of the displeasure they felt at the duty they now performed.

"These fellows were made to look like fools by you. They will welcome the chance to prove themselves otherwise," Seth warned.

"If so, many people were involved in the funeral, how can the steward be lying?" Channing said.

"There is something about Lord Balfoest that doesn't seem right to me," Jared replied.

"I would not say he's virtuous, nor do I believe every word he has told us, but there are only four in our company, and I do not relish the idea of spilling blood in the Golden City," Seth said.

"I would lay bets on our four, against any force he can muster in the short term," Maxwell said, sizing up the men who rode and marched beside them.

"Then let me rush to the infirmary and question the nurses there before they try to force us from the city," Jared said.

"We can keep these fellows occupied here for a bit," Channing said.

Jared nodded. "I'll meet you at the southeastern gate. That is where they wish to take us."

Jared put his heels to the sides of his great horse. Steed responded by surging forward at a gallop. The Windstall stallion raced between the lines of guards. The men on foot jumped out of the way as the charger ran between them. The horses the officers rode suddenly reared up at the surprising approach of the black horse. The guards struggled to control their mounts and then spurred them to follow the escaping Sīhalt Guardian.

A shout rose from the remaining three companions who turned and fled in three different directions. The company of Tyathian guards were confused for a moment and then divided the men in pursuit of each one.

Jared leaned forward, encouraging the black horse to run faster. He knew the direction he needed to go to reach the infirmary. With a few moments of frank discussion with the nurses there, he planned to find out for sure if Kathleen had suffered in sickness.

Jared could hear the hoofbeats of his pursuers. There were no more than a few, and they would not catch him before he reached his destination.

In the tree-lined plaza spread out in front of the house of healing, Jared rode Steed at a full gallop. He swung his leg over the saddle and dismounted at a run. Nurses in large white hats watched in surprise as the tall man in black sprinted up the gently sloping ramp to the front door.

Jared stepped inside the front door of the infirmary. He overheard voices in the next room. He walked to where he could see the people who were talking.

"How on Abboth's green earth do you ever expect to gain your credentials if you cannot do as you're told?"

A large woman gesticulated aggressively in the face of a doe-eyed girl with brown hair pulled up in a bun. The harsh words were answered by a sweet voice that quavered.

"Yes," the girl said as she wiped tears from her eyes, "but the child was still alive."

"I am the Head Nurse and I will tell you when to start and when to stop resuscitation efforts. You will not make decisions of that nature as of yet — if ever!"

The girl cried out, wringing her hands in anguish, looking at the small form of an infant in the crib.

"But, I saved her," she cried.

The older woman raised a hand to slap the girl just as Jared intervened.

"Excuse me," he said in his deep voice.

The Head Nurse jumped and turned to the Sīhalt Guardian.

"Who gave you permission to enter my infirmary?" she said in a loud accusatory tone.

"I am Jared DeTorre, Sīhalt Guardian on a mission for Prince Heathron Dol Lassimer. I need some answers."

"Prince Heathron is dead," the nurse said, emphasizing the word. She narrowed her eyes at him.

"His passing makes no difference in my duty to serve. I have sworn an oath and I will fulfill it."

It was Jared's turn to add emphasis to his words, and he did so with a tone that made the nurse hesitate.

"I don't see how I can help you," she said, motioning for the girl to leave the room. "You look healthy enough."

"Do not leave just yet," Jared said to the young novice when she turned to leave, wiping tears from her cheeks.

"I need to know if the Dal Sundi Princess was cared for by your nurses. How long was she sick before she died?"

"Now you will make demands of my staff? I won't stand for this insult!" the harsh woman said. Two more nurses hearing the exchange came to the door of the room.

"Call for the guards," the Head Nurse said. "This man must be removed from our House of Healing."

"I want to know if any of you have seen the Princess since the day we arrived in the city last summer."

Jared looked from one to the other of the nurses, and they all looked down at the ground when the Head Nurse glared in their direction.

"If it were not for the commands of the imperial family, we would never have lifted a finger to help that witch. She didn't belong here — cursed as she was. I was glad to hear the Sickness took her."

The resounding slap broke the brief moment of silence that had reigned after the nurse spoke. Jared's hand flew and the fat woman reeled unceremoniously and fell to her rump on the floor. The two nurses at the door covered their mouths with their hands in surprise — one to stifle a scream and the other to conceal a satisfied smile. The novice gasped and then began to laugh.

The brown-eyed girl turned to the Guardian and wiped more tears from her eyes, these of laughter.

"I'm in deep trouble, Lord Sīhalt," she said. "So, I might as well tell you that the red-haired Princess has not been seen within these walls since the day you arrived. I was also asked to falsify the records saying that nurses were sent to minister to her in the palace. Instead, those nurses were reading in the park. I know they say she died of the sickness, but if that is true, we did nothing to help her."

"I'll have your commission for this, girl," the Head Nurse threatened, trying to right herself.

"It's okay," the young nurse said, removing her white apron and throwing it toward the woman seated on the floor. "I quit."

As she said these words, a sudden padding of boots followed by a loud crash, resounded as guards burst into the infirmary. They came in like a storm, surrounding Jared with swords drawn. Having assumed their positions, they fell into an intense, contained stillness, and waited, as an officer walked in slowly behind them and surveyed the room.

Jared raised his hands to show he held no weapon.

"I am ordered to remove you from the city," the captain of the City Guard explained.

"Run him through!" shouted the Head Nurse. "He's a demon."

"We will take it from here," the officer replied, turning slightly, and motioning for Jared to walk toward the exits.

"Yes, Captain Bastian," the guards said, saluting their superior.

"Thank you," Jared said, "I remember you from the main gate when I last visited Tyath."

The captain saluted, "Lord Sīhalt, are you familiar with the name Dallin Sarkkand?" he asked. "There is a young noble man and an Imperial Guardswoman who just returned from the contested lands. They were looking for you and insisted that they be able to speak with you."

"I will gladly speak with them," Jared said.

The captain escorted him to the main gate. They were joined by Maxwell, Seth and Channing who lost their pursuers and circled back to meet him. In the gate-house, Captain Bastian closed the door and the shutters of the small window.

In the room stood a tall young man with wide-set eyes and rather curly brown hair. He wore a crimson doublet with his house crest and expensive boots made for traveling.

"I am Dallin Sarkkand," he said, as soon as they entered, "and this is Lilly, an Imperial Guardswoman to Princess Kathleen."

The young woman also stood. Her straight dark hair and

equally dark eyes had a familiarity to them that Jared could not place.

"Hello, Lord Sīhalt," she said, "I will be brief and to the point. I believe the Princess is alive and being held captive in her royal apartments. Perhaps Prince Heathron is alive too. We looked for you on the western reaches of the empire. When we returned, Captain Bastian's men took us in for questioning and we revealed our intentions. Will you help us to free Kathleen Dal Sundi? I know where she might be in the city."

"Lead the way," Jared said in a deep voice, "I too believe she is yet alive."

"Nothing will stop us from going to her," Seth said.

"No matter how many stand in his way," Maxwell added.

"It isn't men, but walls that are the barrier. I think she is being held near the outer wall to the south," Lilly said.

"I cannot ask the guards to abandon their posts," Captain Bastion said, "I would be discovered as an ally to your cause. If we are discreet, I will be able to continue to be of assistance until the Prince and Princess are free."

"Take us to the place," Jared said to Lilly.

"Yes Lord Sīhalt," she replied.

A TREE GROWS IN STONE

The walls of the Golden City were built deep into the foundation bedrock on the Amaranth Plain. The upper reaches of the wall were decorated with cornices and carvings. The watershed for the wall was diverted into channels of stone that protruded outward and the base of the walls were enormously thick. The Builders of the bygone era had created weep holes for the groundwater to find a way through the impenetrable walls. The enormous stones, positioned one upon the other, were set so tightly, that a hand hold could not be found. Over the centuries, additional rooms had been built around the original courtyards making this section of the city a warren of hallways, smaller courtyards, and passageways.

Lilly looked up at the walls of the towers high above their heads, trying to get her bearings.

"This is about where rooms would be," she said.

"I can fly above it, to be sure," Maxwell offered.

"From the secret garden inside, you can see the sky through the windows above," Lilly said.

"Go and take a look, Maxwell," Jared said, his face taut with anticipation.

"I'll go over here before I change," Maxwell said.

"It can be a little unsettling," Channing explained to Dallin and Lilly.

Maxwell walked past the nearest corner of the wall to Shift.

"How are the floors connected? Do you remember?" Seth asked.

Lilly furrowed her brow in thought.

"I don't know," she admitted.

The scream of a rock eagle pierced the air, just before the great bird of prey lifted itself on wings of metallic green.

"Was that....?" Dallin began, as he watched the bird begin to climb to the highest towers.

"Yes," Channing said. "I felt the same way when I first saw it."

Lilly looked on in amazement. "I've never met a Shifter before! The Luzian Church says they don't exist, but the Old Gifts are coming back, just as my grandmother used to say."

"But to what purpose? I hesitate to consider," Seth replied.

Jared scanned the walls. It would be almost impossible to climb. There were no footholds because the stone was so smooth. The height of the walls made those of Altrastadt seem small in comparison.

He used his Senses and listened for anything that might give him a clue to her location. The wind blew softly, and Jared could hear the sounds of the city within. He listened and heard the sound of water moving through the channels. The sun was shining, but the small patches of snow, encrusted since winter, still melted and fed the tiny drips that he heard making their way to the ground.

Jared focused on the fixed stone walls in front, the foundation of the city. Faintly, deep within and below the level on the ground outside, he heard a dog bark. The animal was angrily barking as if it wanted to attack someone.

Why would a dog be found in the deepest levels, if it wasn't guarding something?

Jared held up his hand, "Quiet!" he said. "I hear something."

The strange sound came faintly to his ears. The guard dog's barking had ceased. Instead Jared heard someone struggling to exert himself, followed by the slow, constant sound of wood being slid along stone.

His companions remained silent. Except for the impatient snort of one of the horses, they were still. Then a faint humming sound rose on the wind.

"There!" Jared said. "Coming from over there."

The Sīhalt Guardian jumped down from his horse and ran to the city wall. He placed his hands on the stone and laid his head against the wall. Jared looked at Seth.

"What is it brother?" Seth asked.

"She is near, I can feel it," he said.

Jared rounded the next corner of the wall.

On the exterior, he saw a small tree beginning to grow. The branches unfolded wide and the slender trunk was fixed tightly against the stones. From the foundation, it grew out of a small hole.

Jared walked closer. He could see the tree was not common to the Northern Realms.

"That is a citrus tree," Channing said with excitement.

Despite the coolness of the new spring air, the little tree became covered in blossoms. The flowers opened before their very eyes. A burst of the orange blossom scent cascaded over Jared, washing away his doubts.

Soon small round oranges, the color of the sunrise in the summer, grew rapidly until they dangled from its delicate branches.

"Surely this day will be remembered in my life. I've seen two miracles within moments," Dallin said in awe.

"This was the sign Kathleen promised me!" Jared cried.

Jared reached the lowest edge of the stone skirting outside the wall. He pulled himself up and stood on the narrow ledge. By sliding his feet along the wall, he made his way to the tender young orange tree.

"Kathleen," he called.

Then he waited, listening with his perfect hearing for the response.

Ever so faintly, he heard a voice.

"Jared? Is that you?"

"Kathleen, I've returned!" he said, grasping the branches of the tree to keep himself steady. He leaned down to speak into the opening from which the tree had grown. The channel was obstructed by the roots of the tree, but Jared could hear Kathleen and she him.

"Oh Jared, you've come!"

He heard the words spoken by the voice he so often heard in his dreams. The sound of it warmed his soul, and he felt as if the power of it would give him strength to tear away the immoveable stone between them.

"You're alive," Jared said.

"I didn't give up hope. You're the only one that can save us," Kathleen replied faintly.

"Who else is with you?" Jared asked

The voice sounded very weak. "Larissa and Heathron are here. Melva too. But Lord Balfoest intends to kill us. Please hurry."

Jared heard the dog barking again, more clearly now. The ferocity of the sound urged him onward.

"Hold on, Kathleen. I will come for you."

He leaped down from the wall just as Maxwell flew down from above. The eagle Shifted back into a human form as it landed.

"I saw the orange tree growing from the foundation. Is that her?" Maxwell asked.

"She's inside with Melva and Larissa. Can you get inside?" Jared asked.

"The tree will have to be removed, but I can squeeze through. I've done it before."

"How will we remove the tree? The roots are embedded in the rock," Seth said.

Maxwell looked offended. "I'll tear it away. Just watch."

"Are you okay, Heathron?" Kathleen asked.

"I've got you, I'm braced against the wall," he said. Heathron's broad shoulders were not as muscular as they used to be. The months of imprisonment had taken its toll. Lack of decent food and continued torture left the Prince scarred and somewhat thinner than before.

"Stop now, Kathleen," Melva said. "You are pushing yourself too far in your weakened condition."

"I'm done growing it. He saw the sign I made for him," Kathleen said with excitement in her voice, "Jared is coming for us."

Heathron felt both a leap of hope and a pang of regret fill his heart. The Guardian had returned to rescue Kathleen.

The Sīhalt will do what I have not been able to manage, Heathron thought.

"Jared will save Kathleen from the horrors of Lord Balfoest," Heathron said under his breath, but none of the others heard him because the mastiff in the hall was barking again. Karl was bringing his horrible canine for a visit.

Kathleen slowly climbed down. She looked at the others.

"He said he is coming," she reported.

"Well he had better come immediately or there may be nothing left of us," Larissa said above the savage barking.

Heathron searched in vain for a loose rock or any object large enough to be used as a weapon. The Prince was trained in hand-to-hand combat, but the holds and strikes he had practiced since childhood were designed for a fight with another man, not a ferocious Horming Mastiff.

As the guard came closer, they could hear him encouraging the dog onward.

"Are you ready?" Karl said in a desperately excited voice. "Are you ready to get them?"

The dog, just outside the door, lunged against the restraint of the leash. Heathron could hear the savage barking and knew that he would feel the teeth upon him once more. He felt the pit of his stomach sink, but reminded himself of his need to be brave. Although Prince Heathron stood weaponless before the door, he reached for one of the two emotions that serve as an antidote to fear — love.

He turned his mind toward Kathleen and the adoration he had always felt for her. He considered the good she represented in his life. He remembered the softness of her face, the warmth of her lips, and her high cheekbones that always seemed to give her an aura of resolute courage. The dog barked, now biting the edge of the door outside.

Heathron took a stance in front of the women. He spread his feet wide and bent his knees. Now he reached for that other emotion that leaves a man with no room for fear in his soul. Heathron embraced the rage. He thought of the lies used to isolate him and complete his false arrest. He gritted his teeth and remembered his mother struggling to breath and his father locked in death's embrace. Anger flowed through him like the torrent of a flood.

"Open the door now, Karl!" Heathron shouted. "I am ready for you and your dog."

∾

Maxwell climbed the ledge and took the form of his favorite animal. The wolvermink claws helped him reach the tree that grew from the stone.

"Work quickly, my friend," Jared pleaded.

The beast seemed to be made of all teeth and claws. It looked back at him and seemed to grin. It closed its teeth around the base of the tree and braced its paws against the city wall. A deep-throated growl rose from the wolvermink. Chunks of wood began to fly as the beast shredded the orange tree. The powerful jaws and muscled neck of the wolvermink flexed again and again until it secured the base of the tree in its awful jaws. The wolvermink leaned back with all its strength, and the roots of the orange tree began to give. The animal pulled the roots free and fell back with all its effort, the remnants in its mouth.

As soon as it landed, it raced back toward the hole in the wall. Maxwell Shifted into a long snake — perfectly sized to fit through the wall.

Jared turned to Channing and placed a hand on his shoulder.

"Go and find a boat for our escape. Find one that is fast and light!"

Channing saluted and galloped toward the harbor.

"I'll go gather support, among the loyal Houses where I can," Dallin said.

"If Balfoest and the council learn of your family's loyalty to the Prince, you will be killed. We are not ready to fight. We plan to flee. Be careful," Jared said.

Dallin mounted his horse and looked at the Sīhalt Guardian.

"I will organize the resistance to Balfoest and his supporters. Do not give up on Tyath, Lord Sīhalt. The day will come when you will again be proud to be a Guardian of the Golden City." Dallin touched his heels to his horse and galloped off.

Jared turned to Seth and Lilly.

"We may have to fight our way through the streets to reach the inside of the palace," Jared said.

"It can't be any worse than what we've already been through, brother," he smiled. "I'll race you there."

Lilly pointed to the next tower along the wall. "We can enter at the next gate. I know a way to reach the lower levels. I will lead you there."

THE SERPENT ARRIVES

K athleen and Melva stood on weak legs against the back wall of the cell. Larissa huddled in the far corner trying to make herself small. Heathron stood before them, his hands balled into fists, calling the guards.

"Come and fight me without the dog, Karl. You have already betrayed your Prince, why do you continue to betray your own self-respect? Are you afraid that after all this torture, I can still beat you, man to man?"

Kathleen knew it wouldn't be fair. It never was. She remembered the first time Balfoest had set the dog on the Prince. She shivered and squeezed her eyes shut for a moment, trying to make the image go away.

But there stood Heathron, alone against the enemy, still willing to defend her. Keys rattled in the lock of the door. The timbre of the barking increased. The dog wanted blood, and Karl would give it to him. Kathleen cried out and looked away. She couldn't bear to watch it again.

A strange tearing sound accompanied by a primal growl erupted from the hole in the wall above their heads. The dog paused for a moment at the sound, only to resume it's barking again. Kathleen looked up to see the circle of light streaming in from the hole in wall. The tree she had grown was no longer there. Heathron took a few steps back from the door. He held one hand low and briefly looked behind him to make sure Kathleen was okay.

Larissa gave a shrill scream and pointed toward the back wall. She huddled further into the corner. Kathleen saw the door begin to open but her eyes followed the direction Larissa pointed.

An enormous yellow serpent with red eyes began to enter the cell. It flowed like honey from a spoon.

Kathleen heard Melva say something in her native tongue. It sounded of disbelief. The old woman gathered Larissa and Kathleen to her side. Heathron backed up further, joining the women in a small cluster.

The creaking of the old metal hinges added to the cacophony. Karl entered the room, the mastiff straining against the short leash.

The giant viper slithered to the middle of the room, positioning itself where Heathron had stood just a moment before. The thing coiled its long body and rose up to the height of Kathleen's shoulders before it flared its hooded head and revealed glistening fangs.

The guard released the mastiff whose attention was now focused on the snake. The dog circled and lunged only to draw back, barely escaping the counter strike by the snake. The serpent drew itself up even higher and let out a hiss that matched the dog's bark for volume. The sound filled the air and made Kathleen and the others cover their ears in pain.

The great mastiff attacked again and this time the snake seemed to have baited the dog. As the canine lunged up at the neck, the snake shifted to one side, and the dog just missed being able to sink its teeth into the shimmering yellow scales.

Before the dog landed back on the ground, the viper struck with lighting speed. The long, sharp fangs sunk deep into the dog's neck. The mastiff let out a yip and slid to the ground before turning to face its adversary again. The snake followed the movements of the dog as it circled back to the side of its master. Kathleen saw the guard's terror-filled face. He pointed at the snake and commanded the dog to attack. Instead the mongrel stood quivering at his side, saliva flowing from its jowls, the vicious excitement in its eyes now extinguished.

To Kathleen's amazement the serpent coiled on the ground began to shift. The body widened and the head became more rounded. The tail shrank too, drawing itself inward toward the growing body of the form. Karl's eyes widened, and he dropped his sword.

"It's a person," Larissa said as the outline of the snake now transitioned to that of a young man. He stood naked in front of the guard and the attack dog. The young man raised his hand and pointed at the paralyzed mastiff.

"Bad dog!" he said in a voice of reprimand. Whereupon the animal let out a whine and crumpled to the floor.

Karl stared at the dead animal, then back at the disrobed man standing in the middle of the room.

"You really should have kept your dog on a leash," the young man said.

The guard jumped and ran down the corridor calling for Nich. There was no answer, and his footsteps retreated into the distance.

The strange, young man turned to look at Kathleen and the others.

"Hello, I'm Maxwell," he said without the least bit of embarrassment given his lack of clothing. "Sorry to drop in on you like this but you should gather your things. We will be going now." He gestured toward the open door.

"We don't have any things," Kathleen said, still in shock.

"Right," he looked around the filthy cell, "Then follow me."

"Don't hurt me! I'm here to help," a voice called from the hall.

Heathron helped Kathleen into the hallway. Maxwell took a defensive stance.

"Nich is a friend," Kathleen said to Maxwell.

"Very well," the Shifter said, relaxing and offering his hand to Nich. "We accept your friendship."

Nich's eyes swept up and down the form of Maxwell's frame. The young guard hesitated to shake his hand.

"I'm sorry. Does anyone have a blanket or something?" Maxwell asked. "I lose my clothes every time I Shift. It can be unsettling."

"That is the least of the unsettling part," Heathron said looking down at the carcass lying in the cell.

"But thank you for your help," Melva said as she led Larissa into the hall and handed her tattered shawl to Maxwell.

"I can show you the way out through the tunnels. They will be waiting for us if we go up the stairs," Nich said.

"Lead the way. Jared, Seth, and Channing are following Lilly into the city at this very moment," Maxwell said with a smile.

70

THE MARINE ESCAPE

Channing resisted the urge to run down to the harbor, draw his sword, and commandeer a ship from an unsuspecting merchant. The harbor served as a social gathering place, but also as a commercial and naval hub. He needed to be careful.

"Think man!" he said to himself. "It will not do to ruin the chance you have to go home."

Instead, Channing forced himself to walk slowly and nonchalantly along the wharf as if he had not a care in the world. The harbor at Tyath had a boardwalk that wrapped around the entire expanse. Slips were available and boats of all sizes were moored in neat rows. Channing stood tall and curled his lips up at the corners of his mouth in his most engaging smile.

I need to find someone with a nice boat, he thought.

His brilliant red jacket had a few scuff marks on the sleeves, but he brushed the dust from his shoulders and ran his fingers through his hair. His locks resembled a lion's mane.

Channing made sure that his cravat was loose, lending him the demeanor of a man willing to break the rules. He smiled and waved charmingly to a few of the ladies gathered in groups, some of them struggling under the weight of the shopping baskets looped over their arms.

He tipped his hat to the sailors working to clean the ships before they headed back out to sea.

He whistled a merry tune and even stopped to buy a bouquet of flowers from a vendor along the dock.

"Who are these for?" the woman behind the flower cart asked.

"Not for my mother," Channing said with a wink.

"I didn't imagine so," the woman replied.

Channing moved ahead, like a hunter stalking game in the woods. He scanned his likely targets and decided to move on. The boats in this area were too commercial. They were blunted, squat and sat low in the water.

Those would never do for a man of Marth, he thought, walking further down the pier. He passed other boats and arrived at the farthest edge of the harbor where the quality of the crafts seemed much improved. Very few boats were moored here and those that were represented the highest quality. He needed a boat that was fast, and big enough to carry them all.

"These are more like it," Channing said to himself.

The masts on the boats were taller. They carried more sails, and even the names and paint schemes seemed to fit what he wanted.

"You look lost," a woman said as Channing came strolling by.

Channing looked at the stern of a light blue yacht.

Marine Escape, read the name on the boat.

Looking over the rail was a blond-haired beauty wearing a white captain's hat.

"Who are the flowers for?" she asked as she sauntered down the gangplank.

"Oh, these are a thank you gift," Channing said.

The young woman raised her eyebrows.

"Have you received some favors here in the Golden City? I can see you're not from around here," she said looking at his clothing, inspecting him as if he were a newly sculpted statue.

Channing took it as a compliment.

"I am supposed to meet a merchant woman here from Altrastadt. I've waited for two days, to inspect her wares and show her what I'd like to trade in return. I must be unlucky. I appear to have been jilted again."

The beautiful woman looked at him through lowered lashes.

"My name is Jessica Turlin," she said, "owner of the *Marine Escape*," she extended her hand, "perhaps I can help you."

My thoughts exactly.

Channing smiled and swept the white-plumed hat from his head and kissed her outstretched hand.

"My name is Channing Dur Ruston, Captain of Candoreth, opportunistic merchant and battle-hardened rogue."

Jessica seemed to purr. "Do you have wares you would like me to inspect? You don't look like a merchant woman, but I am desperate to trade," Channing said with a raised eyebrow.

Jessica seemed to find humor in his statement and coyly turned to show off her slender form.

"You might have interest in what I have to offer," she said, responding to his meaning.

Channing held up the bouquet.

"These flowers need fresh water. Perhaps I could climb aboard and place them in a vase for you?"

"My crew would love to be on shore right now. Perhaps I will relieve them of their duties for an hour or so. Then we can ...negotiate."

Jessica looked up and down the dock taking stock of the maintenance work her crew was performing on the deck and hull. The yacht gleamed clean and bright.

"Is there not a captain of the ship?" Channing asked.

The woman looked offended.

"I am the captain of the *Marine Escape*. I would assume a military man such as yourself would know that." She pointed to the anchor and star emblem on her hat.

"I know very little of such things, Lady Turlin. Where I come from, only men are the captains of ships."

"Rest assured, she is mine," Jessica said seductively. "Whatever waves might break against her hull are mine to choose."

Channing placed a hand on the lower back of the woman and leaned in to whisper in her ear.

"Then I shall take these flowers to the captain's quarters," he said, "while you furlough the crew."

Jessica drew in a deep breath and licked her lips.

"Wait here on board, I'll be right back," she said and walked down the dock telling the men they were free to go.

Channing waited and watched until the last of the crew were slapping each other on the back and walking toward the city. Jessica Turlin still had not climbed aboard when he drew his sword, reached over the rails, and cut the mooring lines. The yacht shifted and began to drift away from the dock.

Jessica Turlin called to one of her men, "Manning, you forgot to secure the boat!" she shouted.

"No, Lady Turlin! I tied it right tight, I did," he said.

She glanced down to see the cut mooring line drifting in the water then looked up and shouted in anger.

"What are you doing?" she cried.

"I'm just taking her out for a bit, if you don't mind Captain," Channing yelled back, saluting the enraged beauty.

"I've got some friends that need passage. You can have the flowers, though!" he said as he threw the bouquet. It fell short of the dock and landed in the water.

"So sorry about that," Channing said with smile.

Jessica ran frantically along the dock.

"Stop this right now!" she commanded. "That is my yacht."

"What's that?" Channing said, cupping his hand to his ear. "I can't hear you over the waves breaking against her hull."

Channing turned the boat to angle toward the far edge of the harbor. The wind blew, drowning out the calls from Jessica demanding that he return the yacht immediately.

Channing removed his lucky hat and adjusted the brim and ran his fingers along the white plume.

Works every time, he thought with a grin.

71

FROM DARKNESS TO LIGHT

They ran through the tunnel, Nich leading the way. The young guard held torches aloft to illuminate the passageway cut through natural stone. A faint, cool breeze blew through the expanse of the tunnel. It was large enough to drive a wagon through and tall enough to accommodate a man on horseback. The gradual incline was comforting to Kathleen even though she could no longer walk herself. At least they were making their way to the outside. She could feel it.

"Are you alright, Kathleen?" Heathron asked.

He carried her in his arms because she was too weak to run for long.

"You're the one carrying me," she said with compassion. "Thank you."

"I suppose I'm the one responsible for getting you into this mess," the Prince said. "The least I can do is help you escape."

"Keep moving," Maxwell said and took a few steps back to encourage Melva and Larissa as they hobbled along together.

In the distance, further back down the tunnel, Kathleen heard barking again.

"It sounds like they have brought the other dogs," Nich said.

He paused at a fork in the tunnel and held the torch higher to see the words carved into the rock.

"We go this way," the young man said. "We're not far from the gate."

After several more turns in the tunnel, Kathleen could feel that Heathron was slowing down.

"I might be able to run now," she offered, but the Prince just shook his head, swallowed deeply, and continued to carry her in his arms. The barking behind them, savage as it was, increased.

"I can see the light ahead," Nich shouted and encouraged the group to move faster. Iron grates, far above their heads, allowed sunlight to filter through the tunnel.

"We are getting closer to the exit," Larissa said.

Kathleen tried to ignore the sound of the dogs gaining on them.

"I'm going to run ahead and call for help," Maxwell said as he sprinted past Nich toward the light.

Heathron stumbled for a moment and regained his footing. He was breathing laboriously now, sweat rolled down his brow and a grim determination was fixed on his face.

"If we can just make it outside," he managed to say in an attempt to give her hope.

Karl and his dogs must have entered the straight stretch between the last bend. Kathleen thought she could see movement in the distant regions of the tunnel behind them.

She tightened her arms around Heathron's shoulders and tried to make it easier for him to carry her. As fast as they ran, the tunnel seemed to stretch out further in front of them. The floor of the tunnel still rose, but now it was almost imperceptible.

"Help us!" Larissa began to scream, looking up to the iron grates above. The sound of the city streets filtered faintly down into the tunnel. No one above acknowledged her calls.

Kathleen looked back over Heathron's shoulder. The sound of

the dogs was louder now, and she could hear Karl encouraging them onward.

"Run, run, run!" Nich encouraged them, shepherding the prisoners forward toward the light illuminating the end of the tunnel. "If we get past the doors, we can lock them in!" he shouted.

Kathleen could see two great doors held open at the side of the tunnel with enormous metal hooks. Gears were set in the ceiling and floor to allow each door to rotate open and closed. Nich ran forward and grabbed a lever. After slipping the ring off of the handle, he threw his weight downward against the lever and released the hooks that secured the doors open.

The growls and snarls coming from the pack of Horming Mastiffs sent cold shivers up her spine. Heathron began to pass Melva as the old woman slowed from exertion.

"Come on Melva, you can do it!" Kathleen cried.

Nich was struggling to turn the wheel that would bring the tunnel doors closed. The large metal pins were rusted, and for all the struggle, Nich only managed to move the doors a few inches. The tunnel remained open and seemed to be alive with the vicious sounds of the oncoming dogs.

Kathleen looked toward the light and realized they easily had two hundred more yards to go before they were free of the darkness.

"I've got to help him close the doors," Heathron said as he set Kathleen down and steadied her feet on the floor.

"Lilly and the Sīhalt Guardians are coming!" Larissa said with excitement.

The small group turned to see three figures running toward them. Their shapes were silhouetted against the bright light. They ran forward with capes billowing behind them. Lilly turned and began to fight some of the soldiers as they poured into the tunnel around her.

Heathron joined Nich and tried to close the doors. They

strained against the wheel, and it began to move, slowly creaking as it turned. Shouts from deeper inside the tunnel punctuated the growls of angry dogs as their feet padded quickly behind them.

"Close the doors!" came a faint shout from one of the Sīhalt Guardians as they sprinted down the tunnel. Kathleen could not tell if it was Jared or Seth.

Kathleen saw Nich turn to Heathron.

"It will not close in time," the boy said as they strained against the wheel. Heathron pushed with all his might, trying to use his legs to make the wheel rotate faster, but when Kathleen looked back the mastiffs were almost upon them.

Nich took a position between the slowly closing doors. He held his torch in one hand and drew his sword with the other. The fastest of the dogs sprang and slammed into the young guard. The boy was thrown backward, the sword knocked from his hand. The beast was upon him, savaging him with violent slashing bites. The boy tried to fend off the animal by shoving the lit torch into its face, but the dog ignored the flames and bearing it's teeth, grabbed Nich by the throat. The boy yelped, but the sound was cut short as his body was thrashed from side to side. Another attack dog joined in the kill.

"Nich!" Kathleen screamed.

Melva grabbed her arm and tried to pull her away, but Kathleen shook loose of her hold. Then Heathron let go of the gate wheel. It was too late. The doors to the deep were still open, the demons had arrived.

The Prince stooped down to pick up Nich's sword. He turned to look at Kathleen. Exhaustion rested like a dead weight on his shoulders. She saw his hands trembling as they clutched the hilt of the sword. His expression held her at bay — kept her from running to his side. He raised a hand and pointed toward the sprinting Sīhalt Guardian.

"I love you, Kathleen," he said. "Now go to him."

Heathron turned to face the approaching dog pack. Their vicious howls echoed on the tunnel walls. He shrugged his shoulders back as if to relieve them of the weight they carried. Prince Heathron clenched his jaw and lowered his head toward the attackers. He would give his life for hers.

He raised the sword over his head and stabbed the heart of the first dog that continued to ravage Nich's body. As he made a second swing, the remaining dogs ran through the open gate and surrounded the Prince.

They lunged at him from every side and despite the cries of Kathleen, he did not retreat. Heathron blocked an attack from the knife-like teeth with his forearm, but the enormous dog held on, and in doing so, lowered the Prince's guard. Another mastiff ran in and sunk its teeth into Heathron's leg. The dog pulled and Kathleen saw Heathron go down under the fierceness of the pack's attack.

Kathleen ducked as a shadow passed over her head and a sudden gust of wind blew her hair across her face. A shrill cry like the call of an eagle resounded in the tunnel. Clearing her vision, she saw a giant bird of prey sink its curved talons into one of the dogs.

Just as her mind registered what she was witnessing, the bird transformed into a different beast. An imperious growl rose louder and angrier than the rest. Unlike the dogs, there was no excitement in this sound. The guttural sounding animal seemed deeply enraged by the presence of the dogs. Kathleen saw the hairy beast rise to stand over the fallen Prince.

At first, she thought the ferocious creature would join in the attack, but it did not hurt Heathron who was curled into a defensive position. Kathleen did not recognize the animal. It was as if a man-sized badger had returned home to defend its cub. The dogs continued to bark and some renewed the attack.

"What is it?" Kathleen asked Melva, but the old woman shook her head in confusion.

"I don't know," the old woman whispered.

"It's a wolvermink...," Larissa said, "...a very large wolvermink."

The beast grabbed one of the dogs by the head and crushed its skull between powerful jaws. Another mastiff snapped at the wolvermink only to receive a quick slash from its sharp claws. Then the wolvermink pulled the dog into a violent embrace and bit down on the canine's neck. The dog went limp and made not another whimper.

The Sīhalt Guardians, with swords drawn, fell upon the remaining pack of dogs with twirling cloaks and flashing steel. The Horming Mastiffs did not give up even when the thin *impla* blades laid them open. When the last of the dogs fell, the Guardians helped Heathron back to his feet and finished closing the tunnel doors. They knelt to honor Nich, placing his arms across his chest in final repose.

Kathleen ran to Heathron who moved toward her despite his many wounds. Before she could reach him, Jared came into view. He swept her into his arms and held her close. As the terror of the moment passed, Kathleen realized with joy that Jared had indeed returned. He hugged her passionately, and she felt her body give in to the exhaustion she had tried so hard to stave off.

"You came back," she said, collapsing into his embrace.

"I promised I would," he replied in a voice full of emotion.

"Let me see Heathron," Kathleen managed.

Jared flinched at the request, but he complied.

"Of course, of course," he said and held her so that she might see the Prince, hunched over in pain a few paces away.

Kathleen saw Heathron's countenance, marred by the bites he had suffered, but knew his expression of pain was greater for the embrace that had held her.

"I thought I had lost you," Kathleen said, taking difficult steps toward him.

"And I feared the same," he said, not looking at the Sīhalt Guardian who reached out to steady her arm.

The wolvermink growled deep and low as it looked down the tunnel and lowered to its haunches beside the Prince.

Kathleen put her arms around Heathron despite the blood soaking his hair and shirt. She held his head and hugged him to her breast.

"Channing is arranging passage on a boat for us," Jared said.

Maxwell Shifted into a man. He was not without wounds, himself. Larissa offered him the shawl.

"You dropped this when you ran off," she said.

"I owe you my life," Heathron said to Maxwell.

"I won't forget it," the Shifter said smiling as he tied Melva's shawl around his waist once more. "If I'm going to have someone indebted to me, it might as well be a prince."

"You must be Seth," Kathleen said as she acknowledged the blue-eyed Guardian nearby who resembled Jared so perfectly.

"And you must be Princess Kathleen Dal Sundi — most noble of women," the Guardian said, kneeling before her with a fist across his heart. "We returned with all haste, Your Highness," he said.

"You look so much like your brother. Thankfully, your eyes tell you apart," Kathleen said.

"Nonsense, Your Highness. I am younger and better looking than he is," Seth said with a wink.

"It'll take more than a brush with death or a few arrows to make that true," Jared replied.

Kathleen smiled to witness the banter between the brothers. She felt as if she understood Jared a bit better, having met his sibling.

Lilly interrupted as she came down the tunnel.

"Captain Bastion will keep the horses. He said we have an open path to the gate, and from there to the harbor — but we should go now."

"Thank you, Lilly," Kathleen said and hugged the guardswoman tenderly. "You have been a loyal and true friend."

"I will not leave you now, Your Highness. Your life is yet in danger."

"You would leave your home here in Tyath?"

"Any place where you and Prince Dol Lassimer are treated with such distain is not a place I will call home," Lilly said.

72

FISH BAIT

"Move quickly, Your Highness," Captain Bastion said when he saw Heathron emerge from the tunnel.

City guards assisted Heathron and the women escape. The Sīhalt Guardians kept their swords drawn, looking in every direction as they made their way to the harbor. The companions squinted against the bright sunlight as they raced from the dark tunnel and were bathed in light of day.

They rushed down the tree-lined avenue of Anchorage Park. It led them down to the waterfront. Members of the City Guard, under command of Captain Jarek Bastion, helped them reach the harbor gate.

People on the walk quickly moved out of the way as the group rushed to the water's edge.

"Over here!" a voice called from a distant point along the dock.

Channing waved his white-plumed hat from the deck of a light blue yacht.

A group of men led by Jessica Turlin raced toward them, from the opposite side of the harbor walk.

Even at this distance, Kathleen saw the infuriated look of the noblewoman and began to laugh.

"What is it?" Larissa said. "What is so funny in this crisis?"

"Captain Dur Ruston commandeered the *Marine Escape*," she said through tears of laughter.

"Hurry! Hurry!" Channing called as he looked at the armed men led by a furious, blonde-haired girl.

They moved along a narrow portion of dock that rocked and swayed as they hurried. Seagulls called and took flight, evading the people as they ran toward their waiting boat.

"Maxwell, Channing, help them aboard. Seth and I will delay our pursuers," Jared said.

The brothers turned to face Jessica Turlin and her crew. Lilly joined them as Kathleen and the others climbed up the ladder with Captain Channing and Maxwell's help.

"Welcome aboard," Channing said, taking Kathleen's hand to steady her feet. "We will sail for home as soon as we get everyone on board."

Jessica's men shouted and rushed down the dock, armed with gaff hooks and cutlasses. One held a harpoon. Kathleen watched the Sīhalt Guardians prepare to defend them.

"Just like old times," she heard Seth say to Jared as they pointed their *implas* toward the sailors and stood far enough apart to deny them passage.

"I'm sure I can handle this group by myself," Jared replied. "But it is nice to have you at my side once more."

"We don't want a repeat of Fishing Point, do we?" Seth said.

Seth quickly whipped his thin blade through a pattern in the air, making it sing with the movement.

"You had to bring that up?" Jared said with a groan.

"I don't know. You are not as young as you once were. Maybe you have learned a few things since then."

"I'm in my prime," Jared replied.

Looking down from above, Kathleen had to admit, she agreed.

"You are stealing my boat!" Jessica screamed angrily at the party boarding her vessel.

Kathleen smiled down at the woman who represented what she hated in the Golden City.

"If I recall, you ran my boat onto the rocks, so we are borrowing yours," she said, smiling sweetly. "I'll bring it back as soon as I am able."

"You will hang for this!" she shouted.

"I'll let you know how she handles," Kathleen said. "Feel free to come to Candoreth, and I'll show you around."

Her tone was breathy, sweet as nectar, and exactly pitched to infuriate Jessica even more.

"Stop them!" Jessica commanded her crew.

The men took a half-step closer, but the Sīhalt Guardians shook their heads.

"I don't think the fishermen need more bait, but if you come any closer, I will be happy to cut some for them," Jared said.

The burly man lifted the harpoon above his head and hurled it at Jared, who moved to one side just enough to allow the pointed shaft to bury itself in the wood of the dock. Jared advanced with lightening quick speed, taking short, punctuated steps.

The sailors stumbled backward over Jessica, trampling her a bit while trying to get away from the whistling blade. When Jared stopped advancing on the narrow dock and the crew of the *Marine Escape* regained their footing. Jessica screamed as if she had been run through.

Long, golden locks floated on the water of the harbor. A few small fish rose to investigate and swam away, disinterested.

"You cut my hair!" Jessica screamed, holding up more of her severed curls in a fist of rage. Half of her long hair was cut level with her ear on one side. The singing blade of the Sīhalt had done its work.

"Tell your men to stand down or I'll finish the job. I don't want to see blood in the harbor today," Seth warned.

"You will never make it out of the harbor," Jessica said, trembling with anger.

"Okay, DeTorre boys! Quit picking on the little girl. Time to go," Maxwell said, motioning for them to climb aboard.

Jared and Seth leaped from the dock and nimbly climbed the ladder behind Maxwell. They saluted the angry crewmen of the stolen yacht as they hopped over the rails. The *Marine Escape* swung outward, moving further toward deeper water.

73

WAVE MISTRESS

"We need more wind in these sails. I imagine the navy will be along shortly," Channing said, scanning the horizon.

They added more canvas and the wind thrust the beautiful blue yacht past the towers of the Tyath harbor. The wind blew eastward, down from the mountains, sweeping across the waves of the Clearwater Sea, causing the surface to jump and bounce with white foam.

"My brother Pilus will follow us, no doubt," Heathron said, looking back at the Golden City.

"Do you believe he knew you were alive?" Kathleen asked in surprise.

Prince Heathron shook his head.

"I don't know, but I imagine he grew accustomed to the idea rapidly. He is in the service of Lars Balfoest now. He can't be trusted."

"Here they come," Channing said, pointing to the far edge of the harbor. Sails unfurled with the new insignia of Tyath: a circle of nine triangles adorning the canvas. Oars thrust into the water and drums rumbled.

"We needed a greater head start," Lilly said. Her face held a look of concern as she estimated the distance between them.

"The *Marine Escape* is built for speed. It handles beautifully in the water. It is the only thing I like about Jessica Turlin — her appreciation for the finest watercraft," Kathleen said.

"The bigger ships have more canvas exposed to the wind. Their masts are taller, and they can row if the wind slows," Heathron said. "I don't see how we will stay ahead of them. Look how they gain on us, even now."

"Let's hope this yacht lives up to its name. We will have some safety in the Straits if we can make it that far. They would not dare board us in such turbulent waters," Kathleen said.

"If we can make it to the shores near Windstall Hermitage, there is a channel where the water is too shallow for the draft of their ships. It leads to a hidden harbor," Jared said. "We will be safe there."

The Imperial Navy moved in formation. The larger ships spread out in a line like a net to enclose the smaller boat.

The ships on the outside began to pass the smaller yacht. Water sprayed up on the prow of the naval vessels as the trap was now sprung.

"We will not go back to Tyath," Prince Heathron said, placing his hand on Kathleen's arm. "I promise you that."

"I would die beside you, fighting on this deck, before we allow Princess Dal Sundi to be taken," Jared agreed.

Kathleen noted the use of her title.

Thoughts twirled in her mind. Despite the dangers they now faced, she couldn't help but notice he used her title. Why did she feel a stab of pain when he did not say her given name? Perhaps he did that out of respect for Heathron and the people aboard? Or was he reminding the Prince, in a subtle way, that she was not married?

Heathron did not seem to notice. He looked at the ships coming closer, and Kathleen saw fear in his eyes. She remembered the savagery Heathron had endured to protect her, and she felt closer to him. The Prince kept looking seaward and placed an arm around her shoulders, pulling her close to comfort her like he did that cold night on Winterfest.

She also remembered her own words that night.

"Prince Heathron Dol Lassimer and I will be married."

The memory played in her mind, and she looked at each of the men who held a portion of her heart. Jared, with his dark hair and sharp features carried an air of mystery about him. His deep voice made Kathleen want to shiver with pleasure and yet the subtle gray at his temples was a reminder of how quickly things could change. Heathron smiled at her with a face that was the picture of youthful refinement. His athletic build and easy smile made Kathleen want to smile too. She had been promised to him since childhood, and she had renewed that commitment of her own choice when she considered what marital options were truly possible.

I could have never guessed the twists and turns my story might take. Even now standing beside Heathron, so much is uncertain - a reflection of my own heart, she thought.

"Your Highness...Kathleen," a voice said.

Kathleen turned to Lilly.

"I'm sorry, Lilly. What is it?"

"I could help."

"Take the helm if that is where you can best be used. I don't know how we will get away, but they shall not board us without a fight."

"Princess Kathleen," she said slowly, "I can help us get away."

"What charts do you know? Is there a hidden rock formation just below these waves that we might pass-through? Do whatever you can," Kathleen said.

"I need a rope to be tied around my waist," Lilly said.

Seth grabbed a coil of sturdy rope.

"What is your plan?" the Sīhalt Guardian asked.

"My father's fishing boats are smaller than this, but the principle is the same. I need to touch the water," she explained.

Kathleen furrowed her brow.

"What's going on Lilly?" she asked.

The navy ships drew closer. They could see the faces of the men on board. The fact that no arrows were shot in their direction showed how confident the men were in capturing the *Marine Escape*.

Lilly carefully tied the rope around her waist with a knot that would not slip.

"I am going to repel down to the water," she said. "Secure me when I am just above the waves."

Seth nodded. "I won't let you drown."

Jared prowled the deck like an angry saber-toothed cat. He looked ready to pounce.

"Prepare yourselves!" he called to the rest of the passengers.

Lilly went over the side as the yacht changed direction one last time to avoid the oncoming navy. Seth lowered her until she touched the water.

Kathleen looked at her friend and wondered what she could possibly do to help them. The short sword on her right hip would be little help against a boarding party.

With her feet braced against the side of the yacht, and the rope around her waist, Lilly bent her back and reached down, allowing her fingers to be pulled through the water flowing around the hull. Kathleen thought she heard a humming noise over the surging waves.

A swell of water began to rise behind the ship. The crest of water made an increasingly steep slope that rose behind the boat.

The swell allowed the *Marine Escape* to shoot forward, running like a dolphin. The sails actually became slack as the ship sped forward, sliding down the slope of water. Kathleen and the other passengers staggered as the boat suddenly picked up speed.

"She is a Wave Mistress," Seth said in awe as he saw the rising mound of water behind them.

"They are trying to close the noose!" Channing called as the foremost ships turned on a course to intercept the yacht.

"Prepare to be boarded!" the captain called, sword in hand. He stood tall on the deck.

"It will be close," Maxwell said. "We might smash into the side of that one."

The marines on the closest ship held boarding hooks. When they saw the miraculous acceleration and increased speed of the yacht, they swung the metal hooks and cast them across the narrowing distance of water and pulled hard to engage the hooks over the rails of the boat.

Jared and Maxwell sprang into action, using their swords to cut as many of the ropes as they could. Heathron hobbled in pain from one spot to the next, helping as much as possible.

With some difficulty, Kathleen, Larissa, and Melva threw back some of the heavy hooks before they engaged.

Suddenly, the bow of the navy ship slammed into the stern of the *Marine Escape*. The impact threw Kathleen to the deck. Scrambling to get up, she was thrown down once more — her head smashing against the handrail. Dizzily, she heaved up to her elbows - her eyes burned with saltwater. She could see Larissa and Melva had lost their feet too. Larissa was screaming while Melva seemed to crumple without a protest.

"Look out, Lilly!" Seth cried, as he quickly looped the rope around a cleat to secure it.

The nimble guardswoman swung her rope to the back of the stern just in time to avoid the splintering wood as the spar of the navy ship scraped against the *Marine Escape*. The impact gouged a great hole in the stern that tore into the cabin, but remained above the water line.

"Jessica isn't going to like that," Kathleen whispered to herself as the yacht bucked and tossed. They changed direction and moved ahead of the naval vessels.

Now arrows were being loosed as the distance between the two ships increased. They whistled through the air, puncturing the wood of the ship in short, sharp hisses. Kathleen and Lilly scrambled to the far side of the ship. "Come on!" Lilly said, motioning for the others to follow her lead. She swung around the bow, clinging on with her hands, and dangled near the water. It worked. She was out of range of the arrows that flew from the Tyathian ships, and she was still able to use her Talent to funnel the water under and around the damaged ship. With great effort, the others mirrored the tactic, all apart from Melva, who huddled for refuge against the wheel, arms wrapped around her head.

A minute or so later and Channing gave a long exultant shout as he steered the yacht beyond the reach of the pursuing navy.

"To Caaaaaandoreth!" he called with a giant smile on his face. They flew along the southern coast of the Clearwater Sea. With the help of Lilly's Talent, the Turlin yacht raced downhill on the swell of water rising from the ocean surface. It lifted the craft and allowed it to slide along the continuous wave flowing from Lilly's strong and Talented hand.

When the wind blew in a helpful direction, Channing called for every bit of sail they could manage. When the wind became contrary, all the sails were hauled in and they still sliced the water faster than if they had been propelled by a hundred oars.

"How long can you keep this up?" Kathleen called to Lilly. The guardswoman's hair was wet with spray as she swung from one side of the boat to the other, like a spider dangling from its web.

"I'll come up in a moment," Lilly shouted with a gleeful face. "I never get to do this anymore," she said.

"At this rate, we'll sail all the way to the Straits of Windstall in less than two days!"

"That's unbelievable, yet...there she is," Heathron said of the young girl with a rope tied around her waist. She dangled over the side of the boat. Her wet hair flew in the wind as she skimmed her fingertips across the water.

"She needs to touch the water — like I do the plants," Kathleen said. "I need contact to use my Talent."

The yacht raced in a fashion no one had ever seen. People in two smaller fishing boats gawked as they watched the yacht go by and then braced themselves for the wake that followed, tossing them on turbulent water.

"She will need to eat soon?" Seth asked.

Kathleen nodded.

"Melva is very weak and needs nourishment too," Kathleen said.

"I can no longer see the sails of the navy," Jared said to Seth, looking westward."

"Bring her aboard," Channing called. "I need to shake her hand!"

Seth hoisted Lilly to the deck. She wrung out her hair and accepted a towel from Maxwell.

"I found another reason for you to like Jessica Turlin," Larissa said. "I'm setting out some food for everyone, and I must say, Jessica Turlin knows how to eat well."

"Good. I'm famished," Melva said, looking like she might collapse at any moment.

"We were very fortunate to have the Talents of a Wave Mistress with us," Jared said, looking at Lilly and shaking his head in amazement.

"I prefer the term Water Dowser," Lilly said. "I'm glad I could help."

"Either way, it is good to have you aboard!" Seth said.

74

REPORTS FROM TOVE

"What are you doing? You will run us into the cliffs!" Channing yelled.

"Reef the sails and turn the rudder sharply to the left on my command," Jared said.

The black cliffs rose from the sea in sheer grandeur. The waves crashed against the sharp rocks and jagged boulders jutted above the waves.

"Stay the course — we know this passage well," Seth said.

The yacht lunged foreword as the waves carried the ship toward an extremely narrow cleft in the cliffs.

"I do believe our boat is larger than the cave you are aiming for," Channing said.

"She will fit just fine. Hold the course," Seth replied.

As they drew closer, Channing saw the narrow cleft was wider than it appeared. The walls were staggered, allowing the boat to swing around the outcropping. Heathron looked up to see a person waving high above. Jared signaled to him silently, and the black robed man disappeared from his line of sight. As the boat passed the entrance, the water calmed, and the yacht was able to glide further into the harbor, protected on all sides. A small beach of black sand could be seen at the far end of the secret shelter. Heathron steered the boat toward it and Lilly cast anchor. When the boat stopped, the party waded ashore carrying Kathleen and helping Larissa on unsteady legs.

"Follow me, they will not find us here," Seth said.

"Do you believe we lost them?" Channing asked.

"I can wait here. If they try to come into this harbor, as narrow as it is, they will wish they had not," Lilly said, offering her Talent as a defense.

"Thank you for your willingness to stand guard for our safety, but do not be concerned. We have eyes on this entire area. We will not be surprised by the sudden appearance of our enemy. You should go inside with Kathleen, she may need you," Jared said.

THE GROUP GATHERED in Master Tove's private office, sitting around his large wooden desk. Bookshelves lined one wall, and weapons lined another. It was a secure place, so Jared leaned forward and asked in a low tone, "What can you tell us about the pirates?"

Master Tove shuffled through his papers looking for a report.

"Well, I can tell you that they didn't act on their own. We have reports from our sources within the Golden City — let's say there are factions that probably paid the pirates to abduct her."

"So, the attack that happened when I first arrived in Candoreth was a paid job." Jared replied.

"That's right."

"That explains questions I've had for the past year," Jared said. "Who are these pirates?"

"They come from a group of islands midway on the Eastern

Sea. Their manner of speech is confusing, though. I think they represent more than one people. They are a mix of sailors from allied nations cast off from the old-world continents of Centia, and perhaps Sulia. Some of their ships look like ours, but others have an entirely new design. Only our oldest records have any reference to ships built like the ones our informants described."

"Do you believe they work for the Empire?"

"They work for themselves, but they're willing to be hired—that is evident."

"Why are they here now?" Jared asked.

"I wish I knew. We don't have any informants among them. But we do have reports from the south saying that almost all maritime trade between kingdoms has ground to a halt. The Candorethian navy is trapped among the outer islands, and if many more pirate ships arrive, Candoreth may no longer have a navy," Master Tove said.

"There's no time to lose. We need to sail south," Jared concluded.

"What can one do against so many?" Master Tove mused

"I'm not sure, but Kathleen wants to go home."

"She deserves to be home," Master Tove agreed. "What about the Imperial Navy searching for you? How do you expect to slip by them?"

"I don't think they saw us come into this harbor, but they will be searching for us up and down the coast. We could leave under cover of darkness."

"That's dangerous especially with the rocks."

"We do have an advantage if we reach the open water. Their larger ships won't be able to catch us."

Master Tove raised an eyebrow.

"What gives you such confidence?"

"Master Tove, I would like to introduce Lilly."

The young woman stepped forward and grasped Master Tove's hand.

"She's from Fishing Point. She grew up on the Clearwater Sea, and is Talented with water. She is a Dowser."

Master Tove went a little stiff, his eyebrows raising suddenly.

"Is it true, daughter? Can you command the waves?"

Lilly nodded in humility.

"The water does whatever I ask it to do, when I'm touching it."

Master Tove got up and made his way to the library. He looked up and down the shelves, his fingers dancing along the spines of books that had not been moved for generations.

"I know it's here," he said. "I studied it many years ago. The prophecies are being fulfilled!"

He removed an ancient book and opened its pages. Turning a few carefully, Master Tove read from a page in the ancient script:

That which was lost, has been found.
Water recedes when revealing the ground.
A witch for the timbers tall and lean,
Mast and spar and gunnels clean,
Another as Mistress of water and waves,
Beware and believe when the sea behaves!

"What is that, Master Tove?"

"Some say it is the rantings of a madman. Others call him a prophet. I was divided on the issue, until today."

"But this book is ancient, surely you don't think it speaks of us," Lilly said.

"The Talented are rare as it is. Neither a true Builder nor Wave Mistress has been known for many centuries. And now I have two Talented women standing before me - a Green Grower, and one calling herself a Dowser. What are the chances? How did you come to know each other?" He asked Kathleen.

"I chose her as my guard."

"You picked her from many?" Master Tove asked.

"Yes," Kathleen replied. "I chose Lilly and there was another."

"Talented?"

"No, but a good friend nonetheless," she said.

"What else does the prophecy say?" Jared asked.

"The copies we have are translations from earlier texts. A complete rendering does not exist. There are a few more stanzas after the one I just read to you, but other than that, the original document was destroyed. We don't have the rest of it."

"What does the remnant say?" Jared asked.

They looked back at the manuscript and read:

The ——— will rise, and answer the throne,
With ——————— and bone
A new dawn approaches,
Standing alone.
A girl on the mountains,
Has found her true love,
With death ——— she ——— taken
But by willful return,
Only to see a beautiful city burn.

"THAT'S HORRIBLE," Kathleen said. She thought of Candoreth burning.

"The divination was given in the past, perhaps to see our day," Master Tove explained.

"This could mean anything, though" Seth said.

"Or it could be of prophecy of doom," Jared replied.

"Perhaps I shouldn't have shown you this. I just got excited when I realized for the first time in my life, I was meeting a Wave Mistress, I'm sorry," Master Tove said.

"We need to leave tonight," Channing said.

"We should stay here for a couple days," Seth replied.

"The prophecies spoke of a beautiful city burning. I'll never forgive myself if that city is Candoreth," Kathleen said.

"Don't jump to conclusions," Jared said.

"We can't even tell what half of the words say, but if Lilly is the Dowser and I am the Builder of ships, Heir to the throne of Candoreth — I want to go home as soon as possible. I don't care how far we have to sail to avoid the pirates. If we stay far to the open water, we'll be safe," Kathleen said.

"Can you protect us, Lilly?" Jared asked.

"I'll do all I can," she replied.

Master Tove nodded.

"Take a few days to mend and prepare. The Hermitage is your home for now. Barrett, show our guests to their rooms, and tell the kitchen staff we will need a meal prepared."

The Sīhalt servant led them out of the office.

"Jared, Seth and Maxwell, I need to speak with you three, alone."

The door closed and Mater Tove turned to them. "All my reports say that you have had quite a mission since you left."

Jared nodded. "It was unlike any mission I've been given so far," he said.

Master Tove looked towards Seth.

"I am so pleased to have you back among us," he said, "And Maxwell, thank you for your services."

Maxwell smiled with this gap-toothed grin.

"My pleasure, Master Tove," he said.

"Maxwell, can't you find another face to use?" Master Tove said.

"I rather like this one, Master Tove. It's amazing what people will give you when they think you're old, decrepit, and missing most of your teeth."

"He manages to get himself to smell the way he looks," Jared said.

They laughed and Master Tove placed his hand on Jared's back.

"Take Seth into the courtyard. He will want some time alone at Arabella's grave I think."

Seth embraced the ancient Sīhalt Master. "It is good to be among family again. I will write a full report of my dealings with the Delathranes in the morning," he said.

75

CONFLICT IN THE MIST

Jared made his way to the quiet courtyard before dawn. He walked in the traditional flat sandals and white robe of the Sīhalt. Grabbing the hilt of his *impla*, he drew it silently from the scabbard.

Jared walked over to look at the burial site of Arabella and Tand. He felt grateful that Seth's name did not need to be added to the simple marker at the head of the grave. The penance he had begun so long ago now resumed for the short time he would be home.

"I miss you, sister," he said to Arabella's spirit - if perhaps her soul still walked the Hermitage. He picked a small sprig of leaves and laid them at her headstone. Then he whipped the sword through the air. The morning mists swirled at his feet with the passing of his steps.

Jared sought the quiet contemplation of movement to be found in the forms of his practice with the sword. Despite the coolness of the damp morning, Jared felt a bead of sweat forming on his brow. He moved more forcefully and added kicks both high and low. Jared used his fists to drive the white mist away with a jab and open-handed strike to his imaginary opponent.

Jared struggled but the quiet did not come, neither did the contemplation.

His mind would not be rid of the red-haired girl. Kathleen had ignored him! She ran from him, almost as if she were afraid, into the arms of Prince Heathron.

Why wouldn't she? His inner voice spoke in anger, *she was never meant for you!*

Jared slashed the air. The white robe he wore flew out behind him. He turned and changed the level of his body to the ground. He had imagined it would be different. When he returned, he thought his interaction with Kathleen would be on his terms. His worst scenario included watching her descend the steps of the Great Cathedral, dressed in white, arm-in-arm with Heathron. He had never thought that leaving her in Tyath would result in such a wretched existence for Kathleen. She needed him and he was not there.

You have failed again, the voice in his mind said.

Jared leaped to the top of a stone wall within the courtyard. He balanced as he walked along the wall, not slowing the movements of his dangerous blade.

KATHLEEN WATCHED from above the courtyard. The narrow window had small hexagonal panes of glass set in a pattern with thin, lead strips welded together. Kathleen tiptoed her way a few steps closer to stand beside the window, half concealed as she moved the edge of the drapes to reveal the courtyard below. She held her breath and peered outside. It was early morning and the mists of the hermitage still swirled thick along the flagstones below. She wanted to open the window, to watch him more closely — to have one less obstruction. She felt a craving to watch him as he danced with his *impla*.

Jared was alone. He moved with the fluidity of an angel.

Instead of the black she always saw him wear, the Sīhalt Guardian was dressed in the white robe of Sīhalt mortification. He stepped crisply and thrust the blade toward the mists then whirled and leapt back performing an aerial movement with his feet spinning overhead and landing in a fighting stance, facing the opposite direction.

Kathleen did not dare move. Even from the third level of the hermitage, the abilities of the Sensor were keen. She knew any movement or sound, above that of her own breath, would be heard by the Guardian. As she watched him move across the steps with leaps and kicks, Kathleen realized she was breathing in short, shallow breaths.

In the dim morning light of the courtyard, Kathleen saw another figure dressed in white approach. Jared kept his back to the approaching figure.

At first Kathleen believed it was another Sīhalt Guardian, but as the man approached she drew a deeper breath inward. The man hobbled on a crutch tucked under his right arm. The man was tall, and his sandy blonde hair was in disarray. Kathleen knew at once it was Heathron.

What is he doing at this early hour? He should be resting, she thought.

Jared slowed his movements into a slow-motion turn with gliding steps.

She couldn't hear if words were exchanged, but she saw Heathron raise a hand and point a finger at Jared. The Sīhalt looked around as if to verify they were alone, and then he turned and held both arms out as if proclaiming his innocence.

What are they saying?

Kathleen's thoughts jumped from one scenario to the next and none of them were calming to her. She wanted to fling the window open and lean outward to hear the exchange between the men. Heathron, clearly agitated, hobbled closer to Jared in the courtyard below. He lifted his crutch as if he would strike the

Sīhalt Guardian. Jared did not move. He stood with clenched fists at his sides.

Tears streamed from her eyes. She stepped back from the window and made her way to the wash basin, afraid she was going to be sick.

JARED HEARD the sound of wood on stone well before he heard the footfalls of the Prince. The step-slide, step-slide, pattern of the walk was easy to identify. The Sīhalt Guardian resented the intrusion of both his meditation and solitude.

"I knew I would find you here," Heathron said.

Jared stopped moving and allowed the mists to gather at his feet again. He did not turn to face the man who held Kathleen's heart. He needed a moment to control his features and hide the pain he felt within.

"Master Tove encourages us to seek the quiet contemplation," Jared said as he turned around. He breathed heavily and sweat ran down his neck and chest. Jared wiped his forehead on the white sleeve of the robe and sheathed his thin sword.

"The Sīhalt Guardian," Heathron said slowly, drawing the name out as if to examine every syllable. "I'm glad that you can seek the quiet contemplation in your halls of black stone, isolated from the rest of the world in the Windstall Hermitage. You scheme, plan, and arrive in the very moment of our greatest need!" His voice held a tone of contempt as he spoke.

"Be careful, Prince," Jared said. "You are a guest of our Order this day."

"I speak not of the entire Order, or Master Tove, or even your brother, Seth. They seem to be men of honor - bound to code." Heathron looked at Jared from head to toe - measuring him, finding him wanting.

"What do you want?" Jared said evenly, his blood riled.

"I want you to leave us alone," Heathron said, pointing a finger at the Guardian's chest.

Jared stood looking at him without a reply, his face like stone.

"Do you need me to spell it out for you, Sīhalt?" Heathron said. "Kathleen and I were truly happy together. You promised to go away - I let you go...and we found love."

"You knew I would return," Jared said.

"The year is not over. You came back early."

"It is a good thing I did - I rescued you," Jared said harshly.

"Maxwell broke us out of the prison, not you. It was Lilly who lifted the waves. Captain Channing secured the boat. Where were you when we were broken and bleeding for months on end?" Heathron asked. "You were not there as she cried out in fevered pain, I was."

Heathron raised his crutch and balanced on his uninjured leg, pointing it like a spear.

"I would not have left if I would have known you couldn't protect her!" Jared said. He spread his arms wide in a show of innocence he did not feel.

"Give me what is rightfully mine, Sīhalt," Heathron said.

"Kathleen is not to be bartered for," Jared replied.

"She desires to marry me. She announced it herself during Winterfest."

Jared swallowed, forcing down the lump in his throat. He frowned as his pulse pounded in his ears.

"We will be married as soon as we arrive in Candoreth," the Prince added, aiming it as sharply as a sword, right into the heart of the Guardian.

"Do you feel no gratitude for the role I have played in her safety?" Jared said.

"I have lost my father to an assassin's blade and my mother to the poisoner's cup. My dignity lies broken in the dungeons of Tyath, and my throne has been usurped by the Council. I will not have Kathleen stolen by you."

"I am sworn to protect her until her wedding day," Jared said simply.

"I release you from your duty, Guardian," Heathron said. "Master Tove knows I have already paid you for your services."

"The oath I took was to Kathleen as well," Jared said. "I will not leave her again until my duty is fulfilled."

Heathron took a few pained, awkward steps forward and leaned forward on his crutch so he was a hand's breath away from Jared's face. "Listen here, Guardian, I am going to marry her when we get to her home in Candoreth," he said calmly, quietly, pausing. "Then your duty will be fulfilled. And your time with Kathleen will be at an end."

76

A HOPEFUL HORIZON

Kathleen looked around at the people who journeyed with her on the yacht.

The Shifter named Maxwell sat cross-legged on the deck, wearing a tattered, brown shirt and ragged trousers. He entertained himself by tossing a dagger into the air and allowing it to land point-first between his fingers. The closer the blade came to his fingers, the more he seemed to enjoy the game.

Boys can be so strange, she thought.

Maxwell had been helpful in bringing about the rescue. Kathleen shivered and shook her head, trying to clear it from her memory. She could still see the reptilian face changing into a man. It seemed so unnatural.

Melva and Larissa sat with Kathleen. The old Healer reached into her pouch and pulled out a handful of the journey food. She shaded her eyes with a wrinkled hand and scanned the distant shoreline.

Lilly, ever the sailor, stood confidently at the helm with her dark hair blowing. Her smile was bigger than Kathleen imagined possible. Jared's brother Seth leaned, like a cat, against the woodwork nearest to her. He laughed and chatted with the beautiful

Imperial Guardswoman as if he had known her his entire life. His brilliant blue eyes shone brightly despite the horrors Kathleen knew he must have endured at the hands of the Delathranes. His cheeks were still a bit hollow, but he looked like the food and rest at the Windstall Hermitage had done him good.

Could the two of them be happy as a couple? Kathleen asked herself. The Sīhalt Guardian was handsome, not as ruggedly built as Jared, but he looked years younger than his brother.

Lilly looks happy, and I don't think having her hand on the helm is the only reason she is smiling so grand, she thought. Kathleen wished, not for the first time, that she had no obligations to her people and her country.

"I wish I wasn't a princess, but rather just a girl like Lilly," she said.

"You think you would be more free - just a girl with the wind in your hair?" Melva asked.

"I know I shouldn't covet the circumstances of someone else," Kathleen said.

"Every life lived has its own set of challenges. Your trials are not worse than others I have known," Melva said.

"What are you thinking about?" Larissa asked, holding onto the rail of the *Marine Escape*.

"I was just thinking about the future," Kathleen said. "When will we ever see the Golden City again? How long is Heathron going to live as a deposed ruler?"

"An imperial prince in exile is still a threat to the usurper on the throne in Tyath. Heathron will have to fight to survive. Lord Balfoest, and the renegade Council of Nine, will not rest until he is dead," Larissa said with certainty.

"I don't know how much protection Candoreth can offer, but I will ask my father to give him what assistance we can," Kathleen said.

"We can return this yacht to House Turlin sometime," Melva

said, looking at the flag with the white swan flying in the breeze. "Heathron will be back on the throne before this is all over."

"It was a small contribution for Jessica to make to show her support of the Empire," Kathleen added, smiling.

Larissa looked toward the eastern horizon. The sun was just breaking through the clouds that lay low across the ocean. The blazing orb was making its way slowly, yet perceptibly increasing in strength as it illuminated the morning sky.

"What is it they say about a red sky in the morning?" Larissa asked.

"The sailors take warning," Kathleen finished the phrase.

"It's more a mother-of-pearl pink," Larissa said, looking at the clouds.

"It's good to be optimistic, especially when your heart says you have reason to worry," Kathleen said.

"What worries you most, Kathleen? Is it the thought of pirates surrounding our home or the difficulties of navigating the dangerous waters of love?" Melva smiled slightly as she said this.

Kathleen glanced over at the figure of Jared sharpening his *impla* in silence. She knew he could hear every word of her conversation on the deck. He pushed a small, smooth stone over the shining surface again and again without looking up. His dark hair hung down, hiding his face.

She had hurt him deeply and was not sure what to do next.

"How can I love two men and be one woman?" Kathleen asked both Melva and Larissa.

"You must choose your path," Melva said.

"Is there any way I can choose one of them without destroying the other?"

"In all my life experiences, I have never found a way to fully love two men and be only one woman," Melva said.

"That sounds like something I'd try," Larissa interrupted. "The thought of either of them being lonely breaks my heart."

"I'm glad to see you are getting back to your old self again," Kathleen said to Larissa, shaking her head.

"I lost a couple of youthful years with all that craziness in Tyath," Larissa said, shrugging off the nightmare of their captivity. "I don't have any time to waste."

Larissa looked toward the Captain of Candoreth standing on the foredeck. Channing stood with one hand on the pommel of the sword strapped to his hip. His other hand caressed the silk shirt he wore - a gift from the trunk of Lord Turlin's cabin.

"Lady Albodris," he said, tipping his audacious hat in Larissa's direction, when he noticed her eyeing at him. Then he turned to look out to sea as if he had no cares in the world.

Larissa kept looking at the Captain.

"He's kind of insufferable, isn't he?" she said.

Just then, Prince Heathron came walking along the deck. He skipped the few steps leading to the mid-deck, smiling broadly, and threw the crutch he had been using overboard. Then he dramatically swept Melva up in a joyful embrace.

"Whoa!" the old woman said. "If you break my bones, who will Heal me?"

"Thank you for Healing me, Melva!" Heathron said. "I feel better than I could have ever imagined."

"You've come to your senses regarding the Talents?" she said, smiling. "You seem very happy for a man who has lost his throne," Melva observed.

"I may have lost my kingdom, but that is temporary. As long as I have my love with me, I would trade it all," he said as he swept Kathleen up in a similar embrace. He leaned her back, and Kathleen felt his lips firmly against hers. She put her arms around his neck, but as they kissed, she opened her eyes ever so slightly and caught a glimpse of Jared looking at them through dark hair that fell forward, partially covering his face. The Sīhalt Guardian looked away, but he did so a half second too late.

His storm-gray eyes smoldered with...desire?

Or was it jealously? she thought with a sudden pang in her heart.

"What is the matter, Kathleen?" Heathron asked, sensing her hesitation at their kiss.

"I'm just concerned about everyone...in Candoreth," she said.

Heathron's deep brown eyes searched her face. His eyes flicked briefly toward Jared, but the Sīhalt Guardian had his head bowed again, looking at his sword, testing the sharpened edge with the sunlight dancing across the infinitely smooth surface.

"Everything is going to be okay," Heathron said softly. He pulled Kathleen close to his heart, smoothing her hair as he hugged her close. She wrapped her arms around Heathron.

Kathleen whispered in response, soft enough that only Heathron, and perhaps one other person on the boat, could hear her. "Yes, everything is going to be okay."

THE END of Book Two

AUTHOR'S PROMISE

I hope you loved the story! Help me succeed by leaving an honest review online. Social proof is powerful.

In *Guardian of the Emerald Coast, Book Three of the Sīhalt Series,* we will continue the adventure with Kathleen, Jared, Heathron and the rest of the band of colorful friends. In book three, she returns to her homeland and discovers that all is not well in Candoreth. The tension increases as duty and desire continues to inspire the thoughts, words and actions of our heroes. It will be exciting!

Book Three is coming along nicely. It will be ready next year.

Go to my website AustinRehl.com and I'll give you the earliest updates as well as material related to the Lands of Desnia.

All the Best,

Austin Rehl

P.S. My email is austin@austinrehl.com.

ABOUT THE AUTHOR

Austin Rehl lives in beautiful Marietta, Ohio with his wonderful wife and six talented children. He is a practicing dentist, and also enjoys working on his farm, hunting in the woods, and spending time with friends and family.

Austin considers himself a romantic, and a poet. He enjoys reading and writing fantasy and sci-fi.

Go to austinrehl.com to stay in touch or join his advanced reader team!

www.ingramcontent.com/pod-product-compliance
Lightning Source LLC
Chambersburg PA
CBHW030538020726
47494CB00005B/1426